In Search of Us

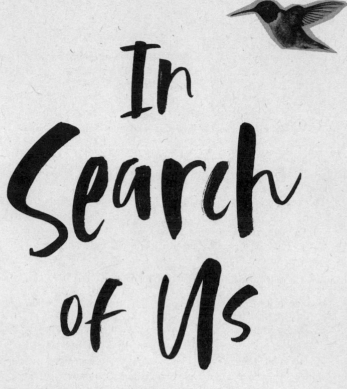

In Search of Us

AVA DELLAIRA

SQUARE
FISH

FARRAR STRAUS GIROUX · NEW YORK

SQUARE
FISH

An imprint of Macmillan Publishing Group, LLC
120 Broadway, New York, NY 10271
fiercereads.com

Square Fish and the Square Fish logo are trademarks of Macmillan and
are used by Farrar Straus Giroux under license from Macmillan.

Our books may be purchased in bulk for promotional, educational, or business
use. Please contact your local bookseller or the Macmillan Corporate and
Premium Sales Department at (800) 221-7945 ext. 5442 or by email at
MacmillanSpecialMarkets@macmillan.com.

Library of Congress Cataloging-in-Publication Data

Names: Dellaira, Ava, author.
Title: In Search Of Us / by Ava Dellaira.
Description: New York : Farrar Straus Giroux, 2018. | Summary: Relates the
stories of Marilyn who, at age seventeen, fell in love with James, left her
stage-mother, and set out on her own and Angie, her now seventeen-year-old
daughter, who returns to Hollywood seeking her father.
Identifiers: LCCN 2017019595 (print) | ISBN 978-1-250-29461-6 (paperback) |
ISBN 978-0-374-30533-8 (ebook)
Subjects: | CYAC: Mothers and daughters—Fiction. | Identity—Fiction. |
Single-parent families—Fiction. | Love—Fiction. | Racially mixed people—
Fiction.
Classification: LCC PZ7.D3847 At 2018 (print) | DDC [Fic]—dc23
LC record available at https://lccn.loc.gov/2017019595

Originally published in the United States by Farrar Straus Giroux
First Square Fish edition, 2019
Book designed by Elizabeth H. Clark
Square Fish logo designed by Filomena Tuosto

1 3 5 7 9 10 8 6 4 2

LEXILE: 880L

For my husband, Doug Hall

In Search of Us

Prologue

ANGIE

> *Behind every man now alive stand thirty ghosts, for that is*
> *the ratio by which the dead outnumber the living.*

—ARTHUR C. CLARKE, *2001: A Space Odyssey*

The living are catching up with the dead. Back when Arthur C. Clarke was writing in 1968, they had us outnumbered by thirty to one. But now, we living humans have multiplied so quickly, we're down to fifteen ghosts apiece. Angie knows the facts: there are over 7 billion people alive, and 107 billion who once were.

Angie's dad is one of the dead, or so she'd believed. She'd often imagined him beside her, the leader of her little ghost tribe, fifteen strong. She pictured him the way he is in the photograph with her mom. He looks the same age she is now: seventeen. His smile wide and bright, his skin dark and his teeth white, his body muscular and long. He wears a backward baseball cap, like a '90s dork, she thinks. In the photo, he and her mom, Marilyn, are at the ocean, on a boardwalk. Her mom's wearing overalls over her bikini, hoop earrings glinting, long sun-gold hair falling around her pale face. She's leaning against him like she belongs there, her head thrown back in laughter, his arm draped over her shoulder. All that blue water behind them, seeming to go on until it meets the sky.

She first discovered the picture a year ago, while she was getting ready for Sam Stone's sixteenth birthday dinner. She'd been rifling through her mom's drawers looking for lipstick while

Marilyn was at work, and at some point the search expanded. She found herself digging, though she didn't know for what. Then, at the back of her mom's underwear drawer, she found a wooden box. Inside was a worn manila envelope stuffed full and sealed, and beneath it, the photograph.

Angie stared down at the grinning black boy who was staring back at her, and though she'd never seen him before, she knew her father instantly. For a split second, she wondered who he was with. As it came into focus, Angie saw that, of course, the girl was her mom. She looked so carefree. Young. Full of possibility. Happy.

Suddenly Angie's chest felt hollow. She wanted to pull the boy out of the photo. To make him grow up into a man, to make him be her dad. To make him make her mom smile like that again.

Instead she tried to put herself inside of the picture—to imagine what it would have been like to be there with her parents—how the sun would have felt, how the ocean might have smelled. And though she's never even been to the beach before, she could almost hear the far-off sound of the waves under their bright laughter.

Angie has one more year of high school, and then comes The Future. She has no idea what she wants to "do with her life," where she belongs, or how she'll ever be enough to make good on everything her mom has given up for her. When she finds herself struggling to breathe, her chest tight, the anxiety nameless and uncertain, Angie thinks of the seven billion humans and counting living on earth. The unfathomable numbers ease the panic, and she starts to feel light—the kind of light-headed that you get from laughing too hard or staying up too late, or both at once. She's smaller than a drop in an ocean. So what does it matter what one girl—Angela Miller—does with her life?

She considers herself average, unremarkable: she likes history and science (particularly biology), running hard, grilled cheese with burned edges, soccer, coffee with soy cream, vinyl records, hip-hop blasting in the privacy of her headphones; she comes armed with lists like this, prepared for the necessary profiles, meant to give some practiced but tenuous definition to "herself," whoever that is. The feelings that loom inside her, threatening to spill over, she had diligently learned to keep at bay. But today, everything will change.

Angie holds the photograph of her parents in her hands now, listening to Janet Jackson sing "I Get Lonely" on a Walkman she found at a Goodwill for $2.99. The song plays from a mixtape labeled FOR MISS MARI MACK, LOVE, JAMES in faded blue pen. The early-morning sun is already turning too hot, piercing, chasing Angie into the shaded part of the porch. Flecks of cotton drift through the warm air, pooling in the gutters like summer snow. In front of her sits a duffel bag with T-shirts and socks, underwear, and her two favorite dresses carefully folded inside, along with the envelope from her mom's drawer and the listings for Justin Bell between the ages of twenty-four and thirty-five, or of unknown age, living in the Los Angeles area.

Marilyn left for work almost an hour ago. When she comes back, she'll find her daughter gone.

Angie has lived in this house with her mom since the day Marilyn picked her up from fifth grade and told her she had a surprise.

"What is it?" Angie asked, when Marilyn didn't produce any of the usual treats—a Milky Way, gummy bears, a chapter book, or a new set of colored pencils.

"Just wait," her mom answered, "this is the best surprise yet."

She got on I-40, then pulled off and drove through Albuquerque's Old Town, a part of the city they visited only when Angie wanted to go to the natural history museum. Were they going now? But no, her mom was weaving through streets with huge cottonwood trees and ivy-covered houses. And then, as they reached the edge of the neighborhood and the houses started to get smaller—little flat adobes with nicely kept yards—she parked in a driveway. The house was short and squat, with a blue roof.

Angie turned to her mom. "Come on!" Marilyn urged, girlish excitement in her voice.

Angie followed her mom up to the front door as Marilyn fumbled with her key ring. Whose house were they at?

As the lock clicked open, Marilyn looked at Angie and said, "Go on, go inside. It's ours."

She was only ten, but Angie understood then that her mom had given her what she herself had never had—a house to grow up in. The two of them painted it together: blue in the living room, yellow in the kitchen. Ocean green in Angie's bedroom.

Angie's always loved the thick walls that stay cool through the summer mornings, the rounded archways, the worn paisley couch where she and Marilyn would stay up on weekends watching romantic comedies, eating popcorn sprinkled with Parmesan or frozen root beer float bars.

When she was little, Angie believed she had the kind of mom other kids ought to be jealous of—one who packed the best lunches, with carefully made sandwiches cut into triangles, and made the best brownies for bake sales. She'd wake Angie in the mornings when Angie didn't want to get out of bed by blasting "Dancing in the Street," and together they'd spin around the house laughing in their pajamas. Her mom decorated for the holidays, including New Year's and Halloween. Every Fourth of July she'd make red-white-and-blue cupcakes and cook hot dogs in the pan. She'd buy sparklers, and once it got dark enough, Marilyn and Angie would stand outside in their garden, writing their names with the glittering wands. It didn't strike Angie as strange then, when she was a kid, that it was just the two of them. That they didn't go to other people's barbecues, that when her mom would drop Angie off at friends' houses, she never stayed to socialize with the other mothers, who often spoke to Marilyn in patronizing tones. That at parents' nights at Montezuma Elementary, she was the youngest mom by far, and though Angie would notice some of the dads being nice to her, Marilyn always turned away to search for her daughter. Even when her mom eventually shut the door on Manny—the first (and last) man to come to their house for dinner—Angie had learned to accept the loss.

Ever since Angie was a little kid, Marilyn has told her she's her beauty, her light, her reason for life. Her precious little angel. But sometimes, when she thought Angie was busy with a coloring book or the television, Angie would see her staring out the window, tears running down her cheeks.

As Sam's Jeep turns the corner and parks in front of the driveway, Angie presses stop on the Walkman and pulls off the headphones. She thinks of her mom coming home to an empty house tonight, and she almost turns to go back inside. But instead, she picks up her duffel and heads toward the car.

Sam wears a rumpled white T-shirt, a pair of cutoff sweatpants that hang on his tall, narrow frame, and mirrored aviator shades. His hair is the same kind of messy it's always been.

"Hey," Angie says, wishing she could see his eyes.

Sam merely nods in greeting, takes her bag from her, and stuffs it into the back seat. Angie climbs into the car, which smells vaguely of marijuana and seems to be storing several weeks' worth of breakfast burrito wrappers. The '90s Cherokee that Sam named Mabel gives an unhappy rumbling noise as it starts.

As they roll down Angie's street, Sam remains wordless and turns up the music. Angie glances back at her home disappearing behind them, and then she looks down at the girl in the picture with her dad. The one who must have sped through the night with the windows down and the music loud, inhaling the

8

scent of the sea, the one who must have known the feeling of free-dom and air rushing into her lungs and a life, a new life, about to start. The one who must have known the way that falling in love brings the world closer, as if everything were in reach. At least that's how Angie imagines it.

MARILYN

18 Years Earlier

• • • • • *Marilyn is seventeen today. She stares back at her* own eyes reflected in the car window, transposed over the man on the corner wearing a CASH FOR GOLD sign and a woman pushing a shopping cart full of clattering bottles. They pass an Arco station where a crew of boys with backward baseball caps carry away cigars and sodas. The backs of her thighs stick to the seat, and she can feel sweat beading around her hairline. The classic end-of-summer Los Angeles heat wave has hit. It has to be at least a hundred degrees out, and the '80s Buick, loaded down with boxes, has no working AC.

"It's just for a little while," her mom, Sylvie, rambles on. "Until we get another break, you know. You have your appointment with LA Talent in a couple weeks."

Marilyn nods without turning her mother's way.

Her last audition (where she was to be one in a family of four out to buy a television) was a downright disaster. She'd understood the stakes, and all morning, sitting in the waiting room with the other girls, her chest had felt tight, her stomach queasy. She tried to concentrate on her book—*The White Album* by Joan Didion—but she'd been stuck on the first paragraph, unable to focus, rereading the same opening sentence: *We tell ourselves stories in order to live.* As she'd gotten in front of the camera, she found she could hardly breathe.

When her mother came to pick her up, Marilyn didn't mention the sense of panic, the dizziness, or the casting assistant who'd brought her a glass of water and shot an *oh god* look to the director across the room. She endured Sylvie's look of deep disappointment—brows arched in tension—when a week later their supper of Lean Cuisines was interrupted by the news that Marilyn had failed yet again. As Sylvie hung up the phone and stared out the window at the pool and its plastic lounge chairs, Marilyn pushed a piece of wilted broccoli around her plate.

After a long moment of silence Sylvie poured herself a third glass of white wine and turned to Marilyn. "It's a wasteland around here, really. I've been thinking we should move up near Hollywood, get closer to it all," she said, too brightly. "I mean, who knows, you could run into a casting director in the grocery store." As if they weren't fleeing the apartment they hadn't paid rent on in months.

Marilyn knows her mom would let her go ass-first in a photo (like the girl sprawled on the billboard over the freeway, advertising jeans) if it meant the money that would get them into a shiny new house in the hills above the city, above everything, where she believes they belong. As far as Sylvie's concerned, a new and better life is just around the corner, the revolving door to the future a mere step away.

As a child, perhaps Marilyn believed in Sylvie's dreams of a better place, but by now, she's given up on ever walking through the door in her mother's fantasies. She holds tightly to the thought that it's only another year until she'll be eighteen, moving away for college, beginning a life that belongs to her. She sees the future like a little diamond of light at the end of the tunnel; she's learned to fix her gaze on it, to struggle toward it, to keep that diamond in her mind.

A car honks at Sylvie as she holds up traffic behind her to make a left turn onto Washington Boulevard. Marilyn takes in the sunburned look of the streets, the smell of meat drifting from a taco truck mixed with the faint scent of the ocean, the bright bougainvillea growing up a chain-link fence.

Sylvie ignores the honking and navigates the Buick onto South Gramercy Place. Marilyn vaguely recognizes the residential street lined with dilapidated apartment buildings. LOW DEPOSIT advertises one banner. She notices a red flower box hanging out of a window, a laundry line where clothes wave like flags. A man leans against the building below, dragging from a cigarette.

"Marilyn, look. You can see the sign from here." The car swerves through the middle of the road as Sylvie turns around in her seat to point to the white letters: H-O-L-L-Y-W-O-O-D on the mountain in the distance, standing stalwart through the haze of smog that comes with the summer heat.

"Mmm-hmm." Marilyn does her best to ignore the dread building in her chest as they continue down the block and pull up to 1814—a two-story duplex at the corner, with crumbling pink stucco and an unkempt yard, where a few orange trees survive nonetheless.

Lauryn Hill's voice drifts up from a radio in the apartment below: *How you gonna win* . . . Sylvie fumbles for the key under the mat, the curls in her dyed blond hair falling loose in the heat and sticking against her pale cheeks. As they enter, Marilyn is transported back in time by the familiar scent—some odd mix of cigars, Febreze, and cooked meat.

Pieces of furniture lie haphazardly about the room—the couch slightly askew from the wall, the coffee table butting diagonally against it, holding a candy jar filled mostly with butterscotch wrappers. Late-afternoon sun streams though barred windows, casting spots of light on the shag carpet.

For a moment they both just stand there.

"Well, this could be worse," Sylvie says with forced cheer. Marilyn wishes that somehow she'd been able to do better. That she could have managed just one more commercial, one more success that would have kept them away from here.

In the tiny bedroom that was once hers and will be again, Marilyn opens the windows, letting in a burst of hot air. It's already past five o'clock, but the heat hasn't let up. She stares out at a distant line of skinny palm trees, their tops wavering. She thinks they look like scattered soldiers, the last ones still standing in the battleground of the city, and raises her hands in two opposing L shapes in front of her eyes—the frame of a photograph. With a blink—her imaginary shutter—she freezes the image in her mind.

"You're so beautiful." Sylvie's voice startles her. She turns to see her mom watching her from the doorway, as the radio from below goes to commercial and a voice instructs her to *double your pleasure, double your fun*. Marilyn wants to collapse on the floor, suddenly exhausted.

As Sylvie moves to wrap her arms around her, Marilyn remembers the day—almost ten years ago now—that they left Woody's and moved into the then-brand-new apartment they've just left behind in Orange County. Sylvie loved the pool and the fresh carpet, but Marilyn's favorite part was the air that didn't smell like anything. She'd been in her bedroom putting her clothes away neatly in a new pink dresser when she heard her mom scream her name.

She rushed into the living room to find Sylvie in tears and her own face on the TV. Marilyn-on-screen opened the top of a My Little Pony and pulled out a jeweled bracelet, exclaiming *There's a surprise for me!* before kissing the top of Twilight Sparkle's head. The image of herself gave Marilyn an uneasy feeling—that wasn't her, was it? Not really. No. She found herself wanting to back away from the screen, but when Sylvie pulled Marilyn to her and said, in whispered awe, "You're so beautiful. My baby girl. You're on TV," she couldn't help but revel in her mom's pride.

Marilyn now lingers in Sylvie's arms, engulfed in her perfume—Eternity by Calvin Klein? Sylvie's scent is a rotating kaleidoscope of samples from the counter at Macy's, where she spends her workdays convincing customers that a bottle of Chanel or Burberry is a potion powerful enough to transform them into the kind of women they want to be.

"It'll all work out. You'll see," Sylvie says, almost to herself.

She releases Marilyn from her grip just as suddenly as she'd embraced her. "Let's unload now, so we have time for the birthday dinner."

Marilyn can see her mom is working, even harder than Marilyn herself, not to crumble.

"Great," Marilyn replies, and kisses her on the cheek.

Moving boxes up the flight of stairs goes slowly. By the time the sun drops and the day starts to give up, the Buick's two-thirds empty and they're both sticky, struggling with one of the heaviest boxes in the load, containing Marilyn's books.

As Marilyn backs up the stairs, the muscles in her arms burning, she sees a man's figure—tall, broad-shouldered, dark-skinned, head down—crossing the street toward them. She blows a strand of hair away from her face and regrets that her hands are full, because she wants to lift them into a frame, to take a picture of him in her mind as he steps beneath a jacaranda tree and into its puddle of purple petals collected in the gutter.

As he walks quickly up the pavement toward their building, she can see that he must be close to her own age: though he looks physically grown, he still has the wide eyes of a boy. He wears basketball shorts, sneakers, and a white T-shirt, soaked down the front with sweat. Tattoos cover his left arm.

"Marilyn! Stay with it! The time to go on one of your little journeys is not while we're carrying a load of your bricks," Sylvie complains. And, perhaps hearing the noise, he turns and sees Marilyn staring. She watches him as she struggles with the weight of the box, manages a backward step up the stairs.

He looks away, but after a moment, he's climbing toward them.

"You need help?" His voice is different than she would have

imagined. Softer, shyer. The sound of it seems to match the gentle blue of the early-evening sky.

"My goodness, yes! What a darling. Someone must have sent us an angel." Sylvie immediately drops the box, never one to refuse the charity of others.

"I'm Sylvie, and this is my daughter, Marilyn. It's her birthday."

Marilyn is grateful for the exertion, which has undoubtedly already turned her cheeks pink, disguising her blush.

"Happy birthday," he says simply. She thinks she can feel the heat radiating off his body.

"Thanks." She lets her eyes drift upward to the gulls floating high against the pink clouds. She tries not to look at his shirt sticking to his muscular body.

"And you are?" Sylvie prompts.

"James."

"James. Good to know we have a strapping young lad in the building."

"You guys moving in?"

"Yes yes. We're up there. My daughter's an actress, we thought it would be better if she were closer to Hollywood."

Marilyn knows how silly this must sound—she's obviously not an actual actress, or they wouldn't be moving here. But James just nods and lifts the box, his body so close to Marilyn's that for a fleeting moment she can smell his skin. Though she can hear the effort in his breathing, his face doesn't indicate any strain as he carries the books into the apartment.

"We've got a few more in the car, you wouldn't mind terribly would you," Sylvie says (more than asks). Marilyn winces.

"Sure," James says, and she can't tell if he's irritated.

Sylvie stays inside, making a show of looking busy as she starts to unpack, but Marilyn follows James up and down the stairs with the lighter boxes, determined to do her part. He laps her on every round and doesn't make much eye contact.

When they've finished, Sylvie thanks James again and Marilyn follows him downstairs so she can lock up the car. The sky's beginning to darken, and the heat of the day has suddenly given way to the empty cool of desert night. She feels a chill, her clothes still damp with sweat.

At the bottom of the staircase, he turns to her. "So, how old?"

For a moment, Marilyn's confused, before she remembers it's her birthday. "Seventeen."

He nods. "Me too."

She looks out at the sidewalk, littered with scattered trash—a Coke bottle, a crushed beer can, a Carl's Jr. bag, of all things. Carl's Jr. was the last commercial she'd booked, five years ago. Residual checks don't last forever.

"So where you guys coming from?"

"Orange County. We're staying with my uncle again. We lived here when we first came to LA."

"You're an actress?"

"No, not really. My mom wishes I were. I was in a couple of commercials forever ago . . . it's her thing, but I've been playing along for so long I guess it's become routine."

"Yeah, I feel that. I mean, you gotta be what you gotta be for the people you love. It's not always *you*, unfortunately."

Marilyn nods. She can smell someone's dinner cooking, can hear a distant siren.

"Thanks again for helping us."

"No problem."

She smiles at him and for the first time he seems to be really looking at her.

"Later," he says.

As Marilyn watches him disappear into the apartment below her own new home, her skin feels prickly, her senses uncannily acute. The building at 1814 South Gramercy suddenly seems beautiful.

· · · · ·

Marilyn's uncle does not look happy to see them when he comes in an hour later to find Marilyn unpacking dishes and Sylvie on the phone with Domino's. Woody's a slight man, with long graying hair pulled back into a ponytail and a tiny gut.

"Hello, ladies," he says dryly. "Welcome back."

Sylvie hangs up the phone and turns to him. "Thank you for letting us stay," she gushes in her best Sweet'N Low voice.

"You were my brother's wife," he says remotely.

Sylvie hides her wince fairly well, but Marilyn catches it. To Woody's credit, he *did* agree to give up his bedroom for Sylvie and sleep on the couch. Marilyn's tiny room, it seems, had mostly been storing boxes, which now litter the hall.

"Like we talked about," Sylvie adds quickly, "it will only be for a bit. In the meantime, we'll make lovely housemates. The place will be spic and span. You won't have to worry about a thing."

"I do love your mashed potato casserole," Woody hints.

"I'm planning on making it for you tomorrow. I've just ordered us a pizza for this evening. You know, it's your niece's seventeenth birthday," she prompts.

Woody looks at Marilyn, sizing her up. Since they moved out, Marilyn has seen him only a handful of times, the last of which was two Christmases ago when he came down to the OC with a twelve-pack and passed out on their couch.

"Well," he says, "you sure have grown up since last you were here. Even since the last time I saw you. Grab me a beer, would you, doll?"

She goes to the fridge and pulls out a Miller Light, briefly pressing the cold bottle against her cheek. She feels vaguely feverish. Though it's cooled down outdoors, Woody's apartment seems to have caged the day's heat.

"Get one for yourself if you like, it's your birthday," he says.

Marilyn does not.

When the pizza arrives, Sylvie insists they put birthday candles in, which she's managed to fish out from one of the unpacked boxes. Marilyn leans over the flames that are starting to drip spots of pink wax onto the cheese: *I wish that by this time next year, I'll be far away from here, in college in New York City, beginning a life that belongs to me . . .* But as she closes her eyes to blow out the candles, it's James she sees behind her lids, the image of him tugging at her like an undertow.

Lying awake atop the creaky single bed, between the worn My Little Pony sheets her mom bought her years ago, Marilyn hears muffled voices floating in through her window. One of them sounds like James's, and there's another, a kid's voice. She strains to hear what they're saying, but they talk softly and she can only make out words: *Nana... shoes... school... promise...* A faint bit of laughter.

The voices go quiet, and she's alone with the emptiness of the room where she once spent her first sleepless nights in the city. She stares up at the familiar patterns in the ceiling as a helicopter circles overhead. Then, moments later, there's music. She thinks she recognizes the melody, and the sweet voice that comes in from the night. *Try me, try me...* She imagines James in bed listening, and the sound becomes an invisible bridge between them. She finally drifts off, sharing his song.

• • • • • *Marilyn wakes in a sweat to early-morning light* flooding in through her window. Outside an ice cream truck plays its song, over and over. She surveys the boxes strewn around her, her chest tightening. She takes a deep breath and holds her hands up to frame a photograph of the detritus of her life, blinks, and takes a picture.

She'd discovered her love of photography when she joined yearbook last year, mostly as a means of having a worthwhile extracurricular to add to her college apps. But instead of simply photographing her fellow students, she soon found herself using the school-issued 35-millimeter camera at every chance she got—capturing a child struggling to be released from his father's grip, a girl tucking a white rockrose behind her ear, the streaks of a plane left behind in the pale blue sky, Sylvie on a plastic lounge chair at the apartment pool leaning down to paint her toes. As Marilyn looked through the lens, her surroundings had become something worth watching. Worth keeping. She began to go to the library to look through photography books, studying the work of Robert Frank, Carrie Mae Weems, Sally Mann, Gordon Parks. She'd discovered that by learning to click the shutter at the right moment, you could make art out of anything. But, of course, she'd had to return the camera to school at the end of the year. In its absence, she's begun taking mind-pictures—an effort to salvage the much-needed connection to the world around her.

When Marilyn slips out of her room, she finds Woody shirtless, smoking a cigar, planted in front of an old computer with a Planet Poker logo on the screen, above a green card table and several animated players.

"Morning," she says.

He coughs. "Dear," he replies, an edge in his voice, "you'll have to make yourself scarce when I'm working. Can't afford to break my concentration."

"No prob—" she starts to say, but the look on his face suggests it would be better to opt for silence.

Woody's made money at cards for as long as she's known him, but apparently "work" now extends to online poker. When he first moved to LA he'd landed a job at the Ford factory, her mom once explained, but when it closed down he gave himself over to gambling full-time, hoping to become the next Amarillo Slim—onetime winner of the World Series of Poker who appeared on talk shows, charming the country with his slow Texas drawl.

Marilyn pockets the twenty-dollar bill Sylvie had slipped under her door along with a list of groceries to pick up for dinner. She steps outside, relishing the slightest lift of a breeze against her skin. The hot air smells of a mix of faint flowers and exhaust. She has no idea where the nearest store is, so she sets off wandering and finally finds a bodega, where she purchases her mom's dinner ingredients plus a Mexican Coke and a banana—her breakfast. By the time she makes it back to the apartment an hour later, she's sweaty and sticky. As she crosses the street toward 1814, she sees James step outside, his shirt off, carrying a hummingbird feeder. As he moves to hang it near a window, she notices a tattoo of the dark outline of a bird on the back of his left shoulder. Without thinking, she sets down the heavy bags and lifts her hands, framing his V-shaped back, the shadow-bird on his shoulder, a real live hummingbird hovering uncertainly some distance above it. Just as he starts to turn, just as his eyes become visible, she blinks and snaps the imaginary photo.

It takes her a split second to reemerge into reality and realize how odd she must seem, standing at the edge of the driveway staring at James through her rectangular hands. She quickly drops them and waves. He frowns and does the same. His gaze leaves her feeling naked, as if with a single glance he could strip away her layers of defense.

As he turns and goes inside, the hummingbird that was hovering descends on its feeder, tiny wings fragile and fluttering.

Marilyn tiptoes past Woody, who's exactly as she left him, and spends the rest of the day cleaning and unpacking. Still looking at the image of James behind her eyes, she scrubs away the layers of dust on the sills, the hidden grime on the floors. She scours the bathroom with bleach, and is oddly soothed by the smell that erases the scent of the house, creating a blank chemical slate. She puts her mom's clothes into drawers and then unpacks her own.

She lines her books in neat, single rows against the walls and tapes up her photographs—favorites she'd copied on the Xerox machine at the library.

From the bottom of the last box she pulls out a stuffed lion with matted hair, holding on to a red heart, now just by a thread. Though she doesn't remember getting him, she knows Braveheart (as she'd named him long ago) was a gift from her father. She tries to recall his face, as she often does, and feels the usual sense of vertigo. He can't be seen head on; he's like a turning kaleidoscope, a boat drifting farther out to sea. Her memories of her youngest years all feel that way—fuzzy and fleeting, as if she were recalling a childhood that hadn't belonged to her.

When Marilyn thinks of her father's death, it's Sylvie's scream she hears. He'd had a heart attack while he was at work. In the following weeks—or months, she couldn't know—there was the murmur of the television, their small Amarillo home filling with the scent of Sylvie's Salem Lights, possessions sold off at a yard sale, neighbors with uneasy smiles who came to wish them farewell. The quiet dread that crept in and nestled in Marilyn's chest as she stared out the window of the car moving over the sun-bleached, wide-open desert landscape—an earth without borders. On the second day of the trip, she fell asleep beside the boxes and woke in the night as the car climbed a dark road, revealing an ocean of dotted lights spread in the distance. For a moment, in her half sleep, she was disoriented, thought she was seeing stars. Were they upside down? Had the sky fallen to the ground? The touch of her mother's hand, squeezing her own. "Look, baby. We're here. City of Angels."

Sylvie's starting supper—the mashed potato casserole Woody's so fond of—when she turns to Marilyn, who's sitting at the table peeling potatoes. "You forgot the milk!"

"It wasn't on the list," Marilyn says, sure of it, because she'd checked the basket against her mother's scrawl twice.

"Yes, it was. Now what? Woody will be back any minute . . ."

"I can go get some," Marilyn offers, though she resents being blamed for the oversight.

"There's no time. It'll take you half an hour at least. Go ask that boy—the one who helped us with the boxes."

She's embarrassed by the thought of knocking on James's door asking for milk, but Marilyn knows her mother's worried Woody will have had one too many drinks during his "shift" at the casino, that she hopes to keep things calm with the promised casserole.

So she steps into the sticky twilight and hurries downstairs. As she stands in front of the door next to the hummingbird feeder and knocks, she's surprised by the intensity with which her heart pounds against her chest.

A few moments later a boy answers. He looks maybe eleven—on the very precipice of adolescence, without having yet crossed its border. His features are a near-perfect copy of James's, minus the self-possessed reserve, plus a layer of baby fat.

"What's up?"

"Hi. I'm Marilyn. We just moved in upstairs."

"I know. My brother said."

"Oh." Her heart rate doubles. What exactly had James said? Enough for his brother to recognize her at least.

"You live with the weird old dude."

"Um, yeah. He's my uncle."

"Justin? Who's there?" A man's deep voice comes from inside.

"The girl!" And just like that, Justin takes her hand and pulls her through the doorway.

An older man in his late sixties sits on the couch watching *Jeopardy!* He's tall, broad-shouldered, with a bald head and a warm smile. Their grandfather, Marilyn guesses.

"Hi, um, I'm Marilyn. We just moved in upstairs?" For some reason it comes out as a question.

He nods. "Alan Bell."

"James! The girl's here!" Justin calls out. He drops Marilyn's hand, leaving her standing in the center of the living room, smells of dinner drifting in. The colorful furniture is worn in a nice, lived-in way. The bumpy walls, so ugly at Woody's, are hardly noticeable beneath the family photos, children's handprints in clay, and carefully arranged artwork.

Alan looks at her expectantly. "You're here for James?"

"No, I—I was just, um, I forgot milk at the store today and my mom needs some for her recipe, just a cup and a half. I didn't know if you had any . . . we could borrow."

"Of course," Alan says, just as James emerges. The way he eyes her makes Marilyn feel like an intruder.

"James, get her a glass of milk," his grandfather instructs. A woman in fuzzy pink slippers and a matching pink robe shuffles in from the next room, her eyes creased with smile lines, hands covered in flour.

"And who's this?" she asks. Marilyn's surprised by her voice, which is soft and high, like a young girl's.

"Marilyn. She's just borrowing milk," James says.

"You're a pretty girl. Don't let him get after you." The woman grins as James disappears into the next room. If he heard his grandmother's comment, he doesn't acknowledge it. "I'm Rose," she offers, and then calls out to Justin to set the table while Alan calls out to the television: "Gin!"

Marilyn turns to see the clue on the screen: *It's the liquor you might drink while playing a card game of the same name.* When a bespectacled contestant guesses the same right answer, Alan slaps his hand on his knee.

Marilyn feels a hot kind of longing arise in her chest. Longing for a family like this one, a family that laughs and shouts and sets the table for dinner together, a family that lives in a place that smells good, that feels like a real home. She can't help but let her eyes drift toward the photos on the wall. There's one of James and Justin as young boys, with a woman in a red flowered dress and a brilliant smile.

James approaches with the glass of milk and catches her lost in the picture.

"Here."

"Thank you."

As his hand brushes hers, she feels a spark. But he looks away, toward the TV: *A fisherman tricks one of these creatures into letting itself be trapped in a bottle.*

Alan is stumped.

"What is a genie," James says quietly.

Marilyn studies his face.

"Later," he says.

"Bye!" Justin calls.

"Nice to meet you," Marilyn stutters out to the room, but James is already opening the door to let her out.

••••• *Early-morning sun dapples the sidewalk, the smell of* exhaust mixing with the sweet scent from the doughnut shop across the street. Marilyn peers into the stream of traffic on Washington, searching for the bus she hopes is about to arrive, and tucks her freshly blow-dried hair behind her ear. She wears jeans and a white T-shirt, black Converse, face free of makeup— a carefully crafted look she hopes will make her appear normal enough to get by without question, but plain enough not to solicit much interest.

After a week at Woody's, she's begun to look forward to the beginning of school, daunting as it may be. Anything seems better than being cooped up in that apartment. She's spent most of her time with her door closed, reading and rereading *The White Album*. After she'd failed to get through the first essay during her last audition disaster, she hadn't been able to bring herself to return the book to the Orange County Public Library when it was time to pack up and go, so she'd tucked it into the bottom of her suitcase.

Joan Didion describes, in the title essay, a time in which she felt she was merely going through the motions of life—she was giving an "adequate enough performance" but had "mislaid the script," no longer understood the plot. Marilyn understands—she studies for the SATs, buys the groceries, does the laundry at the coin-op down the street, but she feels as if the invisible thread that's meant to attach her to the world has been severed, if it were ever there.

When she steps onto the campus of Los Angeles High, she sees an endless stream of kids pouring into the building, dotting the lawn, sending shouts and laughter ringing through the air. The school must be twice as big as her old one in the OC. All the better, she thinks. Among two thousand students, it will be easy to be invisible.

And it's true. From the moment she steps through the doors, she becomes only one of many in the packed hallway. She frames imaginary photos of the girls pushing and giggling in midriff shirts, in short shorts, in baggy pants, owning their space, owning their bodies and what they are becoming. She feels passing stabs of jealousy toward them and their vibrancy, but there's no point in trying to make friends. Marilyn's here for just a year, then she'll be gone.

Even at Orange High, she'd often had the sensation that she was standing behind an imperceptible screen, separating her from her surroundings. But at least she'd had a group to hang out with, a place to sit at lunch and invitations to movies or bonfires on the beach. Tiffany Lu had been her closest companion; they'd bonded over their mutual obsession with getting into a good college, though while Tiffany spent her weekends at debate club tournaments and violin lessons, Marilyn's time was taken up by a stream of failed auditions.

Just one more year, Marilyn tells herself again, as she navigates the overcrowded cafeteria. She's interested in only one person: James, though she hasn't seen him all morning. Part of her wants to skip the issue of lunch altogether, but in preparation for her meeting at a new talent agency, Sylvie's been making her diet shakes, eyeing every bite of food she eats skeptically until she'll finally admonish Marilyn, "That's enough," and clear her plate. As a result she's been constantly hungry and decides now to take the opportunity to eat all she can in private. Marilyn buys a bag of Cheetos, a bag of Ruffles, a Dr Pepper, two slices of pizza, and an apple. She carries her loot across the lunch yard, then wanders through the main building, opening doors to empty classrooms. The arts budget has been cut and along with it the photography class (she'd inquired during registration last week), but there's still a small darkroom, which Marilyn discovers at the end of a long, empty hall. She inhales the scent of the chemicals lingering in the air, slumps down against the wall, and spreads her lunch before her, staring into the glow of the red safety light.

As she eats, Marilyn calls up images of the great buildings of Columbia University from the brochure she keeps carefully pressed between the pages of her dictionary—students poring over books on the lawn, leaves falling along brick pathways, city skyscrapers. She imagines the people she'll speak to across the tables of New York restaurants one day—artists, gallery owners, magazine editors—and takes comfort in the idea that this moment in her life, sitting alone in the defunct Los Angeles High School darkroom, and all the moments she's lived thus far, will disappear into a remote past. She will no longer be the child who played with My Little Ponies in the commercial, nor the preteen grinning at a Carl's Jr. cheeseburger. Not the girl who lived in the boxy apartment in Orange County, nor the girl going home to the musty, shag-carpeted space where she stays with her mother and her alcoholic uncle. Not the child who was once trapped in a talent agent's office, ostensibly to work on her "audition skills," not an aspiring model, not even her mother's daughter. Instead, Marilyn imagines a self, a hard, brilliant kernel, waiting patiently somewhere in her depths to be revealed when she arrives into the future.

· · · · ·

Still. There is another year left to survive, and James, in the apartment below, becomes her private life raft. She sees him coming home in the afternoons wearing navy slacks and a pale polo top—a uniform, clearly—so she's gleaned that he must go to a private school. But her days—blurs of classroom lessons, bus stops, still-stifling summer heat, homework done on her single mattress—are punctuated by the sounds of him. She learns to pick out his footsteps, the light, purposeful clip he makes when walking up the drive; the particular jangling of his keys as he unlocks the apartment door; the way his voice drops deep when calling out a name; the softer murmurs of conversation, often accompanied by Justin's playful laughter.

He appears sometimes in the mornings, taking down and rehanging the hummingbird feeder, which Marilyn finds devastatingly charming. He often goes out in the early evening, dressed in sneakers and shorts, and comes home an hour later, T-shirt soaked through with sweat, the light of the sky dimming to a pale glow. She routinely peers out the window, watching him walk up the drive, his body singular in the dusk, the *Jeopardy!* tune leaking out as he opens his apartment door. But her favorite time is just before she falls asleep, when his music drifts into her room with the night air. She imagines he's playing it for her to hear, that the voices of Erykah Badu, 2Pac, Wyclef, Prince, are his way of speaking to her.

Two weeks go by before Marilyn finds the courage to manufacture another encounter with him, but finally, dizzy from the crash diet Sylvie has her on, last night's song still playing in her head on repeat, she decides to take action. She waits as the sun drops and the sky turns soft; when at long last she sees him walk out (later than usual today), she jumps up. But by the time she gets outside, he's already at the end of the block, taking off in a jog. She can't exactly run after him, can she? So instead she continues to the bodega and buys a Mexican Coke, a much-needed rush to her blood sugar. She sips slowly, soothing herself with the pleasure of the fizzy taste mixing with twilight. It's on her way home, when she passes the park, that she sees James sprinting back and forth over a section of blacktop, his body slicing through the air, before he bends to catch his breath. *My god, he's beautiful.* She stops, stares.

Finally, she calls out, "James!"

He lifts his hand, waves. In a burst, she runs over to where he stands.

"Thirsty?" Marilyn asks.

She can hear his panting breath (the heat of his body, so close). She offers the Coke.

"Thanks." James takes it. Tilts his head back. Chugs. She watches his Adam's apple moving up and down his throat, exposed.

He hands the bottle back and looks at his watch, and again, he explodes into a run.

• • • • • *Marilyn and Sylvie sit in a giant waiting room with* leather chairs imposing enough to swallow them, and wall-size windows offering views of the mess of traffic on Sunset Boulevard. Sylvie flips through a magazine with Drew Barrymore on the cover, shot to look as if she's topless, and the headline "Secrets to Hollywood Survival." Drew Barrymore is one of the actresses Marilyn admires—she's adored her since she saw *E.T.* as a girl—but she could do without Sylvie's running commentary: *Did you know Drew uses lipstick on her cheeks—for blush! I thought I invented that trick . . .* Marilyn knows exactly why they are here, what they've come for, and yet part of her feels that it is utterly pointless, that there's no reason at all for them to be in these chairs, in this waiting room, in this city, on this planet. When she catches her reflection in the glass, she sees someone she doesn't recognize—her pale blue eyes painted smoky, lips a deep berry color that Marilyn thinks makes her mouth look like a gash.

Sylvie's rubbing a perfume sample from the magazine on her own wrists and Marilyn's struggling to breathe through the tightness in her chest when a girl with a pencil skirt and pouty lips appears and calls Marilyn's name. The girl escorts them up an elevator, gives them glasses of water, and seats them on a less imposing leather couch in an office full of orchid plants—five to be exact.

"Well, this is very classy," Sylvie comments when they're left alone in the room. "I love those flowers. We should get some of those, don't you think, Mari?"

Because the question seems rhetorical, Marilyn only nods in response.

This place is certainly a departure from that of the previous talent agent she'd worked with in the OC, the one who booked her first commercial, the one who began to lose interest in her as she grew out of childhood, the one who Sylvie finally fired after the last audition didn't pan out. He'd been a short, round man, who always wore a three-piece suit, had an office with '70s wood paneling and a yellow paisley couch that Marilyn never wanted to sit on, due to its subtle but suspect stains. Marilyn can still recall his prickly, pungent smell, which, as a child, made her think of porcupines; she can still recall the dread at entering his office, the feeling of spiders crawling under her skin, the way she wished she could curl into a protective ball like the roly-polys she liked to play with in the grass outside their apartment.

After some time a small-boned woman with an expensive-looking pantsuit, a close-cropped pixie cut, and a no-makeup face comes in, all at once, as if she'd blown the door open.

"Hello, hello, hope I didn't keep you waiting. I'm Ellen, obviously." She speaks quickly, so that the words blur together, Ellen-obviously sounding like a single name.

Marilyn wipes her sweaty palms on her skirt and stands to shake Ellen-obviously's hand. Sylvie launches, automatically, into a too-eager soliloquy on her daughter's value and merits, but Ellen-obviously quickly interrupts and directs her attention to Marilyn.

"Tell me about *your* aspirations, dear. How hard are you willing to work?"

Marilyn thinks of waking up to the smell of Woody's cigar smoke, of his eyes following her around the kitchen, of his voice demanding that Sylvie clean the bathroom, and takes a deep breath, willing herself to focus. At once, she floats successfully above herself, watching as she performs her role (which is possible, she's learning, even if she's mislaid the script, even if it's only an improvisation).

"I'm willing to work as hard as necessary," Marilyn hears herself saying. "As for my aspirations? I want to make money."

Ellen-obviously laughs, an abrupt laugh that stops as quickly as it began. She studies Marilyn, letting the silence hang in the air for a moment before she says, "Well, you're honest. I like that. I saw your reel, of course—very cute. Clearly you've grown out of the kiddie stuff." She makes a circular gesture in the direction of Marilyn's face. "No Disney here, uh-un. But you've got a rather interesting look. Blond but not blond. I can work with that. And you have a vibe—a je ne sais quoi. You should lose ten pounds, but not more—don't lose your glow—and we can start putting you up for some modeling gigs."

"Terrific!" Sylvie says. Ellen merely nods in her direction, indicating they are free to go.

"Just like Marilyn Monroe!" Sylvie squeals as soon as they step out of the building. "She—"

"Started as a model, you've told me."

"Baby, it's all happening!" Sylvie squeezes Marilyn's hand, and Marilyn smiles at her weakly in return.

"I don't know, Mom."

"What do you *mean* you don't know?"

"I mean, I'll try, I know we need the money, but it's not . . . I just don't want you to get your hopes up . . ."

"Oh, Marilyn, where's your optimism? Positive thinking is half the battle. You have to believe it to make it real. We should be celebrating!"

As they arrive at the old Buick, Marilyn pulls an ad for a local BMW dealership from the windshield. It's not an uncommon thing, flyers like this one left on dusty, beat-up cars parked in the lots of fancy hotels, pre-furnished condos, talent agencies—the assumption being that here, in this city, your life can change overnight. Yesterday you may have been broke, living in your uncle's run-down apartment. Tomorrow, you could be "someone," someone ready to buy a new car to fit your new status. She balls up the paper, tosses it in the nearest trash.

Sundaes from Dairy Queen are her and Sylvie's usual celebration treat, but those are a no-go based on the weight-loss recommendation. It's just as well, because Marilyn feels like throwing up. Instead, Sylvie suggests, they ought to celebrate by looking at houses.

Not up for protesting, Marilyn sits in silence as they turn into the narrow streets of the Hollywood Hills. Sylvie drives slowly, precariously, as she leans out the window, making running commentary on each of the homes. A BMW honks, speeds around her. Sylvie pretends not to notice. When she spots a house with a for sale sign, she pulls into the driveway. Little white statues—identical replicas of Michelangelo's *David* in miniature—are lined up and spaced at even intervals at the edge of the lawn.

"Oh my god, they're so cute!" Sylvie exclaims, and tells Marilyn to hop out and grab one of the brochures beneath the image of real estate agent Rod Peeler's smiling face. Marilyn does, as quickly as possible, hoping this means they can go home.

But Sylvie idles, studying the brochure, which tells them the asking price is eight hundred grand. There will be an open house the following Sunday. Sylvie declares, with delight, that they ought to go. Just to "see what's out there," so that they'll be "educated" when they're "ready to buy." Marilyn shuts her eyes, reminding herself that there is one thing she must focus on: the diamond at the end of her tunnel. Next year. College. Getting the fuck out of here.

• • • • • *Saturday morning Marilyn sleeps as long as possible* and wakes to the relentless sound of the ice cream truck, which has taken to parking regularly outside the apartment. Sylvie's already at work, and Woody's at the casino. Marilyn tries calling Tiffany, and listens while she recites updates about their old group—who's dating who, who hooked up at the beach, who'd gotten suspended for weed in their locker. Marilyn's side of the conversation consists mostly of a bunch of *uh-huh*s, *oh cool*s, *no way*s. It's painfully obvious that whatever her connection to that world, it was fleeting. Now that she's lying on her single bed in her stuffy room at Woody's, none of it seems to matter.

She hangs up with Tiffany and fishes for change at the bottom of her purse, ready to give in to the call of the ice cream truck. She steps outside, and there, sitting at the bottom of the steps, is Justin, reading a comic book. When he sees her, his round face lights up with an open grin.

"It's hot as a devil's butt." He giggles.

"Yep," Marilyn agrees.

She gestures to the ice cream truck. "Any recommendations?"

"Get Pink Panther. That's the best."

Marilyn does, but instead of eating it herself, she gives it to Justin.

"Thanks," he says, eagerly devouring the panther's ice cream ears.

"So, what grade are you in?" Marilyn asks, sitting down beside him on the steps.

"Sixth."

"Do you like middle school?"

Justin shrugs. "I guess."

"It's a little scary?"

He pauses. "Naw." He turns to her, his mouth full. "You gonna kiss my brother?"

Marilyn laughs. "Um. I don't think so."

"You want to, though. I can tell."

"And how's that?"

"You were all nervous when you came to our house that night." Marilyn feels herself blush.

"He kisses lots of girls," Justin says. "Once I made him tell me all the names, and I counted. There were twenty-nine."

"Oh. Wow. That is a lot." Marilyn supposes it shouldn't be shocking. He's beautiful, after all, even if he's reserved. But in all the time she's spent listening for him, she'd somehow imagined him as hers alone.

"He'd kiss you too if you want to."

"And how do you know that? What if he doesn't think I'd be nice to kiss?"

"I asked him."

"Oh." Her cheeks go hot again, her heart swerving like a car speeding around a sudden bend.

"I'll start kissing soon. James started in middle school."

"Well, that seems okay. But you don't have to kiss that many girls. Maybe you'll wait and find someone you really like."

Justin shrugs, seemingly unconvinced. "Me and James are going to the beach."

"That sounds so nice." She imagines waves, and the smell of ocean air breaking through the suffocating heat.

"You wanna come?"

She does want to, very much, but she remembers James's face when she walked into his apartment without invitation, and worries about intruding again.

As if on cue, he steps out the front door, carrying two bath towels and a boogie board. He pauses when he sees Marilyn, gives her a sidelong glance. "What's up?"

Before she can respond, Justin chimes in, "Can she come?"

Marilyn smiles nervously. James raises his eyebrows, and turns to face her.

"We're leaving now. You ready?"

"Just one sec." She runs back up the steps and hurries into her room, quickly digging through her dresser until she finds her only swimsuit—an old black bikini whose elastic is starting to give out. She puts it on and throws a pair of overalls over the top, grabbing her shower towel off its hook on the way out.

James's eyes follow Marilyn as she rushes down the steps, but his gaze is a closed door and she can't tell what he's thinking. She follows him and Justin to an old red Dodge, dented on the side. Justin moves to jump into the front seat, but James stops him.

"Where's your manners. Let her get shotgun."

Justin pouts.

"It's okay—" Marilyn starts, but Justin gets in back as James opens the door for her.

She turns in her seat to offer Justin a smile, hoping he's not regretting inviting her along. He punches her lightly on the arm. "Slug bug," he says, and points to an old Beetle parked up the street.

James turns "California Love" up loud on the radio, eliminating the need for conversation, and they speed down the 10 freeway, the windows down, her hair blowing around her wildly, sweat collecting under her thighs. James is a sexy driver, she thinks. He goes fast, weaving around other cars, but not too fast; he's focused, in control. Marilyn tries not to stare. Instead she searches the road, and when she finally finds another Beetle she turns around and taps Justin on the shoulder. "Slug bug," she shouts over the music.

As they get closer to the ocean, the sky goes white, a layer of marine clouds blocking the sun. By the time they park, fog rolls off the water. Bodies move, ghost-like, in the near distance. Justin jumps out and tears across the sand, disappearing into the fog. Marilyn and James follow, set their towels out on the crowded beach. A moment later, Justin reemerges, dripping water.

"Are you coming in?" he asks Marilyn, not waiting for her answer as he grabs her hand and pulls her toward the sea. She laughs and struggles out of her overalls, throwing them down on the sand behind her.

A shot of electric happiness overtakes her as she dives under a wave and rides it, Justin beside her, to the shore. They do this over and over until she's finally exhausted and shivering, having forgotten completely the feeling of heat that's overwhelmed her for the past few days.

When they walk back to James, who's lying on one of the towels, eyes closed, Justin jumps on him and they wrestle until James has Justin pinned, but he quickly lets him up. Justin grabs the boogie board and heads back out. Marilyn stays beside James, her towel wrapped around her body, strands of long wet hair sticking to her face.

"He's so cute," Marilyn says, and then thinks the word sounds stupid. Cute is too inconsequential—Justin's wide-open charm is more than that.

"He likes you," James says. "He's not like this with everyone."

Marilyn smiles and for a while they're just quiet, James looking outward, seemingly hardly aware of her presence, though his body beside hers causes a rush of warmth to run under her goose-bumped skin.

Eventually he turns to her and says, "So tell me something about yourself."

"Um. I don't know. Like what?"

"Whatever you got."

"I was born in Amarillo, but I barely remember it. We came here when I was six. My full name is Marilyn Mack Miller."

James cocks his head at her.

"I know, it's odd. Apparently, my dad had been hoping for a boy. He was so sure I'd be one, he'd already picked out the name.

Mack seems a little unfortunate even for a guy, but it was my great-grandfather's name. When I came out a girl, my mom let him use it as a middle name—a sort of consolation prize. She got her way and named me Marilyn after Marilyn Monroe, who she was—well, still is—basically obsessed with. She forgets about the tragic death, and uses Marilyn as proof that anyone, from anywhere, can be beautiful and famous . . ."

Marilyn trails off, worried that she's in danger of saying too much, but James is still looking at her, as if waiting for more. "Anyway, since the commercials aren't working out anymore, my mom wants me to do modeling now. She'll be like, '*Marilyn* started as a model, and it helped her get discovered.' My mother isn't exactly stable. She believes in fairy tales."

It occurs to Marilyn that it's been a long time since she's talked to someone like this. Even with Tiffany, she hardly divulged anything about her family life.

"What about you? What's your full name?" she asks James.

"I'm James Alan Bell. Alan's my grandpa's name. My mom named me after James Brown, who was her favorite."

Marilyn thinks of the picture of James and Justin with the beautiful woman in red hanging on their wall.

"So we're both named after famous people. But yours is cooler," she says.

James gives her only a half smile in response. Marilyn thinks of the voice that drifted through her window the first night at Woody's, and retroactively recognizes it as James Brown. *Try me, try me . . .*

She wants to touch James. Instead, she studies the patterns

of tattoos on his arms—roses winding around each other, flames morphing into ocean waves, the hummingbird on his shoulder, the name "Angela" on his bicep surrounded by stars.

As she's considering asking who Angela is, Justin dashes back toward them, boogie board under his arm. Without thinking Marilyn lifts her hands into a frame, and in a blink she snaps a mind-photo of the grinning boy emerging from the fog. James turns to her before Justin's on top of him, tackling him once again.

"Come on! Race you!" Justin exclaims, trying to pull his big brother up. James puts him in a playful headlock, which Justin squirms free from.

"He's afraid of the water," Justin tells Marilyn gloatingly.

"I'm not afraid of it."

"He can't swim. Not like me."

James gives in. "True. Not like you."

Justin smiles back, dashes off.

"What's that thing you do?" James asks. "With your hands?"

Marilyn feels her cheeks burn. "Um, it's just, like I'm taking a mind-picture. . . . That sounds stupid. I love photography, but I don't have a camera to use anymore. So I practice just framing moments, and snapping the shutter at the perfect second . . ."

James's gaze is now fixed on her in his impossible-to-read way. She's never told anyone about her imaginary photos before, and she begins to wonder if it was better that way.

But then, he breaks into a smile. She realizes that this is the first time he's smiled at her—really smiled with teeth and all—and it has to be one of the most beautiful things she's ever seen. His whole face comes alive, bright enough to burn through the fog.

"That's really cool," he says. "I admire that."

Marilyn feels herself beaming at his approval.

"If you want to be any good at anything, the only way is to practice," he continues.

"Yeah. I've always been in front of cameras, for commercials or auditions or whatever, and I've always felt like . . . I don't know. Like I wasn't really there. When I started taking my own pictures, it was like I was getting these pieces of myself back."

"Because you're looking instead of being looked at. Because you're in control."

"Yes." She hadn't known how to say it so plainly, but that was exactly right.

When they pull up to the apartment hours later, the smell of salt water still in her hair, sand stuck between her thighs, shades of electric pink across the sky, Marilyn does not want to get out of the car. She does not want the day to end, does not want to go back inside to the reality of her life.

"Where have you been?" Sylvie asks when she walks through the door.

"At the beach with the neighbors."

Sylvie frowns.

"You know, the boy who helped us?" Marilyn prompts.

"Yes, I remember." Sylvie pauses. "I didn't know you were so-cializing with him."

"Okay, well, I guess I am, as of today."

Sylvie is silent. Woody's still at the casino, so they don't cook, instead eating cold cuts for dinner.

Marilyn doesn't shower before bed, doesn't want to wash the ocean from her, the quiet proof that, at least for the afternoon, she had belonged somewhere.

• • • • • *Sunday afternoon Sylvie drives herself and Marilyn* up into the hills. They get lost, Marilyn fumbling with the map in the passenger seat, before they arrive back at the house with the miniature *David*s on the lawn.

"There's our friends!" Sylvie says as she parks the old Buick in the long driveway. The real estate agent, Rod Peeler, greets them with a white-toothed smile.

"Howdy, folks," Rod says, in what Marilyn thinks sounds like a faux Southern accent.

"Come on in. Are you with an agent?"

"No, we're just starting to browse," Sylvie says. "My daughter's a model, and she's just booked a big job, so we're looking to upgrade."

Marilyn thinks he must see through the lie, but Rod Peeler continues to smile and ushers them into the living room with a glass wall looking onto the city. Rod tells them he's an expert in the area and hands over his business card, tells them to "make yourselves at home." Sylvie puts on a show of inspecting the rooms where others mill about—a young couple in expensive-looking sweats with expensive-looking haircuts, a man in his fifties with a sullen toddler in tow.

The kitchen is filled with the kind of golden California light that feels cleansing. There are cookies and lemonade laid out on a silver tray on an oak dining table. Sylvie pours them both cups from the glass pitcher, but shoots Marilyn a warning glance as she takes a chocolate chip cookie and nibbles. They step out through the open double glass doors to the backyard, the majority of which is taken up by a small crystal-blue pool, its oblong shape cut out of the concrete and surrounded by well-kept greenery.

Sylvie squeezes Marilyn's hand and whispers, "Just imagine, baby. A pool of our own."

Marilyn nods and eats the rest of her cookie, biding her time until Sylvie finally bids farewell to Rod, telling him how much they love the house, that they'll "be in touch."

Rod winks. "Please do."

When they're back in the car, descending from the hills, Sylvie turns to Marilyn and asks, "What'd you think?"

"Why do you do that?" Marilyn replies.

"Do what?"

"Lie like that. That I got a job and whatever."

"I'm not lying," Sylvie answers. "I'm willing that truth into existence."

"Mom . . ."

"That's your problem. You're a cynic. Sometimes, you have to believe in something, you have to *act* as if it's true, in order to make it so."

Marilyn sighs and stares out the window.

"Try it. Say it, Marilyn—I'm a successful actress. I live in the beautiful home that I deserve."

"Mom, I can't say that. It isn't true."

"Say it, Marilyn! Say it. It's important."

"No!" she spits out.

Sylvie abruptly pulls the car over on Hollywood Boulevard, causing the driver behind her to honk. "We're not going anywhere until you say it," she says, her voice wavering like a flame.

"I'll walk." Marilyn opens the door as abruptly as Sylvie pulled over and gets out. She moves to the sidewalk, doesn't look back at her mom's car.

A man with a Kangol cap hands her a tape with his face printed on the cardboard sleeve.

"My debut," he says.

"Thanks," Marilyn answers, and takes it, hurrying on.

He catches up to her. "It's ten dollars. Support the artists?"

"Oh, sorry, I don't have ten dollars," she says, and tries to hand the tape back.

"You know what, keep it. If you like it, spread the word."

"Okay," she says, and offers a fleeting smile before continuing down the block. She pauses at the crosswalk without letting herself look back to see if Sylvie's still parked behind her. A woman at the bus stop holds a crying baby. A truck makes a left turn, nearly hitting a Range Rover that speeds through the yellow light. She continues for three more blocks, reaching the beginning of the Walk of Fame, where her footsteps punch down against the dirty stars. She's just passing Liza Minnelli's when Sylvie pulls up to the curb in front of her. The passenger-side window rolls down, revealing her mom's face covered in tears. Marilyn forces a deep breath. She gets back in the car.

"Marilyn, say it, please. It's so important."

Marilyn swallows, shuts her eyes. She lets herself leave her body, focuses on the promise of next year, when she'll be a student at a university, living her own life. She says in a near whisper, "I'm a successful actress. I live in a beautiful home."

Sylvie stares back at her for a moment, then wipes her eyes. "See, that wasn't so hard, was it?"

· · · · ·

Woody's drunk when they get back. Marilyn can tell by the way he eyes her when she walks into the house. That and the several bottles of beer piled around him. He sits slumped back on the couch, cleaning his nails with his switchblade.

"Wherey'allbeen?"

Sylvie ignores the slur in his question. "We had an appointment."

"What kind of appointment?"

Marilyn knows Sylvie won't mention the house in front of him. Instead, she says, "Your niece had a winning meeting at one of the biggest talent agencies last week. She's steps away from becoming a successful print model, so we'll be out of your hair before you know it."

Woody raises his eyebrows. "Is that so?" he asks as Sylvie picks up the empty bottles around him. "Get me another, would you?"

Marilyn goes into her room and shuts the door. She's quickly become accustomed to reading Woody's signs: when he's like this, it means he's lost money at cards that day.

Moments later the shouting starts. "The goddamn drain is clogged up! It's all her fucking blond hair!"

Marilyn steps out of her room, not wanting to leave her mother alone with the mess of the bathroom, and especially not with Woody, but the moment Sylvie sees her, she waves Marilyn away.

So Marilyn puts on her Walkman, trying not to hear Woody's lumbering footsteps, trying not to anticipate his next outburst. She inserts the tape from the man in the Kangol cap. As he sings, *Can't afford to lose myself*... in a pretty falsetto, she does her best to focus on *The American Pageant*. The AP US history textbook reports on the Dutch ship that arrived off the coast of Virginia and sold the colony its first slaves in 1619. When the colony established a parliament, representative self-government was born in Virginia "in the same cradle with slavery and in the same year," the book states, with a cool distance that makes Marilyn furious. She tries her best to imagine her way into the reality evoked by the short sentences, and by ten o'clock she's only made it twenty pages into the forty-page chapter. As she's in the middle of flipping the tape over, she hears a door open downstairs and then slam closed. The particular footsteps, accompanied by a jangling of keys, that she knows belong to James. Marilyn peeks into the living room to find Woody now passed out on the couch and Sylvie's bedroom door closed—hopefully she's also asleep. Before Marilyn can talk herself out of it, she rushes outside.

"James!"

He's already halfway down the block, unlocking the red Dodge with the dent. As he turns to face her, she feels suddenly foolish. Stupidly, she thinks, she waves, just now registering the fact that she's in sweats.

He stands looking at her, as if trying to discover what she'll do next.

Finally, she walks toward him. "Where are you going?" she asks.

"To the store."

"Can I come?"

He shrugs and walks around to the passenger side to key open the door.

A silence descends as he starts the engine. She stares out the window as they roll down their block, onto Washington, up Vermont. *You are on my mind,* Soul for Real sings on the radio. James changes the station, scrolling through restless snippets of songs that move in and out of their frequency.

"Sorry, I just needed to get out of the house," Marilyn says finally.

"That's cool," he answers. "That uncle of yours seems like he might be a tough dude to live with," he adds after a moment.

"Yeah."

James pulls into Vons, the nearest supermarket. "Anyway, I get needing to get out. Sometimes it feels like it's so small in our apartment, it's like there's literally not enough air."

Like no matter how deep I try to breathe in, I can't fill up my lungs, Marilyn thinks, but stops herself from saying out loud.

"This is your car?" she asks.

"Yeah. Well, actually, it used to be my mom's. My grandma used it for a while, but she doesn't drive much anymore. So I guess it's mine now."

"It's embarrassing, but I don't know how to drive yet," Marilyn says. "I mean, I took the class at school last year, so I did the whole going-around-cones thing. But the one and only time I got behind the wheel with my mom, it was a disaster. I don't think she even wants me to learn. She'd rather drive me around to all these stupid meetings and stuff."

James parks. "What about you?" he asks. "You wanna learn?"

Marilyn shrugs. "Yeah. But I'm leaving next year for college, so it doesn't really matter."

"Where?"

"New York would be the dream—Columbia. But it's almost impossible to get into. NYU doesn't offer much in the way of scholarships or financial aid, which I'll definitely need. I might try Barnard or Sarah Lawrence, but I want somewhere big enough that I don't feel like I'm being watched. I could also see myself in Boston, or Chicago. Maybe the U of C, and then there's Boston University, Emerson . . ."

"So you're smart."

Marilyn shrugs.

"And you've done your research."

"I've pretty much memorized the *Fiske Guide to Colleges* . . ."

"Do you have a copy?"

"I used one from the library, near where I used to live." Marilyn pauses. "We could go together sometime, if you want? I mean, to a library around here."

"I'm down," he says, and they walk into the cool, air-conditioned store. He picks up a basket and heads for the produce section, where he grabs three apples.

"You didn't even check them," she says.

"Huh?"

"You have to test them first."

Marilyn picks up an apple, places it by his ear, and gently presses on the skin with her thumb.

"If you hear a snap, you know it'll be crispy. If it's just more of a thud—it's gonna be a shitty apple."

He laughs, but tries it.

She lifts her hands into a frame to take a picture of James listening to the apple in the produce aisle. She blinks her eyes at the moment he turns to her.

"I think this one's good," he says. And then, "You're so fucking weird, but I like you."

Marilyn grins.

On the way home, James puts in a tape, and Otis Redding begins singing midsong: *burning, from wanting you . . .* As he pulls up to a light, he tips his head back, his face softening as if to allow the sound in. After so many nights of listening to his music drifting up to her, seeing him like this disarms Marilyn completely.

"I don't wanna go home yet," she says softly as they park outside the apartments on Gramercy.

James hesitates for a moment, but he gets out of the car. Marilyn follows, only to find he's still holding the driver's door open.

"Let's see what you got," he says.

"Really?"

"Get in!"

Marilyn glances up toward Woody's apartment and sees the light in Sylvie's bedroom window is, luckily, still off. She steps in and moves the seat forward, carefully adjusting her mirrors the way she remembers learning in the class. She glances over at James, to find him watching with amusement. He reminds her of where to put her feet—gas and brake—and she pulls off down the street, ever so slowly, and a little shaky at first. She stops at the stop sign several yards too soon. James laughs. But after a few circles around the block, she gets the hang of it, and has to keep herself from pushing the gas pedal all the way to the floor; she wants to fly.

As she carefully parks against the curb and shuts off the ignition, she turns to James. And all at once his hands are in her hair, his wide, dark eyes searing. She feels her heart beating in her throat as he twists her long hair into a ponytail that he uses to gently tug her face toward his. His mouth is on her mouth now, and it's not a safe kiss, not a gentle one. It's a hungry kiss, full of a deep need.

He releases her suddenly and runs his fingers along her cheek. "Fuck."

She's still breathing quickly, longing for the touch he's withdrawn.

"You're my neighbor . . ." he says. "This is a bad idea."

Without thinking, Marilyn leans forward, this time placing her mouth on his, her hand on his chest. He puts his hands on her waist, and pulls her closer to him. He turns her, so her back is pressed against the seat, his body pressed against hers.

"You taste like ocean," he says.

She smiles. "Salty?"

"Not exactly—you taste the way the ocean looks."

She stares into his eyes. He leans back, away from her, against the other seat. "I'm not trying to get into anything too serious, alright. I'm focused on doing what I gotta do, keeping my grades up, college apps and all that."

Marilyn ignores the part of her that feels like it's drowning and wants to grasp onto him. "Yeah, me either," she says. "I'm counting down the days till I can leave."

He gets out and opens her door for her before unloading the groceries. They walk up the sidewalk together in silence, until they reach the steps that lead to Woody's.

"Good night, Miss Mari Mack," he says, and her stomach flips.

Marilyn gets in bed that night, her body still humming. She listens for the sound of James's music, and eventually, hears the first chords of the Fugees' "Ready or Not." She imagines he put the song on just for her, that he can picture her hair splayed over the pillow as she stares out at the night, still burning from his touch. A helicopter circles overhead. She gets up to see that the door of her bedroom's locked.

As Lauryn Hill sings *make you want me . . .* she slips back under her sheets and lets her hand move under the elastic waistband of her mesh shorts, the soft worn cotton of her under-wear. James was so sure of his movements, as if he was able to read the space of her desire and fill its form perfectly. She can still feel his mouth, his hands . . . but most of all she can feel the thing he woke up inside of her, her body alive and disorderly and irrevocably *hers*. As if she were, for the first time, aware of her own presence. As the last notes of the song play, she gasps with release and falls slowly back into the world—the sound of a dog barking, the hum of the helicopter overhead, the day's heat gone soft with the night, coming in through the window and brushing against her skin.

• • • • • *Marilyn wakes on Saturday morning to the sound of* knocking on the metal screen door. She rolls over and reaches for her shorts crumpled by the side of the bed, pushes the tangled hair out of her face.

"Oh!" she says, when she opens the door to find James standing right in front of her.

"Late sleeper?" he asks with a smile.

She glances at the clock and sees it's already eleven.

"I'm jealous, I've been up since seven. You wanna go to the library?"

She looks back at him, distracted by the fact of his body so close to hers. "The library? Sure."

". . . We were gonna work on college stuff, remember?"

"Um. Yeah! Let me just—I'll just get dressed real quick."

"Cool. I'll be downstairs."

Marilyn had hardly noticed Woody, planted in front of his computer, but when she shuts the door and turns around, she finds him watching her, a deep frown etching itself into his face.

"Sorry," she says quietly, remembering his admonishment to keep out of sight. Since Sylvie's already at work at Macy's, Marilyn gets ready and slips out of the house.

As soon as they enter the central library—three stories, sprawling, packed with what feels like an infinite number of books—Marilyn's in her element, soothed by the order, the idea that any information you could need is readily accessible, organized neatly into card catalogs.

She'd spent many evenings in the refuge of the smaller public library in the OC, and had even had a special spot, next to a window looking onto the courtyard where gulls fought over apple cores and other lunch debris left behind. It was there that she'd read the *Fiske Guide to Colleges*, front to back and back again. At the description of each school—"*lovely path-laced campus set amongst trees and lush green hills*"; "*students are academic and proud of it, even discussing Max Weber at their parties*"—she'd close her eyes and imagine herself in the "there" of her possible future.

"So," Marilyn asks James as they ride the escalator to the top floor, "where are you thinking of going? What do you want in a school?"

"I don't know," James answers. "I'll hopefully get into UCLA."

"What do you have in the way of extracurriculars and stuff?"

"You playing college counselor?" he teases.

Marilyn blushes. It's true—she's eager to show off the knowledge she's acquired, to help him find his perfect match.

"Sorry," she says, following him to a table tucked into the corner.

"No, it's cool. I'm a runner. A sprinter. I placed in state last year, but my numbers aren't enough for a scholarship. I could probably run at a D3 school, but they don't give money for sports.

I do it 'cause I love it—keeps me sane. When I'm running, I don't have to think of anything." He looks off. "And, unlike with almost everything else, there's such an obvious goal."

"Well, even if you're not getting a scholarship, it can still look good on your apps. How about your grades?" Marilyn asks, playing the part now.

James frowns at her and lets out a half laugh. "My grades? Isn't that kinda personal?"

"Well, you know—I'm just trying to see where you're at."

"My grades are good."

"Really good?"

"I've gotten straight As since I was a little kid . . . My mom was big on school. She used to, like, figure out who were the best teachers at my elementary and pester the principal till he put me in their classes."

Marilyn smiles. "So, I mean, you could probably do even better than UCLA. You could go out of state if you wanted."

She senses the tension gathering in his body as the words leave her mouth.

"Look. I'll be the first one in my family to go to college. UCLA would be a huge deal. It would be a success."

"I know—I didn't mean that—"

"And tuition is more affordable for residents, obviously. I don't just, like, have money. My grandparents have already bent over backward to send me to Immaculate Heart, even with the aid we get. I can't take any more from them next year."

"But there are scholarships, and loans. You don't wanna get out of LA?"

James shrugs. "We live in the version of LA that we live in, which is not even the same city as the one in which UCLA exists. You know that as well as I do."

A long moment of silence passes.

"I will be too," Marilyn says. "The first in my family to go to school."

He nods.

"I haven't talked to my mom about any of it," she confesses. "I think if it were up to her, I'd stay with her forever. If she even agreed to college, I'm sure she'd want me to go somewhere local, study acting. But I want to—need to—get out of here."

James stares at her. "Well, you don't need her permission. You'll be eighteen," he says eventually.

"I know," Marilyn says. "But it's gonna break her heart. She still thinks I'll be a famous actress who can buy her a mansion . . . I mean, maybe I can help her, eventually, after I graduate and get a job, and . . . it might not be the fame and fortune she imagines, but it would be something . . ."

"What are you gonna study?"

"Art history, I think . . . I want to be a photographer." It's the first time she's stated this out loud. Perhaps the likelihood of her actually becoming a photographer, she worries now, is not much more than her mother's fantasy of her becoming a famous actress.

But James smiles. "Right, the 'mind-pictures.'"

"It's probably dumb," she says. "But, I mean, at least I could work at a museum or a gallery or something if it doesn't work out."

"If you know what you want, you have to go for it. You're lucky. I have no idea."

"What's your favorite subject?"

"Right now? History. We're carrying it with us either way, so it's nice to at least know what's on your back."

"Maybe you could be a history professor or something?"

"Sounds boring, though." James laughs. "I can't really imagine myself staying in a classroom forever. I like history 'cause it helps me understand the world we're living in, which I guess is really what I'm interested in."

"So maybe you'll become a journalist? Or write books—have you ever read Joan Didion?"

"Who?"

"Joan Didion. She's a journalist, kinda—she writes like nonfiction essays and things. They're amazing. I have one of her books you could borrow? Actually, I wanted to check out another while we're here."

"Cool."

"Are you taking AP US?" she asks.

"Yeah."

"Me too."

"We should study together," James says. "We probably have the same reading and stuff. *American Pageant*?"

"Indeed." Marilyn smiles.

"Have you done the SAT?" James asks. "I'm taking it on October twenty-fourth."

"Oh. Cool. Me too. Well, I haven't signed up yet, but I obviously need to." Marilyn grows anxious at the thought of it. She needs fifty dollars to register to take the test, but after the failure of her last audition and their return to Woody's, she hasn't been able to bring herself to ask Sylvie for the money.

"Maybe we could study for that together too?" she suggests.

"I'm down."

And so that's what they do. Marilyn pulls out the vocab flash-cards she's made, and they take turns quizzing each other. She's impressed by James—after twenty words, he's missed none.

"Talisman?"

"Lucky charm," he replies, without a beat.

"Laconic?"

"Brief, like to the point."

"Covert?"

"Hidden."

"Abstruse?"

A pause. "Hard to understand," he says finally. "Like, 'The inner workings of her mind are abstruse.' "

Marilyn grins. "How do you know all these already?"

James smiles back, playfully smug. "I've been studying all summer."

"Me too, but still!"

After vocab, they move on to grammar, and Marilyn allows herself to show off the tricks she picked up at the free after-school classes she and Tiffany took at Orange High.

Eventually she gets up to find Didion's *Slouching Towards Bethlehem* on the shelves and, upon James's request, reads the first essay to him: "Some Dreamers of the Golden Dream." She loses herself in the story, hardly aware of time passing, until she sets down the book and sees the sky paling outside the windows, the underbellies of scattered clouds going pink, the gulls that arrive with evening.

"She's a dope writer," James says, and Marilyn senses that he's

been affected by something in the book beyond what he can—
or will—express right now.

After she gets a card and checks it out, Marilyn offers to let
him take it, but he says, "No, let's read it together."

On the way home, there is the music on the stereo—the Roots
singing "You Got Me"—warm air through the windows; the
city cast under the sunset sky; streets crowded with liquor stores,
bakeries, nail shops, boys riding bicycles, children holding on to
the hands of their mothers, men in cowboy hats smoking cigarettes, women in hoop earrings and heels stepping carefully out
of cars.

"She's sharp," James says abruptly. "Her writing. That's the
word for it."

"Yes!" Marilyn agrees. ". . . Those are the sorts of pictures
I want to take, the kind of pictures of people she makes with
language. Nothing fuzzy or too pretty—I want my pictures to
capture that way something can be beautiful because it's human,
even if it's all botched up."

As James stops at a light he looks at her. "She can keep her
cool even while she gets right into the heat of something. It feels
like you're in good hands—like you can trust her."

Marilyn feels her fingertips tingling—literally—with the desire to touch him, and tucks them under her thighs to avoid the
temptation as James pulls onto Gramercy Place. He parks the car
in front of 1814, but doesn't turn the ignition.

"I guess maybe the idea of UCLA stuck," he says eventually,
" 'cause my mom took me to visit the campus when I started

first grade. She told me I was gonna go to college when I got older, that I could be whatever I wanted to be . . . It's weird, to finally be at this moment—makes me wish she was here to see it."

Marilyn can feel the heaviness of his words, the way they shift the charge of the air.

"It's like when she used to look at me, she saw this amazing thing. Sometimes I feel like I'm still clinging to that image of myself in her eyes, but it's so hazy now. The further away she is, the further away it is, the further away I am."

He turns away, stares out the window at the purple flowered tree across the street.

"I remember this one time, I got into trouble at school, and she sat me down and told me, 'You can't afford mistakes, James. Some people inherit a future, but you've got to make your own.' Even then, as a little kid, I understood what she was getting at . . . Anyway, I try to keep it tight and be good, so that if she is, somehow, looking down on me, she could be proud."

"She's so proud, James. She must be."

James nods, and it's like he's pulling the flood of emotions he'd let loose back into himself. He opens the door to get out of the car, and then turns back to her.

"Thank you," he says, "for listening." To Marilyn, those words gleam.

"Let's study together again next week, yeah?" he asks.

"Yeah." She smiles, and already the next Saturday cannot come soon enough.

• • • • •

When Marilyn goes inside, she finds Sylvie on the couch in front of *Unsolved Mysteries*, a glass of white wine in hand, the open, half-empty bottle beside her.

"Where have you been?" Sylvie asks.

"At the library."

"Well, you know, Mari, your uncle doesn't—he's not really fond of the neighbors, which I didn't know when James helped us out a while back."

Marilyn feels stunned into silence. "Why not?" she finally stutters out.

"I don't know, Woody's not always a reasonable man, obviously, but we'll be out of here soon anyway. Until then, it's just better if he doesn't see you hanging around with them. James can't be coming up here and knocking on the door. We're guests and I don't want any trouble. Besides, you've got other things to focus on. We have another appointment with Ellen this week, and hopefully she'll arrange for new photos."

Marilyn clenches her jaw. James is the *one* good thing about their move here, about anything in her present life. She will *not* give that up. She will *not* let her uncle get in the way of that. She forces a swallow. Takes a deep breath and gathers the heat of her anger into a tight ball.

"I need to take the SAT . . . it's fifty dollars," she blurts out.

"Fifty dollars for a test? What do you need that for?"

"To apply for college."

"Well, chances are by next year you'll be well on your way to becoming the next great Marilyn. I don't think you need to run off to college." Sylvie always thinks everything will happen *just in time*. She'd thought Marilyn would land an audition *just in time* to allow them to pay rent on their apartment. Now she thinks Marilyn will become famous *just in time* to keep her from leaving, to keep her within Sylvie's own orbit.

"Mom," Marilyn says, more quietly, "I want to go to school. It's really important."

Sylvie's face freezes over into the familiar mask she wears when she's upset.

"Meg Ryan went to NYU," Marilyn tries. "Claire Danes goes to Yale." She hates herself for this approach—though she likes both actresses, she doesn't aspire to emulate either. But she's desperate for the shortest route to her mother's agreement.

"Well," Sylvie says finally, "I think you should focus on something local—LA is *the* place to be, after all, in your line of work."

Marilyn just nods. As Sylvie refills her wineglass, Marilyn goes, closes herself into her bedroom.

The next morning, when she finds a fifty-dollar bill pushed under her door, she shuts her eyes in silent gratitude.

• • • • • *Marilyn moves through the days at LA High, focusing* on her classes, opting to eat lunch alone in the empty darkroom with her schoolbooks, conjuring images of James like a secret survival tool as she navigates the crowded halls. In AP US history, she hears his voice, his imagined responses, during their discussions. She does her work, watches him through her bedroom window, waits for the next Saturday to arrive.

When it does, she wakes at 7:54 a.m., before her alarm. The sunlight streaming through her window looks deliciously buttery today, instead of suffocating. Or maybe it's just her mood—summer's heat has clung relentlessly to the first days of October, and this one's no different. She chooses a cotton dress, twists her hair into a bun, puts on lipstick and a pair of hoop earrings she'd slipped into the cart when she went to the 99-cent store with Sylvie this week. She likes the shiny glint of the cheap metal, the way it brings out the gold in her hair. Marilyn's never wanted to be "sexy," never tried at it; fussing over her appearance has always reminded her of auditions, of anxiety. But she feels something within her starting to shift: she wants to look pretty for the day with James, yes, but even more than that, she wants an outward expression of the way his presence makes her feel inside of her body—both newly self-possessed and ravenous.

When she comes out of her room, she finds Woody asleep on the couch and Sylvie dressed for work, eating a raspberry Yoplait and staring out the barred window, where the sun's heat now announces itself on the street.

"Morning," Marilyn whispers, and kisses Sylvie on the cheek.

"You look nice," Sylvie says. "Where are you headed?"

"I'm going to study with a friend," Marilyn says, a polite half lie. She's invented a few companions for Sylvie's sake—extrapolated from girls she sits with in the library during free periods. Easier not to confront her mother with her truth of the fact she'll spend the day with James, though she assumes Sylvie must at least suspect.

"Well," Sylvie says, after a pause, "it's nice that you've started . . . taking an interest in your appearance."

Marilyn smiles at her mom, privately wishing her out the door.

"You want a ride?" Sylvie asks with a sidelong glance.

"No, it's okay. I can take the bus."

Marilyn makes coffee, and when Sylvie finally leaves for work, she pours it into two mugs, adds cream to both.

She packs her bag and heads out, where she sits on the shaded part of the steps, sipping her coffee and waiting for James to emerge—this way he won't knock and risk waking Woody. By the time he steps outside half an hour later, she feels herself already beginning to sweat through her dress. His gaze catches on hers like Velcro, and for a moment they're stuck like that, staring at each other.

"What's up?" he asks. "What are you doing out here?"

Marilyn considers telling him what her mom said about

Woody, but she's too ashamed by it. "Just wanted to get out of the house. I brought you a coffee?" She offers the mug. He smiles the smile she loves and sips. They get into his Dodge and ride to the library with the windows down, hot air loosening strands of hair from her bun. She wishes his hand that rests on the shifter would brush against her bare thigh.

And this is how they spend the next three Saturdays: together in the library, studying for SATs, comparing notes on the reading for their US history classes, thumbing through the *Fiske Guide*. Since the night they kissed, they haven't so much as touched again. *Why not?* she wonders. During one of their study dates James made reference to cruising the mall for girls with his friends—"They're hella thirsty," he'd joked, " 'cause Immaculate Heart is an all-boys school." Why not just make a move herself, then? She doesn't know; perhaps she's afraid of growing attached to him. All her life, she's only allowed herself one hunger: for her own distant future. But now, her vision blurs; she wants James.

The most maddening: the occasional trace of his lingering smell. What to compare it to? For Marilyn he conjures the clean cool of the fall air she longs for, burnt sugar, a penny in a fountain—copper and water at once. And yet, she can get so wrapped up in showing off during the vocab quizzes they give each other, so lost in a conversation with him over colonial history, or in a discussion of the latest from *Slouching Towards Bethlehem,* that she can nearly forget the ache of desire inside her. They've taken to reading one essay aloud every week; when the afternoon begins to shift into evening, they buy coffees from the snack bar downstairs and go out to the courtyard, where they settle on a bench beneath the wide leaves of a travelers palm, and Marilyn's voice carries them through magic hour. Often, on their way home, with just the littlest light left in the sky, James pulls over in their neighborhood and lets her drive the rest of the way. She loves the feel of the wheel in her hands, the gas pedal against her sole. Most of all, she loves the sound of his voice, deep and calm, as he gives her instructions, and finally congratulates her on a job well done.

SAT day: the twenty-fourth of October brings the relief of one of the season's first foggy mornings. The low clouds and chilly air are a salve to their nerves as Marilyn and James drive to Los Angeles High School, sharpened number two pencils in their bags, "Can't Nobody Hold Me Down" turned up on the stereo for motivation, bananas in hand. (Marilyn brought one for each of them after reading they're good for the brain.) Just before they go into the testing room and take their seats, James reaches out, squeezes her hand. Marilyn feels it like an electric shock. Her body is still buzzing as she finds her desk, grateful that James sits behind her so she won't have the opportunity to stare at the perfect back of his neck (she loves the half-moon curve from his head to shoulder, the exposed skin at the end of his hairline). Instead, she channels the energy of his touch, still hot inside of her, to focus; she feels laser sharp.

When they're released four hours later, Marilyn finds him waiting for her at the door.

"How'd you do?" she asks.

"I don't know, my brain feels like jelly."

76

But Marilyn can see from his expression that he's confident. She grins back.

"You wanna get some food?" James asks.

She does. (She would go anywhere with him, wouldn't she?)

The fog has burned off while they've been inside, leaving the sky a clear California blue, pouring out golden light. When they step into the crowded parking lot at In-N-Out, Marilyn can feels the hints of fall in the softest touch of sun on her skin, the leaf-like smell in the air mixing with the scent of grilled meat. People spill out the door, crowd around the tables outside. James goes in to get lunch while she saves the only open seats. She raises her hand and takes a mind-picture of a woman in a blue hijab, printed with moons and stars, holding a french fry, a wide-eyed boy next to her, staring up at the sky. Groups of dreamy, greasy teenagers sit on the lawn of the park across the street with their burgers in baskets, palm trees overhead to match the ones printed on their cups. Marilyn takes another mind-picture of a girl in braids, swaying with her arms around herself—*Holding Her Own Body and Learning to Dance* would be the title of the photo, Marilyn thinks.

"Mari Mack, I wish I could see the pictures in your head," James says, coming up beside her with the food.

"One day." She smiles.

When they finish eating and walk to the car, James reaches out, hands her his keys.

"You drive," he says.

"What? I can't." She's practiced only in their neighborhood.

"Yes you can. You're getting good."

She wants to validate his confidence in her, so she gets into the driver's seat, adjusts her mirrors, and starts the ignition. But as she reaches the edge of the lot and waits to turn into traffic, her heart thuds too loudly, her chest tightening around it like a cage. The truck behind her honks impatiently.

James puts his hand on hers over the wheel.

"Take a deep breath," he says. "You got this."

As she exhales and pulls onto Sunset Boulevard, like magic, a sense of calm comes over her, a singular focus.

It's not until she parks back on Gramercy that she allows herself to feel the exhilaration—she *drove*! For real. On busy city streets. She unbuckles her belt and turns to James, grinning. She leans forward and impulsively places her lips against his neck. All at once, they are devouring each other. Lips on lips, hands grasping, his biceps in her grip, his shoulders, his hand on her waist, in her hair, breathless. All the pent-up sexual tension of the past month coming out in a series of sustained explosions—she feels it like a fireworks show—burst after wondrous burst setting off inside her body. She doesn't know how long they are locked together like this, soaking in flame.

ANGIE

• • • • • *Angie's not sure where the story starts—the one that's* led her to this moment in Sam Stone's Jeep, speeding down I-40, whatever sense of security she's been able to take for granted melting away as quickly as the city dissolves into desert. Perhaps there's a beginning somewhere, but it stretches into a past she can't see, through the lives of her parents, her parents' parents, and generations of invisible ghosts.

She glances over at Sam, his mirrored glasses reflecting the distant mountains, his hair falling messily over his forehead, his arm resting casually on the steering wheel. He has not yet uttered a single word to her. *Certainly almost all of the seven billion people in the world have been heartbroken before, but how many of them have been stupid enough to do it to themselves?*

Angie first met Sam five years ago, the same day she learned to shave her legs. She'd been one of the few girls in her sixth-grade class who still had hair (as a consequence she wore only pants that year), and she was determined to get rid of it before seventh grade began. Marilyn insisted she was too young; she was perfect as she was, her mom said. But after weeks of pestering, Marilyn finally caved, and Angie sat on the edge of the bathtub with her leg lathered in shaving cream as Marilyn showed her how to glide the blade. She passed Angie the razor, and after a magical stroke the hair was gone. Delighted, Angie turned to her mom, only to find her eyes were full of tears.

"What's wrong?" Angie asked, her chest tightening as it always did at her mom's unpredictable sadness.

"Nothing," Marilyn replied quickly, as she reached out to brush Angie's forehead. Angie understood then, even if she didn't have the words for it, that every step she took forward into the world of being an adult would hurt the person she loved most.

On the next stroke she cut herself. She could hardly feel it, but there was so much blood, pouring bright red down her leg. Marilyn stopped crying and went into mother mode, like she did when Angie was a kid with a scraped knee.

That afternoon Angie wore her favorite pair of cutoffs, and though she had a dull, lingering feeling of guilt, she kept running her hands over the smooth silkiness of her legs. She was at the park with Vivian, a girly girl whom she'd been friends with since the fourth grade, when they'd choreographed a dance routine to Rihanna's "Umbrella." They were lying in the grass drinking slushies and watching a few boys kicking around a soccer ball.

When the ball flew in their direction, nearly hitting Angie in the face, it was followed by Sam—tall, lanky, thirteen, with a huge grin, floppy hair, and golden-brown skin.

"You guys wanna play?" he asked.

Vivian half tried, her boobs (which were much further along than Angie's) bouncing as she squealed and chased. But Angie lost herself in the game, laser focused on the ball, her body pushing against its limits. She scored the winning point, and bent over to catch her breath, when all at once she was aware of Sam looking at her new legs falling out of her shorts. Where just moments ago they'd felt strong—inevitable and invisible—suddenly they felt like Jell-O. When he looked up and his eyes met hers, she thought of the summer lightning storms she'd watch with her mom from their porch.

Angie and Vivian started coming nearly every day to join in the soccer games, until school started back in the fall and Sam returned to his mom's. After his parents' divorce earlier that year, his dad had moved into an apartment at the edge of the park, but Sam was only there for summers and weekends. Though Angie often ran by just to check, she didn't see him again until one Saturday in November, when, miraculously, he was in the park dribbling the ball around by himself. Something about him looked at once beautiful and terribly lonely under the falling leaves, the gray sky.

"What's up," Sam said as he kicked the ball to her.

She shrugged and kicked it back. They passed like that, until Angie called out, "Goal between those two trees!" She kicked hard, Sam blocked, and they played until they both collapsed onto the grass from exhaustion. Angie was aware, with every sense she possessed, of his body breathing next to hers. And then his hand came to her face. His lips were on her lips, and she could feel herself falling through space.

"Sam!"

They both looked up to see Sam's dad, Mr. Stone, standing

at the edge of the park, leather jacket slung over his shoulder, car keys in hand. "Let's go!" Angie later learned that Mr. Stone is considered a "sexy" English teacher at Albuquerque High, known for his meandering poetry lectures. He has a pale face and dark, mussed hair, a tall frame usually draped with a rumpled linen shirt. Sam looks a lot like his dad, though his skin is a shade darker to match his mother's—a petite woman from Oaxaca, Mexico, who'd been a bodybuilding champion back in the day and now runs an art gallery.

Angie could see the blush rising into Sam's cheeks. "Gotta go, I'll see you later," he said, and jogged over to his dad, leaving her in the grass. She stayed like that until it started to get dark, staring up at the leaves falling in slow motion, the branches growing slowly naked against the paling sky. She kept brushing the tips of her fingers over her lips.

When Angie finally got up and ran home, Marilyn was already there, back from her Saturday shift.

"Where've you been?" she asked.

"Playing soccer in the park. With Sam."

Angie remembered the look on Marilyn's face when they shaved her legs, and decided against telling her she and Sam had kissed.

But later that night, when Angie was lying under her covers retracing the details of the afternoon in her mind—the way he tasted like the clean air of a forest, his warm breath on her cheek—Marilyn knocked on her door and came in to sit on Angie's bed.

"So do you like this Sam?" she asked.

"Yeah." Angie was surprised—she felt like somehow her mom could see inside of her.

"And what do you like about him?"

Angie thought about it for a moment. "We match."

Marilyn looked back at her, eyebrows raised in curiosity.

"We're the same speed. We're the same height," Angie said.

She knew it was more than that, but she couldn't find the right words. Finally she told her mom, "We kissed." A pause. "And our lips fit."

Marilyn looked stricken. "I love you so much," she said.

Angie was afraid her mom might cry, but then she smiled.

"This calls for a celebration. Your first kiss!"

Angie got out of bed and they drove to Baskin-Robbins, hurrying in before closing time. She got a waffle cone with pink bubble gum ice cream, which has been her favorite since she was a kid, and her mom got mint chocolate chip. They ate them in the car together, trading a bite for a bite. They kept the heater running and rolled the windows down, and though it was fall, the air smelled like fresh grass. It was a perfect night.

Two hours into their trip to LA: a blast of warm air hits Angie as Sam cracks his window, lifts his sunglasses, and rubs at his eyes. Angie stares out at the red cliffs rising in the distance and remembers how she went to search for Sam at the park after their first kiss. They'd never actually exchanged numbers, so she spent successive Saturday afternoons sitting on the swing, her nose growing cold, hoping for him to appear.

Weeks later, she finally discovered him huddled behind a

tree with a girl who looked older, a full figure visible under her hoodie, smooth hair rippling over her shoulder. Sam looked up; Angie thought he saw her on the opposite side of the field before she turned and ran.

Stop it, she'd said in her head, wiping the tears that had sprung to her eyes. *Stop it.* And she did. She stopped crying. At thirteen, she was already becoming well versed in the art of self-control, taking the unwanted emotions, stuffing them into little boxes, and sending them into some unreachable depths.

· · · · ·

Sam didn't reappear in Angie's life until winter of Angie's ninth-grade year. On the surface, her transition into high school had been a smooth one: she'd made varsity soccer and had become close with the other two freshmen on the team—Mia Padilla, brown bombshell and daughter of the deputy mayor; and Lana McPherson, fearless lesbian (as she would introduce herself, superhero style), a freckle-faced white girl. Angie had sleepovers with them on Saturday nights, finished her homework Sunday afternoons, and arrived at school Monday mornings with a carefully chosen outfit and a smile on her face. She was one of only a handful of black students at Albuquerque High (the population of the city is roughly split between Hispanic and white), but Angie fit in; she would be considered popular. She couldn't say why, then, she so often felt her chest growing tight, her breath coming too fast.

On New Year's Eve, Angie and her girls had scored invites to a senior party, thrown by one of the goalies on their team. At some point, Lana was making out with Sandy Houston in the back seat of her car (unbeknownst to Sandy's boyfriend), and Mia was inside playing beer pong. Angie had joined in the game for a while, but she didn't want to end up too drunk—she'd promised her mom she wouldn't drink to begin with, and each sip had given her a spike of guilt. Half buzzed, she wandered outside into the cold January night, grateful for the protection of her red puffy coat, which she wore everywhere like a suit of armor.

In the corner of the yard was an old cottonwood. Angie, in childhood, had been a masterful tree climber. She hoisted herself up and scaled as high as she could. She watched her breath on the air, the branches clinging to their dried brown leaves, the old swing set in the corner of the yard showing off its metal to the moonlight. She wondered about the people who'd built this house—it was one of those historic adobes that must have been more than a hundred years old.

"Yo!"

Angie looked down to see the figure of a tall, skinny boy standing below her. She lifted her hand to wave. And then he was— rather clumsily—pulling himself onto the lowest branch.

"Remember me?"

Of course she did. The face looking up at her was Sam's. A laugh of surprise escaped her lips.

"Wanna come any closer?" he asked.

"No."

"Okay, then, I guess this is where I risk my life for you."

Angie watched as he managed to make it up to the branch just below hers.

"What are you doing here?" she asked.

"My boy Leo's stepsister is on your team, I think. Jana?"

"Oh, right . . . but what are you doing here, like in this tree, though?"

Sam shrugged. "Looking for you."

"Aren't you freezing?" Angie asked. He was wearing only a hoodie.

"Yup."

He scaled the final branch, wedging himself beside her. "Wanna warm me up?"

She raised her eyebrows, but as he reached out his hand she took it between her own, rubbing them together.

"You still play soccer?" she asked.

"Yeah. At El Dorado."

Angie nodded. They sat in silence for a long moment before Sam said, "Let's play a game?"

"Um, okay."

"It's called the opposite game. My dad does it with his creative writing class."

"Okay."

"Say something, like anything."

"I don't know."

"Just pick something you see."

"The moon."

"Okay, so I have to say the opposite of the moon. A pebble. Now you say what's the opposite of a pebble."

". . . A mountain?"

"Okay, the opposite of a mountain is a crater," Sam said.

"The opposite of a crater is a comet," Angie answered.

"The opposite of a comet is . . . the night sky, but not the stars. Just the black parts in between."

Angie laughed. "Okay, the opposite of the dark part of the night . . . has to be sunlight."

"The opposite of the sunlight is . . . the bottom of the ocean."

"Nice. The opposite of the bottom of the ocean is the dirt on the ground."

"The opposite of dirt is chocolate."

"The opposite of chocolate is a brussels sprout," Angie said.

"The opposite of a brussels sprout is . . . mmm, something good," Sam said, and leaned toward Angie, tentatively brushing his lips against her lips.

"A kiss," he said in a whisper.

"The opposite of a brussels sprout is not a kiss. That one doesn't even make sense!"

"You're right. I was looking for an excuse."

Angie smiled. "I cried over you, you know, when I saw you in the park with that other girl."

"I was a dumbass back then."

"You better not break my heart again," she teased, pulling back from him.

"I won't." He looked so earnest, it shocked her; she nearly lost her balance on the branch.

As much as her boyfriend, Sam became her best friend. Angie discovered that all the itchy questions, just below her surface, faded when she was with him. He told her she was beautiful, he told her she was perfect, he loved to fall asleep in the afternoons with his legs wrapped around her body and his head tucked into her neck. Sam played his dad's vinyl records for her, read her passages from *On the Road*, poems by Pablo Neruda and John Ashbery. He told her about watching his father read at open-mic nights to meager crowds, about visiting Mexico with his mom when he was a kid, about his cool older cousin in Los Angeles, about his heartbreak over his parents' divorce.

When he'd asked about her dad early on, Angie had told Sam the same thing she told anyone. "I don't have one. He died in a car accident before I was born."

"I'm so sorry," he'd said.

"It's okay," she'd replied. And it was. Mostly. Kind of. Maybe.

• • • • • *Angie's now 207 miles away from her mom and* counting, the farthest she's ever been in her life. You'd hardly be able to guess at the world's unfathomable population, here in the empty middle of the desert—nothing but a few scattered cars passing, a billboard advertising an Indian trading post, an endless expanse of land so flat it feels like you could fall off the earth, broken by purple mountains in the distance like a mirage.

Sam leans over and reaches across Angie's lap, pulls a CD out of the glove box. Angie feels a twist in her stomach at the smell of him—clean laundry and Old Spice deodorant, and something else, something indefinably him.

Sam fumbles with the CD player. A moment later, she recognizes the opening chords of "Maps" by the Yeah Yeah Yeahs. The sound throws her back in time, into Sam's dad's apartment, shaped like a hallway, long and narrow, with chipping white paint and little paper lantern lights. Angie's heating frozen pizza and searching the fridge for odd toppings; Sam's laughing at one of her more failed creations: blackberries plus green olives. Sam and Angie are half-naked under the turquoise Mexican blanket on the couch, watching *Drive*; they're tangled in his navy-blue bedsheets, Karen O's voice the soundtrack to their discoveries. It couldn't be coincidence. He must have done it on purpose. Or perhaps he's forgotten?

Angie turns to him as Karen O cries, *Wait!* But Sam is still hidden behind his glasses, focused on the road.

The next track is "Beast of Burden." Another one of her and Sam's songs. This must be the CD she'd made him for his sixteenth birthday last summer—almost exactly a year ago. She'd worked on it for days, arranging and rearranging the song order; she'd wanted his birthday to be perfect. But when she'd been getting ready for his dinner that evening, rifling through her mom's drawer for lipstick, she'd started searching—or maybe snooping's the word—and discovered the photograph of her parents on the beach. The simple fact of her father's smile began to unravel all of her carefully constructed defenses: the moment she saw his face, he became, at once, a person. A person who looked like her. A person, who, obviously, had made her mother happy. Her grief for the beautiful boy staring back at her was breathtaking.

Literally. She felt her chest collapsing; she could not get enough air. She began to distract herself from the irretrievable image of her parents by imagining her way outside the frame of the photograph. Who else might have been there on the beach that day? She pictured a mother wearing a straw hat, bending to give her son an ice cream cone. Beside her, two boys on skateboards with long '90s chains. A couple walking hand in hand, wearing matching mirrored aviator sunglasses that reflected palm trees. Beyond them, a lifeguard—an older man trying to stay awake in his tower, after having been up late the night before with a woman who offered a second chance at love.

She started to think of all of the other beaches along the California coast, and then the ones farther south in Mexico, and on the opposite side of our country, in Florida, North Carolina, Maine. Beaches in Peru, in Spain, in South Africa, and all the people who'd populated them on a single day, seventeen years ago . . . As she, her parents, and the world she knew got swallowed up in the sheer magnitude of human life, Angie found she could breathe again. *There are now more than seven billion people on the planet, more than one hundred and seven billion people who have lived on this earth*, she told herself.

Angie remembered the opening line from the introduction to *2001: A Space Odyssey*, which they'd read in her sophomore English class: "Behind every man now alive stand thirty ghosts." She ran the numbers and calculated that, as of now, forty-seven years after the book was published, we each had about fifteen. The ghosts she'd always sensed surrounding her were anonymous, but at their helm, she could now see her father, seventeen and grinning.

Ding.

Angie picked up her phone to see a text from Sam: *You on your way?* Shit. She was late. How long had she been sitting there? Angie shoved the photo back into the drawer and dashed out of the house, having forgotten about the lipstick she'd been looking for in the first place.

She arrived at Sam's clutching the CD she'd made him and put on her best smile. Mr. Stone took her and Sam to Scalo, where they sat at a table tucked into a corner, soaking bread in dishes of olive oil, candlelight dancing across the room. He let them drink from his glass of red wine big enough to stick half your face into. It made Angie's cheeks hot and the world soft and swimmy and twinkly.

Mr. Stone talked about the Black Mountain poets, which he was in the middle of teaching, and how the kids of this generation didn't get it because of cell phones, but that maybe we'd reinvent poetry, for the digital age.

Angie tried to focus, could feel Sam running his hand up her tights under the table, but (maybe it was the wine now?) she felt so far away, surprised they could hear her voice at all. She was staring down at a world where she was too small to see. She felt dizzy.

"What do you think?" Mr. Stone asked Sam, but before he could answer, Mr. Stone turned to Angie and told her he thought Sam had the soul of a poet. "It's a blessing and a curse," he said. "But you have to take it seriously. We need our artists, our writers, now more than ever."

Sam beamed at his father.

"Not that practical types aren't important too," Mr. Stone went on, looking to Angie. "Like Sam's mom, and yours. Somebody has to run the banks or everything would crumble. Somebody has to *sell* the art, at least in our world."

"She used to be a photographer," Angie blurted out. "My mom. She was really good." Angie knew this based on the single photograph of an empty beach that hung in their hallway.

When Angie was little, Marilyn had waitressed, leaving Angie at daycare or trading babysitting with Gina, who also worked at the diner. Once Angie started elementary school, Marilyn had enrolled at the community college, juggling a class or two with her job. After five years she got her associate's degree, and then a job working as a teller at Chase. Only a couple years later, she became the branch manager. Angie knew it wasn't her dream job; she knew her mom did it all for her. Angie knew that even if she'd learned to be practical, deep down, her mom had a wandering-forest kind of soul, an open-desert-road kind of soul, a crashing-ocean soul. She wanted Mr. Stone, and Sam, especially Sam, to know about the girl in the picture—the girl who looked happy.

But before Angie could get any further, the waitress came up holding a piece of chocolate cake with a single candle and burst into an operatic version of "Happy Birthday." Sam's hair fell over his forehead, same cut as his dad's, his cheeks pink from the wine. He looked at Angie and for a flickering moment, the hollowness in her chest filled up with him. She wished she could have stayed in the soft place where the whole world seemed to be made up of only them, but it no longer felt sure. The billions of lives lived and lost now crowded in. He blew out his candle. She couldn't shake the vertigo.

● ● ● ● ● *The day after his sixteenth birthday, Sam left to* visit his cousin in LA, and Angie went back into her mom's drawer as soon as she left for work. She noticed the sealed manila envelope again, but she couldn't figure out how to open it without getting caught. Or maybe she was afraid of what she'd find inside. Instead, she pulled out the photo and carried it into her room. She spent the morning lying on her stomach, studying her father's face. How can you miss someone you've never known?

That evening, Angie and Marilyn sat at the kitchen table eating breakfast for dinner—Angie's favorite. She was in the middle of cutting her waffle in perfect lines when she looked up and choked out the words "What was my dad like?"

Marilyn's voice stumbled for a moment, like she'd tripped on the question, and then she replied, in a tone that was slow and measured: "He was kind, and so smart, just like you. He was a runner too. He cared about history. He loved hamburgers from In-N-Out and Chinese food. He loved the ocean—" And that was as far as Marilyn got, before the tears started streaming down her face.

She said she was sorry and wiped her eyes, but the tears didn't stop. She excused herself and went into her bedroom. Angie

cleared the plates and washed the dishes and waited, but her mom
didn't come out.

The last time Angie had attempted the same question was
years ago, circa eighth grade. She'd gotten a slightly different
set of information then: "He loved music. He wrote beautifully.
The beach was his sanctuary . . ." And then the same tears.
She'd come, long ago, to understand that talking about her dad
caused her mom pain. She shouldn't have brought it up, she
told herself.

But she couldn't help wondering why her mom had never
shown her the photograph. Lying in bed that night, she thought
back to the day in preschool, when, after Marilyn had chaper-
oned a field trip to a goat farm, Angie's friend Jess had asked
Angie, "Are you adopted? You don't look like your mom."

For a panicked moment, Angie wondered if Jess was right.
Before Angie could come up with an answer, Jess went on:
"Where are you from, Africa? My sister's friend was adopted
from Ethiopia." Jess pursed her lips when she said it, like she was
proud of herself for the knowledge. She was a precocious girl
who wore outfits that echoed her own mom's business casual in
miniature.

"I'm not adopted," Angie finally replied, suppressing the desire to grab hold of Jess's long hair and yank.

After school, Angie ran to her mother the moment she arrived.

"There's my girl!" Marilyn exclaimed as Angie leapt into her
arms, clinging tight.

"I wish I looked like you," Angie said as Marilyn strapped her into the car seat.

Marilyn paused. "You do," she said finally, and pulled a mirror from her purse. She told Angie to make a dinosaur face, and did the same. With their lower jaws stretched forward and eyes bugged out together, they *did* seem nearly identical. Angie dissolved in laughter.

"Besides that we both make good dinosaurs," her mom told her. "You have the shape of my eyes, and my widow's peak. But you also look like your dad."

Her mom checked out *The Colors of Us* and *Black, White, Just Right!* from the public library that day, explaining that Angie's father was African American, which meant that Angie was too. It was special, beautiful, Marilyn said, something to be proud of. She bought Angie a black Barbie the following week—a rare gift, since they couldn't usually afford new toys.

Still, Jess's question left Angie with a lingering sense of uncertainty. Unlike her other fears, which she could bring to her mother to be soothed, this was something she had no words for—an anxiety that she thus learned to tuck away into the unreachable folds of her fledgling self. Sometimes, lying in bed or staring out the window on the way to school, she'd try to conjure an image of the dad who would have looked like her, but she couldn't see him—he was too fuzzy, coming into focus only when he ended up resembling the father character on her favorite show, *That's So Raven*.

Marilyn never discussed her dad with her, really, beyond the same explanation, over and over: he had died in a car accident, he loved her, was proud of her, and was looking down on her from heaven. (Did her mom even believe in heaven? They didn't go to church.) "He gave me you, the greatest gift of all," Marilyn would say, and Angie learned the statement was like a ribbon on a package that could not be opened.

Angie once tried to talk to her dad, when, in first grade, she'd been invited for a sleepover at the house of her friend Megan, who was a Ouija board aficionado.

"You need to think of someone who's dead," Megan explained. "Close your eyes and ask them something."

"Dad?" Angie asked, feeling shy in front of her friend. "Are you there?" A wild thrill ran through her body when the planchette began moving, finally landing on YES.

"Ooouuu!" Megan exclaimed. "Ask him something else."

Angie wasn't sure what to say. "Um, do you miss Mom?"

"No," Megan interrupted. "Something like—like how he died."

Angie frowned but gave in. "How did you die?" She looked down at the board as the planchette began to move in circles. Was it Megan's fingers pushing?

"Oh my god!" Megan screamed. "It's haunted! It's an evil spirit trying to break out!"

"He's not evil!" Angie exclaimed. "You're cheating!" She ran out of the room and told Megan's mom to call her mom. She wanted to go home.

Still, that night Angie begged Marilyn for a Ouija board of her own. She begged and begged until she got one for her birthday two months later. She sat alone in her bedroom, her small body bent over the board.

"Dad?" she'd asked in a whisper. "Are you there?"

She waited in silence, but there was nothing.

"Dad? Will you talk to me?"

Thinking he was asleep, maybe, she decided to try the next day. But still, he didn't come. Finally Angie shoved the board into the back of her closet, and did her best to shove her dad out of her mind.

But why wouldn't Mom give me something I could see? Angie asked herself again, now lying in bed and staring down at her parents in the ocean picture. It would have helped. Angie looked like their daughter.

She opened a population clock online, watching the numbers of people on earth grow faster than the second: 7,435,678,912 . . . 7,435,678,914 . . . By the time her eyes began to shut, the population had jumped by more than 10,345—just in the single hour she'd been buried under her comforter in the adobe room on Los Alamos Avenue.

The next morning, Marilyn set a plate of scrambled eggs with buttered toast cut at a diagonal and melon sliced halfway off the rind in front of Angie.

Angie managed a bite before she heard her mom's voice come out, wavery: "I'm sorry I got sad last night."

"It's okay, Mom."

"I loved your dad, very much. I still do. But sometimes, we let ourselves forget, in order to move forward . . ."

Angie saw the broken-open look on her face and she knew her mom hadn't forgotten at all, not really.

"It's just—hard for me—to go back to that time . . ." Marilyn turned, staring out the window. "The first day we met . . ." she began, but Angie could see waves crashing in her mother's ocean-blue eyes, sending tears to their corners. She stood up, pretending it didn't matter.

"You can tell me later. I don't want you to be late."

As soon as her mom left for work, Angie went into her drawer and pulled out the manila envelope that had been underneath the photograph. Her heart pounded as she got a butter knife and took it into her room, sliding it carefully along the seal. The glue must have been worn from age, because it popped right open.

She reached in, carefully, and first pulled out a tape with a worn label, starting to peel off: FOR MISS MARI MACK, LOVE, JAMES.

She next pulled out a stack of papers and photos, at the top of which was a sheet torn from a notebook, where the words *I love you* were written in now-faded pen, in a boyish hand. Beneath it, an old brochure for Columbia University, starting to split at the creases. Her mom had wanted to go to Columbia? Angie had no idea.

Under the brochure was a stack of photos—black-and-white eight-by-tens that looked like they'd been printed in a darkroom. The first was of her dad, standing at the end of a pier. It was taken from far away, his arms stretched upward, his figure small against the ocean, seemingly suspended in midair.

Next an older woman stirring something on a stove, her dad watching from a doorframe. Could she be Angie's great-grandma?

Her dad, lying on a mattress, tangled up in My Little Pony sheets. He was asleep, or looked it. Soft light streamed through the window, falling around his face, which was open, exposed.

Then, a photo of a boy, maybe eleven or twelve. He looked just like a younger version of her dad, she thought, with chubbier cheeks. Did her dad have a brother? Where was he now? Why hadn't her mom ever told her about him? The boy sat on the front steps of an apartment building, holding a half-eaten, melting popsicle and grinning at something to the left of the camera. The steps receded behind him in a perfect line, going slowly out of focus. Only his face was sharp. She loved his face.

In the last photo, her dad was lying on a couch. His chest was bare and his legs, which looked skinny in the picture, tumbled out of basketball shorts, capped by sneakers that hung over the edge of the armrest. The same boy—now she was sure it was his brother—tugged on his foot, trying to pull off the shoe. They were both looking at the camera, as if surprised by it.

Though Marilyn didn't appear in a single photograph, it felt to Angie as if she were looking at her, backward, through a lens. These photos were her mom's way of seeing the world; Angie fell in love with the version of her hidden behind the camera.

If it weren't for her, Angie wondered, might her mom have recovered from losing her dad? She might have gone to Columbia

University. Angie wondered if her mom would have become a photographer, with her pictures hanging in galleries in LA and New York City. Or a photographer for magazines. One who travels around the world, capturing moments, feeling alive. *If she hadn't tied herself to me*, Angie thought, *maybe she would have become who she was meant to be.*

• • • • • *Clouds gather in the wide-open sky ahead, casting* shadows on the land. When the first chords of James Vincent McMorrow singing "Cavalier" come on, Angie looks over at Sam, his skin glowing in the light of the midday sun. She wants to reach out and touch him. She wants to reach through time—to pull the boy she knew to her, to be the girl she was with him.

"Is this the CD I gave you?" she finally says aloud.

"Yeah."

For a moment it seems as if the conversation will end there, but Angie pushes ahead. "Why'd you put it on?"

"I don't know. Want me to shut it off?"

"No."

So the song plays through their silence—*I remember my first love* . . . A freight train passes alongside the highway, soft, dusty shades of blue, red, and brown swaying over the landscape. She feels unhinged.

"I know this is weird, but we have another eight hours to LA and then, well, more than a week in which you're planning to let me stay at your cousin's. So I—I feel like we have to talk to each other, eventually."

Sam doesn't take his eyes from the road, but finally he speaks in a voice that bites: "I'm sitting in a car with the only girl I've ever been in love with, a year after she decided she didn't love me back. I'm sorry I don't know what to say. A long time ago I promised you I'd be there for you, no matter what. I'm someone who keeps my promises, for better or worse, so here we are. But if there's gonna be any talking, that's on you."

He's right. Angie knows he is. She wants the words—any words—that could break the silence that's now heavier than the distant, dark clouds, but they flee from her, leaving only shortness of breath, an awareness of her shortcomings.

"I'm sorry. I'm fucked up, Sam."

"Everyone's 'fucked up,' Angie. That doesn't mean anything."

The road continues to roll away behind them, to stretch out ahead, uncertain. On the horizon, streaks of rain evaporate in the desert air before they can reach the ground. Angie doesn't want to think of the last night, a year ago, that she spent at Sam's apartment. But she can't help it.

The evening Sam returned from LA, a week after his sixteenth birthday, Angie went to meet him at his dad's apartment. Mr. Stone was out on a date, so Sam and Angie had the house to themselves. Sam's skin had tanned, his brown hair streaked with sun. He brought Angie shells collected from the beach. She held them to her nose and smelled them, wanting to imagine the ocean where her parents were in the picture.

"What does it look like?" she asked Sam.

"Endless," he said. "But it's not so much the way it looks as the way it feels. You can get high off it."

Angie smiled, trying to imagine it.

He pulled her to him, both of them tumbling onto his bed. "I missed you," he said.

"I missed you too."

"Come here."

"I'm here!"

He squeezed her tighter. "No, closer!"

He kissed her neck, her mouth, smiling between kisses. Angie and Sam had never had sex; he'd pester her about it and she'd throw pillows at him, telling him it was off-limits, no way, not yet. Instead they would do everything else they could think to do, perpetually amazed by the discovery of their own bodies and each other's.

But tonight, as she felt Sam's breath on her neck, his skinny chest pressed against hers, it wasn't enough. She needed something big enough to make her forget there was anything outside of this room with its vintage Rolling Stones poster, its milk crate of records, its Virgin of Guadalupe throw tacked to the wall, its never-made bed. She needed the world to be as beautiful as it was in her mom's photographs.

Sam's that beautiful, she thought, looking at him naked on his comforter that smelled like dusk, beside the lava lamp his dad had given him for his twelfth birthday. She stared into his specked green eyes, glinting in the dark, and said, "Let's do it. I'm ready."

"You're sure?" Sam asked.

Angie laughed. "Hurry before I change my mind."

"Yes, ma'am." Sam grinned back. He pulled a single

condom—handed out in health class—from inside his dresser drawer. She knew where it would be; he'd often joked with her that he was saving it for just this occasion, reminding her that whenever she was ready, so was he.

There was the fumble of getting it on, the uncertain mechanics. What might have been awkward made them laugh. They knew each other's bodies so well by now, had been naked together countless times.

Still.

Sex was different.

After it was over, Angie felt wide open—like her borders had been taken down, and anything could get in.

"I love you," Sam whispered. He spooned her from behind, his long legs wrapping around hers, his breath warm on her back. And she felt it too—I love you—spreading open in her body like a web of cracks through her heart, like a bird's wings, like something newborn. She wondered if this was how Sam's parents once felt, before they got divorced, if this was how her mom used to feel with her dad.

Suddenly Angie wanted to get out. Out of his house and back to a room where she could close the door, where she could be alone, just a drop in the ocean.

Angie turned to face him, but she couldn't—she couldn't say it out loud. She made herself smile, trying to make a joke of it. "How many people, of the seven billion in the world, do you think have ever said that to each other?"

"Probably all of them," Sam replied. "It's human."

"Yeah." She turned to the window. The light from the

streetlamp spilled in around the edges of the curtains. "How many do you think had happy endings?"

Sam paused a moment. "Endings aren't happy." He propped himself up on his elbow. "Even if you fell in love and got married and had kids who grew up into good kids, and in your old age you still made love and finished each other's sentences and went to Europe together and drank red wine looking out at the Eiffel Tower, one of you, most likely, is gonna die first. And the other is gonna be left heartbroken. Loss is a fact of life. You can't avoid it."

"Yeah, but it's not the same," she said. "It's not the same as losing someone when you're—just starting out. Before you got to live your life."

"But then maybe you recover. Maybe there's someone else."

"There's not," she said quickly, hotly, without thinking. "Not for my mom."

Sam inched his body away from hers. "Oh."

Suddenly there were hot tears in her eyes. She rested her head on the pillow, facing away, willing herself not to cry.

She felt Sam's stillness beside her. "But don't you think," she heard him say eventually, his voice gentle, "that if your dad were here, I mean, if he could talk to you, don't you think he'd tell you that love's worth it, for however long it lasts? That he'd want you to let yourself feel that?"

"I have no idea what he'd want," she said. "I don't know him."

Sam was quiet.

"I'm sorry. I should go." The words felt like a mouthful of stones.

"Let me walk you." He sat up, looking for his shirt.

"No, I'll be fine."

"Okay," he said, and lay back down. The kaleidoscope of his eyes had stopped turning, and in stillness, the need in them was piercing.

She got dressed in the dark, the silence in the room heavy as water, pulling her under.

Sam held out his sweatshirt, offering it to her. "It's cold out."

She took it, though something about the gesture felt heart-breakingly final. It smelled like him. He rolled over, pulling the covers tightly around him, and he seemed like a little boy then. She wanted to tuck him in, to stay with him, to stroke his head and make him laugh, but instead she closed his bedroom door quietly behind her, and let herself out.

As soon as she stepped into the night, the sob that had been building in her chest came pouring out. The stars that are other suns with invisible planets, light-years away, looked down at her indifferently. She ran the whole way down Sam's block and onto the next and the next, pulling his sweatshirt against her body. She told herself, *I'm one in more than seven billion—other people have felt worse pain, are feeling it now. Get it together,* she told herself. *Stop it, stop crying.* But she couldn't. *How many of the seven billion alive today had never known their fathers?* She imagined her ghost dad, his footsteps trailing behind hers, and she wondered if Sam was right, if he'd tell her it's better to love and lose—if he could honestly say her mom was better off for having loved and lost him, for having had her, than she would have been without either of them. She wondered if he'd be the type to tell her to tighten up and shake it off, like she tells herself, or if he'd be the type to hug her and start to cry, like her mom would, or if he'd be the type to make a joke. She hoped he'd be the type to make a joke, but it didn't matter. She didn't know what he'd tell her, because her ghost dad had no voice. He only had a face. And a few shaded lines of personality: likes for Chinese food and the ocean—who doesn't like those things? An interest in history and the body of a runner. (At least she knew he'd be able to keep up with her, sprinting through the neighborhood.)

When she turned onto her block, she paused, made herself take deep breaths. She didn't want her mom to see how upset she was when she walked in.

"Baby! Is that you?" Marilyn called from the other room when she heard the door.

"Yeah, one sec, I have to pee!" Angie went into the bathroom and ran the tap, put eye drops in her red eyes, smoothed her bun.

She found Marilyn on the couch with a little bowl of popcorn, watching *Grey's Anatomy*. Angie gave her mom a hug and sank down beside her.

"How was your night?" Marilyn asked.

"Good," Angie lied as she rested her head against her mom's shoulder, like a little girl. She was suddenly so tired.

She didn't move, didn't meet her mom's eyes, when she asked, moments later, "Did my dad have any brothers or sisters?"

She'd vowed not to ask any more questions, but she had to know if the boy in the photo was alive. Angie couldn't see Marilyn's face, couldn't see if tears were starting to run down her cheeks. She didn't want to know. But it took her mom a long moment to reply.

"Yes, a younger brother. Justin. He was really special . . ."

Finally, as if sensing Angie's question, Marilyn said softly, "He was in the car with your dad that night."

● ● ● ● ● *Another sixty-three miles without a word between* Angie and Sam, and then in the middle of Christine and the Queens singing "Saint Claude" on the birthday CD, Sam makes a sudden exit off the highway.

"I'm hungry. Let's get some food."

They drive by a Dairy Queen and a Denny's before he pulls up to Joe and Aggie's Cafe, a pink-painted building decorated with an old Coke logo, a portrait of a man in a sombrero, and a large map of Route 66.

Inside, a single waitress presides over the empty restaurant decked out in Southwestern memorabilia. She waves her hand to indicate "sit wherever," and saunters over to their booth in the corner. Sam orders a carne asada burrito (Angie knew he would, knows it's his favorite). Angie gets tacos.

And then there's nowhere else to look but at each other. Angie feels for her photo in its envelope inside her purse. After a moment, she pulls it out and hands it to Sam. It seems the only thing to do, the only truth she can offer to break the silence between them.

"I found it last year, on the night of your birthday dinner."

Sam stares at the photo. "You have your mom's widow's peak, and her chin. Your dad's mouth, and his cheekbones."

Angie unconsciously raises her hand to her face.

"They look happy," Sam adds. The matter-of-fact longing in his voice tells Angie he understands: the shadow of what her parents once were, of what's been lost, stretches ahead of her as if it were her own shadow.

"They do," she says.

"They're at Venice Beach. I recognize it. My cousin always takes me there."

Though Angie had envisioned all the other people on the beach with her parents that day, she also imagined it to be some-how secret—almost as if it were in another dimension.

"Can we go?" she asks quietly. "When we get to LA?"

"Yeah," Sam replies. "Sure." And the waitress arrives with their food. Angie hadn't realized until just this moment that she's starving.

• • • • • *Sam and Angie's official breakup was uneventful.* After the night she lost her virginity she'd avoided him for days, wishing she could find a way to go back to the time when they were easy with each other, when he made her feel safe.

"You know," she told him finally on the phone, heart thudding, "only two percent of high school relationships end in marriage. So, I mean, maybe it's for the best if we're just friends. Maybe—"

"Fuck that," Sam interrupted. "Fuck your meaningless numbers. I told you I love you. If you don't feel the same way, at least have the balls to admit it."

"Sam, I—it's not that—I just, I don't think I'm ready for love."

"Okay, Angie," he said. "Guess this is it, then."

"I guess."

"Thanks for the past year and a half." He hung up.

She didn't know how to miss her dad, but the ache of missing Sam, which stayed with her when she went to bed at night, became almost like an anchor. On her early-morning runs, she'd sometimes find herself at the park where they first met, bent over, out of breath, staring at apartment 3D, trying not to imagine Sam asleep inside, the rise and fall of his chest. She'd painted and repainted the memory of him so many times she could no longer see what was really there. Only thick layers of feeling on top of each other, indecipherable color.

She got through her junior year. She kept her grades up. She avoided her mom's questions about college. She took refuge with Mia, Lana, and Lana's new girlfriend, Abby. They spent Saturdays at Mia's house, giving each other avocado masks, baking brownies, skinny-dipping in Mia's pool, watching old movies— *10 Things I Hate About You*, *Almost Famous*, *Romeo + Juliet*. Angie laughed with them; she joined in on dance parties; she played along. But she avoided saying much about her and Sam's breakup: *We just kind of outgrew each other, I guess*. And she never did talk to them about her father, or the photographs she'd abandoned back in Marilyn's drawer.

She felt, often, that her ghost dad was standing beside her, just out of reach, obscured by the light, one with the air. She wondered after the rest of her ghosts, but try as she might, Angie couldn't visualize their faces—those invisible ancestors remained blurry, uncertain, haunting her with stories she did not know.

Her English class was assigned a project on immigration after reading *Call It Sleep*, in which they were meant to interview a member of their family about how their ancestors came to America, and write a fictional re-creation of the journey. Angie's first thought was that one could hardly call being kidnapped and sold into slavery "immigration," as her father's ancestors likely were. She wished she could talk to her ghost dad about it, but of course she could not.

She didn't really want to interview her mom, either, since Marilyn always tensed up at the mention of her own parents. Marilyn's dad had died when Marilyn was a little kid, and Angie had never met Marilyn's mom, who was a Jehovah's Witness. She lived with her husband in a complex in the Dominican Republic as part of their "Bethel Family," having dedicated herself to supporting God's will (and missionary work). Ever since she could remember, Angie had gotten a birthday card from Grandma Sylvie with a five-dollar bill inside, and every so often her mom would get a piece of mail addressed in loopy script. Marilyn would set it aside by carefully pinching the envelope between two fingers as if it could burn her. Once Angie had walked in on her mom reading one of those letters; the look on her face was one that Angie had never seen before: something like an abandoned child.

Angie decided to try doing some research for the assignment, even going so far as to join Ancestry.com. She knew that her dad was James Bell, that his mother was named Angela and that she'd died when Angie's dad was a kid, but it wasn't enough info to turn up anything on the website. She asked Marilyn for her dad's father's name, but Marilyn didn't know. His grandparents, Marilyn said, had been Rose and Alan Jones.

"Where are they now?" Angie ventured.

"I have no idea, honey." Though for once her mother didn't resort to tears, Angie could hear the strain in her voice, could see her grip tighten on the knife she was using to chop cilantro from the garden. "I'm not sure they're even alive. We didn't keep in touch."

As Marilyn turned, the bowl of almost-finished ceviche she was holding slipped from her hands and shattered on the floor.

Angie helped her clean it up, then retreated to her bedroom while Marilyn ordered a pizza to replace the ruined dinner. When Angie typed Rose's name into the online family tree, the website said only, *There aren't any hints available for Rose Jones yet. To get hints, try adding details to her profile.* Same for Alan. Her mom's side of the chart practically filled itself in, however. She entered Marilyn's name, Sylvie's, and Marilyn's dad Patrick's, along with their birthplaces and years. The website found Patrick's death records and suggested matches for his parents, who were also born in Amarillo, Texas, and then his parents' parents—father from Georgia and mother from Mississippi. The generations of white southerners kept hopping backward, until she got to her great-great-great-great-grandfather, William Isaac Cheney, who'd been a general in the Seventy-Fourth Regiment of the Georgia Militia during the Civil War. Angie felt dizzy. So she had ancestors who were more than likely slaves, and others who fought against their freedom in the Confederate army? She shut the computer screen and tucked her head down to her knees.

Eventually she read a couple Wikipedia articles about the arrival of the Puritan pilgrims and wrote some bullshit about the *Mayflower.* A generally good student, she got a C, with a note from her white teacher: *Dig deeper.* Angie balled up the paper and threw it in the trash.

She ran. She loved running. She loved how it allowed her to become a blur. She won track meets, but they didn't matter. What mattered was the way it felt to put on headphones and sneakers and loud music—"Backseat Freestyle," "Black Skinhead," "16 Shots"—the pounding rhythms taking over her body until she was hardly herself anymore. She understood the anger deep inside of her muscles, of her lungs, but she never allowed herself to feel it outside of the confines of the songs that pushed her to go harder, go faster, her feet hitting pavement.

And, when she arrived at the end of the school year, seventeen years old, with only one more year left until she'd graduate, the ground was tipping beneath her.

• • • • • *Angie sees the sign on the highway:* WINSLOW 23 MILES.

"Look," she says to Sam, trying to maintain their tentative truce. She begins an off-key rendition of "Take It Easy."

He cracks a small smile in spite of himself.

"Should we stop?" Angie asks.

He shrugs.

"Come on!"

"Alright, alright."

So when they arrive at the exit, Sam pulls off the freeway and drives through the streets of the small town, until they see a brick building, WINSLOW, ARIZONA painted on the side. By the stop sign is metal sculpture of a man, leaning against a pole holding a sign that reads STANDING ON A CORNER.

"Think that's your spot," Sam says, and parks at the curb.

Angie gets out of the car, drapes herself over the man, and throws up a peace sign.

"Hold the pose." Sam snaps a picture on his phone.

"Now you!" Angie insists.

Sam shakes his head no.

"One together at least?" she asks.

Sam rolls his eyes, but comes to stand beside Angie. She takes his phone and captures a shot of the two of them on either side of the metal man.

They wander into the trading post across the street. As they wait in line Angie glances over Sam's shoulder and catches him studying their photo. He buys a bottle of water, and Angie buys a postcard—GREETINGS FROM WINSLOW—thinking she'll send it to her mom.

Her mom. Angie's stomach tightens at the thought of her. Marilyn will be getting home from work around now, discovering she's gone. Angie reaches into her bag, pulls out her phone, and looks down at the black screen. She'd shut it off this morning, not wanting to hear from her mother, not wanting to be found.

She thinks about turning it on, dialing "Mom." But she can't. She knows she can't. She can't hear the way her mom's voice would break, the way she'd say, "Angie, where are you?" The way she'd say, "Stay right there. I'm coming." Angie knows (without even thinking it), that if she hears her mom like that, she won't be able to carry on.

She's managed to suspend the reality of her decision to leave, to suspend the reality of her separation from her mom and the pain it will cause her. She's allowed herself to think only of the version of her mother in the photo, the version of her mother she's fallen in love with, the version of her mother she's gone to look for—the version of her mother that, deep down, Angie imagines she can bring back to life.

• • • • • *On her first day of summer vacation, Marilyn took* Angie out to dinner to celebrate the end of her junior year.

"Let's go to the diner," Angie had said.

"You don't wanna go somewhere nicer?"

"You said anywhere I want! You knew I'd pick that." Anytime there was a cause to celebrate that allowed Angie to select a restaurant—including birthdays, track trophies, and good report cards—Angie chose the 66 Diner, with its infamous slogan: Get your kicks on Route 66. Mostly because she wanted to see Manny Martinez, the manager, and to make sure her mom did too.

As they stepped through the doors they were welcomed by a blast of cool air-conditioned air, the smell of hamburgers and fries, and by Manny, hovering over the hostess stand.

"If it isn't my girls!" he said, a reference to their old song— "My Girl."

Angie smiled at him. "Hi, Manny."

"You look older every time I see you. You guys don't come to visit me enough."

Marilyn offered a conciliatory smile, her head bobbing back and forth in a girlish way like it did when she was nervous. Angie thought how young she looked in that moment, and for a second, she thought she saw a glimpse of the girl she'd once been, the girl in the picture with her dad.

"Not much's changed around here, as you can see," Manny said. "Just got a little more of this"—he patted his small belly—"and a little less of this," he said, referring to his barely receding hairline. It was the same joke he'd made on and off for the past several years. But he still had the same handsome face, kind brown eyes, and easy smile, and whatever the indefinable quality was that had made Angie, as a kid, wish her mom would fall in love with him.

Marilyn had worked at the diner until Angie was nine. When Angie used to walk over after school from Montezuma Elementary, Marilyn would set her up in a corner booth where she'd get to order a red cream soda and grilled cheese on sourdough while she did her homework. Angie had felt special, part of something. She hadn't just been in a restaurant. She'd been the waitress's daughter.

Manny used to make a fuss over Angie, sneaking her tastes of milk shakes when there'd be extra in the bottom of the frosty silver cups, asking her about her books, pretending to find a quarter behind her ear, which he'd give Angie to put in the old '50s jukebox. She'd loved "Dancing in the Street" and "Baby Love" and especially "My Girl." If it was slow, when the song came on her mom would pull her up from the booth and lift her into the air, singing along—*Talkin' 'bout my girl* . . . Angie *was* her girl, and in those moments she was so proud to be. As they'd bounce around the dining room, she could sense Manny's eyes on them, how he watched her mother with what she now knows looked like longing.

Every so often, when they were closing, he'd pop open beers and put on the radio the cooks kept in the kitchen, and get Marilyn to salsa dance with him. He moved like magic, Angie thought, twirling and dipping and making her mom laugh with her head thrown back.

A week after Marilyn left the diner for her new job at Chase, she'd told Angie in a cautious voice, "Now that I'm not working with him anymore, Manny wants to be friends. He's going to take us out to dinner on Saturday."

When Angie and her mom would stay up late having slumber parties, eating popcorn, and watching movies, Angie used to imagine the actors as possible suitors for her mom. She'd wanted Marilyn to have someone to swoop in and give her a happy ending, and she hoped Manny might be him. Though Marilyn was careful to say it wasn't a date, Angie had never seen her mom act that way before—nervous and fluttering, like the hummingbirds she loved to watch through the kitchen window, flitting back and forth uncertainly before they'd finally land on the feeder and drink from the red plastic flower.

Angie watched her mom dig out things she'd never worn before—a maroon dress with long sleeves that she said was too tight now, a faded one with flower print ending at her knees, and Angie's favorite, a black velvet one with a swingy skirt. But when Marilyn stared at herself in the mirror in the black dress, she seemed to see something beyond her own reflection, and

Angie worried she'd go through the looking glass like Alice. Finally she took it off and put on her jeans and the soft blue button-up blouse she wore to parent-teacher conferences. She brushed mascara on the lashes over her ocean-blue eyes and painted on lipstick from her tube with the perpetually pointy tip. Then she started acting busy, folding the laundry, tidying the kitchen.

Angie put on her favorite dress—a purple Mexican one that her mom had bought her at the flea market, which she saved only for birthday parties and other special occasions—and sat in front of the window of their apartment building, waiting.

She watched as Manny pulled up in a baby-blue '80s convertible Cadillac (or the Caddy, as he called it) and walked across the lot toward their apartment, smoothing his hair with the inside of his palm. Angie was used to seeing him on his motorcycle, but he also kept the older car, which had been his dad's. By the time the bell rang, Angie was already poised to open the door. He lifted her up, told her how pretty she looked. When Marilyn appeared a moment later, he said the same to her, but in a whisper-voice. He was wearing a button-up shirt and a tie. Angie thought he'd dressed up like the men in the movies on purpose, to show her mom that the story didn't end just as friends; maybe Manny was the star of their own romantic comedy.

They went to a restaurant called the Town House. The dim lighting and dark red vinyl booths made it seem impossibly fancy to Angie. She ordered a Shirley Temple with extra cherries, and to her delight the glass was chock-full of them. She sat on the same side of the booth as her mom, and together they looked across the table at Manny, as he lifted his martini glass.

"I can't believe I've taken for granted every day I've gotten to spend with you," he said as he met Marilyn's eyes. "You blow me away. Here's to the next chapter in your life."

Marilyn blushed, her cheeks turning red under their rouge, as she lifted her own glass to meet his.

"And here's to Angie," Manny said, smiling at her, "the coolest girl I know."

After dinner, when they arrived back at the apartment, Manny walked them up to the door. Angie said good night and slipped inside, hoping he and her mom would kiss. In the movies, people always kissed on the porch. She rushed to the window to watch, just in time to see their lips meet, just for a moment.

Manny now led them to the best table in the 66 Diner, next to the window, asking Marilyn if work was going well, asking Angie about school.

"Are you thinking about colleges already?"

Angie only nodded.

"Where do you want to go?"

"I'm not sure," Angie said. "I'm applying to a bunch of places."

At the beginning of junior year, Marilyn had given her a package wrapped in purple paper and tied with matching ribbon. Angie opened it to discover a *Fiske Guide to Colleges*.

"This is such an exciting time in your life, Angie. The whole world ahead of you," Marilyn said as she reached out and pushed the curls from Angie's face. "I'm so proud of you."

Her mom was always telling Angie this—I'm proud of you—for things that Angie didn't believe merited pride. It was her mom, not Angie, who spent hours poring over the *Fiske Guide*, adding flags to pages, highlighting passages she'd read aloud. Marilyn got Angie a tutor they couldn't afford for the SATs, which Angie took twice this past year; Marilyn insisted they spend hours watching virtual tours of various schools on YOUniversityTV; she made too many appointments with the college counselor at school, who could never remember their names. Still, for all of Marilyn's excitement, Angie didn't miss the sadness in her mom's eyes when she would talk about Angie going away, and she worried about leaving her alone.

Angie's grades were good, though she wasn't an overachiever with APs and all that. She should have been able to do well on the SAT, she thought, what with all the extra tutoring, but while her score did go up a few points between tests, it wasn't in "Ivy League range." Still, when her mom suggested she consider Columbia, Angie thought of the worn brochure tucked into the manila envelope, and she agreed to apply.

"Are you sure?" Marilyn asked. "I—when I was your age, you know, my mom put a lot of pressure on me, and I never want to do that to you. I want you to feel free to make your own choices. As long as you're happy, Angie—that's what I want for you."

Angie fought her frustration—she'd just agreed to her mom's suggestion! Part of her wished that Marilyn just wanted her to be a doctor or lawyer or something like that—at least then the path would be obvious.

"I am happy, Mom," she'd said, and forced a smile.

Angie now looked up at Manny, hovering over their booth.

"Do you girls want your usual?" he asked.

They did. For Angie, it was the same grilled cheese meal she'd had since she was a kid, and for Marilyn it was a green chile cheeseburger and a glass of white wine.

A moment later, "My Girl" came on the jukebox, and Angie looked up to see Manny smiling at them from across the restaurant. The early-evening sunlight spilled onto the checkered linoleum floor. In the next booth over, a little girl shared a sundae with her father.

The back door opened, and in walked Sam Stone, in a blue diner uniform, tying an apron around his narrow hips. Angie felt like her breath had been vacuumed out of her chest. Aside from a few times she'd spotted Sam from a distance outside Mr. Stone's apartment, she hadn't seen him since they broke up almost a year ago.

"Angie?" her mom asked. "Are you okay? Where'd you go?"

"I'm fine." She stared down at the table. Moments later, there was Sam's hand—the hand that had held her own, the hand that used to sweep across her stomach—right in front of her, setting down a water glass.

"Oh, Sam!" Marilyn said. "Hi! I didn't know you were working here." Angie was grateful for her mom's voice right then, cheerful and kind, because she couldn't find her own.

"Hi, Marilyn. Hey, Angie." Angie could see a spike of barely perceptible emotion in his face, like the tiny needle of a Richter scale, but his expression quickly settled into something neutral.

Marilyn continued, "How long have you been—"

"Since winter break," Sam answered before she could finish the question. "Busing. I've been mostly working weekends."

"I worked here for years," Marilyn added.

Sam smiled at her mom. "I know, Angie told me. It's a great place. Though I have to say, their grilled cheese isn't as good as yours." Angie remembered the afternoons they'd spent at her house, when Marilyn would make them lunch and Sam would make her laugh by eating three grilled cheeses at once.

Marilyn smiled back at him, but before Angie could think of anything to say, she heard his voice again. "Well, we're getting busy. Dinner rush. Good to see you guys."

"Bye," Angie said, the single word to come out of her mouth.

As Sam walked off, Marilyn looked at her with sympathy, which only made Angie feel worse.

"Was that hard for y—" her mom began to ask, but Angie just shook her head and said, "I'm fine. Can we not talk about Sam right now?" The tiny interaction had been enough to tear something inside of her, and she felt herself splitting open.

When they finished eating, it was Manny himself who came to clear the plates, and then he sat down in the booth beside Marilyn, telling her about his idea to start a pop-up restaurant that would open in various locations around the state. He'd work with local farmers; his grandmother's mole verde recipe would be their specialty.

Her mom was polite, kind even, but Angie could see she was

holding the door shut. Each time Manny saw Marilyn, he pressed, just gently, to see if it would swing open, but it never did. Angie didn't know why she'd made them come here tonight—or why, after all these years, she still insisted on making them visit him.

After their first not-a-date to the Town House, there had been a few more weeks of outings with Manny—a movie, the Tramway, bowling at Silva Lanes—and Angie watched her mom begin to open up, laughing, acting silly and giddy—a version of her that Angie had only ever seen when it was just the two of them at home. And then, Marilyn had invited him for dinner. Angie helped her mom grate the cheese for enchiladas, mash the guacamole, mix the batter for her strawberry shortcake in preparation.

He got there twenty minutes early, with a box of brand-new colored pencils for Angie, a bouquet of lilacs—Marilyn's favorite—and a bottle of red wine. Aside from her old babysitter Gina or occasionally one of Angie's school friends, they hardly ever had people over. As Marilyn showed Manny around, her body was tense, her voice suddenly formal. When he'd paused in front of the photograph of the ocean that hung in the hallway, her mom seemed eager to move on, tucking her hair the way she did when she was nervous. In the image, the sky was full of clouds with heavy gray bottoms. There was a kid's swimsuit at the edge of the shore, about to be sucked up by the waves. A bird dove into the water, almost out of frame. The photo had always made Angie think of ghosts. She sometimes stood in front of it for forever, staring at the place where the water met the sky.

"Wow," Manny said. "This is beautiful."

"Thank you," her mom replied.

"Where'd you get it?"

"I took it," Marilyn said, but her voice sounded like something shutting down.

"I knew you were a lot of things, but I didn't know you were a great artist too."

"Well," her mom said quickly, "not really. It was a lucky shot, anyway, and it was a really long time ago. I don't take pictures anymore."

"That's a shame," Manny said. He sounded like a doctor who was pressing gently on an old injury to test how deep it went.

"I just keep this one to remind me," Marilyn said finally.

"Of what?"

She stared at the photograph as if she thought she could step into it. "All the drops that fill an ocean."

While her mom went to finish dinner, Angie pulled Manny into her room, showing off her books, her stuffed animals, her set of paints, anxious to make things go right. They ended up on her floor in a stiff Chinese checkers competition until Marilyn called them to the table.

The food was meticulously arranged on the plates. Manny complimented the meal, asked for seconds, poured Marilyn more wine, told them funny stories. Her mom finally started to loosen up.

After dinner, Manny insisted on helping them clean, and when he finished drying the last dish, he pulled a *Jerry Maguire* DVD from his suit jacket, his eyebrows arched.

"I brought a movie—I know you like this one."

Marilyn looked momentarily off balance.

"I mean, if you're in the mood," he said. "I can always leave it for you, pick it up next time."

Marilyn glanced uncertainly at the clock. "Well, Angie and I usually read before bed . . ."

"That's okay," Angie said quickly, feigning a yawn. "We don't have to read tonight, I'm tired anyway."

Her mom paused a moment. "Alright, then," she said, a small smile forming on her face. "Why not . . ."

So Angie got ready for bed and hugged Manny good night. Her mom came into her room, folding the covers over her. "I love you more than the whole universe," she said.

"I love you more than infinity times infinity," Angie replied—a bedtime exchange that had been part of their routine for as long as Angie could remember.

Her mom kissed her forehead, and then Angie asked, all at once, "Do you think Manny will be like my dad?"

"Oh, honey. I don't know."

Angie sensed her mom rolling backward down a hill, moving away from Angie, from Manny, from the night. Angie couldn't catch her.

"Your dad was . . . Manny and I are . . . just friends. He's a very nice man, but you're my family." Angie felt a sudden, crushing weight on her chest. She nodded and closed her eyes, pretending she'd drifted off to sleep.

But in fact, she stayed awake, listening carefully to the hushed voices coming from the living room, listening for the sound of the movie starting that never came. Instead there was the sound of her mom crying quietly—a noise she'd become attuned to—and eventually, the sound of the door opening and then closing.

In the weeks that followed, Angie asked her mom when they were going to hang out with Manny again, and she'd say vague things like "Not this weekend" or "He's busy with work, baby." In an attempt to change the subject, Marilyn would say, "Let's go to Chuck E. Cheese's! You and me." Though her voice was full of forced cheer, the light that Manny turned on in her eyes had gone off. Angie felt if only her mom would let Manny come back, she'd go bright again. But finally, Angie agreed to Chuck E. Cheese's, and lost herself in the Skee-Ball game and the quest for tickets, trying to forget Manny who knew how to salsa dance, Manny with his movie outfits and big smile.

• • • • • *Angie managed a wave at Sam as she and Marilyn said* good night to Manny and walked out of the 66 Diner, to discover the sky lit up in classic New Mexico fashion—brilliant oranges blooming from lavender blues, the Sandia Mountains glowing the watermelon pink of their namesake. Angie let her mom take her hand and squeeze it like she had when Angie was a child.

"It's beautiful, isn't it?" Marilyn said.

"Yeah." Angie sensed her mom saw some deeper meaning in the spectacle of color, something secret that she wanted Angie to see too.

In the minutes it took them to drive back, the sunset slowly extinguished itself, leaving the sky in twilight. Angie bent herself away from the sadness in her stomach and into the safety of their home. Not everyone had what she did, she reminded herself—a loving mom, a house they'd lived in long enough that it had been imprinted with the shapes of her childhood.

As soon as they walked inside, Marilyn began lighting her candles. For as long as Angie could remember, their house had been full of them—the kind you'd see in Catholic churches, the kind you could buy at the 99-cent store. It used to be a regular weekly stop, after Marilyn picked up Angie from school. She'd get toilet paper and paper towels and bags of rice and oranges and cleaning products, and she'd let Angie pick out a treat—flip-flops or a pinwheel or a pack of colorful erasers. And then she'd load up the rest of the cart with votive candles.

The night is good, Marilyn had said to Angie, more than once. It's a clear dark, a clean dark, but the moment before it's arrived, when you sense yourself losing the light—that's when Marilyn would replace the sun with tiny indoor flames.

She would leave them burning in their tall glass jars—it's bad luck, she said, to blow them out—and since Angie was a little kid, she got used to living with the flickering lights and their ghostly shadows that would accompany her when she'd get up to use the bathroom in the middle of the night, or when she used to come in late from Sam's house, her mom already asleep. The scent of wax smelled like home.

This evening, while Marilyn lit the candles, Angie made popcorn, with butter and Parmesan cheese the way Marilyn had taught her, and they curled up on the couch together. Angie felt like something familiar and chose *Breakfast at Tiffany's*.

Halfway through the movie, Angie could hear Marilyn snoring softly. It used to be Angie who would fall asleep during their movie nights, and her mom would carry her to bed. But these days, more often than not, Marilyn was the one who dozed off before the credits rolled. With her head on the armrest of the couch, her eyes fluttering in sleep, she looked, as she did more and more to Angie recently, very young. As if she were a girl, rather than the mother who'd taken care of Angie since she was born, who'd fought to give Angie this very home. Angie pulled their favorite fuzzy pink blanket around her and tiptoed to her room.

She got in bed but felt wide awake. Her iPhone screen was the sole light in the dark room as she began fiddling around, and then, as she found herself scrolling through Sam's Instagram—his only social media profile and thus her only tie to him. His last post, a week ago, was of an outdoor concert—the Madrid Blues Festival, full of bikers and hipsters alike. The image showed a picture of Sam's dad holding up a plastic cup of beer. She scrolled through the rest of Sam's photos—trains tagged with graffiti art, Latin American soccer stars, a still image from the movie *Boyhood*, and one from *Sunset Boulevard*, the neon sign for the El Don motel on Central where a cowboy wields a red lasso, his mom making dinner, an image grab of a song on Spotify: "Some Dreamers" by a group called Fly Boys, with the text "gets me every time."

Angie hadn't heard of the band before. Sam read all the music blogs, and though he also had a penchant for his dad's '60s folk, he was always introducing her to new stuff when they were together. She opened her browser to Google "Some Dreamers" and clicked on the link to the video.

The music was haunting—mostly instrumental, the lyrics sparse: *An inch of moonlight, rattled green, quiet, quiet, the night is coming, dream you're rising, this is your own ragged sky . . .* In the video, there was a boy Angie's own age. He was brown-skinned, with big, pretty eyes, eyes that looked sad. The camera followed him moving through a pool party—kids stuffed into a sun-blasted backyard, drinking from Solo cups and passing joints, wearing board shorts and bikinis, their bodies perfect in the way that all young bodies are perfect. The boy, our boy, was apart from the crowd. He climbed up to a tall diving board. He looked up and jumped, his arms spread, flying through air. Angie waited for the splash—but as the camera followed him down, there was no water; his body flattened against the concrete bottom of the pool. Angie gasped in horror. A line of blood spread from the back of his perfect head like an inkblot. The world lingered in a long stillness, the other kids now vanished. A lone helicopter circled overhead. Power lines crossed each other. Palm trees shuddered in the breeze.

And then, at once, the boy got up and began to dance. At first he danced as if invisible strings were pulling his limbs, lifting him, moving his body to the rhythm, and then, slowly, he began to break free of them, to move effortlessly, powerfully, joyfully.

Angie watched it three times, in a frozen trance. It was uncannily beautiful, and it felt *true,* in a way she didn't have words for.

It wasn't until she'd watched it for the fourth time that she read the text below. "A short film by director Justin Bell featuring music by Fly Boys." Justin Bell. Justin Bell. Her dad's brother's name. That was the boy in the picture. Of course, it couldn't have been him. Her mom said he died . . . and yet, Angie had a feeling, a feeling she couldn't shake, that it was.

She Googled "Justin Bell, Some Dreamers video," and found several links. The first article she opened, a blog post by a DJ for KCRW—a Los Angeles public radio station—referred to Justin Bell as an important up-and-coming LA-based music video director with "modest brilliance." The video had won the audience choice award for best short film at the Los Angeles Film Festival. There were several other articles on music websites. But none of them came with a photo. One article noted that despite his growing relevance, even Google finds Justin Bell elusive. Another article noted that personal questions were returned unanswered. But that same article did note his age—twenty-nine. He'd looked about eleven or twelve in the pictures, so that would be right for her dad's brother.

She watched the "Some Dreamers" video again, and it felt clear. The name was not a coincidence; it couldn't be. Justin Bell who lived in LA and had made the music video with its images that cut right to Angie's center, he was the Justin from the pictures, the round-faced boy on the steps with the melting popsicle. He wasn't dead like her mother said. He was her father's brother. Her uncle. He was alive.

So if he wasn't dead like her mom said, Angie thought, her heart suddenly trying to leap from her chest, what if her dad wasn't either?

Angie did what she always did when there was too much feeling, when she needed to lose herself. She put on her running shoes and slipped out her window, taking off into the night. She hardly saw the houses in the neighborhood where she'd always lived flying by her, hardly saw the moon or the trees or the windows where lights flicked off, hardly felt the collected heat of the sun rising from the blacktop, hardly heard the crickets with their thrumming songs. Instead, she heard the lyrics of "Some Dreamers," the chords of the song already etched into her. She saw the video bright in her mind. Her mom lied to her, she thought, and this fact was as stunning as the hope of finding Justin, as the chance her dad was alive. She pushed past the burn in her lungs and her limbs, past the pain, past the limits of her body, until she knew what she had to do.

Angie was high from exertion, sweaty and still breathless, when she stepped onto the porch of apartment 3D with the cracked white paint. She saw the lights were on inside and rang the bell.

Sam opened the door in sweatpants and a hoodie. His eyes looked bloodshot. A moment passed before he seemed to register her on his doorstep.

"Angie?"

"Hi." She landed halfway back in the world again, realizing the strangeness of her showing up at his house like this, a year after they'd broken up.

"Are you okay? What's wrong?"

"I'm—I— Sorry. To just be here. I need to talk to you. Can I—come in?"

"Okay," Sam said, his body guarded as he stepped aside to let her pass.

The apartment was almost exactly as it had lived in her memory, shaped like a hallway, long and narrow, with strings of paper lantern lights. A giant arched mirror leaned precariously near the door, reflecting the prints hung on the walls—Miró, Dalí, Marcel Duchamp.

It smelled like weed. It always had, vaguely, because Sam's dad smoked, with his door closed and bedroom window open, imagining he got away with it. She glanced at the joint in an espresso mug being used as an ashtray, and guessed Sam had taken up his father's habit, and now neither of them needed to hide it.

Sam settled onto the couch and pulled the blue Mexican throw blanket against him—the same blanket that he and Angie used to lie under together. He picked up a half-finished beer and began peeling at its label.

"Is your dad home?" Angie asked.

"On a date."

She wasn't surprised; Mr. Stone had often been on dates, which meant she and Sam had had the house to themselves many nights.

"What's up?" Sam asked, a sharpness in his voice.

Angie moved toward him and took a seat at the very edge of the couch. She suddenly felt as if she were walking on a frozen pond, unsure how well the ice would hold, unsure if she cared.

"Are you—going to see your cousin in LA this summer?"

"Yeah. Next week. Why?"

"I know that this is a little weird, but I have to ask you for a really big favor. I mean, you're the only one I can ask, but—I—can I come with you? You're driving, right?"

Sam squinted at her. He sipped his beer. "We haven't talked in a year and you show up at my house at midnight asking me to drive you to LA?"

Angie took a deep breath. She wanted to tell Sam everything, wanted to make him understand, but the losses began to fall into each other—Sam, Manny, her mother's talent for photography, the shape of childhood—leaving Angie with a gaping hole. She turned toward the missing space left by her father, whose absence, at least, had a form.

"I think my dad could be there. He could be alive."

"What?"

"You know the song you posted a couple weeks ago? 'Some Dreamers'?"

"You were looking at my Instagram?"

"Yeah. But the point is—I saw the video, and it's—I think my uncle made it. The video, not the song. My dad's brother. My mom told me he died too, but he's alive."

Angie waited for Sam to react. "Wow, Angie. That's—that's crazy," he said finally. "I get why you'd want to find him, but I don't know that you should just up and go to LA. I mean, how do you know it's him? Have you talked to your mom?"

Angie shook her head no.

"Well, what's your plan when you get there? You're just gonna— go where? Find him how? You should at least get in touch with him first."

"If I can, will you bring me with you?"

Sam was silent.

"Please," Angie said. She could hear the desperation in her own voice and tried to swallow it. "My mom lied about my uncle, which means she could have lied about my dad too." She glanced at Sam. "He could be alive. I have to go. I have to find out."

Sam was looking away from her, still tearing at the label on the beer.

"I know that there's no reason for you to say yes," Angie continued. "I know you don't have to do this. And I wouldn't ask if I didn't—if it wasn't—important, but I—I need you."

Sam picked up the joint from the espresso cup and lit it.

"Don't say shit like that, Angie." He exhaled. "You can come. But don't give me that I-need-you bullshit. Don't pretend it's like that again. You need my fuckin' car."

He looked at her. "And I suggest you come up with an actual plan. 'Cause LA is a big-ass city, so you're not gonna just walk down the street and find this guy. I'm not getting involved. But my recommendation, for your sake, is that you don't make this trip unless you know what you're doing. And that you talk to Marilyn."

"Thank you," Angie said, unsure how to respond.

"I'm leaving Thursday. I'll pick you up at ten." He looked away, exhaling smoke in the direction of the white linen curtains that shuddered against the night breeze.

"Okay. Thank you, again."

He nodded. She let herself out.

She stepped onto the porch, her clothes still damp with sweat, and shivered against the warm night breeze. As she walked home, now taking in the sound of the crickets that felt as loud as engines, the rustle of summer-green leaves in the dark cottonwood trees, the innumerable stars in the sky, she thought of the last time she'd left Sam's house, late at night, the year before. And in that moment, she had the sense that if she could find her dad, it could change her into the girl who'd know how to say "I love you" to Sam.

• • • • • *Sam and Angie are just past a town called Needles, in* the long, empty stretch of road that runs through the Mojave Desert, when the gathered clouds begin to pour. Angie holds her breath as the rain comes down in sheets; the patter on the metal roof of the car makes its own rushed music that plays over Alabama Shakes singing "Sound & Color." The windshield wipers work overtime, but Angie can't see more than a few feet ahead of them, and she knows that Sam, seemingly calm behind the wheel, can't either. A semitruck zooms by, dousing them.

Without breaking concentration, Sam carefully guides the car to the shoulder of the road.

"Guess we'll just wait it out," he says, and Angie's happy that he's speaking to her now, at least sort of normally. He reaches over her lap to open the glove box, and pulls out a little tin meant for mints. He takes out a joint and lights it. Angie watches the desert getting drenched, the soft browns and yellows stretching outward as far as she can see.

"I Want a Little Sugar in My Bowl," the last song on Sam's birthday CD begins. Angie looks over at Sam, his eyes now shut in the driver's seat. *Come on, save my soul* . . . Nina Simone sings, as if she were pulling the notes up from deep water.

Sam opens one eye and sees Angie watching him. A look of

uncertain longing passes between them, before Sam shuts his eye again. Angie wants him; she can feel her body insisting on the truth of this fact. She wonders if she's gotten a contact high. She read somewhere that the concept is just a myth, but she feels suddenly light-headed.

"How's your dad?" Angie asks. It's the only thing she can think of.

"Fine. Good. He's got a girlfriend now. A proper one. They've been together almost six months."

"Do you like her?"

"She's alright. Young. And pretty. Of course. I think I make her nervous. Her voice goes up like two octaves when she talks to me." He looks off and says eventually, "She's Italian. A great cook. Sometimes I watch them together in the kitchen, chopping stuff, singing to my dad's old LPs, him spinning her around, her dumping pasta in the strainer. I can't remember my parents ever being happy like that."

He seems vulnerable, the same kid Angie once knew. She has the overwhelming desire to wrap her arms around him.

He holds in the smoke before he exhales. "You want?"

"No, I'm good," Angie says.

He takes a final hit, then puts it out. Nina keeps singing. Another truck rushes by, momentarily blinding them with its wake. Sam rubs at the fog on the window and peers into the rain.

"A few weeks before my parents told me they were getting a divorce," he says, "Mom was having these friends over for dinner. She'd spent all day preparing, and my dad started complaining about it—he hated guests. She cracked, saying how he never appreciated her, how he saved the best parts of himself for his students and had nothing left for her. Dad pointed to her enchiladas and guacamole, to the pitchers of drinks and flowers in vases, and he was like, 'But, Camila, this isn't for us. You're trying, but you're not trying for *us*.' She was in the middle of setting the table and she rushed out of the dining room in a fury, so that a plate slipped from her hand. She just bent over the porcelain pieces and started sobbing. The plate had belonged to her mother, and to her grandmother before that. They were gifted to her, after she and Dad got married, and she'd brought them from Mexico. It was hand-painted, with a guy and a donkey on it. I was trying to make her feel better. I was like, 'It's just one. We have a bunch more.'

"She didn't look up. She just said, 'But it's not a full set anymore. There will always be something missing.'"

Sam turns to Angie, but doesn't quite meet her eyes. "I don't know why," he says, "but I keep thinking about that plate lately. It seems like the saddest thing."

Angie doesn't remind him that he's told her the story of the plates before, but she thinks of the first time she heard it, the first time they'd been in bed in his room.

"You know, when we were together," he says, "I used to feel like it was proof that I didn't have to be like them . . . I thought we could be different . . ."

Angie watches him as he continues rubbing fog off the window. The rain stops as suddenly as it began. "You still can be," she says. "I know—I know you're mad at me. I know you have every right to be angry, and I know it was fucked up, the way I left. But I didn't do it because I didn't love you. It was just that I didn't know how to say it. I guess I still don't . . ."

Sam's now looking back at her, really looking, for the first time since she got in the car.

"I would say I'm sorry—I am—but I know that it doesn't make anything better. So I'll just say thank you for letting me come to LA with you."

Sam nods back at her.

"You're welcome," he finally says, and it feels like a gift. He rolls down the window, and Angie does the same. Light breaks through the cloud bank at the other end of the sky, as they lean their heads out into the desert air, still electric from the rain.

"Okay, then," Sam says. "Guess it's time to get going."

He must be high, Angie worries. "Why don't you let me drive for a little? You've been driving for like eight hours."

"I'm used to it," Sam says. "Made this trip a bunch of times on my own."

"Come on, I want to. I miss Mabel." Mabel, the name of his Jeep.

Sam looks at her for a long moment. "Alright," he says finally, "you can drive for a couple hours, but we'll switch again before we get close to the city. It'll get a little hairy."

As Angie turns the ignition, Sam pushes his seat back. "So, what's up with your uncle? You talk to him?" he asks.

Angie focuses on merging back onto the freeway, reluctant to admit the truth to Sam.

"Not yet," she confesses. "But I've left messages . . . Actually, he may have called back already. My phone's been off." Angie hopes that when they arrive in LA tonight, she'll turn it on and, like magic, there will be a voice mail from her dad's brother, telling her he can't wait to meet her.

Sam studies her for a moment before asking, "What do you wanna hear?"

She knows what she wants to hear; she wants him to hear it too.

"I brought this old tape that my dad made for my mom. Maybe we could put that on?"

"Where's it at?" Sam asks.

He fishes it out of Angie's bag, and moments later the Fugees are singing "Ready or Not." Sam smiles at the first chords, and Angie grins back at him, as they head into their last 210 miles toward the City of Angels.

• • • • • *The day after Sam agreed to bring her to LA, Angie* had scoured the internet for Justin. She tried Facebook and came up with nothing, nothing that looked liked it could have been him on Twitter or Instagram either—apparently he didn't do social media. On the White Pages website, she found eight listings for Justin Bell between the ages of twenty-four and thirty-five, or of unknown age, living in the Los Angeles area. She pulled out her debit card and paid the $1.99 each to see contact info. Only five out of eight had phone numbers listed, but she found addresses for all.

As she prepared to dial the first number, her palms started sweating. What if he answered? What if it turned out to be him? What would she say? She put down the phone, deciding she needed to practice. After she'd rehearsed several times, pacing around her room, she called.

It went right to voice mail. This Justin Bell had a British accent on his message, so she was pretty sure she could cross him off the list.

The next Justin also went to voice mail, but it was automated. She left a stumbling message. "Hello, my name is Angie, and I'm calling for Justin Bell, to see if he may be related to a James Bell, who's my dad. Call me back please, if so." She gave her number and hung up.

She left another message for the next Justin.

The fourth one picked up. "Hello?" The deep male voice sounded suspicious.

"Hi, I'm, um—my name is Angie, and I'm calling to see if you're related to James Bell?"

"Huh? No, sorry, kid, you got the wrong number."

The space of hope that had spread open in her chest collapsed.

The fifth number yielded only a similar conversation. But she had two messages out for Justins who could be *her* Justin, she comforted herself, and three addresses with no numbers that she'd have to check out in LA. Something would pan out. She'd find him; she had to.

Luckily she'd saved plenty of money from last summer's baby-sitting gig—more than enough to eat and chip in for gas during the trip. While Marilyn was always generous with her, Angie had hated having to ask for cash for new clothes or dinners with friends, considering she knew how hard her mom worked just to get by. So Angie had spent the first week of last year's summer vacation riding her bike around, dropping into restaurants with her résumé. She'd worn her most professional-looking outfit—black slacks and a collared jacket—but she'd gotten only a bunch of noes and a couple indifferent shrugs from bored hostesses: "You can fill out an application if you want." She began to wonder if the sweat stains, which seemed to be an inevitable result of biking in the June heat, were hindering her. So when her mom said someone from Chase was looking for a summer nanny, Angie immediately called Linda Bennet to set up a time to meet.

Determined to impress her potential employer, she'd arrived fifteen minutes early. She walked up the drive: a terra-cotta birdbath placed awkwardly in the middle of a perfect green lawn, rows of pansies planted in brick flower beds, a white Range Rover. She smoothed her cardigan (god, it was already so hot at 9:15 a.m.), then rang the bell.

A white woman with a perfect blond blowout opened the door. "I'm sorry, but we don't accept solicitors."

Angie stood frozen on the BE HAPPY welcome mat, trying to find her voice.

"I said"—the woman's voice became sharper, shrill—"I said, we don't accept solicitors."

"I'm not—" Angie tried.

"Please, get off my property!" Her voice rose at the end into a high-pitched squeal.

Angie could feel hot tears behind her eyes. "I'm here to interview for the nanny job," she'd managed to get out.

The woman turned nearly as red as her pansies. "Oh. Oh, of course. I—I'm so sorry. I, well, I just, I didn't know you were—I mean, your mom, you and your mom don't—"

"Look alike." Angie finished the sentence.

The woman fixed her face into an overly bright smile. "Right. Okay! Let's start over, then. I'm Mrs. Bennet. Please, come in." But it took her a moment to move her body, which was blocking the door.

The den was decked out with framed, studio family portraits, matching floral cushions, and little signs over many of the room's objects, in case one forgot what they were for, Angie supposed:

keys written in cursive on the key hook, *coats* over the coat rack, and, in an offbeat gesture, *harmony* over the piano.

"Can I get you some lemonade? Really, I'm so sorry about that—Angie, right? I just—you have to understand, your mom didn't tell me you're—I mean—I wasn't expecting—"

Mrs. Bennet was saved by the little girl who came bounding into the room, wearing *Frozen* pajamas.

"Wanna see my little ponies?" she asked Angie, already tugging at her hand.

It turned out Angie and Mrs. Bennet's daughter, Riley, got along famously. When it was time for Angie to go, Riley threw a fit of protest.

"Well, sounds like she likes you!" Mrs. Bennet said, and she asked how much Angie charged.

"Twenty an hour," Angie said after a moment. It was a lot of money, certainly more than she would've requested in a different circumstance. She figured Mrs. Bennet would never go for it.

Mrs. Bennet's face did register some alarm, but she fixed it into a smile. "Oh, okay, then! Well, you're hired!"

Half of Angie wanted to tell Mrs. Bennet to forget it anyway, but twenty an hour—that was way more than she could make doing anything else this summer. She thought of Beyoncé's line: *Best revenge is your paper.*

When she got home and Marilyn asked, "How did it go?" Angie answered only, "Good. I got the job."

"That's great, honey!" Marilyn exclaimed, and hugged her. "I'm so proud of you!"

Angie made herself smile and didn't say anything more—maybe because she was afraid Marilyn wouldn't understand. Maybe because although Marilyn had made an effort to point out African American heroism to Angie throughout her life, she'd avoided talking about racism, and Angie instinctively believed she had to protect her mom from such realities.

In the end, Angie grew to adore Riley, who was full of energy and curiosity. Mrs. Bennet, for her part, was perfectly, almost formally, polite to Angie and had asked her back this summer. Angie was due to start Monday.

She picked up her phone to text Lana. *Could you do me the hugest favor in the world? I need someone to cover my babysitting next week.*

Lana texted back, *What's up?*

Kind of a long story. I'll tell you later . . . ?

Tell me now bitch! Or no dice.

I'm going to LA with Sam?

STFU. Sam, THE Sam?? You're a thing again?

Angie paused, purposely taking her finger off the cursor so her thought bubble graphic wouldn't linger. The truth felt like too much to tell Lana. She didn't want to submit the mission to her scrutiny, didn't want to hear Lana muse about her uncle Justin, who Lana would undoubtedly judge to be "ridiculously cool" based on the video. It's not that Angie didn't love Lana, it's just that she didn't necessarily trust her to understand—Justin wasn't just *cool*, he was her first chance to understand where she came from, her key to finding her father.

Angie finally typed back, *IDK, I ran into him at the 66 Diner, and . . . it sorta happened from there?*

She fell back onto her bed and tried to focus on breathing.

Okay, I'll cover you. Want all the deets please!

Thank u ur the best.

The only question left, the biggest question, was how she could convince her mom to let her go. After Sam had agreed to bring her along, it took three full days to work up the nerve, but finally, when Marilyn came home in the evening, Angie followed her into her bedroom. (The first thing Marilyn always did, when she set foot in the door, was give Angie a kiss, then go immediately to her room to get out of her work clothes.)

"How's my girl?" her mom asked.

"Really good."

"And why's that?" Marilyn smiled.

"I actually—I spent the day with Sam," Angie lied. She needed her mom to believe they were rekindling their friendship, at the very least, if she had any hope of getting Marilyn to buy Sam as her reason for wanting to go on the trip.

"Oh! Really? That's great, baby. How was it?"

"It was good. We just hung out and talked. I guess after I saw him at the diner, I thought we should get back in touch. Try to be friends. I don't know. I missed him."

Marilyn pulled a worn Montezuma Elementary T-shirt over her head. She turned to Angie and gave her a soft smile. "That's great, sweetie. I'm proud of you."

Angie felt her usual shame at those words. She wished she were more worthy of her mom's pride. But maybe, now, she could be. Maybe she was about to do something that would matter, and even if it made her mom unhappy at first, maybe in the end it would be worth it.

"Tell him he can come for grilled cheese anytime," Marilyn joked.

"Actually, Mom, Sam's going to LA next week to see his cousin. Remember, he always does that at the beginning of the summer? And, well, he invited me to come along."

Marilyn's face shifted, awash with anxiety. "Oh, Angie, I don't think that's—"

"It would only be for eight days. I've never even been out of the state—I could finally see the ocean, Mom!"

"Angie, I—I can't just let you go off, to some other city, without an adult, or . . . Where would you stay?"

"With his cousin. You keep saying I have to think about college. I could get him to show me around some of the campuses while I'm there."

"I didn't know you were interested in going to school in LA," Marilyn said, her voice careful, as if trying to conceal an incredible fear.

"I just mean, it would just be good to start looking, to get a sense . . ."

"Well, I was planning on taking you on a college trip this fall. I thought we'd do that together."

"Okay, well, I won't look at the campuses, then. We'll just do, like, touristy stuff. Go to the beach and all."

"Honey, I don't—I don't think it's a good idea. I can't give you permission to go off like that . . . It would be different if there were a parent, or . . ."

"His cousin's like twenty-four. He counts for an adult."

"LA is a really big city, Angie. A lot could happen, things you might not be prepared for."

Angie looked away.

"Listen, honey, next year you'll be eighteen. You could be gone forever if you wanted to be . . . You'll be going off to college, on your own, and—well, I'll always be here for you. I'll always do everything I can for you, okay, no matter what. But it'll be up to you to make your own decisions soon. In the meantime, I'm your mom, and it's my job to protect you, and I can't do that if you're—in a big city, far away from me . . ."

"It's not that far away," Angie mumbled. "Only like an eleven-hour drive."

Marilyn paused and turned to Angie, her eyes almost pleading. "You'll have all summer to reconnect with Sam, when he's back."

There were so many things Angie wanted to say, but before she said any of them, she got up and walked out of the room.

Angie *had* briefly considered telling Marilyn the truth— *I know that my dad's brother is alive.* But she didn't want her mom's explanation, wouldn't be able to trust it. She knew she had to find out for herself. Her mom had been lying for her entire life—why should Angie be honest now?

Marilyn came into Angie's bedroom later that night, where

Angie was halfway working on her college apps. "Are you still upset with me about LA?" she'd asked.

"No," Angie answered, thinking, *It's so much more than that.*

This morning, she'd woken with a start from some kind of nightmare. She couldn't quite remember, but she knew she'd been swimming in the sea, pulled, suddenly, by a strange undertow. She could still feel herself choking.

Seven billion, Angie repeated in her head as she lay in bed, trying to calm herself. *Seven billion. You're just a drop in the ocean. Seven billion.* She gasped for breath. Her technique wasn't working the way it usually did. Something was different now. She was going to LA. She was going to look for her father.

After Marilyn left for work, Angie packed her things, ignoring the heavy pounding of her heart, ignoring the shortness of breath. She went into Marilyn's room, opened her drawer, and took out the photograph of her parents at the beach, along with the manila envelope holding the rest of the black-and-white pictures. She looked at the collection of things on her mother's dresser: the pink soap in the shape of a piglet; the turquoise earrings; the ceramic heart box filled with tiny, colorful clam-shaped seashells; a half-used jar of "Sylvie's Lemon Lift," with a homemade label that had been there for as long as Angie could remember; a laminated card with a hand-drawn picture of Marilyn and Angie on the front that Angie had made as a child. She picked it up, opened it, and read:

Dear Mommy,

You are very, very, very special to me. You are kind, loving, caring, wonderful, tremendous, understanding, and I could go on forever. You make everything fun. You are good-natured. Mom I love you more than you could ever, ever imagine. You are a million times better than any other mom. Happy Mother's Day.

Love, your daughter Angie

Angie swallowed and replaced the card. As she walked into the kitchen, she saw the plate of eggs her mom had left her, covered to keep them warm, with a melon slice cut off the rind. A spike of pain—literally—shot through Angie's chest. She ate the food, though each bite was a struggle, and washed the dishes. She took out a pad to leave a note, but couldn't think what to say. Finally she wrote,

Mom, I went to LA with Sam. I'm sorry because I know you'll be upset, and I don't want to upset you. I love you more than the whole universe, like we always say. I know you love me too, but sometimes, the best thing you can do for someone is to let them figure stuff out on their own. I'll be back in 8 days. I'll be careful, don't worry.

Love, Angie

• • • • • *Angie feels Sam's hand on her leg, gently shaking her* awake. "You should see this," he says. She opens her eyes, bleary, to the pitch-dark. They seem to be on the freeway, in the middle of the mountains somewhere. The windows are cracked, letting in a rush of warm air. It smells the way she's always imagined the ocean would. "At Your Best (You Are Love)"—her favorite song from the Miss Mari Mack tape—is playing on the stereo.

Sam must have started it over after she fell asleep.

As the Jeep crests the hill, suddenly millions of lights appear in the distance, scattered over the land like a magic trick.

"It's beautiful," Angie breathes.

"It's beautiful," Sam agrees.

Aaliyah's voice is sweet, clear, weightless as light: *Stay at your best, baby . . .* Sam turns to Angie and smiles a small, slow smile. "Welcome to LA."

Angie's come here, to this sprawling city of seven million, to chase down a single ghost. As they drive through the night toward the seemingly endless city, she feels it. Her father is here, hidden somewhere among all those lights.

MARILYN

• • • • • *"Is she your girlfriend?" Justin asks his brother. He* sits between James and Marilyn in the dark theater, the three of them halfway through their giant bucket of popcorn before the trailers have even begun.

Marilyn tentatively chews on a kernel and looks to James, waiting for his response.

"No," he says, and her heart contracts, a hand in her chest tightening its invisible grip. "We're friends."

Justin raises his eyebrows. "But you've kissed her?"

James rolls his eyes. "Gimme one of those Milk Duds," he tells Justin as the lights dim.

Marilyn attempts to focus on the previews. She herself would not have answered the question any differently, right? But since their second kiss three weeks ago, they *have* kissed— furtively and fervidly—several times. She's begun to become familiar with the fact of his moodiness: like a morning glory missing circadian predictability, he blooms and closes according to his own internal rhythms, which she's struggling to intuit. During their Saturday study sessions, some days he hardly looks up from his books, but other days, he's eager to talk— about US history, college essay topics, jokes passed on from friends.

As *The Mask of Zorro* begins with a flaming *Z*, Marilyn looks to Justin. He doesn't notice; his gaze is glued to the screen. Instead, it's James who catches her eye. He gives her a small smile, and it's enough to unclench her heart.

The movie's good, but mostly Marilyn loves how much Justin loves it. As the two of them wait in the lobby for James to use the bathroom, Justin swishes an imaginary sword through the air.

"The only sin would be to deny what your heart truly feels," he says in his best Zorro accent. As Marilyn laughs, he leans in and asks, "So has he kissed you?"

She can't help but give him a small nod of confirmation.

"I knew it!" Justin cries as James walks back to join them.

"Knew what? Who's starving?" he asks.

"Me!" Justin replies, despite the fact that they devoured a large popcorn and two boxes of Milk Duds. So they stop at a taco truck and drive to Elysian Park, where they eat, splayed on the grass.

Her belly full, early-November sun in her hair, Marilyn watches James and Justin beside her tossing a football, until Justin runs over, recruiting her to play. The three of them stay as the sky begins to dim, the prism of the evening breaking pink against the mountains. Driving past parks like this with her mom, Marilyn had often felt a stab of jealousy at the people barbecuing, hosting birthday parties, hitting piñatas. But now, James and Justin beside her, their laughter pealing into the fall air, she feels something she cannot remember having felt ever before, that is yet somehow familiar. It is the feeling of belonging distilled—clarified, purified; it is the feeling of family.

· · · · ·

By the time they arrive back to the apartment, Marilyn's face has bloomed with a sunburn. Thinking they were going only to the movies, she hadn't bothered with sunscreen this morning, and now the boys tease, calling her Strawberry Shortcake.

"I'm not short!" she insists with a laugh as James parks. But when he goes to open the door, Marilyn freezes. Across the street, there's Woody, pulled jaggedly into a spot, getting out of his truck. She can see by his zagging walk that he's been drinking—doubtlessly returning from a bender at Commerce Casino—and she knows what alcohol does to his temper.

"I can't go in yet," she says, her breaths shortening, as James opens her door. He follows her gaze. Woody seems not to have noticed them, not yet, but if they walk up the driveway, he surely will. Marilyn's heart pounds desperately against her chest.

"What are you guys doing?" Justin complains.

"Go inside," James says, his tone measured. "Tell Grandma I went to the library and I'll be back later."

"I wanna come!" Justin protests, but James refuses firmly.

As they drive off down the block, James looks at her. "What happened?"

"Um—just my uncle. I—I guess he doesn't want us to hang out, I don't know why. He drinks sometimes, and he gets . . . bad."

"I know."

"You do?"

James stares out the windshield. "He's a total prick," he says finally.

"What?" Marilyn tries to swallow her rising anxiety.

"Years ago he was coming home drunk and hit my grandma's car in the driveway. That's where the dent came from. She was calm about it, asked him to pay for the repairs. He refused, tried to spin it like somehow it was her fault because of how she'd parked. My grandpa was pissed, of course, and confronted him the next day. Woody said some really fucked-up shit—"

"What did he say?"

James looks at her, shakes his head. "Nothing I actually wanna repeat. We tried to get him kicked out, but it didn't work. Ever since, he's been ugly to us. He called the *cops* last year when we had a birthday party for my grandma. It was family. Old people. They busted in, broke our door—Woody apparently said there were drugs, which they searched for. Finally they realized they literally had nothing on us and left, only after wrecking the place."

"I had no idea. I'm so sorry," Marilyn says, a vise grip on her lungs. A hot, dangerously hot, anger toward Woody burns in her center.

"Yeah, shit's fucked up."

"I can't believe your family was so nice to me that day."

"It's not your fault you live with him . . . they probably felt bad for you."

A stretch of uneasy silence unfolds as James circles through the neighborhood.

"What do you wanna do?" he finally asks.

Marilyn shrugs. She feels ill, seasick with guilt. "We can go back, I guess. He'll be inside by now."

James looks at her for a moment, and then, instead of turning toward home, he makes a left onto Washington and gets on the 10, driving toward the coast.

• • • • • *In the nine o'clock moonlight, the beach feels vast and* private. There are a few scattered bodies—a jogger, a man sleeping on the sand, a group of kids huddled around what must be a joint—but they feel unreal to Marilyn, part of the backdrop. As if it were only her and James. He offers her a hoodie she pulls over her head—big enough she drowns in it. She inhales his smell, mixing with the salt scent of the seawater, and feels as if she can breathe again. She pulls off her sneakers and takes off running toward the water, leaving the ugliness of Woody, the anxiety, the anger behind.

James walks up, takes her hand.

"It's so quiet," she whispers.

"It's the best time to be here. I come when I've gotta get out of the house. I'll show you my spot," he says. They walk along the edge of the shoreline, the waves leaving stains on the sand that reflect lights of a passing plane. She stops to pick up a mussel shell, the tiniest one she's ever seen, and puts it into the pocket of his sweatshirt.

He leads Marilyn into the shadow beneath the pier, the old wood planks over their heads. Without saying a word he sits down and leans back on one of the poles, the moonlit water ahead of them disappearing into the night sky. And then, his hands are on her shoulders, pulling her to him, his mouth pressing against her mouth. She could handle James, beautiful James, kissing her—the intoxicating smell of his body, the fullness of his lips on her own—but it's the childlike quality of his need that undoes her. She wants, in that moment, nothing more than to give him everything—whatever goodness can be pulled from within her, whatever grace lurks in the ocean echoing in her ears, in the curve of the open horizon visible through the slits of wood. His kiss is not just a kiss, Marilyn thinks. His kiss is the only kiss that's ever changed everything.

He reaches his hand beneath her shirt, along her stomach. She arches her back. He kisses her breasts. She wants more but doesn't know where to begin. She lets out a soft moan. She bites gently at his neck. Her body seems to move with the waves, pulling slowly back, then crashing with expectation against the wall of him. She wants to break through. She *wants*.

It's James who regains himself first, who starts to smile between kisses, who pulls away from her and says, "I'm hungry, are you?"

Marilyn nods, but walking across the sand, she finds herself unable to recover from the absence as he recedes back into his own impenetrable skin. She longs for the blurred lines, the bleeding edges that open them to each other when their bodies take over.

They stop at a tiny stand, the only thing still open at this hour, where a girl with a bored look and a striped paper top hat gives them french fries and corn dogs. They sit on a bench and

Marilyn devours her food too quickly. Her cheeks burn, maybe from the day's sun, maybe from the lingering heat of him.

All at once, she finds herself blurting out, "So have you kissed any of the other twenty-nine girls there?"

"Huh?"

"I mean, that's what your brother said—there have been twenty-nine? So I make an even thirty, right? That's a good number. A lucky one?" She senses something bad creeping into her voice—insecurity, fear, a strange dread. She wants to push it down, but she can't.

He looks at her for a long moment. "No, I haven't kissed any other girls there."

"But it's true, though? You've kissed that many girls?"

"I haven't counted. Why does it matter?"

She doesn't know.

"That's my spot. It's where I go alone," James says finally.

"Oh."

"It was my mom who showed it to me."

He shared something important with her, and she'd ruined it. "Well I—I loved it," she says, but can't make her voice convey the sincerity of the statement.

He smiles at her, not his bright-light smile, but a guarded one that won't give itself over, and kisses her quickly on the forehead. It's like the doors behind his eyes are slamming shut.

"We should get back," he says.

"Okay." She turns to the ocean, as if it has the answers. But from this distance it's only a mass of darkness, bleeding into the night sky, pulling at the shore.

•••••

When she arrives back at the apartment after ten, she finds Woody dozing on the couch, and Sylvie, still in her work clothes, cleaning up from dinner. She gasps when she sees Marilyn.

"Where have you been? Your face! What happened to you?"

"Nothing, Mom, I got a sunburn at the park today."

Marilyn turns to escape into the safety of her room, but Sylvie follows.

"Ellen called, and she's made you an appointment for new pictures for your book on Wednesday, and you can't very well show up like that; what are we going to do?"

Marilyn sighs. "I'll put aloe on it. We'll use makeup if it's not better."

"Your skin will be peeling off. I need you to—I need you to be straightening your priorities, Marilyn, I—" Her voice drops to a whisper. "Were you with *him*?"

"Who's *him*?"

"You know who!" Sylvie whispers back vehemently.

"He has a name. Yes, I was with James."

"I thought I told you to stay away from him!"

Marilyn pulls the sleeves of James's sweatshirt over her balled-up fists.

"Well, you didn't. And I won't. You told me to keep it away from Woody, which I was trying to, but I can't believe—I didn't realize what he did to James's family."

"Which is what?"

"He ran into their car and then said some shit that was so

169

bad James wouldn't even say it back to me. He called the cops when they had a birthday party for James's *grandma*! I knew he was messed up, but I didn't know—"

"I don't want to be here any more than you do, but if you hate it so much, maybe you should be less focused on James and more focused on your career."

Her mother, of all people, will not be the one to help her process this. Marilyn takes a deep breath. "I know we have nowhere else to go right now, so I'll try not to cause any trouble with Woody, but James is my—my friend—and you can't change that."

Sylvie's posture stiffens as she walks out of the room.

She returns, minutes later, with a cup of cool milk she insists on dabbing over Marilyn's face. (*Disgusting*, Marilyn thinks.) The next day Sylvie keeps Marilyn home from school, applies masks of blended cucumbers, black tea, oatmeal, and by the time they arrive at picture day, her face is again pale, her fragile new skin ready to be photographed.

• • • • • *Marilyn stares at the camera, blank-faced. She wills* her brain to turn to static, white noise. She follows the instructions. She smiles. She looks fierce. She changes outfits. She allows herself to be photographed in underwear. She arches her back; she juts her hip; she puts her hands in her own hair. She imagines James's hands there, and small, shy roses bloom in the apples of her cheeks.

"That's it. That one's golden," the photographer calls out.

She puts on the sweatshirt borrowed from James, listens to Sylvie gush her thanks to the photographer.

"You've found a whole new way of being in your body," Sylvie says to Marilyn as they walk out. Marilyn imagines she's right—James has woken up every nerve within her. But since the difficulty of their last night together, she feels those nerves standing on end, anxiously awaiting the renewal of his touch.

When they arrive back at the apartment, Sylvie opens the miniature door on the mailbox, carries the stack of paper into the apartment. She piles the bills for Woody on his desk, keeps the mailers to cut coupons from, sets aside the *People* magazine wrongly delivered to their address, then turns to Marilyn and hands her an envelope.

"For you," she says, purposely nonchalant.

Marilyn looks at the return address: The College Board. She carries the envelope into her room, and, as soon as she's alone, tears it open.

She's done well. She's done very well! Her first thought is that she has to see James. He must have gotten his today too. This is just what they need, she thinks—something to celebrate together. Searching for an excuse to get out of the house, she finally gives up and tells Sylvie only, "I'll be back in a little bit."

Sylvie looks up from the *People* magazine she'd begun flipping through. After a long moment, she just nods and moves her eyes back to the page.

Marilyn hurries down the stairs, knocks on James's door. Rose answers, wearing her pink sweat suit.

"Come in, sweetie." She moves aside to let Marilyn enter.

"Is James home?"

"He'll be back in a half hour or so. You're welcome to stay if you like. I sent him to the store to pick up chicken for dinner, and of course his brother tagged along. Anywhere James goes, Justin wants to go."

Marilyn follows Rose as she moves into the kitchen and pours glasses of lemonade.

"Justin's quite fond of you as well," Rose says with a girlish smile. "I think he hopes you'll be James's girlfriend. But you have to be careful with that one," she cautions. "He has a great big good heart, but he has a hard time settling. After his momma died, you know he didn't talk for nearly a whole year? Of course that was a long time ago . . . He's doing well now, but he still misses her."

Marilyn just nods, surprised, startled even, by Rose's candor.

172

As if reading her mind, Rose says, "I can tell by your eyes you're one to trust. Nothing like your uncle. I've always had that power, since I was a girl. Could read people—pick out the good ones—in a matter of moments." Rose sets out two glasses of lemonade and a plate of cookies before disappearing from the room. When she returns, she's carrying a huge stack of slim photo albums.

"I've got one for every year," she says, "since 1956, when I married Alan. Their momma, Angela, came only a year later. She was our only one." Rose sifts through the stack. "These here are from when James was a baby boy."

Marilyn begins to flip through the first album Rose hands her. It's like reading the story of James's life. She's arrested by the beauty of his mother holding him as a newborn; her face, serene, open, seems to glow even through the faded film. Another photo shows baby James on his grandpa's lap. James wearing mouse ears at Disneyland, James with cheeks puffed up to blow out three birthday candles, James in the bath. She wants to wrap the little boy in her arms, to keep him close to her, always. In another photo, James sits atop a man's shoulders, smiling. This must be his father; she recognizes the shape of his mouth, the familiar way he tilts his head to the left.

"They split up," Rose explains. "When Angela was pregnant with Justin. He lives in Texas now, remarried, with two little girls. They go visit him in the summers. Luckily after Angela passed, he didn't fight us for custody. I don't know what I would've done without the boys. They've been my reason to get out of bed in the morning ever since we lost her."

Marilyn turns the page to find a photo of young James resting his head in the crook of his mom's shoulder. He looks so innocent, so satisfied. Like he knows he'll always be held.

At that moment, the front door opens. James and Justin walk in, carrying grocery bags. James stops midstride when he sees Marilyn.

"Hey," he says, his voice guarded.

"I was just showing your friend my books." Rose smiles.

James looks over Marilyn's shoulder to the picture of him with his mother. Marilyn glances back at him, but he's wearing his closed-door face. He moves away to the kitchen, starts to put up the food. Justin, on the other hand, rushes over.

"Where's the ones of me?" he asks. "Did you show her when I was born?"

"Not yet, baby," Rose says as Justin begins rifling through the albums.

Marilyn isn't sure if she should get up, follow James. But now Justin has the page open, pointing to a photo of him as a baby in his brother's arms.

"Wow," she says to Justin, his eager eyes on her. "You were insanely cute." Justin skips forward, comes up with a photo of him as a toddler with a plastic baseball bat.

"This is when I won the Little League." He pages through the album until he arrives at a studio portrait of James, baby Justin, and their mom, dressed in matching red polo tops. And then another one, where James, maybe eleven, stands beside Justin, five or six, both of them dressed as Ninja Turtles for Halloween.

"Which turtle are you?" Marilyn asks James as he reenters the room.

"He was Michelangelo," Justin chimes in. "But *I'm* more like Michelangelo; really he'd be Donatello."

James doesn't respond to his brother, but instead goes out the front and brings in the hummingbird feeder. He fills it and hangs it in its place.

As he comes in and closes the door, Marilyn thinks she can feel a heat like anger coming off him.

She turns in her chair. "Sorry," she says, "I just—I got my scores, so I wanted to—I just got excited, so I came down. I figured you'd maybe have gotten yours too."

"Mail come?" he asks Rose, his voice neutral. She points to a pile of paper on a stand near the door. James sifts through until he finds the envelope he's looking for and opens it, neatly along the seal. From the look on his face—almost blank, a hint of fear around his eyes—Marilyn thinks he hasn't done well.

He hands her the paper. He has an almost perfect score.

"James," she says softly. "This is amazing. I mean—congratulations. I'm so happy."

He just nods. "Well, thanks for helping me study. You did good?"

"Yeah. I mean, not quite as good as you, but yeah."

Rose and Justin watch them curiously. "A test we took," James says, "to get into college. The SAT."

Rose nods. "He's got his momma's brains. She was brilliant too."

"To college where?" Justin asks, his face scrunched into a frown.

"I don't know yet, Jus. Nana, you need help with dinner?"

"Peel the potatoes, will you? Marilyn? You want to stay?"

She glances to James, but he doesn't meet her eyes.

"No," she says. "I mean, thank you so much, I'd love to, but I should get home." She wants nothing less than to leave, but what can she do? He didn't invite her here. He's closing every door; she can almost hear the echoes of him slamming himself shut.

She reminds herself that she's leaving in less than a year—nine months, at most—alone. To start *her* life. Her own life.

But when, an hour later, in her room after an American cheese sandwich, Marilyn smells the scent of Rose's chicken drifting in through her window, it smells so good, so much like home, it almost makes her cry.

● ● ● ● ● *The next day the winds start. Santa Anas. In Joan* Didion's words, *drying hills and nerves to flashpoint.* Panes rattling, branches scraping, sirens all through the day and night. Dirt in Marilyn's eyes waiting for the bus from school. Dirt in her mouth. Only a glimpse of James through the barred glass, walking up the driveway, face sheltered by hand. Too gusty, even, to open the window, so there is no music that night. People are wrong to say there's no weather in California (notes Joan Didion, and Marilyn agrees). You have to know the city, have to live within its unpredictable rhythms, to understand how deeply they can run, how they can get into your blood. *The wind shows us how close to the edge we are.* A fight in the high school hallway. At home, the sound of breaking glass. Marilyn cracks her bedroom door, peeks into the living room to find her mother cleaning up the shattered remnants of Woody's beer bottle. An accident or not, she doesn't know. He's popping open another. Marilyn feels the wind blast through her, imagines the landscape of her body catching fire. Disaster weather. It hurts.

When Saturday finally comes, Marilyn steps silently past Woody, who doesn't turn from his computer screen, and sits outside on the steps, shielding herself with her hand, a scarf tied too tightly around her throat, waiting for James. She can feel the wind drying her eyes, can taste its cry.

She doesn't know how long she sits there, but it is long enough to know James will not appear. Still, she can't bring herself to turn back and climb the steps to Woody's apartment. She feels a kernel in her chest heat with anger to the point of popping, as the voice of something small and abandoned within her pleads, *No, you cannot leave me.*

She finally stands and knocks on his door.

A long moment later, he answers. "Hey."

"Hey."

"Sorry, wasn't sure if it was cool for me to come upstairs to tell you, what with the bullshit with your uncle and all, but I can't do the library today. I've got a bunch of stuff I have to take care of around the house. My grandma's not feeling well."

To skirt the risk of him hearing her voice break, she just nods, turns, and goes home.

· · · · ·

By the time Marilyn wakes on Sunday morning, the wind's passed, having left behind only traces of its presence—palm fronds littered over the streets, trees bent to their knees, candy wrappers and takeout bags blown into bougainvillea bushes. What they need is rain, something to cleanse the air, but too-hot sunlight rules the now static sky. She cranks her window open and then opens her schoolbooks, forcing herself to focus on *The Grapes of Wrath*.

There is no sound of James until late in the afternoon, when she hears the familiar rhythm of his footsteps. She watches him walk down the drive in his basketball shorts and sees him burst into a run—as if there were a tiger chasing—the moment he hits the blacktop.

She doesn't change out of her cotton shorts and old T-shirt. She only puts on sneakers and takes off toward the park where she'd seen him a few months ago. Her breath is ragged in her ears, her cheeks pink as the clouds in the evening sky, when she arrives and spots him sprinting across the cement, racing against a ghost, against his shadow, against the blazing sunset, brilliant in color because of the wildfires broken out in the hills—a repercussion of the wind.

As he bends to rest, hands against his knees, Marilyn walks forward, his eyes now locked on hers. His breath is loud enough it could be echoing in her own body. As she searches for words to break through the wall between them, she takes in the curve of his bicep flexing as he stands, his hand tensing into a fist, his beautiful eyes watchful from behind their closed doors.

At once, she stands on her toes and kisses him, her face trying to find the right angle. He kisses her back, and their sparks are not gone, certainly not, but somehow they cannot land in each other's presence the way they so easily had.

He pulls back, glances at his watch. (His rest between sprints has already gone on too long, she realizes.)

"What's up?" he asks.

"James, what's wrong?" she replies, her voice threatening to split with a sob.

"What do you mean," he answers, but it hardly sounds like a question.

"I'm sorry," Marilyn says finally. "About Woody. And the

beach the other day, when you took me to your spot—I loved it, and I'm sorry I—I just—sometimes I just want you so much. I mean, I like you so much, I get afraid, and . . . I said the wrong thing."

"Don't worry about it," James says, and gives her a quick kiss on the forehead.

But it's not enough.

"I don't get what's up with you—with us," she blurts out.

He looks off toward the invisible smoke coloring the sunset sky, doesn't meet her eyes.

"Why were you so weird when I came over the other day?" she pushes.

"You can't just open the door and walk into someone else's house like that," James says, remote.

"Not everyone has somewhere they belong like you do," Marilyn exclaims. "Not everyone has a perfect family. Sorry I was enjoying talking to your grandma. She invited me in."

"Perfect family? My mom's dead. My kid brother's growing up without ever having known her, with a father we only see for two stupid weeks in the summer. And you weren't just talking. You were going through my childhood pictures—pictures of me and my mom, like it was just some casual entertainment."

Marilyn fights away tears. In the distance, the sunset now begins to extinguish itself.

"I said I didn't want a girlfriend, okay. I said from the beginning it wasn't gonna be like that—we both have other shit to focus on. You're leaving next year. Whatever happens, we're probably not gonna be in the same place, so it just—it doesn't seem like a good idea to get too attached."

She feels it in her chest, the sudden, sharp pain, followed by the shortness of breath. Is it because of Woody that he doesn't want to get too close to her? Is it because he lost his mom that he's afraid, thinking she'll leave too? She wonders this in a whisper of empathy, but her fear, her hurt, raises its voice first: "Look, if you—if you don't want to hang out with me anymore, that's fine. I mean, I can handle it, you don't have to spare my feelings." She feels the heat building in her throat. "But you can't just— disappear and pretend it doesn't mean anything. 'Cause we both know there was something between us, something that mattered. At least it did to me. We could help each other. We *have* helped each other."

She turns and walks away as the tears finally escape her eyes. She stares at the sky gone soft with before-nightfall blue, feels the chill of fall sneaking into the air. Though she forbids herself from looking back at James, she can see him, in her mind's eye, tearing across the concrete, moving near the speed of light.

• • • • • *Marilyn's hair smells like mayonnaise—Hellmann's* brand, to be exact, which has its own particular scent. Sylvie never cheaps out on the mayo for the hair mask. In the middle of the bright aisles of Smith's this afternoon, Marilyn suggested they go with the generic store brand, since it was only going on her head, but Sylvie rejected the notion.

It's been one of their rituals ever since she was a little girl: the evening before an audition, Sylvie measures out a perfect cup of mayo and works it into her hair, starting from the scalp and moving down to the ends. She then twists Marilyn's mane into a mayonnaisey mess on the top of her head, wraps it in cellophane, and finishes by covering it in a warm towel. The first time they tried the mask was before the My Little Pony audition, and ever since Sylvie's thought it brings good luck. Despite the fact that Marilyn shampooed her hair three times after the treatment, she can still detect the smell that makes her think of a picnic gone on too long.

Ellen-obviously has booked her an audition for a Levi's super-low-jeans commercial—the girls are simply meant to walk around in the jeans and midriff tops, she'd explained. (Later animation will make the belly buttons of the chosen girls appear to be doing the talking—or, rather, singing a rendition of "I'm

Coming Out.") Sylvie went to bed by nine o'clock, and sent Marilyn to do the same, warning she needs her "beauty sleep" for tomorrow.

But Marilyn's been wide awake for what feels like hours, staring out at the moon as it travels into the corner of the window visible from her bed, rising in the night until it crosses the distance of her little pane of glass. She watches it now halfway out of view on the other side, slipping into the portion of sky beyond her. We move from one point to another, into and out of view, but the shifts are impossible to track with bare eyes. When had James slid into her heart? What gravity has pulled him away?

Finally she flips on the light and picks up *Slouching Towards Bethlehem*. She opens to the essay she and James were meant to read together last Saturday when he didn't want to go to the library, and begins it on her own. "On Keeping a Notebook" turns out to be one of her favorites so far, but it's these lines that take hold of her: *I think we are well advised to keep on nodding terms with the people we used to be, whether we find them attractive company or not. Otherwise they turn up unannounced and surprise us, come hammering on the mind's door at 4 a.m. of a bad night and demand to know who deserted them, who betrayed them, who is going to make amends.*

Marilyn reads the lines again and again; she begins to thinks of the girl of seven on her mother's lap, watching herself on television with a brand-new My Little Pony. How little care she's given to that girl, how easily she's banished her. She thinks of that girl's fear, of her longing for her mother's love. Of how she woke screaming from nightmares she could not remember. She thinks of the talent agent in Orange County and his disgusting couch. She thinks of the rage she felt—at him, yes, but also at her mother, who had left her in his charge when he said he wanted to work with her on audition skills "in private," the mother who, when Marilyn said she did not like the man, told her she must be imagining things, the mother who twirled her hair during meetings, discussing her daughter's "potential." She thinks of that childhood rage, of how she swallowed it up and stuffed it down. So abandoned, it grew its own tiny beating heart in her belly, which she's become obliged to carry.

She thinks, then, too, of the girl of thirteen who was overcome with anxiety when she started to grow breasts. The girl who, for a period of time, stopped eating to see if it would make those breasts fade back into her body, the girl who could no longer say her lines without a flood of panic in her chest.

Becoming someone else does not happen in an instant. No, the steps to reinvention are slow. Marilyn thinks of the western migration—endless miles to cross, only a covered wagon for shelter. But if you survive, before long the cold winters of the East are only a distant memory. You are somewhere, someone, else.

And yet. What the mind allows to pass through time, the body does not forget.

Is it hours later? Just minutes? Marilyn glances at the window to find the moon gone. Eventually her eyelids grow heavy enough to stay shut, and she starts to sink into the quicksand kind of sleep.

Until she is startled awake again by a thud against the glass.

She sits up abruptly to see a sneaker falling from the window. She watches it descend back to the cement, where James stands in the drive looking up at her, one foot left with only a sock for cover. His dark eyes are their own glinting moons, suddenly and all at once in view.

She feels herself orbiting them as she gets out of bed, still in a half-dream state. She dresses and cracks her door open, cursing its perpetual creakiness as she peers into the living room. Woody snores lightly on the couch, his dirty-socked feet askew on the armrest.

She starts to tiptoe across the shag carpet but freezes as Woody's snore stops, his arm dropping toward the floor.

Finally, the snore begins again. Marilyn holds her breath and ventures to open the even squeakier front door, and—thank god—the snores continue. She steps into the night and looks down to see James, still standing in the driveway, his shoe returned to his foot.

"Hey," he whispers as she walks up beside him.

"Hey."

"I couldn't sleep, so I went for a run. I saw your light on."

"I couldn't sleep either. Though I was starting to, before you woke me up."

"Sorry."

"It's okay."

"I mean I'm sorry I was a jerk."

She nods. Though she still feels the wound of his withdrawal, here he is before her, the only salve.

"I wanna take you somewhere—"

She hears half a question mark at the end of his statement, the worry that she will not follow.

But she will. She cannot resist the pull to him; it's magnetic, nearly scientific.

· · · · ·

It must be close to two a.m. by the time they arrive at Runyon Canyon, where they climb over the park's gated fence (locked at dusk) and halfway up the steep side of the trail. The letters of the Hollywood sign loom large off to the side, the hill below dotted with homes and the small black rectangles of their swimming pools. James waits for Marilyn as she makes her way over a boulder, her heartbeat in a hurry, her lungs sucking in the cool night air. It smells faintly of fire smoke and seawater, and of the late-night Chinese takeout James carries alongside a six-pack of beer.

"Don't turn around," James tells her. "Not till we're at the top."

And when they are, when she does, she finds LA's sprawl transformed into something sparkling and miraculous, spread below them. Tiny cars form crisscrossing lines on the roads, the lights in thousands of homes become twinkling stars. From this vantage point, as she leans her head against James's chest, Marilyn can understand the city's promise.

"What does your hair smell like?"

Marilyn winces, leans away from him. "Mayonnaise. Sorry."

"Mayonnaise?"

"It's supposed to make your hair extra shiny. Sylvie's audition ritual. I have one for Levi's tomorrow."

"White people are crazy."

Marilyn laughs. "My mother is, at least."

James pulls two beers from the bag and pops them open on the side of a rock. He unpacks the Chinese—kung pao chicken and lo mein—and hands Marilyn a Styrofoam box.

"I could not want anything less than to do this thing," she says.

"So why are you?"

"I don't know. I have to try and make some money so I can at least leave my mom with something before I go away next year." She sips her beer, feels the alcohol starting to loosen her grip on herself. "And I guess I don't know how to say no to her."

"But what about you—some money to help yourself?"

Marilyn shrugs and looks away, overwhelmed by a sudden, restless desire to break free of her own skin.

"You're mad?"

"I don't know. I guess I am, but I feel like I shouldn't be."

"Why not?"

"Because there's no point. There's nothing to do with that kinda feeling."

"Sure there is. Anger can be fuel, like anything else."

They sit in silence for a moment. Marilyn pulls at the label of her beer.

"My first agent—this guy in Orange County—used to make me watch him jerk off." It's the first time she's said it out loud, and the words feel gummy in her mouth. She wants to spit them out, to be rid of them. ". . . I tried to tell my mom, but she didn't listen. She was too caught up in hoping he'd make me a star.

I just got really good at leaving the room, you know, just going somewhere else. I think I used to go back to our old lives in Amarillo, before my dad died, but now I can hardly remember that stuff . . ."

"Fuck that guy," James says, his face hard. After a moment he reaches out to her and brushes a lock of hair from her face. "I'm really sorry."

But Marilyn doesn't want sympathy. She doesn't want him to stroke her head. She wants him to push her back against the dirt, to press his lips to hers, to let her lose herself in him.

"I don't want it to change how you think of me," she says.

"It doesn't," James replies. "But you know you don't have to do that audition," he adds eventually. "You don't have to do shit. You're in control."

"That's not exactly true."

"I get it's a bad situation. I get you feel all kinds of pressure. But you still have a choice."

"I guess."

"Be practical," James says. "Is there something in it for you? If you get the part, can you use the money to fly to whatever school you're gonna go to? To cover the cost of whatever a scholarship or loan won't? Tell your mom you're not just handing it over anymore. You'll only do it if you get to keep half."

Marilyn swallows. James looks at her for another moment, then finishes off the rest of his beer and hands her the empty bottle.

"Here. Break it."

"Break it?"

"Break it."

"Um."

"You're fucking mad. I can see it. Break the bottle, Mari Mack."

Marilyn looks back at him uncertainly.

"You keep that anger all buried, and it won't be useful to you. Eventually you'll do something that'll hurt you or someone else, maybe without even meaning to. Think of that fucker and break the bottle."

Marilyn reaches up and hurls it with more force than she knew she had. It smashes against a rock, making a perfect shattering sound.

She swigs the rest of her own beer.

"Think of your asshole uncle," James tells her, and she breaks the second bottle. The anger begins to feel good, like it belongs in her body.

She pulls the image of an open road, barren land and endless sky, from somewhere in the depths of her memory. She thinks of the girl who crossed that desert with her mother at age six, of all of the children she used to be, and for the first time she doesn't want to turn away.

"It's pretty, isn't it? The glass," she says. "I feel bad, though, leaving it all there like that."

James pulls the rest of the bottles out of the cardboard six-pack, gets up, and uses it to sweep the glass into the paper bag that had carried the food.

She wishes she could be inside his mind, to hear his thoughts, to see the world through his eyes.

"What are you thinking?" she asks him as he walks back to her.

"I love you," James says.

Marilyn tries to study his face, but he stares outward to the city below, as if it were an ocean hundreds of feet below that he was preparing to dive into. But he's already leapt, hasn't he?

She gently reaches out, puts her hand against his cheek, and turns his head toward hers. It is precisely the distance between them, she thinks then, that makes their connection all the more beautiful. The thin thread, however delicate, that ties them to each other—it's made of gold. It matters more than anything else at this moment.

"I love you too."

She does not know if it's true, not yet, does not know if she even understands what love is—but it doesn't matter. She knows she could love him. She feels sure now that she will.

ANGIE

• • • • • *It's just after eleven p.m. when Angie and Sam arrive* at his cousin's, but the neighborhood is wide awake. They park down the block next to a row of palm trees. To Angie, they look magnificent and exotic; she's surprised to see that they just grow, right there, between apartment buildings and the corner grocery. *I love LA*, she thinks as they step out of the car into the city-dark tempered by streetlamps and headlights and the distant neon of bars. There's a passing siren; a beat-up car parked nearby blasts Chance the Rapper singing "Angels." Angie thinks she can smell the ocean on the warm night air, though it must be miles from here.

Sam takes her bag and his own.

"Let me get something," she offers.

"Naw," he replies. She doesn't fight him on it.

He leads the way to an old brick apartment building with arched windows and rusted fire escapes. He goes around the side and knocks on a door. The man who answers—well, if you'd call him a man, he's just twenty-four—bears a family resemblance to Sam, though he's much shorter and stockier.

"Cuz!" He hugs Sam and slaps him on the back, then turns to Angie with a warm smile. "I'm Miguel."

"Angie."

As he ushers her inside, the first thing Angie notices is that it smells like something delicious has been cooked recently, the scent of warm spices lingering in the air. Her stomach growls.

"Nice job," Miguel says to Sam with a grin. "This is your mamacita?"

A moment of awkward silence ensues. Finally Sam smiles. "We're just friends."

Miguel raises his eyebrows. "But she's the little girl you got all those shells for?"

Angie's not sure about being called a little girl—she definitely towers over Miguel—but she's distracted by remembering the pain of the night, almost exactly a year ago, that Sam returned from LA with the collection of seashells—the night they had sex, the night she left.

Miguel speaks before Angie can find the right words. "Okay, I get it, it's 'complicated,'" he says, making air quotes. "You guys had a long drive, more on this later."

"I've gotta piss," Sam says, and takes off, leaving Angie alone in the living room.

"Welcome," Miguel says, "to our humble abode."

The apartment is fairly small, with plaster walls, but it's full of life and color. Lines of empty Coke bottles holding single paper flowers line the windowsills; the gray-carpeted floors have been brightened by Mexican throw rugs. One of the walls has been tacked with push-pinned sketches, notes, fortunes from cookies. The opposite wall has been painted with a mural of a woman's face, beautiful and haunted, emerging from a bed of silver roses. One of the thorns has made a gash under her eye, and a teardrop-shaped bead of blood runs down her cheek.

"That's me."

Angie turns from the mural to see a girl in her early twenties with rumpled, bright red hair emerging from the hallway. She wears hoop earrings, tights, and an oversize man's T-shirt.

"Don't worry." The girl laughs. "I didn't paint a picture of my own self in the living room. Miguel's the artist."

Angie nods.

"I don't live here," the girl continues, with another giggle, "though I admit the mural makes me feel at home."

"As if you needed help with that," says Miguel. "You pay no rent, and yet, you're always here."

She swats his shoulder. "You're grateful for my feminine touch."

Miguel turns to Angie and says good-naturedly, "Angie, this is Cherry. If you hadn't guessed, I'm madly in love with her, but she refuses to move in with me, despite the fact we've been together since college."

"I'm old-fashioned-ish. Not until you put a ring on it. Or," she teases, "get a tattoo to match mine."

She reaches a hand out to Angie and flips her palm up to show the inside of her wrist, tattooed with twin cherries on their stems.

"In case I forget my own name." Sam returns, and she rushes to give him a kiss on the cheek. "My favorite cousin's here!" she exclaims, mussing his hair.

"Hey, Soda," he replies with a smile.

"Like cherry soda," she explains to Angie.

Miguel's in the kitchen, popping Dos Equis and stuffing little triangles of lime into the necks of the bottles. He passes them around the room. Angie sips timidly, liking the explosion of bubbles against her tongue.

"You hungry?" Miguel asks.

Angie nods. Actually, she's starving.

"I saved you guys some food."

Moments later, they're sitting around the table eating chicken mole.

"How is this even real? This is basically the best thing I've ever tasted," Angie says.

"I like her," Miguel says to Sam. "You sure she's not your girl?"

Sam ignores him and explains to Angie, "He's a chef on a taco truck."

"A yuppie one." Miguel smiles. "Day job."

Everyone chatters on, and Angie learns that Miguel has recently gotten a commission to do a mural on the side of a new health food store on Melrose, and that Cherry has an internship at the city's public radio station. To make money, she bartends at a small nightclub. Light-headed from the beer, Angie feels as if she's landed in a foreign place where real lives happen. For a moment, she can almost forget about her mom alone tonight, about the anxiety of how she'll find Justin, and whether she'll ever find her dad.

"We've got one sofa bed," Miguel says, "so y'all are gonna have to figure it out."

He hands them sheets and a couple of blankets and disappears into the bedroom. Cherry kisses the top of Sam's head, and then Angie's too, before she bounces off after Miguel.

"I can sleep on the floor," Sam offers.

"No, I can. You let me tag along, I'm not taking your bed."

"Well, I'm not gonna be the jerk who lets the girl sleep on the floor."

"It's fine," Angie says finally, "we can share the bed. We're just going to be sleeping, it's not that big a deal."

Sam stares at her for a long moment, until finally she gets up and goes into the bathroom to change into the green zebra pajamas that her mom bought her at Target.

By the time she comes out, Sam's made up the bed, and Angie hurriedly gets under the covers as he disappears into the hallway. She hears the sink turn on in the bathroom and remembers the playful arguments they used to have when she'd chastise him for wasting water by letting it run while he brushed his teeth.

She reaches for her phone, stares at the black screen. She needs to find out if Justin's called back, if he's emailed. Her pulse rises as she pushes the on button.

The screen shows only a single message from her mother. *Are you safe?* Nothing more. She'd expected panicked voice mails, a stream of texts. Is it possible Marilyn has just . . . let her go? Angie feels queasy as she types back, simply, *Yes.*

The thought bubble appears. Angie waits. It disappears. What is her mother thinking? What did she type and then delete? The thought bubble reappears, and, after what feels like an eternity, the words: *I want you to tell me every day that you are safe.* Angie replies, *Okay.* And that's it. No more thought bubbles, no declarations of love, of anger, of anything. She tries to imagine Marilyn in their home. Is she popping popcorn for a movie night alone?

Does the house feel empty without Angie, too quiet? In her daughter's absence, can Marilyn sense the ghosts? Angie thinks of typing, *Good night, sweet dreams, I love you more than infinity times infinity*, which she's said to her mom every night before bed since she was a child. But she does not; she cannot say one thing without saying everything.

She checks her voice mails again, wishing that one from Justin would have magically appeared, but there's nothing. She shuts off her phone and faces the wall, pretending to be already asleep when she hears Sam come out of the bathroom. The weight of his body sinks into the other side of the bed. The lights of passing cars cast shadows over the walls, reminding her of the flicker of her mom's candles. "Friends" by Francis and the Lights blasts from an open window: *Remember who you know . . .* The song fades as the car moves into the distance. Muffled voices from a nearby apartment. Another siren. Finally, Angie drifts off. She wakes in the night to the weight of Sam's arm over her body and turns to see him, mouth parted, eyelids closed in dream. She watches him for a moment, and then, not wanting to wake him, not wanting him to move from her, she repositions herself carefully. She must lie like that, wide awake, breath shallow, for hours.

Finally she sleeps, and when she opens her eyes to the morning light, Sam's side of the bed is empty. She hears voices in the kitchen, smells coffee.

"Damn girl, you could sleep through a car crash," Miguel says as she walks in to find him and Sam finishing breakfast.

He hands her a cup of coffee. "Beach day. You in?"

Angie glances to Sam. "Well, actually I have to . . . There's someone I'm looking for."

"Oh, right, Sam said. Your uncle?" Miguel asks.

Angie nods and turns on her phone to check again for anything from Justin, but all she finds is a meme from Lana: Napoleon Dynamite with the text *Don't be jealous that I've been chatting online with babes all day.* She's too consumed by worry to even laugh.

If one of the people she left a message for was *her* Justin, he'd have called her back by now, right? He'd want to meet her, right? So maybe her Justin is at one of the three addresses with an unlisted number. He must be. But what if she can't find him? What if . . . what if he's out of town, or worse? . . .

"You hear from him?" Sam asks.

"Not yet. If you're going to the beach with them could I maybe use your car? I have a few addresses I need to check."

"I'm not letting you go to strangers' houses by yourself," Sam replies.

Miguel raises his eyebrows.

"Sam . . . it'll be okay. I'll be careful."

"Angie. That's crazy."

Angie's face twists up with urgency. "I'll just take the bus, then. Or, like, an Uber."

"Jesus fucking Christ!" Sam explodes. "Why don't you just come to the beach with us, and we can drive around looking for Justin afterwards. I thought you wanted to see Venice anyway."

Angie begins, in spite of herself, to breathe too quickly. He doesn't understand; it's not some casual search.

Sam sighs. "Fine," he says, before Angie can gather herself to reply. "We'll go check your addresses first, then we'll go to the beach. Cool?" He cuts eyes at Miguel. "I'll meet up with you guys there."

"Thank you," Angie says quietly.

• • • • • *The late-morning sun slowly burns through the fog* that hangs over the city. It's the marine layer, Sam tells Angie, that on summer mornings extends far inland from the beach. It gives the light a certain half-awake softness as they drive up from MacArthur Park, past Sunset Boulevard. A man in a shirt cut to his midriff crosses the street; a young woman jogs up the crowded sidewalk with a tiny bulldog; a boy with headphones dances under a stoplight, spinning a Jiffy Lube arrow; palm trees preside over it all.

"So this is Hollywood," Sam says. "Not exactly the most glamorous."

But for Angie, it is. She feels as if the LA whose streets they drive through contains both the city in present tense and the city of her invisible past, the city where her parents fell in love.

"I can't believe I've never been out of New Mexico," she says as Sam pulls onto the 101 North. "Before now."

Sam looks over at her, and she senses him softening. She rolls down the window. Rihanna's on the radio singing "Higher," and Angie loves the crackling longing in her voice, feels it all the way through her body. They're speeding into possibility, toward a man who could be her uncle. *Uncle Justin*. Angie tries the words out in her mind as she leans out the window, letting the air rush into her lungs.

She thinks of a camping trip she went on with her mom when she was little, the feeling of freedom in her body as they drove on the highway through the mountains, the windows open and the piney smell of air rushing down their throats as Angie stuck her head out and opened her mouth, singing along to the folk song from her kids' tape: *In my hear-art, in my hear-art, there's a little song a-singing in my heart . . .*

By the time Sam pulls off the freeway twenty minutes later, the fog is gone; sunlight gleams insistently along the wide boulevard with rows of palms and strip malls. The first Justin Bell on Angie's list lives in Reseda. Angie stares out the window and makes a private game of counting the car washes (five) and nail salons (seven), a way of soothing her increasing nervousness as they near their destination. She's been a counter ever since she was kid: the stars in the sky, the streetlights on the highway, the freckles on her mom's pale face. When she was ten, she made it a project to count the leaves on the elm behind their new house. Lying on her back, she'd move from branch to branch, noting where she left off when her mom called her in for dinner. It calmed her, making her world into something to be kept track of. Now (the last time she checked) 7,505,201,954 people on the earth.

How many of them are caught in the strange feeling between hope and fear? How many are about to meet someone they've never met before, someone who could change their entire lives?

Sam turns left into a neighborhood and pulls up to 8956 Valero Street, a low house with gray stucco and an old red Ford parked outside, a tiny sapling tree bending forward in the yard. Angie half expected to see the kid from the photos sitting outside on a stoop eating a popsicle, but the yard is empty.

Sam shuts off the ignition.

"Okay," he says. "Guess we're here."

"I'll just run up. I'll be right back."

Sam shuts his eyes. He keeps them closed for a long moment, and Angie's not sure whether or not to get out of the car.

Finally, eyes still closed, Sam says, "So I'm just your chauffeur, then?"

"What?"

"I drive you all the way out to Reseda when I could be at the beach, and you want me to just sit in the fucking car?"

Angie chokes back the automated response, the defense: *I didn't ask you to come. I could have gotten an Uber.* Instead, she says, "I'm really grateful you brought me. I just—if it's him, it's something I need to do alone . . . I mean, it would be the first time I'd meet my uncle."

"Whatever," Sam says. "Go ahead."

She tries to think of something to say, something to fix it, but her throat has closed in on itself. She only sees the bright sun glaring back at her through the windshield, the fact of the house that could be Justin's. Finally she opens the door and walks up the path. She can feel herself sweating through her T-shirt.

She rings the bell.

A fortyish white man with a deep bronze tan and cutoff shorts answers a moment later, blowing on hot-pink-painted fingernails.

"Yes?" he asks, a note of irritation in his voice.

Angie opens her mouth, but only silence falls out. *Breathe,* she tells herself, fighting the weight on her chest. She glances back at the Jeep, but can't see Sam through the reflections in the windows. He was right, she realizes; she should have let him come with her.

The man drops his pink-painted hand to his side and stares back at Angie, his eyebrows raised. All at once, she wants her mother. She wants her mother the way she wanted her mother as a child. *Mommy!* Angie thinks. *Why did you leave me here alone?* But of course her mother didn't leave her; *she* was the one who left.

Angie hears footsteps on the path behind her. As she turns around to see Sam walking up, slowly her body comes back to her, and then her voice.

"Um, sorry to bother you," she stutters, "but I'm looking for Justin? Justin Bell? Does he live here?"

"He went to Gelson's."

"Gelson's?"

"A grocery store," Sam says as he comes up behind her.

"Um, is he—is he black?" Angie blurts out.

"Huh? No, honey. That man is whiter than rice. A little red at the moment—idiot went out sans sunscreen."

"Oh. Okay." Angie tries not to let the disappointment crush her. There are still two more addresses, she reminds herself. But she'd thought, she realizes now, that somehow, as soon as she arrived in LA, he'd be right there—as if she were *meant* to find him.

"Sorry to bother you. Wrong address, I guess," she forces herself to say, and even manages a polite smile. "You have a nice day."

Sam follows her back down the path and reaches out to put a hand on her shoulder.

This city is so big, Angie thinks as they get back on the freeway.

· · · · ·

The next Justin on Angie's list lives in the Pacific Palisades. After forty minutes in the car along busy freeways and then through winding tree-lined streets, Angie can start to smell the ocean in the air. They pull up a long driveway to a two-story home.

"Will you come with me this time?" she asks Sam, swallowing her pride.

He gets out of the car and follows Angie up the path through a perfectly manicured garden—roses, birds-of-paradise, lavender bushes. Angie picks one of the purple flowers, pinches it between her fingers. The scent reminds her of home, of her mother's garden that she left behind—was it only yesterday morning?

She rings the bell and glances back at Sam. A moment later, the door opens, and Angie's nearly knocked over by a white Lab puppy. She bends to pet the dog, who plants kisses on her face.

A girl, not more than seven, shouts, "No, Ollie! Come here!"

She looks like she's mixed race, which makes Angie hopeful. "Cute puppy," Angie says with a smile.

"You're not Jenna." The girl frowns.

"Um, no, I'm not. I'm actually just—I'm looking for someone. Justin? Is that your dad?"

An older white woman in expensive-looking workout clothes appears behind the girl, her voice sharp. "Can I help you?"

"Um, sorry to bother you, I was just looking for Justin? Is he home?"

The woman squints at Angie. "He's dead."

Angie feels as if she's falling through space, the ground below her gone for good. Her voice comes out in a rough whisper. "Dead?"

"What are you doing here?" the woman asks. "Who are you?"

"I—I'm sorry. I—I just, I thought he might've been my uncle."

"No. He was my son, I should know."

"Oh. I'm so sorry."

The puppy darts between Angie's legs.

"Ollie!" the woman calls, and runs into the yard. Sam goes after her. The little girl stays in the doorway, staring at Angie.

"What's your name?" Angie asks.

"Mary."

"That's a pretty name."

The woman returns with Sam, Ollie squirming in his arms.

"I'm really sorry to bother you," Angie says.

The woman only nods. She takes the puppy from Sam and shuts the door.

Angie ignores the lump in her throat as she follows Sam back to the car. She imagines he must be thinking how wrong it is for her to intrude on people's lives like this. She knows she should give up for the day, offer that they go meet Miguel—they're already near the beach anyway—but her desperation to find her uncle has only increased. She has to know if the last place will be his. Sam asks Angie for the address, types it into his phone.

As they drive away, Angie pulls her knees to her chest, resting her feet on the cracked leather seats, staring down at her toes, which are still painted apple red from when she went to get a pedicure with her mom to celebrate the first day of summer. Her mom, who's adored by the women at the nail salon, who always goes in with a bright smile and asks about each of the women's children, who likes to put her newly painted foot next to Angie's and admire them together—Angie's always felt proud of her kindness, her care.

But getting her nails done with her mom often reminds Angie of the day Marilyn had taken her and Vivian to get their first pedicures. Angie was maybe ten, and she'd been excited. They all walked into the shop together, and sat in a row in big leather chairs, Angie and Vivian playing with the massage buttons, their feet dipped into bubbling water. Angie had chosen the same teal blue as her mother's; she always wanted to look like her back then. But the woman who sat on a stool with Vivian's foot in her hand had looked up at Marilyn and said, "Your daughter's very beautiful." Angie knew the woman was referring to Vivian, who was blond like her mom.

"This is my daughter's friend," Marilyn said. "And thank you, yes, I agree she's beautiful, just like *my* daughter." She reached out and put her hand on Angie's leg, as if to claim her. "Two beautiful girls." The woman squinted for a moment in confusion and nodded, then went back to cutting Vivian's toenails.

Similar mistakes had been made over the years, involving nearly every white girl Angie had ever been close with—in the checkout at the grocery, with waitresses in restaurants, even last year when her mom took Angie and Lana to Dillard's to pick out dresses for homecoming. When Lana stepped out of the dressing room and twirled, the clerk had commented on how wonderful it was to see such a beautiful mom and daughter shopping together. Marilyn corrected the clerk, who nodded and grew quiet. On the way out Lana leaned into Angie and whispered, "God, lady, didn't you get the memo? This is the twenty-first century." Angie knew Lana must have been trying to tell her she was on her side, but it didn't make Angie feel better. *You don't get it,* she'd wanted to say. *You have two parents, and you look like both of them.* Instead she smiled back at Lana, trying to laugh it away.

• • • • • *The last Justin on Angie's list lives in K-Town, short* for Koreatown. LA's downtown buildings rise up just ahead as they drive past a dog-grooming shop, a grocer, more nail salons, clothing stores, a Korean barbecue restaurant. Finally they pull onto Fedora Street and park in front of an old stone apartment building with a green awning and a for rent sign out front. A tall palm tilts in the breeze.

Sam and Angie walk up to the building, only to discover the front door locked.

"Which one is his?" Sam asks, looking to the buzzers.

"I don't know," Angie admits with regret. Her listing shows only the street address.

Just then a woman wearing sweatpants comes out with a small fluffy dog on a leash, talking on her phone. Angie rushes forward and grabs hold of the door before it can shut, and she and Sam slip into the foyer, which looks like an old-fashioned hotel, with thick flowered curtains, a gold-rimmed mirror, gold vines carved into the crown molding.

"I guess we can try them all," Sam says. "There's probably only ten or so in the building."

So Angie knocks at the nearest apartment. Just when she's about to turn away and move on to the next, a young woman—she must be in her early twenties at most—opens the door, a baby held tightly to her chest in a sling.

"Hi, I was wondering if you know if there's a Justin Bell in the building?" Angie asks.

"I just moved in, sorry." As the baby begins to cry, her mother lifts her from the carrier and shuts the door.

At the next apartments, they meet an old Korean man who opens the door wearing pajamas and puppy slippers; a Hispanic woman with a bright smile; a white dude who appears in sweats and no shirt, the bones of a rib cage tattooed over his chest; a pretty Korean teenager with tortoiseshell cat-eye glasses; a young black woman with flour on her hands and a T-shirt that reads NAH.—ROSA PARKS, 1955; another white dude who's in the middle of watching *Keeping Up with the Kardashians*, audible in the background.

With each new person, Angie's voice rises with hope: "I'm sorry to bother you, but do you know if a Justin Bell lives here? In this building?" And each time, the reply is the same. Some version of *Sorry, don't think so. Not that I know of.*

Two doors have no answer. At the final apartment, a Hispanic guy in his midtwenties opens the door. Behind him, Angie glimpses a girl walking through the apartment in a T-shirt and underwear. She can hear the note of desperation in her own voice as she asks, "Do you know if a Justin Bell lives here?"

"I just moved in and I get mail with his name on it sometimes. He must've moved out recently."

"Oh," Angie replies, crushed. There's no way to know if the Justin Bell who moved out of this building is her Justin Bell, but either way, she's run into a dead end. No more addresses to check. No way to verify that he's even real.

As the guy shuts the door, Angie turns and hurries toward the exit. She doesn't look at Sam, doesn't want him to see her fighting tears. How stupid to think she could just walk into a city of seven million and find a single man.

She checks her phone as she steps into the bright sun, hoping for an email back or a message from her uncle, but there's nothing.

"Hey," Sam says as he walks up. Angie still cannot bring herself to meet his eyes.

A siren passes in the distance. Sam unlocks the car and opens the door for her.

Just as he starts the ignition, Angie sees the woman with the fluffy dog walking back up to the apartment building, carrying a little plastic baggy filled with poop. Angie had forgotten all about her, but she must be one of the people who hadn't answered.

As the woman opens the front door, Angie jumps out of the car and rushes up. "Sorry! Excuse me!"

The woman turns around and the fluffy dog begins barking.

"Sorry to bother you, but did you know Justin Bell? I think he used to live here?"

"Justin? Sure. Yeah. He moved out, I don't know, maybe six months ago? He was a nice dude. Used to look after my dog sometimes if I was out of town."

"Was he black and, like, around twenty-nine?"

"Yep."

Angie could kiss the woman and her yapping dog too. "He's a director? For music videos?" she asks, just to be sure.

"Yeah, that's right. You know him?"

"I think he's my uncle. Did he say where he moved?"

"He might've said something about Melrose? Or maybe it was Highland Park. I'm not sure." She turns to the dog. "Beau, shush! Anyway," she says to Angie, tugging on the leash, "we haven't kept in touch."

"Thanks for your help," Angie says, and runs back to the car to tell Sam the good news. He *exists*! Her Justin, he's here in LA.

Sam smiles and reaches out, almost as if to hug her, but he ends up patting her leg.

"But how will we find him?" Angie hardly realizes she's started using "we" instead of "I," as in she and Sam, as in they're in this together.

"I don't know. If he's a director that lives in the city, there's gotta be a way to track him down . . . Maybe you could find someone from the LA Film Fest where he won? Or maybe we could ask Cherry. She works at the radio station, she might have an idea."

"Of course!" Angie exclaims. "I can't believe I didn't think of that. There was this article about him online, on the blog for KCRW . . ."

"Cool. We can ask her tonight," Sam says. "In the meantime, I'm starving."

"Me too," Angie realizes as he turns off Fedora Street. "Did you want to go to the beach?"

"Naw. It's past five and we're already near the apartment. Let's just chill."

"Frozen pizza?" Angie ventures, with a cautious smile.

"I'm down," Sam says, his voice neutral.

At Vons they get three small frozen pizzas—Newman's Own, the brand that Mr. Stone had always stocked at Sam's—and then start exploring the aisles for toppings.

Salami, olive, and jalapeño will be the first; it was one of Angie's more successful creations from back in the day.

For the second, extra cheese—cheddar—and apples. Angie stands in the produce section, carefully selecting the apples the way her mom taught her: Gently press on the top and hold it to your ear. If you hear a snap, the apple will be crisp and sweet. She thinks of how her mom would often bring fruit salad for potlucks at Angie's elementary school. They never knew—the other mothers, the fathers, the teachers—how carefully Marilyn had picked every single piece of fruit, listening to the apples, smelling the skin of the mangoes, knocking on the watermelons. But Angie did.

They decide they'll top the third pizza with whatever they can find at Miguel's, in the spirit of their old game. It turns into a taco pizza—ground beef, sour cream, and shredded lettuce— one of their best creations yet. When they're stuffed, sitting on the couch and laughing, Angie realizes that for the past hour, she hasn't thought of anything but being with Sam; in this strange city, alone with him, she feels at home. She wants to say it out loud, but doesn't dare.

Instead she asks, "Do you still play soccer?"

"Not officially. I quit the team."

"Really? When?"

"After we broke up."

"But you loved it. You were so good."

Sam shrugs. "It wasn't the same as it used to be when I was a kid. It lost the purity."

Angie remembers going to watch him at Eldorado High, sitting on the metal bleachers with Lana and Mia eating nachos, the smell of fall leaves in the air, the rush of pride she felt when he'd score. He was a rising star by sophomore year, playing varsity, same as her.

"I'm not like I used to be, Angie."

I know, but you're still Sam, she wants to say. *I still see the you I knew.*

Instead she replies, "Neither am I."

He only nods. The silence starts to pool around them.

"I bet I can still beat your ass, though," she says.

A smile spreads across his face. "Bet not."

He gets up and a moment later returns with a ball. "You're on."

· · · · ·

Angie and Sam walk through the crowded dusk, populated by car horns and the scents of dinner wafting out of apartments, ice cream trucks and vendors selling clothes from the backs of vans, until they arrive at MacArthur Park. Even in the middle of the city, it smells like summer nights and fresh-cut grass. Families feed ducks at the edge of the huge pond, kids race by on scooters, men play soccer on a field while others watch from lawn chairs tucked below palms. Angie and Sam find an empty stretch of grass and choose makeshift goals between trees. They lose themselves in their game, running, kicking, sweating, their bodies locked in a dance. Angie notices Sam frequently coughs and bends to catch his breath—it's the pot, she thinks. But he always pops back up, matching her speed.

First to ten wins, and they're tied at nine. He kicks. She runs, slides, and catches the ball before it goes into the "goal." And then she's dribbling back across the field. He runs at her, but she kicks just in time and the ball sails over his head.

He grins. "I forgot how good you are."

Angie laughs. Sam lies down and she follows, the damp grass soaking through their shirts, the sounds of the city singing a distant chorus, tiny scattered pinpoints of stars appearing above.

"Did you know the earth is four and a half billion years old?" Angie asks.

Sam looks at her and tosses the ball into the air.

"Humans have only been here for twenty thousand. When you look at the time line of the planet, we're too small to see on it," she adds.

The ball lands with a thud in his palms. "It's all a question of perspective, isn't it?" he says. "From where I'm lying, we're as large as life."

"We're as large as life," Angie says back to him in a whisper. Those words feel like the solution to an equation she's still searching for. Their eyes lock. And then.

She does it because there are seagulls circling in the night sky, because there are palm trees rustling in the warm breeze, because the moon is almost full and huge between the buildings ahead. She does it because she's just beaten him at soccer, because he's still the best friend she's ever had, because she can feel the blood rushing through her body. She does it because a feather floats through the air and lands in his hair, because amid all of her uncertainty, his smell is sure. She does it because when she showed him the picture of her parents, he understood. Because he makes her feel less alone. She does it because she's trying to outrun her fear that she will never recover her parents' once-upon-a-time happiness—she does it without thinking. She kisses him.

He tastes like he always has and more: like her first kiss, and like there's something new and foreign hidden under his tongue. A sweet musk, a lemon drop, a teardrop. Salty. Clean. He tastes like a memory and a beginning.

He pulls her closer, and they're tearing at each other, at once fierce and gentle. She runs her hands under his shirt, across his narrow waist, the muscles of his stomach. He shivers. They come halfway undone on the grass in the night, the city swarming around them.

· · · · ·

When they get back to Miguel's apartment, Angie and Sam find him popping beers in the kitchen, still in his board shorts, and Cherry lying on the couch. Angie thinks she looks even prettier with her lightly burned cheeks and hair dried into messy waves.

"Cuz!" Cherry cries.

"What's up, Soda."

"We missed you," Miguel says.

"Sorry," Angie answers. "It was my fault."

"You find him?" Miguel asks.

"Not yet." Angie glances at Sam. She feels suddenly off balance.

"Cherry, you ever heard of a guy named Justin Bell? Directs videos. He did the one for Fly Boys?" Sam asks.

"Don't think so," Cherry says. "Why?"

Angie tentatively goes to sit beside her at the edge of the couch. "He's my uncle. I think. Could I show you the video? In case you recognize it?"

Cherry sits up and looks at Angie. "Your uncle you think? You're not sure?"

Angie tells her and Miguel the story of why she'd believed both her dad and uncle were dead, and why she now thinks Justin is alive, here in Los Angeles, and maybe even her dad too. She's never been one to open up, but something about the way they act as if her find-my-ghost-dad project is completely normal soothes her.

When she plays the video, after a few moments Cherry says, "Oh my god! Right. That one. Yeah. I work as a production assistant for Malcolm sometimes, and I remember him playing it for me after it came out."

"Is there any way . . . do you think he has Justin's number or email or something?"

"I have work tomorrow, so I'll ask around, see if anyone knows him. Maybe there's a chance his contact info's in our system, if he's ever come in for an interview," Cherry says.

"That would be—amazing." Angie can almost feel the earth rotating—how quickly, how strangely, everything spins around. She's been in LA for a single day, and already she feels as if she's made a thousand revolutions around the sun.

Before bed, Angie remembers her promise to her mom and types *I'm safe* into her phone, then slides under the covers that already smell like Sam. After the kiss in the park, the prospect of sleeping beside him has taken on a different meaning. If she lets herself slip back into their old intimacy, will she know how to sustain it this time? And if she lets herself fall into Sam, will she lose the self-possession she needs to discover what she's come for? She's afraid that she will not find her father, and, she realizes for the first time, afraid that she will—afraid that he will not want her, that there will be a tidal wave of anger at him for whatever caused him to leave her.

"Sam?" she whispers through the dark.

"Yeah?"

"Can we just . . . lie together?"

"Okay."

She scoots closer to him. The weight of his arm around her is comforting, and she lies as still as she can, for fear of disturbing what feels like the fragile peace between them, the tenuous bridge of connection. She listens to his breath long after it deepens into sleep, and tries to match hers to his. The city leaks into the room in little sounds—cars passing, snippets of songs, voices from the street. She thinks of her dad, her mom, Justin . . . until it all becomes an abstract entanglement of feeling, lines crossing each other, loves crossing each other, hopes and fears and deep uncertainty carrying her late into the night, and finally into dreams she cannot remember when she wakes the next morning.

• • • • • *When Cherry comes in the door from work at four in* the afternoon, Angie pauses the TV. She and Sam are still in their pajamas, three and a half episodes into Neil deGrasse Tyson's *Cosmos* on Netflix. (Angie's already seen the whole series more than once; it's like her comfort food.)

"Listen. I've got good news and bad news," Cherry says, dropping her keys on the counter.

Angie gets up from the couch and follows her into the kitchen. "Bad news is no one at work's got your dude's contact info. I mean, no one knows him personally. Good news is there's a party tonight I can get you guys into."

That doesn't sound like good news to Angie. She needs to find Justin, not go to some dumb party!

But Cherry continues, opening the fridge. "There's a chance he might be there."

"Oh! Really?" Angie's heart picks up speed, starting to gallop forward in her chest.

"Yeah. The LA Film Fest starts tomorrow. This is like a kick-off thing hosted by one of the directors on the board. He's a big sponsor of KCRW, so he sent over an invite for everyone there. Despite the fact I don't get paid, that includes me, and since I was the one to RSVP with the names, I emailed back the assistant this morning and asked him to add you guys to the list. He has no idea whether or not there's *actually* a Samuel Archuleta Stone or an Angela Miller who works at the station." Cherry starts eating yogurt from a container, and continues between mouthfuls. "You said that Justin won something at the festival last year, right?"

"Yeah, that's what I read," Angie says. "He won best short film for the video I showed you."

"Okay, so, there's no way they wouldn't have invited him to the party, then. I say let's go, have fun. There'll be lots of free drinks and fancy-ass food on little trays, and good music too, 'cause one of the DJs from our station is DJing there. You keep your eyes open, maybe with any luck Justin shows. If not . . . well, if not, we'll work on plan B."

"Thank you *so* much," Angie says.

Sam gives Cherry a hug. "That was super cool of you. I owe you one."

"I'm gonna go home to get ready. You want to come with, Angie? I'll lend you something to wear. The boys can pick us up in a few hours, yes?"

"Okay!" Angie replies.

Cherry's cream-colored Beetle weaves in and out of traffic on Sunset Boulevard. She speeds through a yellow light, ashing her cigarette out the window, "Partition" blasting on the stereo. Here, Angie thinks, is a version of "growing up" she could almost imagine.

"Are you from LA?" Angie asks over the music.

Cherry laughs. "No. I've been in this city for five years, but sometimes I still feel like a tourist. I mean, in certain moments, in my head I'll still be like, *I'm driving on Sunset Boulevard! Wow! Look at those palm trees! There's the Hollywood sign!* And then, also, I still have moments where I feel totally lost—despite the help of my Waze app—where it's like I can barely get through navigating traffic or dealing with the parking lot at the grocery store."

"You *look* like you'd be from here. I mean, you seem so—so much like you belong."

"That's one of the great things about LA. Anyone can look like they belong here. It's a place where you can reinvent yourself, or invent yourself in the first place, maybe, if you know what I mean. I'm from Kansas. I went to school at Occidental, and stayed in the city afterwards. I miss those crazy skies. I miss the thunderstorms. I miss my brothers. But missing something is okay. It's better, anyway, than feeling stuck somewhere. I'll take longing over boredom any day."

Angie watches Cherry as she changes lanes, tosses her half-smoked cigarette into a glass Pressed Juice bottle.

"Me too," Angie says. "I mean, I'd take longing over boredom too."

"Do you know where you want to go to college yet?"

"No," Angie admits. "But I like it here. Maybe I should come to LA too . . ."

They turn onto a residential street, where purple flowers rain over the parked cars.

"What do you wanna do?" Cherry asks. "What are you into?"

"I'm not sure," Angie says. "My problem is I can't picture any of it. I can't imagine myself in the future. Not even for a second." She looks to Cherry, suddenly self-conscious. "How did you know—you know, what you wanted to do, or, like, how to become a grown-up?"

Cherry laughs. "I'm not sure that I do." She backs into a parking spot and shuts off the ignition. "I think growing up is something that keeps happening, that's always happening, at least if you're living an honest life. And look, you're already on your way. You made the choice to come here to try and find your dad. Good or bad decision, I don't know, but you did what you felt like you needed to. *Do the next right thing*—someone said that to me once. I find it comforting to think about things that way."

As Cherry opens the car door, Angie looks at the chipping red polish on her hands, at the cherries tattooed on the inside of her wrist, at the cigarette left in the juice bottle, and she sees that Cherry's right, she's not Grown Up, not with capital letters at least. She thinks of her mother and wonders if maybe she feels the same way Cherry does sometimes; maybe her mom is still growing up too.

They walk up to a stucco building with pink awnings on Beachwood Drive. Cherry unlocks a door on the side and leads Angie into a tiny studio apartment. The whole thing is as big, probably, as Angie's bedroom back home. She takes in the collections of objects: seashells laid out in a row on the windowsills, along with the same kind of votive candles her mother loves. Wood shelves stained red, holding jars of ink and slim journals and books—Isabel Allende and Sandra Cisneros and Elena Ferrante.

The single bed carefully made with Aztec print sheets, colorful scarves for curtains, fairy lights strung everywhere, giving the room a magical glow.

"So, this is home," Cherry says. "First place that's all mine."

Though the image is blurry in her mind, Angie can almost picture walking into an apartment like this one, an apartment of her own. She can imagine stepping over the threshold of the door, alone, hanging her bag on a hook, flipping on the twinkling lights, turning up her music. She wonders if this is a sign—the first time she's been able to really imagine a piece of the future, even in a small way.

"What size shoe are you?" Cherry asks, interrupting her thoughts.

"Eight and a half."

"Perfect. I'm an eight. I'm sure I've got something you can fit into."

Angie tentatively takes a seat at the edge of the bed as Cherry strips down to her underwear, starts rifling through her closet. She's surprised by how comfortable Cherry is in her own skin, and perhaps a touch jealous. The other girls on her soccer team are as timid as Angie herself, expertly putting on their sports bras under their T-shirts, going into bathroom stalls to change their bottoms. Cherry, though, simply pulls her bra off and throws it on the bed, stepping into a little leather-fringed dress.

She frowns into the mirror. "What do you think?"

"It looks great."

"Here, try this," Cherry says, tossing a long, shiny black T-shirt out of the closet, its back scooped out all the way down to the waist. Angie tentatively takes off her own shirt, quickly pulling Cherry's over her head. Luckily she's wearing her only actually nice bra—black and scalloped.

"It totally works with those cutoffs," Cherry says, and hands Angie a pair of high black heels with ribbon laces.

"I'm so tall already . . ." Angie says uncertainly.

"Which is awesome. Own it."

By the time Cherry declares Angie "ready"—her lips painted a dark crimson, lashes blackened with mascara, curls piled on top of her head, gold earrings dangling, back muscles exposed, long legs accentuated by stilettos—she feels as if she's stepped into another body. As she examines herself in Cherry's mirror, she almost doesn't recognize the woman looking back at her. *Woman*—that's it, isn't it? Dressed this way, she could be at least five years older, just like that. She allows a small smile to play across her lips.

"Sam's gonna die when he sees you," Cherry says as she grabs her leather purse.

Angie follows her out, typing quickly: *I'm safe*. Not waiting for her mom's reply, she shuts off her phone and rushes into the night, out to the street where the boys are waiting in the car. *I am going to meet my dad's brother*, she says to herself, willing it to be real.

• • • • • *I'm going to meet my dad's brother,* **Angie thinks again** as she steps out of Sam's car, valet parked at a house in the hills above the city, and the thought is like a hot coal she can't grip onto for too long, for fear of burning herself.

She waits beside Sam, Cherry, and Miguel for the man at the door to check their names off a list.

"Do you know if Justin Bell has arrived yet?" Cherry asks the bouncer.

"Hmm?"

"Justin Bell? He's on the list, right?"

The man frowns and stares down at his paper. "Yeah. Not here yet."

Cherry turns to Angie, leading her through the door. "So, let's chill awhile. It's early, he'll hopefully show up in a bit," she says.

Angie feels like a kid walking into a grown-up world for the first time. The living room is already filling with bodies, people collecting in the corners, women dressed in designer everything, men laughing.

"Look, there's Malcolm!" Cherry says, pointing to a DJ in the corner of the room playing "Purple Rain." "Let's go say hi."

Miguel shrugs to Sam as Cherry pulls him off.

"You wanna look around?" Sam asks Angie.

"Sure."

They take mini quiches and skewers of shrimp off a passing tray and climb a set of stairs that leads to an indoor atrium–turned–dance floor, which is thick with the scent of jasmine and, more faintly, gin. A retractable roof leaves the night sky as their ceiling. An older woman with a platinum pixie cut rushes over and flings her arms around Angie, reeking of smoke and soapy perfume. She holds on for a moment before she drops her arms to her sides with a high-pitched giggle. "I thought you were—someone else."

"I hope you find her." Angie smiles at the woman and moves through the heavy backbeat of the party, Sam following. She scours the room, wondering at each turn if Justin has arrived.

"Maybe he's not coming," she says to Sam.

He puts a hand on her shoulder. "It's still early, Ang. Let's get a drink, relax. He'll show up in a bit."

"Okay."

She follows Sam to the bar in the corner of the garden room, where he orders lemon drop shots. The bartender—a semi-skinny dude with a beard, bobbing his head to the music in a lazy-cool way—sets them down without actually making eye contact. Next to Angie a curvy girl in a little dress gets lifted up by a little guy and squeals. Angie takes the shot. It burns.

Cherry appears behind them, a hand on each of their shoulders.

She leans over the bar, making herself visible among the collecting crowd.

"Four French 75s, please!" she calls, and collects the drinks from the bartender, who's still bobbing his head.

"Have you ever had one of these?" she asks Angie. "They're my favorite."

Angie shakes her head—in fact, she hardly ever drinks. When she went to the usual high school parties she'd sometimes have a beer or two to make the night go by, but Lana and Mia had always teased her for being a lightweight.

Cherry raises her champagne flute, clinks it against Angie's.

"God, if you could see yourself right now!" Cherry says. "You look hot."

"You do," Sam says quietly.

"Thanks," Angie manages, wishing the powerful feeling she'd had standing in front of Cherry's mirror would return to her.

"Let's dance!" Cherry declares.

Angie slips her hand into Sam's, needing to hold on to something as they navigate through the crowd. She gulps her drink, eats the cherry, and abandons the flute. She begins to move, tying and untying the stem between her teeth until it's shredded. She swallows it. As the booze starts to hit her blood, the air becomes thick, her body fluid. She slides into a slow dissolve. A dream. She's the electric-blue sapphire of dusk. She circles her hips against Sam. Cherry puts another drink into her hand.

The music's sweet and heavy. She's the steam pressing itself to a mirror; she's the heat of breath condensing in the air; she's the red of the roses in her mother's garden, collecting dew. She loses herself. When the thought surfaces—*Where's Justin?*—she lets it linger for a moment, scanning the room, but when she does not see him, she sets down the hot coal of anticipation as she feels Sam pulling her back to him, sees the boyish need in his face.

"Stay with me," he whispers.

How long has it been? An hour? Two? The room has continued to fill with bodies, crowded together, and Angie still feels liquid, but dizzy now. *Where's Justin?* She has to find him.

"Let's walk around!" she shouts to Sam over the music. Sam makes a pit stop at the bar, and hands Angie a new drink. The lights are dim everywhere. She tries to get closer to the faces they pass in the hall, people laughing, drinking, dancing, in a blur. Angie recognizes a famous-ten-years-ago actor with hair dyed the color of a wheat field. A tall dark-haired woman appears out of nowhere by his side, sipping from a martini and fixing her eyes on the point where the wall turns into ceiling. There are so many faces. Will she even know which one is his? Will she recognize him? Will she feel his presence, the blood they share? There are so many people now. She should have been more careful. She should not have lost track of herself. She should have stood by the bouncer at the door, waiting for him to walk in. It's too dark. So many people. She'll never find him. She's breathing too fast. Too fast.

"Angie. Angie. Come on. Let's get some air."

Sam's hand is on her shoulder, guiding her.

They step outside. The lights strung across the deck glint off highball glasses and dance over partygoers' heads like fuzzy, uncommitted halos. An infinity pool spills its water onto bamboo slats. The city's own lights spread below, persistent in the theory that they own the rights to the stars. People exhaling smoke gather around a fire pit, flames dancing over little pieces of broken glass. Angie looks up to see the wavering branches of the palms reaching for the crescent-shaped moon stamped into the sky.

"Sit down," Sam says, and she allows herself to fall onto the wooden step. Cherry's shoes have blistered her feet. She can't catch her breath.

"Here," Sam says, pulling a half-smoked joint out of the mint tin in his pocket. "Take a hit of this. It'll calm you down."

"Will I find him?" Angie asks, in the voice of a child.

"You'll find him. We'll find him," Sam says as he lights the joint and inhales.

He passes it to Angie. She pulls the smoke into her lungs, coughs. Almost instantly, she feels her body relax, her limbs heavy. The music spilling from inside tells her to *levitate, levitate, levitate . . .*

She gets up, walks through the crowd of people gathered near the fire, trying to see their faces, trying to see *Justin's* face. No matter how close she gets, none of them seem to notice her. She blends like clear liquid dropped into a puddle of blue water. Feeling herself disperse, she moves to peer into the pool, where a few people splash their feet. She remembers, for some reason, the day she learned to swim. Each time she'd launched from the steps into the water alone, there was the feeling of exhilaration when she made it safely to her mother's arms. Until the moment she swam out and found nobody there to catch her. Angie can still feel herself sinking, choking. It must have only been a split second—and then, there was her mom, pulling her out of the pool, wrapping her into a towel. Marilyn had been distracted by a conversation with another mother, she explained, apologizing. Angie's anger was eclipsed by relief. She knew she was safe then; her mom had not let her go.

But now there are no mother's arms to catch her, no song to soothe her, no hand to stroke her head. Angie realizes, for the first time, she really could drown.

"Hey. You alright?" Sam asks as he walks up behind her.

"It's so funny, I mean, it seems like there are *so many people* here, but Sam, there are *so many people* in the world, I mean, seven billion five hundred and five million two hundred and one thousand nine hundred and fifty-four . . . except that was last week. By now, there are more and—god—I mean, every second I'm speaking there are more people . . . we don't even matter. We do not even matter." She laughs like it's funny, but there's an odd weight pressing itself onto her chest.

The effort of simply taking in oxygen is strange. She asks her heavy lungs to suck in air, which is then gone again. The breaths won't come without being bidden. She's scared she'll stop breathing altogether, which is making her breathe too fast again, and the thought of the seven billion people is no longer soothing, it's not helping, it's terrifying. Somewhere, in the distance, she can hear Sam saying her name, but she can't grasp it. Who is she? Who's Angie? The sounds don't compute, don't add up to a person.

That's when she sees him.

She knows. She *knows*, she knows. That's him. That's Justin Bell, maker of the "Some Dreamers" video. That's *her* Justin Bell.

He's real. He's alive.

She'd expected him to look . . . different. Older—like a dad.

And yet, the resemblance to her father in the picture is uncanny.

He's muscular and broad-shouldered. He wears ripped black jeans, suede boots, a T-shirt with a picture of an angry-looking dinosaur, black-rimmed glasses. His arm is covered in tattoos. There's a woman with him, a woman with curly hair like hers, a woman who sparkles.

He's walking away from Angie. Why is he walking away from her?

"Angie!" Sam calls.

"Sam, it's him. It's him," she says in a whisper as he appears behind her.

"How do you know that?"

"I recognize him. He looks—he looks like my dad," Angie says, her eyes filling with tears. She can't think straight. Her head is too clouded. "Why did you make me smoke?"

"You were panicking. I thought it would help you chill out."

"How can I talk to him now? I might never see him again! How will I ever find him again?"

She takes off around the side of the house, in the direction Justin went. She feels as if she's spilling out of herself.

In the front yard, the valet attendant is holding open the door to a black Mustang. Justin is getting in the driver's side, the girl already in the passenger seat. Angie wills herself to call his name, but she cannot. Why can't she?

She turns to Sam. "Please. Get the car, quick!"

"This is crazy, Angie."

"Please!"

"We can't just leave Cherry and Miguel."

"We can come back for them! Please!"

Sam walks up to the valet as Justin's black Mustang pulls out of the driveway.

• • • • • *Angie and Sam speed through the hills, taking sharp* turns, until they empty out onto Sunset, and there, at the stoplight, is the black Mustang. A hand, the woman's, out the window, playing with the wind. His elbow, Justin's, resting on the sill. As they pull up behind, Angie can hear the music drifting from his car, a voice singing—no, declaring, pleading—*Someday the sky above will open . . .*

The sky above *is* opening. Angie does not need to look up to know it.

He is here. He's right here. Justin is in the car ahead of her.

The light turns green and the Mustang speeds off. Sam pushes on the gas, keeping up.

The night is dry, but in Angie's eyes, the city lights swim like they do in rain. She stares at the black Mustang.

There's a sudden turn that Sam follows, the sound of honking cars.

There's a yellow light the Mustang speeds through.

"Sam!" Angie cries as Sam stops at the red.

"Angie, I'm not going to risk killing you."

Angie does not answer. She stares at the red light, willing it to turn, willing it with all her might, feeling Justin drifting farther from her. *What if he slips away?*

But then they are moving forward, and at another light several blocks ahead, she sees the Mustang, just now moving through the intersection. Sam sees it too; he must, because he speeds to catch up. They're still a couple blocks behind when the Mustang turns right onto a side street.

Sam follows and they drive down the street, which is full with parked cars, which is quiet and dark, which could be any street. *How many of the seven billion people have clouds in their heads, have longing in their hearts? How many are chasing strangers? How many are searching for fathers?*

As they arrive at the end of the block, they can see no sign of the Mustang.

And then, there he is. Walking up the sidewalk, his arm around the woman. She carries her shoes in the hand that's not around his waist. They are speaking words to each other that Angie can't hear.

Sam pulls over against a red-painted curb. "Angie," he's saying, "he's right there. What do you want to do? What do you want me to do?"

Angie opens the car door and leans out.

She feels like she might be sick, but she doesn't throw up. She takes deep breaths. She holds her head in her hands. She watches Justin and the woman as they turn up a brick pathway to an old Spanish-style, ivy-covered apartment building, as he unlocks a door.

As he disappears inside.

Angie steps out of the car, wavering unsteadily in her heels, and walks up to the building, close enough to see the address.

Taking a pen from her purse, she writes it down on her hand: 179. She looks again, writes it again on her other hand this time, to make sure her brain is not playing tricks: 179.

As she gets back in the car she asks quietly, "Sam, what street are we on?"

"Sycamore."

Sycamore. A street in LA, a street with leafy trees that are its namesake, a street with rosebushes, a street where specific people live, people whose lives Angie knows nothing about.

"Thank you," she says to Sam. "For helping me." She leans into him, resting her head on his shoulder, suddenly so tired.

"I love you," she says.

But the next day, she will not remember saying it. She will not remember much.

MARILYN

• • • • • *Marilyn can hear Diana Ross blasting over the speakers* from the next room, singing "I'm Coming Out." Inspiration for the prospective belly buttons, she supposes. She sits in the waiting room, trying to focus on studying for the US history test she'll have to make up early tomorrow morning, on the last day before Thanksgiving break. *He has compelled her to submit to laws, in the formation of which she had no voice*, she reads, practicing multiple-choice questions based on a passage from the Declaration of Sentiments and Resolutions from the Seneca Falls Convention.

At the sound of her stomach growling, Marilyn glances down at her too-pale exposed skin. Wanting her to look skinny in the crop top, Sylvie allowed her only a SlimFast shake for breakfast, and that was hours ago. As she easily marks off the answers about the first women's rights convention, Marilyn smiles wryly at the irony. The private joke makes her feel a bit better, and the book becomes a kind of armor.

As her stomach growls again, more emphatically this time, her name is called. Marilyn's led into another room, where she shakes the hand of the casting director, a woman in her forties who eats from a bag of fat-free Lays. Her bare feet rest on a chair, their abandoned stilettos on the floor below. Behind her a row of five men in suits sit on a leather couch, all of them looking bleary eyed. The casting director wipes her hands on her pants and instructs Marilyn to simply walk around the room, which is stark white—the walls, ceilings, and floors gleaming—while a dude behind a camera records audition tape. Marilyn wishes she herself were looking through a lens instead of parading around on display.

"A little more bounce, honey," the casting director tells her. "Shake your hips—not too hard—not like you're trying to be sexy, but like it just happens that way. You're with your boy toy. Imagine he's just behind you, staring. You're showing off for him, but not letting on."

Marilyn thinks of James's voice—*You have a choice.* She tries the woman's instruction, as absurd as it might be. She imagines she and James are at the beach. She hears the waves. She turns around and sees him lying in the sand behind her, propped up on his elbows. She imagines walking down to the water, how she moves when she knows his eyes are on her. It makes her stand up straighter, makes something under her skin light up with a heat, soft like the late-day sun.

She's pulled out of her fantasy when the casting director tells her, "Thank you, lovey."

And then it's over.

Marilyn zips up her hoodie as she steps out through the revolving glass door. It's a cold late-November day, cold for Los Angeles anyway. At only three thirty, the sun's already dropping low and thinning out across the sky. Marilyn spots Sylvie parked at the curb in a yellow zone, flipping through *US Weekly*.

"How did it go?" Sylvie asks as Marilyn opens the passenger door.

"Okay, I think."

"I have such a good feeling about this one!"

"I'm starving," Marilyn replies.

They go to the drive-through at Wendy's, where they each get chicken sandwiches (supposedly a healthy alternative to a hamburger, according to Sylvie). Marilyn's sucking at the straw of her Diet Coke when Sylvie turns left out of the driveway onto Sunset; she should have made a right.

"Where are we going?" Marilyn asks.

"I feel like doing something fun. Let's go look at our house," Sylvie says.

Our house is how Sylvie's come to refer to the home in the hills they went to visit after Marilyn's first meeting with Ellen. They've driven by a few times since, Marilyn silently bearing Sylvie's wistful gaze as they pass. On their last visit, Sylvie noted that the price went down to a "very reasonable" $750,000.

"Mom, I'm really tired."

"Oh, come on, we'll just go by real quick."

Marilyn can't help the sigh that escapes her lips.

"Please?" Sylvie adds, a girlish, lilting sound in her voice. She's already making the turn up into the hills, so Marilyn just nods.

As they ascend over the city, the sun fades and scattered displays of Christmas lights begin to come on, identifying the homes of overeager decorators. Marilyn holds the map, but Sylvie doesn't have trouble with the complex set of turns, and Marilyn wonders how many times she's been back there on her own.

They pull up to 5901 Hill Street to find a BMW parked in the driveway, the picture of Ron's grinning face and the for sale sign gone. The last of the day's sunlight glints off a second-story window. Each of the miniature *David* statues wears a Santa hat.

Sylvie bursts into tears.

"Mom—" Marilyn starts, but finds she doesn't know what to say. She stares out at the house as the sun extinguishes itself from the windowpane and the little white lights strung along the rooftop appear in its place. She sees herself and her sobbing mother sitting there in the car as if she were outside of it, staring down from that window in the house her mother so desperately wanted. They look adrift in the boat of the Buick, lost in a sea of expensive homes they will never own. It's so easy to be nothing. To be nobody, Marilyn thinks.

In an effort to stay connected to her own perspective, she raises her hands to take a mind-picture of her mother's profile, framed against the car window, looking out at the house golden with Christmas.

As Marilyn lowers her hands, Sylvie turns to her and says through tears, "It's the Santa hats, you know? That's something I would have done. If the house were ours."

"There are other houses, Mom," Marilyn finds herself saying.

"We'll get one that's even better?"

Marilyn brushes the thinning, dyed-blond hair from her mother's face, baby fine between her fingertips. "We'll try."

• • • • • *Thanksgiving morning is gray, but Woody is unchar*-acteristically cheerful. When Marilyn comes out of her room, rubbing sleep from her eyes, she finds him in a blue suit she's never seen before, making coffee and whistling to himself. Commerce Casino is hosting a poker tournament today, and he's dressed to win.

"Happy Turkey Day," he says.

"You too," she answers.

"Gotta be on my way; that Buick's not gonna win itself."

"Good luck," Marilyn says, and moves off to find Sylvie in her bedroom, painting on lipstick. "James's grandparents invited us down for dinner," Marilyn tells her mom, keeping her voice low. "Do you wanna go?"

Tension draws itself around Sylvie's eyes. "I thought we'd go out for sandwiches." When they lived in the OC, their Thanksgiving tradition had been turkey sandwiches at Ruby Tuesday on the pier.

"You don't want to try something different this year? Rose is a really good cook."

"I don't think so. I have a bit of a headache. You go if that's what you want."

"Are you sure?" Marilyn asks.

"I guess this will just be our first Thanksgiving apart," Sylvie says.

But you could come! Marilyn thinks, trying to push away the guilt. She'd expected her mom to talk about next year, as she does every Thanksgiving, when they'll host the holiday in their own grand home, with a beautiful turkey and all the trimmings. But instead Sylvie just turns away from Marilyn and changes back into her nightgown.

Once Woody's out of the house, Marilyn kisses her mom and leaves her on the couch with the Thanksgiving Day parade on TV and a bottle of white wine by her side.

Dressed in her black velvet dress with the swingy skirt, saved for special occasions, Marilyn knocks at the Bells', shivering under the blank white sky as a gust of wind comes up. A moment later, Justin swings the door open wide.

"Wanna play Operation?" he asks by way of welcome.

Marilyn laughs. "Sure!" she says as she follows him into the warm home, the echoes of the cold day instantly fleeing from her bones. "But I should see if your grandma wants help first."

She hugs James, and finds Rose in the kitchen, in the midst of pulling a turkey from the oven. It smells rich and golden, the way she imagines the kind of Thanksgiving dinners you see on television must. Rose kisses her on the cheek and shows her how to use the baster to gather the turkey juices from the bottom of the pan and squeeze them over the bird.

"It stays moist this way."

"Let me show her," Justin says, taking the baster from Rose's hand.

"He loves this part." Rose laughs.

Marilyn looks to James across the room, in front of a basketball game with Alan but, at the moment, watching her with his grandmother and brother, a smile on his face.

"Boys!" Rose calls to her husband and older grandson. "I'm about to put you to work." She delivers a giant bowl of green beans along with a paper bag and instructs them to snap the ends off. Marilyn peels potatoes, then gets pulled into a game of Operation with Justin, who dissolves in hysterics every time she sets off the terrible buzzer. And like that, the afternoon passes in warm chaos—eager voices, stolen bites of food, laughter.

Still, Marilyn can't help but think of her mother alone upstairs. She feels herself starting to drift away, as if on a one-person boat, and excuses herself for the bathroom, where she catches the vague scent of cologne left in the air, a smell both familiar and far off, triggering a memory stored deep within her body. Though she can't place it, the scent is of her father's cologne (Old Spice, also Alan's). She splashes water on her face, trying to wash away the lingering malaise.

And when she returns, she's pulled back into the room by James's hand on her leg under the table, by Justin's laughter as he gloats over beating her (again), by Rose's careful cooking lessons as she shows her the right amounts of butter and cream (lots) to make the mashed potatoes delicious. They are keeping her afloat. And then, finally, the turkey is carved, the table set. And by the time they sit down to eat, Marilyn's safely docked on their shore, grateful for the sense of belonging that they so readily offer to her.

I'm kissing you . . . Des'ree sings, as Claire Danes blinks at her Romeo, bright blue fish swimming through the tank between them, angel wings spread around her. As James kisses the back of Marilyn's neck, fireworks explode into the on-screen sky. Marilyn feels no less in love than Juliet looks. The movie was her pick—she'd wanted to see *Romeo+Juliet* in the theater when it came out two years ago, but the afternoon her friends went she'd had an audition for a Neutrogena commercial. When she showed James the video box in the aisles of Blockbuster, after pie and coffee and good-nights, he groaned but agreed to watch it with her.

By the final scene—the lovers lying lifeless in each other's arms, bathed in candlelight—tears stream down Marilyn's face. When James leans over to wipe them away with his thumb, she sees he's also crying. A sound of sniffling comes from behind the couch and Marilyn turns to see Justin in his pj's, tucked into the corner of the doorway.

"What are you doing?" James whispers. "You're supposed to be asleep."

Justin wipes at his eyes. "Why couldn't he have just waited another minute?" he asks. "If he'd just waited a minute more, she'd have woken up. Why didn't he check first, to make sure she wasn't breathing? Or listen to her heart?"

"Come here," Marilyn says, and Justin gets up, curls between them on the couch.

She strokes his head, the way her mother had done for her when she was a girl on the sick days she had cherished, and minutes later, Justin's asleep with his head on her lap. Here, eyes fluttering in dream, he could be baby James.

James gets up and lifts his brother off her lap, carries him into bed.

"I should go," Marilyn whispers when he returns.

"No. Don't."

Marilyn smiles. "I have to!" She knows she's already pushing it by staying out this late. Rose and Alan have been in bed for hours—she can only hope Sylvie is too.

"Don't go," James insists again, and lies down on top of her, in that moment no less boyish than Justin. "I wanna sleep by you."

"Come on, I'll tuck you in," Marilyn whisper-laughs.

She scoots out from under James, who grips onto her, pulling her back.

"Come on!" She grins and puts her arms around his shoulders, trying to pull him up, but he lets his body go heavy, and she's hardly a match for all six feet, one hundred and eighty pounds of him. They play like this—her trying to pull him up, him letting her get halfway there before he tugs her back onto the couch—until James finally gives in and lets her pull him to his feet. She follows him to the end of the hallway, where there's a sign on the door marked JAMES in wooden block letters.

"Don't make fun of me," he says. "My mom got it for me when I was a kid, so."

Marilyn smiles, eager to see the bedroom she's imagined him in so many times while listening to his music drifting up to her.

It's small like her own, with a single bed pushed against the

247

window, neatly made with a checkered quilt. White Christmas lights strung along the ceiling illuminate the space. The desk, holding a stack of schoolbooks, is made from old wood, sanded smooth to show its grain. On the opposite wall, there's a huge, perfectly painted black rectangle, and beside it a tiny shelf installed for chalk (two half-worn pieces rest there). He's written, "*Through every dark night, there's a bright day after that.*"—*2Pac*. And, below it: "*I am still committed to the idea that the ability to think for one's self depends on the mastery of the language.*"—*Joan Didion*. A small bedside table with an incense holder, a half-finished glass of water. She wants to run her fingers over the mouth of the cup. When she looks up, she sees constellations of tiny black stars painted against the white ceiling.

Inside of the space where he lives with himself, it feels as if she's thwarted the reality of their separateness, or at least as if she's taken one step closer to him than she's ever been allowed before. He kicks off his shoes, lies down. She raises her hands, takes a mind-photo of his body filling the whole of the perfectly made single bed.

"Come here," he asks her, and she lies beside him, propped on her elbow, engulfed at once by his scent worn gently into the sheets, the years of dreams that won't come out in the wash. James rests his head on her chest and she leans back against his pillow, comforted by the weight of him. The look on his face reminds her of the photograph of him as a boy, resting on his mother's shoulder. She strokes his head, forcing her eyes to stay open as his breathing slows, deepens. When he lets out a little snore, she has to stop herself from laughing. As his eyes move below closed lids, she studies the delicate skin that darkens nearest to his lashes, the eyebrow hairs that grow together in a soft shadow, the way his muscles clench as if holding on tightly to what's hidden beneath. She traces the tattoos on his arm, the cursive of *Angela*, his mother's name.

When she's sure he is deep within a dream, she carefully moves her body from under him, scoots a pillow beneath his head where it had been resting on her chest, buries her face in his neck, taking in his smell before she tiptoes away. He moans softly, shifts his weight. She closes the door behind her, lets herself out.

She shivers in the night air and climbs to the apartment upstairs. She unlocks the door, to find Sylvie sitting alone in the dark, staring out the window at the moon, a glass of wine resting in her hand. She turns to Marilyn.

"You had a nice Thanksgiving, then." The question is not a question. It is an accusation.

"I didn't know you were up," Marilyn says quietly.

"I'm not," Sylvie answers. "I'm somewhere else. Not even in this room at all."

At a loss, Marilyn kisses her mother's forehead. When she gets no response, she goes, washes up, and falls so deeply into her own dreams that she will not remember them on waking, locked as they are into the unconsciousness of the night.

• • • • • *Marilyn wakes to the sound of rain. She tiptoes out of* bed, checks the house. Empty. Woody must still be at the casino, and Sylvie's at work all day for Black Friday. She hurries into the kitchen and starts coffee, dials James's number. It's Rose who answers, in her girlish lilt.

"Hi, Rose, it's Marilyn. Is James home?" When he comes to the phone, she says in an urgent whisper, "It's me, come upstairs, come get in bed, I'm alone."

Moments later, as she's pouring two cups of coffee (cream for both, lots of sugar for his), she hears the knock on the door, rushes to answer. James is there in his basketball shorts, T-shirt stained with beads of rain, tiny droplets in his hair.

"Morning, Miss Mack," he says, his voice low and gravelly, cutting against his boyish smile. At once, he picks her up—sweeps her off her feet, literally!

"Which way?" he asks through her giggles, and carries her down the hall to her bedroom, which is just above his own. He plops her on the mattress, climbs on top of her. He kisses her stomach. He takes off her shirt. She shivers. The rain patters. His hands on her breasts, then his mouth. Her body's so wildly awake, she wonders if she will burst out of herself. She pulls his shirt off, runs her hands over the muscles of his back, nails gently dragging. As she kisses his neck, he lets out a soft moan. His hands move inside of her, do what her own fingers did when she lay in bed and thought of him. And then, a release.

He brushes the hair from her forehead, kisses her temple. She reaches out for him.

"How do I make you feel like that?" she asks in a whisper.

James laughs. "I'll show you if you want."

He does, and it nearly undoes her all over again, witnessing his pleasure, knowing she has caused it.

When they are quiet, her head resting on his chest, his hands in her hair, the rain steady in its rhythm, the sweet heat of his skin against her own, she falls asleep; never has she felt so completely contained in a moment.

She wakes in the early afternoon, eyes blinking open to find James beside her, still sleeping. She gets up, reheats the forgotten mugs of coffee on the stove, fries grilled cheese sandwiches, and brings them back to bed. She nudges him awake, kissing his eyelids, his forehead, his cheekbones, and they picnic together in bed.

"I like your pictures," he says, examining the black-and-white copies on her wall. "Especially that one."

He points to a photo by Gordon Parks, of Eartha Kitt emerging from a bank of low trees caught by sun, hands raised in a dancer pose over her head.

"I love that one too," Marilyn says.

"Now I see where you are, when I hear you at night. I'll be able to picture you."

"You hear me?"

"Your footsteps." He smiles. "When you first moved in, to be honest it annoyed me."

She punches his shoulder.

"I wasn't used to it," he says. "The room's been empty I guess for as long as we've lived here, and my bedroom is where I go when I need things to be quiet. So at first, when I'd hear you moving around, it threw me off. But then . . ."

She looks back at him, waiting.

"Then it started to be comforting. Knowing you were just above me, hearing the little sounds of you. I started waiting for your movements, loving them."

"You know I listen to your music? Through the window. It was so lonely when we moved here, that was the one thing that made it better . . ."

James smiles. "At first I didn't think of it, but I admit, the night after we first kissed when I put on 'Ready or Not,' I turned it up, I wondered if you could hear it . . ."

Marilyn blushes at the memory. "I did."

James sits up and kisses the tip of her nose. He wraps her up in his arms, squeezes tight.

"I can't breathe." She laughs, and squeezes him back.

"Harder!" he says. "Squeeze me like a bear!"

She tightens her grip, using all the strength in her arms to pull him against her body. When she releases him, he buries himself under the blankets. She follows him into the cave of covers, and they become children, playing together. He wrestles her, pinning her down. She wriggles free, tries to pin him.

"Grrr," he growls at her.

"Grrr," she growls back through laughter. She comes up for air, pats for his body under the blankets.

"Grrr," she growls again, and pounces onto him, only he doesn't move.

She lifts the sheets and finds him frozen, curled into himself. "What's wrong?"

"Nothing—I—nothing."

But his playful sense, his smile, is lost.

He rolls over and closes his eyes.

After a moment, she gently rolls up behind him and puts her arm across his chest, spooning him from behind. At first he doesn't move, but eventually he reaches up and takes her hand in his own. They breathe together like that for what feels like hours, though maybe it's only minutes later when James says, "When I was a boy I used to get in bed with my mom in the morning. I'd crawl under the covers and wait for her to be like, 'Where's James?' She'd start feeling around on top of the blanket, and when I felt her hand on me I'd move away real quick, and then she'd get under the covers and chase."

Marilyn smiles, kisses the spot on his neck where his hair stops. She traces the outline of his back, but his body tenses below her hand.

"My favorite part of the game was being caught. I loved the feeling of her weight on me—it felt safe. I loved her voice when she'd say, 'I found you. You know you can't get away from your momma.'"

After a long moment, he continues, "But that morning, her

body started shaking. It was a seizure, but I didn't know that then. To me it felt like an earthquake—like the earthquakes we'd learned about in school. I imagined some fault line inside of her had split open. I panicked. I was too terrified to move. I screamed for help, but my grandparents were out. Justin was just a baby. He'd been sleeping in his crib, but eventually he started crying. Finally I managed to get out from under her, but her body was so heavy. I ran into the next room and called 911. I can't remember much after that. She died in the hospital that night—a brain aneurysm."

Marilyn holds on to him, her arms wrapped around his body, her face pressed into his back. "James, I'm so sorry."

When he finally turns to look at her, she sees the tears running down his face. She runs her hand along his cheekbones, his brow. "She must have been amazing," Marilyn says quietly, "to have kids like you and Justin."

"I don't know that I believe in heaven, at least the way most people do, but there have been times—I've never said this to anyone, but there have been times where I swear I can tell she's here. I can feel it . . ."

He rolls onto his back, stares up at her ceiling. "She loved hummingbirds, for some funny reason. They were her favorite animal. She put out a feeder every spring and filled it with sugar water, like religiously. When we moved in with Nana and Poppa after the divorce, she was all excited about hanging it up—but she had the thing out there for months, and they never showed. She'd change the water and put it back, and I'd be like, 'What are you doing? The birds aren't coming.' And she'd be like, 'Have faith.' And then one morning, I'm in front of the TV with my Cap'n Crunch, and she's squealing, 'Jamie, Jamie! Look!' And she sounds so excited that I run over, and there's this tiny little bird, its wings going maybe a trillion miles an hour. It sees our faces, right up next to it, right against the glass, and it darts away for a minute, and then it turns back. We keep real still and it goes up to this feeder and just starts eating. Right there. Like, inches in front of us. And pretty soon, that one bird must tell its friends where the food's at, and there's this whole posse of them that starts showing up. We watch them every morning—it never gets old. It makes my mom so happy.

"So after she dies, you know, the sugar dries up, and nobody puts out the food anymore. I mean, I'm like eight, so I don't even think of it, and the birds stop coming. But one morning, maybe half a year later, I'm in the kitchen getting a soda, and I turn and out the window I see this little hummingbird staring back at me, its wings beating fast as ever, only it's not going anywhere. It's not darting around. It's just there, looking at me, and I know it's her. My mom. I mean, not literally like she's the bird, but—somehow, I knew she was telling me something. Reminding me. It was just a feeling. I don't know." He pauses. "I hadn't said a word in months, but I whispered to the bird. Just a simple hello, but it broke the silence.

"After that, I started filling up the feeder." James smiles. "The first time I tried to boil the sugar water I didn't ask my grandma or anything first—I just pretty much dumped the whole bag in, thinking I'm gonna make it extra good. And Nana comes in and catches me and she freaks, but in the end she showed me how to make the nectar, and the birds started showing back up."

Marilyn hugs him, and he rests his head against her. She sees the rain has stopped, the deep gray clouds breaking up, letting in the soft blue of the evening sky. She traces the arcs of his body with her fingers, his muscles softening as he shuts his eyes.

"If I ever have a daughter," he says, his gaze drifting toward the window, "I'll name her after my mom."

• • • • • *Marilyn's always imagined a part of her would die* and be reborn into someone new as soon as she left for college, but now the transformation's already taking place. Only it's less like death and more like waking up. Whatever's been there, buried, has begun to surface in James's presence.

The childhood memories that had been fuzzy and distant, like an out-of-focus movie of someone else's life, have started arriving unexpectedly, bright and true in her body. Lying on James's shag carpet, languid after their still-startling intimacy, Marilyn remembers the simplicity of the smell of summer grass from the yard in Amarillo, the desert heat that seemed weightless even as it scorched, the sky she'd imagine swimming through, the smell of her dad's cologne (yes, now she can recall) when she'd jump into his arms—these pieces of herself from another time and place tie her to James now, leaving her with the feeling that all her life has been leading to him.

His lips on her temples, on her eyebrows, behind her ears, little kisses everywhere.

Then Justin, banging on the door. "Are you guys almost ready?!"

"We'll be right there, Jus! Get your shoes on."

This Saturday, two days after Thanksgiving (the holiday

weekend she will look back on and remember as the time in which she fell in love with James), is a rare day when Rose and Alan are both out—a date to the movies—leaving the brothers alone. Marilyn came downstairs in time to see Rose dolled up with pink lipstick and a pink sweater, big gold earrings studded with gems, rose-scented perfume, and she loved the still-girlish way Rose flirted with Alan (who was himself dressed up in a sport coat), holding out her hand for him to take it.

Marilyn came over, ostensibly, to study—she and James both want to make progress on their college essays—with a promise to Justin they'd get ice cream afterward. James set Justin up with a movie and they went into his bedroom, but before they even managed to pull out their papers, they could not keep their hands off each other. That's how it's been these days—a constant hum of electricity (they hope audible only to them), perpetual restless hunger, deep in their bodies. He locked the bedroom door. She had to bite down on his sweatshirt, balled up and stuffed into her mouth, to keep silent.

"We should probably still get some work done, no?" he says, his voice breaking into her reverie.

"But I don't think your brother's gonna wait any longer for Baskin-Robbins," she replies in a whisper. After they go out for cones of mint chocolate chip (Marilyn), rocky road (James), and Neapolitan with sprinkles (Justin), Rose and Alan have returned and James suggests going to the library.

As they set up in their usual spot, James asks, "You wanna look at a draft of this essay?"

"Of course." Marilyn takes the pages that he pushes across the table.

As she starts to read he gets up, mutters something about the bathroom. When he returns, he opens his calculus book and pretends to be absorbed in it, but she can feel his eyes, continually fluttering upward to her. He's written his college essay about his mother. He tells the story of her love for hummingbirds in stunning detail, going back to what he knows of her own childhood in North Carolina, through her family's move to Los Angeles as a teenager, up to the birth of her children, and the bird that arrived at James's window six months after her death. *The funny thing about beauty,* James writes, *is that in no way does its presence negate the truth of suffering, of injustice, of pain, but it does stand stalwart in its own right, as its own truth.*

Marilyn wipes her eyes as she reaches the end. "James," she says. "This is so good. I mean, Jesus, you could be the next Joan Didion."

James laughs, but she can see the pride shining behind his eyes.

"I'm really glad we're reading the book. It helped. It inspired me. I didn't want to write the same old boring stuff."

"It's anything but boring—it's—it's beautiful." And she means it. He's made something so personal bigger than himself, bigger than his own loss, bigger than his own family. He's made it into a story.

"What about you? Have you started?" he asks.

"I have, but this makes me wanna start over. I could do better. I could be more honest. It's easy to forget sometimes how much power there is in saying what you mean instead of what you think someone wants to hear."

"For sure."

"It's like it's become so ingrained in me, trying to please other people, or just—finding the path of least resistance. But that's not who I want to be."

"It's not who you are—look how much work you've put into this whole process already. *That's* not easy."

"Thanks."

"If you want any help, I'm here," he says.

I'm here. Those words have never sounded as good as they do coming from James.

Marilyn spends the next hour making edits to his essay, suggesting cuts and additions and searching for grammar mistakes, and when she hands the papers back to him, he looks up from his textbook and says, "I don't want to let you go."

"What do you mean?"

"Next year. I don't want this to be over."

"Neither do I," she says, her throat tightening.

"What if it didn't have to be like that? What if we went together?"

"That would be amazing . . ." She checks his face, sees her own uncertainty, her own hopefulness reflected. "I could apply to UCLA. You're right, it's a good school," she says.

"I know how much you want to get out of here. I'll apply where you're applying. We'll see what happens . . ."

It takes Marilyn a moment to process his words, and then she begins to swell, filling with helium. She could float to the top of the glass roof above their heads—beyond it, into the outer reaches of the atmosphere.

"Okay," she says, "I love that, but I mean, you have to make sure you think they'd be good places for you. That it's what you'd want—"

"I don't know what I want. But I know I want you."

This is what it feels like to be in love with James Alan Bell, in Los Angeles on the first day of December of 1998, she thinks, as they drive away from the library and merge onto the 101, a huge moon hung in the sky ahead, his hand on her thigh, Aaliyah singing "At Your Best" on the radio.

"This could be our song," she says quietly.

James does not take his eyes from the road, but she feels him weave his fingers through hers. "Yeah."

That night, Marilyn stays up late, adjusting her college list to fit what she believes will be best for James too, searching for their intersections. She drops Smith (all women) in favor of Boston College. She adds UCLA. She also adds Harvard (though she knows she won't get in) just so he'll apply, thinking she could be nearby at another school in Cambridge, maybe Emerson. Columbia, though—Columbia would be the dream. She falls asleep, imagining them arriving in New York together, hand in hand, the diamond at the end of her tunnel now turning into the spectacular lights of the city she could see with him.

• • • • • *At the first ring, Sylvie pushes the worn fake Christmas* tree into Marilyn's arms and runs for the phone.

"Hello?" Her face falls. "Mm-hmm. No thanks. Please put me on your do-not-call list." Sylvie hangs up and turns to Marilyn. "Welp, no news is good news for now!"

Marilyn had a callback for the Levi's commercial last week, but she's already reminded her mom they aren't likely to hear anything until after the holiday.

"We're about to turn a corner. I can feel it in my bones," Sylvie says as Marilyn props up the tree—the same one they've had since the year they moved into the OC apartment. The branches are beginning to seem bare, having slowly shed a portion of their silver "needles" over the years.

Marilyn wishes she could retreat to her room to work on her college essay, but as she looks over at Sylvie in the kitchen starting hot chocolate—their tree-decorating tradition—she softens and opens a ziplock bag full of ornaments. Sifting through the haphazard collection of Play-Doh hearts, candy canes, and silver stars, she finds the My Little Pony ornament that Sylvie had made for her by attaching a hook to the back of a smaller toy. As Sylvie brings her a steaming mug, Marilyn hangs the pink-haired horse on the tree, although she thinks Fluttershy is looking a little worse for wear.

By Christmas morning, they've managed to stock the tree with a few presents. As Sylvie checks the ham in the oven, Woody opens his gift—a personalized mug reading WOODY WINS! They'd bought a plain white coffee cup at the dollar store, and with permanent marker Marilyn carefully stenciled the letters, along with several colored stars. They put it in the oven to bake, and—as Sylvie said—voilà! The marker had become permanent.

Woody's lips turn in a sort of downward smile as he examines it, and Marilyn can see he's restraining emotion. "Well then," he says, "this is very nice, isn't it. Very nice, ladies. How 'bout that. First Christmas gift I've gotten in years, isn't it. Thank you."

"I think I'll put it to good use right now," he adds, getting up to pour coffee, which he finishes off with a shot of Baileys. Though Sylvie says nothing, he turns to her defensively.

"It's a holiday."

Sylvie only nods, and says to Marilyn, "Help me with the salad, will you?"

The "salad" is a Jell-O salad, the same one Sylvie makes for Christmas every year. They stir pineapple, cranberries, and walnuts into the hot liquid and put it in the fridge to set, while Woody works on his Baileys and coffee and pours another, this time with a shot (or two) of whiskey. Marilyn eyes him as she hears the familiar ding of the dial-up, which means he's likely beginning an online poker game.

"Woody . . ." Sylvie says, her voice soft. "It's Christmas. Take the day off . . ."

"It says right here, on my mug. 'Woody Wins.' I've got good

263

luck." Woody smiles, but Marilyn can hear the booze starting to creep into the edges of his vowels.

Sylvie shuts her eyes and then flips on the TV. *A Charlie Brown Christmas* plays in the background while she and Marilyn finish making the lunch. By the time the table is set, the ham, green bean casserole, and Jell-O salad served, Woody's still staring intently at his computer screen.

"Shall we open our presents before we eat?" Sylvie asks.

So Marilyn retrieves the rest of the small packages from under the tree. One for Sylvie, two for her. She opens hers first to find a collection of perfume samples inside a CK One tote. She gets this same gift every year for Christmas, or a version of it. (The brand of tote bag changes.) She dislikes wearing perfume, but still, there's something comforting in the familiar package, and she goes through opening each scent, commenting on which are her favorite. From the bottom of the bag she pulls out lipstick samples. She knows Sylvie gets them from the women at the makeup counter, then carefully slices off the tops with a sharp knife to make a clean surface. Marilyn's mostly only ever used the lipsticks when her mom puts them on her before an audition or meeting, but in the past months, since James, she's started experimenting with her own makeup. She discovers a deep purple and paints it on, grins at her mom.

"You like?"

Sylvie smiles at her smiling. "You know I prefer more traditional colors, but I've noticed you branching out, so who am I to say. I'm just an old lady."

"You are not." Marilyn gives her mom a purple kiss on the cheek.

Marilyn knows what the second gift will be also. She opens the package, carefully wrapped in thin shiny paper, to uncover three jars of Sylvie's famous holiday lemon scrub. Though the recipe is fairly simple, her mom makes it only once a year, perhaps to preserve it as special, and prints out labels—SYLVIE'S LEMON LIFT—that she pastes onto the mason jars. As Marilyn inhales the scent—summer in the middle of December—she wishes her mother *would* have her house in the hills, or at least a home of her own, the money to buy nice dresses, to eat in restaurants with linen napkins, to fill the hole that takes the shape of longing for such things.

"Smells amazing," Marilyn says. "Now open yours."

Sylvie unwraps the tiny gift to reveal a set of careful ornaments made from ribbon and Scrabble letters glued together. The set spells I LOVE YOU, MOM. Marilyn knows it's not much, it's nothing really, but she tries to come up with a new little gift to make her each year.

Sylvie comes over to hug her, and Marilyn can almost feel the lump in her mother's throat as she whispers, "Thank you, baby."

"What's that?" Woody asks, turning from his computer, his voice taut like a bow waiting to release its arrow.

"A present. Marilyn made it for me."

Woody crosses to the kitchen table where they sit. "And where did you get those Scrabble letters?" he asks Marilyn.

"Um. I—found an old game, in the back of the closet."

"You mean *my* old game."

"Sorry, I—I didn't think anyone was using it. It was all the way in the back, covered with dust and stuff."

"You are a *guest* in this house, and you have no right to take what belongs to me!" Woody explodes.

Marilyn shuts her eyes, escaping to her brick pathway, her fall leaves, her stone library, to her future dorm room where she imagines James, asleep in her bed, no one to bother them.

"Put it back," Woody says.

Marilyn glances toward Sylvie, sees the tears gathering in the edges of her eyes.

"Uncle Woody, please," Marilyn says softly. "We all—we all got presents. That one's for my mom."

"You have no *right*—*y*ou don't know where that game came from! You don't know what that game is."

Wordlessly, Sylvie starts snapping apart the letters, freeing the small wooden tiles, the tears now having escaped her eyes, running down her face.

She gets up and goes to the closet. Marilyn can hear the tiles dropping back into the box.

Sylvie returns to the living room. "Let's eat," she says. She moves into the kitchen and begins to cut the ham.

The clink of their forks is the only break in the silence. Marilyn takes a second slice of Jell-O salad for Sylvie's sake, forces the jiggly substance down the back of her throat.

"This is really good, Mom. Thank you," she says in a whisper.

"Mmm-mhmm," Woody agrees. He pours another shot of whiskey, no coffee now, into his homemade mug.

"You bet," Sylvie says, forcing a smile as she gets up to clear the plates. "Mari, are you still going to the movies with your friend?"

Though Sylvie had pouted yesterday when Marilyn told her she had plans this afternoon, she knows her mom's giving her an out. Marilyn washes the plates, and then goes into her room and packs a few things into the CK One tote.

When she kisses her mother goodbye, Sylvie whispers in her ear, "Next year it will be better. We'll have our own Christmas. A real tree. Real presents and all."

Before Marilyn can reply, Woody says, from across the room, "That game was your father's. He got it for his tenth birthday. We used to play together."

Marilyn only nods, feeling herself splitting into pieces.

She steps outside into the bright, two p.m. LA Christmas day sun. She rushes toward James, who's already waiting at the end of the block in the driver's seat of his red Dodge. Upon opening the passenger door, the sight of his face feels like her first breath of air.

"You escaped," he says.

"Thank god."

"Merry Christmas." He pulls a tape from the pocket of his pants and hands it to her.

Marilyn looks at the label—FOR MISS MARI MACK, it says. LOVE, JAMES.

She kisses the corner of his mouth, which breaks into a smile. "Can we put it on?" she asks.

"Try Me" begins as they pull off, and the day transforms. Woody and his drunken slurring, the faltering fake tree, the pain in Sylvie's eyes—they slowly fade as Marilyn watches James behind the wheel. His hand moves to rest in her lap, and she lets her head find his shoulder as the cool wind brushes over her cheeks. The roads are quiet, and they sail down the 10 freeway toward the water in the golden winter light.

By the time they reach the ocean, Des'ree is singing "I'm Kissing You," and Marilyn is wholly inside the feeling of being in love. The beach is nearly empty, the sky soft. They cross the sand, carrying bags and a boom box James brought. He lays out an old quilt while Marilyn puts the tape on and Des'ree continues midsong, crooning to the crystalline turquoise water.

"I pilfered this from Nana," James says as he pulls a bottle of strawberry wine from his bag. "It's been collecting dust in the cupboard for as long as I can remember." He brings out two mugs printed with Christmas trees and pours.

They cheers each other, and the smell of the ocean water mixes with the sweet scent of the pink wine. After a few sips, Marilyn starts to feel her cheeks flushing, the softness of the hazy golden light, the coastal winter sky filling her up.

"This is suddenly the best Christmas I can remember," she says. James grins back at her, his perfect white-toothed grin, as TLC starts singing "Diggin' on You." Marilyn laughs, sings along, *Baby bay-ooo-baby baby . . .*

Holding their mugs, they walk down to the edge of the water, where the waves leave stains on the sand that reflect the floating clouds above.

"Look!" James cries.

He gently scrapes the sand with his foot, to reveal thousands of small, colorful clam-shaped shells. At once, they begin to burrow back into the ground as the waves come over them.

"Wow. What are they?"

"Coquinas. When I was a kid, me and my mom would spend hours pulling away the sand, watching them dig themselves back under. They're not here always—only once in a while, usually in winter—so we'd get really happy when they'd surprise us."

As James squats to the ground and scoops up a handful of the tiny creatures, washing them in the water, Marilyn takes a mind-photo of his body bent toward the shore.

"They're kind of magical," she says, kneeling beside him and sifting through the intricately patterned shells.

"So are you."

Marilyn laughs. "Are you ready for your present?"

"Sure." James smiles.

Marilyn walks back to their spot and wraps the blanket around her shoulders, picks up the bags.

"What are you doing?" he asks.

"Come on!" she says, taking his hand.

"Where are we going?"

"You'll see!" she shouts playfully as she rushes ahead of him.

When they arrive below the pier, she guides James into the secret space of shadow cast by the wooden boards. She spreads the blanket onto the sand and hits play on the boom box, and, to the sound of K-Ci and JoJo singing "All My Life," she whispers, "Come here," as she bends to her knees. James does, wordlessly.

She hasn't done this before, but encouraged by his moan, she grows more confident; she feels a thrill deep in her belly as the physical evidence of her effect on him deepens; she loves the rough-edged vulnerability in his voice when he moans, "Goddamn,

Mari," and then the convulsions of his body as he grabs onto her, pulling her closer.

"That's the best Christmas present ever." James grins as he comes back into himself. He lies down on the blanket and Marilyn rests her head on his chest, the sound of the waves gentle underneath Aaliyah's voice singing, *At your best, you are love . . .*

"I think this is what it's like to be happy," Marilyn whispers.

"I think so too." He smiles at her. From his bag, he pulls a gift messily wrapped in brown paper, topped with a red bow.

"What? You didn't have to give me anything else. I love the tape."

"Just open it," James says.

She takes the heavy package in her hands, peels away the brown paper, and finds a camera.

A real camera.

A 35-millimeter Canon with a beautiful lens, along with a package of film.

"Oh my god, James. I can't believe you did this. How did you—where did you get it?"

"My cousin owns a pawnshop in Long Beach, and I asked him to tell me if he got one in. I picked it up a couple of weeks ago. You have no idea how hard it was to wait to give it to you! I'm gonna do some work for him, man the store on Saturdays for a while in exchange."

"James, I—I don't know what to say," Marilyn stutters. "Thank you."

"It's not totally altruistic. I'm excited to see what those pictures you're always taking look like. I wanna see what you see."

James gently brushes the hair from her face. "I wish I could get inside of that head of yours—I mean, all the way inside of it—but if I can't, at least maybe I can see through your eyes a little bit."

Marilyn is already loading the film into the camera.

• • • • • *Click. James stands at the end of the pier, his body* hovering between ocean and sky.

Click. The ball of sun suspends itself halfway underwater, fingers of light reaching across the sea.

Click. James emerges from the night into a puddle of brightness cast by a streetlamp.

Click. Rose stirs a pot on the stove, her grandson watching unnoticed from the doorway.

Click. Two teenage girls lean against the wall outside of Hope's Mini Mart, one holding a Coke, the other holding a smoke.

Click. James stares back from behind a pane of glass, hand pressed to the car window.

In the three days since Marilyn has gotten her new camera, she's gone nowhere without it. Looking through the lens makes her feels wide awake, wild with possibility.

Click. Justin sits outside their building eating a popsicle, his frank gaze teetering between innocent child and budding adult.

"Can I see it?" Justin asks as she walks up beside him, the ice cream truck's music playing incessantly in the background. She's just returned from a walk to the store to pick up milk and beer for Woody, and of course she brought the camera.

"Yeah," she says. "But you have to finish your popsicle first and wash your hands!"

Justin inhales the rest in one bite and runs off. A moment later he reappears, fingers clean, red ring still around his lips. She flips the aperture and f-stop settings to automatic and hands it to him.

"I'll take a picture of you," he says.

"Okay." She smiles and shows him how to focus. Justin steps away, his face disappearing behind the camera. After a moment, he lowers it, shakes his head. Marilyn watches as he scans their surroundings. Finally he points to the ice cream truck.

"Stand over there," he says, and she obeys.

"Lean against the truck," he instructs. "And look away. Like— like you're waiting on someone who's not coming."

Marilyn does, impressed by his directions. She hears the click, and Justin lowers the camera with a grin. When she returns to him, he's slow to hand the camera back.

"When can I see the picture?" he asks.

"I'm going to print them myself after we get the negatives developed, but the roll's almost finished, so hopefully soon. I put the settings on automatic for you, but there's more stuff you can control. Do you wanna learn?"

He nods eagerly, scoots closer.

"There's something called the depth of field," Marilyn tells him, "that determines how much of the picture will be in focus." She thinks it would be easier if she could show him in an image.

"Wait here," she says.

Forgetting about the groceries abandoned on the steps beside her, Marilyn runs upstairs and pulls a few of the copy machine photo replicas off her wall, hardly taking notice of Woody at his computer. When she returns to Justin he peers over her shoulder as she flips through the pages.

"That's cool," he says. "You collect pictures?"

"Yeah." Marilyn smiles.

Justin points to a photo of a girl in front of a small, rural house. She wears a tiara, her hands in a loose prayer shape over her mouth, her eyes tilted upward.

"I like this one," he says, staring back at the girl as if he could discover something in her gaze.

"Me too. It's by a photographer named Robert Frank."

Next Marilyn finds a Gordon Parks photo of a young boy lying on his back in a field, a june bug crawling over his forehead. The plants in the foreground and the brush growing just behind are blurry, but the boy's face is crystal clear.

"See," she says, pointing at the picture, "this has a shallow depth of field, meaning that not a lot of the picture will be in focus."

She flips to another page, pointing out a picture of a desert road, with a single car, that extends like a sharp line of light into the distance. "And here, everything's in focus, so it has a deeper depth of field. Does that make sense?"

Justin nods, absorbed.

Marilyn opens the back of the camera. "The aperture is the opening that lets in the light. The bigger it is, the more shallow your depth of field, and the smaller it is, the deeper it will be."

She shows him where to set the aperture on the ring of the camera, how to set the f-stop and measure the light. The concepts are complicated—at least she'd thought so when she first learned in her photo class last year—but Justin seems to understand intuitively.

She watches him hover over the camera in concentration, lifting the lens to his eye, setting and resetting the functions.

"Reach out," he says. "Like, toward me. Like you're waiting for someone to hold your hand."

Marilyn hears the click as Justin takes the shot, and turns to find Woody standing at the top of the steps glaring down at them. He locks his gaze on Marilyn's before he moves to go back inside.

Anxiety webbing through her lungs, Marilyn glances at Justin, whose brow furrows above his wide eyes. "I'm sorry, Jus, I gotta go. I'll see you later," Marilyn says, retrieving the groceries and the camera.

She steps into the apartment, her heart loud in her ears. Woody looks up, his eyes narrowed to slits. At once, her fear is eclipsed by rage. Who would find it possible to have anything against her hanging out with the sweetest kid she knows? She thinks of what James had told her: anger can be fuel. And so, jaw clenched in determination, she puts the milk and beer in the fridge, then, without a word, she straps her camera to her body and walks back out into the day.

She stands in front of the building and aims her lens at their duplex, Woody's shadow figure in the window. She knows as the shutter clicks that the picture will be perfect.

• • • • • *A woman paces outside of Mr. Steve's 24 Hour* Pawnshop. She couldn't be too much older than Marilyn and James are—just barely enough to have decisively crossed the border into adulthood. She wears tennis shoes with neon laces, a jean skirt, and pearl-colored studs, her hair pulled back tightly from her face into a neat little bun on the top of her head. She has the straightest posture Marilyn has ever seen.

"Wait," Marilyn says as James opens the car door. He sits back in the driver's seat, watching as she pulls her camera out of its case. She focuses on the woman standing in the shade under the sign for the shop, the window glass between them offering a reflection of a nearby palm. *Click.*

"Morning," James says to the woman as he unlocks the door.

"You're late," the woman replies, looking at the watch on her wrist. "Thought y'all opened at nine. It's nine-oh-six."

James smiles. "Sorry," he says as she follows them in and drops an engagement ring on the counter, a simple gold band with a diamond at its center.

The woman watches him, wordless, as James takes the ring and examines it under the loupe the way his cousin taught him. As the woman shifts her weight, shoulders still back and upright, Marilyn has a sudden memory—it must be from her earliest days in LA—of looking over the counter of a shop just like this, Sylvie passing her own engagement ring. Marilyn can see it perfectly now. It was silver, with tiny diamond studs across the band and a large blue stone—must have been sapphire—at its center. Hazily, she recalls how she'd hold on to her mom's hand, twisting the blue stone round and round on Sylvie's finger. How much she'd loved its dusky gleam, the way it caught the dim light in her bedroom.

But mostly, she remembers the vacant expression on her mom's face when she'd collected the money from the bearded man on the other side of the counter.

"Didn't work out, huh?" the man asked.

"He died," Sylvie replied bluntly.

The man handed over a business card. "Let me take you out sometime."

Sylvie took the card with a polite smile, but as soon as they walked out the door into the too-bright strip mall parking lot, silent tears had started to fall across her face, leaving little trails in her makeup. She threw the card in the nearest trash. Marilyn felt her own hot tears on her cheeks. After they got back into the Buick, Sylvie started the ignition and turned to her, wiping her eyes and then her daughter's.

"Don't cry, baby. We're on to better things. One day, we could have a hundred of those pretty rings if we want to."

"I can give you two hundred," James says to the woman.

A moment of silence, and she nods. He opens the register and counts the cash, hands it over. She takes it and goes, the door chiming behind her.

The rest of the morning is quiet as they work on tweaking their college apps. Marilyn's still unhappy with her essay. All she's been able to think to write about is why she wants to go to college, but each time she rereads her own words, she sees only a girl hungry for escape. School is about more than that for her, she knows it, but she can't place her finger on what it is she wants to say.

"Don't get so anxious about it," James has advised her countless times. "It'll be harder to think straight." So she picks up *Slouching Towards Bethlehem* and begins rereading, hoping for inspiration. A man comes in and buys a power drill. Marilyn walks across the lot and buys tacos for lunch, and they picnic in the cool interior of the shop. James's cousin, Eric, walks in, swinging his hips in exaggerated circles to "Si Te Vas" on the radio. Marilyn bursts out giggling.

"What up, cuz?" Eric says in greeting.

"What up," James replies as Eric turns to Marilyn.

"So this must be the photographer who's smitten my cousin." He raises his eyebrows toward her.

"I'm trying," she says shyly. "Thank you so much for the camera—"

"Don't thank me. Your boy's working for it." He turns to James and winks.

James gives Eric the rundown of the morning, after which Eric says, "You lovebirds are free to fly, then. See ya next week."

And so they flee the shop, into the Saturday-afternoon sun-light.

·····

As soon as James pulls into Fotek, Marilyn jumps out of the passenger door and hurries inside, composing herself before the French-accented man behind the counter, handing over her $3.25 and taking the neat cardboard cylinder containing her film.

"Got it?" James asks as she gets back in the car.

"Got it." She grins, and as he pulls off she breathlessly unspools the roll and holds the negatives up to the window, peering at each tiny translucent blueprint of the picture that has been stamped there. She moves through them one by one, trying to imagine what they'll look like on a contact sheet, trying to guess which she'll print. It feels like magic, the moments taken from their fleeting days and pressed into permanence.

They've already gone over the question of where she can print the photos, since she wants to do it herself: Immaculate Heart, unlike LA High, has a functioning darkroom, and James has planned to sneak her in with the help of his buddy Noah. Noah's taking a photo class, and the school lets their students have access on the weekends.

When they pull up at James's school, Noah's already waiting in the parking lot, leaning against a newish-looking truck. He's a short black guy with big curly hair, unlaced green Adidas, and a bright checkered shirt.

"What up," he calls as they walk toward him.

He gives James a hand slap and turns to Marilyn.

"You stole my boy," he says with a smile, "but I guess I forgive you." To her surprise, he wraps his arms around her in a hug. "You smell good." He makes a show of sniffing her hair, flirty in a benign way.

"Thanks." Marilyn laughs.

"She's cute," he says to James over her shoulder. "Very white, but cute."

"Alright, yo, enough. Back off my girl." James gives him a playful jab.

"We all used to be out chasing the ladies every weekend, but now this one's always like, 'I'm hanging with Mari,'" Noah complains as they walk across the campus, pretty with old brick buildings, a wide green lawn, and palm trees.

He lets them into the darkroom, and it's even better than the one at Orange High. He shows her where the chemicals are and tells her she can use his photo paper.

"Thank you *so* much."

"No worries. In exchange, you only have to lend me James for a trip to the mall."

"Just make sure he doesn't find any girls to replace me," she jokes.

"Don't worry, I'm wingman." James smiles at her.

When they go, Marilyn gets to work, setting up her baths and slicing the negatives into six square rows. After making a test strip, she lays them out on a paper over the contact printer. She hopes, a deep, hungry hope, that she will find at least one image that looks like her mind-pictures, that there will be at least one that will make James proud, that will be enough to satisfy whatever he'd imagined when he said he wanted to see through her eyes. She exposes for nine seconds and moves the sheet to the developer bath, watching the translucent frames make their marks. It nearly stops her heart, those miniature squares bursting full of James, of the texture of their lives together. When she's pulled the sheet out of the fixer, she hangs it to dry and uses a pen to dot the photos she'll print.

Marilyn obsesses over exposure times and framing, trying to make each image as sharp as possible. She puts James's Christmas mix on the tattered boom box somebody's left behind, and flips it over and over again, listening to each side who knows how many times. Erykah Badu's singing, *You know that you got me . . .* when James comes in.

"Hi, Mari Mack."

"You scared me!"

"It's already been four hours."

"Are you serious? I had no idea!" Marilyn says as she pulls her print out of the developer.

"Noah had to take off. He said we should just lock up when we go." He moves to peer over her shoulder. In the photo, James stands at the end of the pier, floating between water and sky, almost as if he could step into the horizon.

"No, don't look yet!" she says as she drops the paper into the stop bath.

"The anticipation is killing me," James jokes.

She pushes him back against the wall and kisses him, their faces illuminated by the single infrared light.

"Well, don't get too excited. I'm still learning," she says, a wave of nervousness coming over her.

She moves to place the picture in the fixer and swishes it back and forth. Finally lifting it out, she hangs it on the line to dry beside the others.

Something about pictures, at least the ones that matter—they seem to store memory, not just of a single moment, but of all of the invisible moments that led to it. She looks at her work: James on the pier. Justin eating a popsicle. James lying on his couch, arms in a cross over his bare chest while Justin tugs on his sneaker, looking coyly at the camera. James's silhouette, seeming to swallow the sun as it sets over the water. Their building from the outside: orange tree, chipping pink paint, scattered petals, wash waving from a line, and a dim figure, impossible to identify, behind a second-story window.

"Okay," she whispers quietly. "You can look."

James comes up behind her, stares at the photos.

"What do you think?" she asks after what feels like an epic silence.

"I think they're beautiful."

"You do?"

"I do." He turns to her with a smile. "Is that what I really look like?"

"Yes and no."

"What do you mean, no?"

"This is still. You're always in motion."

"That's what I love about your pictures, though. I mean, one of the things I love. They aren't stuck. You can feel the movement that's happening, or about to happen."

Marilyn grins. Though the tangible film version is imperfect compared to the moments she's frozen behind her own eyes, these, at least, she can share. They *exist*.

"I just have to print one more," Marilyn says. "Then we can go."

· · · · ·

Later that evening, when Marilyn delivers the black-and-white print to Justin, he looks as if he's seen a unicorn. In the image, she reaches out to the camera, her fingertips in sharp focus, her face blurring softly behind—cheekbones, lashes, jaw, all as if rendered with soft brushstrokes.

"This is the picture I took," Justin says, as if to confirm the truth of this fact.

Marilyn laughs. "You like it?"

"Yeah."

"You're really talented, Justin. You have a great eye."

"Can we go take more?"

"I have to work on finishing my college applications, but next week, I promise."

"Maybe you'll be a photographer like Mari," James tells his brother.

Justin looks to her, as if for confirmation of the possibility. She smiles at him. "You could be."

He nods, suddenly serious. "How did you decide that's what you wanna be?" he asks.

And in the question, suddenly Marilyn knows what she will write in her college essay.

· · ·

Six hours later, after midnight, she rereads her words, written and rewritten by hand, detailing how her experience as a commercial actress and model has inspired her love of being behind the camera. At first, she explains, taking pictures gave her a sense of agency she didn't otherwise have, of control (as James had said all that time ago on the beach).

She writes about her countless "mind-pictures," describing the image of the palm trees standing like soldiers out the window of her tiny bedroom; the grief on her mother's face, staring out at her dream home lit up for Christmas by another family; her neighbor hanging a hummingbird feeder, a bird tattoo on his shoulder and a real live bird in the air, hovering just above. When his eyes met hers and she "snapped" her picture, it was her own version of love at first sight.

She writes about how she believes all these invisible photographs began to change the way she sees—being behind even an imaginary lens had seemed to bring the world within reach. Now that she's in possession of a camera, she's grateful that she will be able to learn to translate that into something concrete, tangible. *I often think about taking pictures,* she writes, *like snatching an image out of the hands of time that would toss it away. A picture can be held, shared, passed on. It can exist anew in each viewer's eye.*

She doesn't know if the essay's perfect, or if it will be the key to open her future. But she knows it's what she wants to say.

• • • • • *December 31: Marilyn and James sit in the library* with a stack of nine-by-twelve manila envelopes and a pile of papers before them, carefully going through each other's applications, checking for errors. Marilyn relishes reading James's boyish handwriting organized into neat lines, his thoughts on the value of music and running and his responsibility to his younger brother. He finds a single error on one of her short answers (where she's written *aperature* instead of *aperture*), so she pays the ten cents to the library printer and recopies the page.

Then, together, they address their ten envelopes. Marilyn insists they save the best for last, where they finally write, *Columbia University in the City of New York, Office of Undergraduate Admissions, 212 Hamilton Hall, Mail Code 2807, 1130 Amsterdam Avenue, New York, NY 10027.*

Marilyn looks up as James sets down his pen, meeting her eyes across the table.

"So," he says. "Guess we're ready?"

"Yep."

In line at the post office, Marilyn kisses each envelope.

"For good luck." She grins at James.

"Don't get lip gloss on my college apps!" he jokes. "I might get disqualified."

They're still laughing off their nervous energy when the clerk signals them to an open window. They stand side by side and hand over their envelopes.

"Bet you both get in," the clerk says as James gives her thirty-two dollars, part of a small loan from Eric that he'll work off with an extra morning at the shop.

As they walk to the car and pull onto Olympic Boulevard, the day is impossibly wide open—the space that they had filled with their hours of work suddenly empty.

Marilyn takes James's hand, squeezes it.

"What do we do now?" he asks.

"I guess we should celebrate, right?" Marilyn replies. "It's New Year's Eve after all."

"I have an idea," James says after a moment. He flips on the radio, where Prince is singing *Party like it's 1999*. He turns it up, and they drive, one instant at a time, into the future.

· · · · ·

The sun sets over the ocean in the distance, leaving traces of soft pink light in the sky as Marilyn and James hike up Runyon Canyon, carrying burgers from In-N-Out and a six-pack of Woody's beer that Marilyn snuck from the fridge, reminding herself to replace it tomorrow. While it's not champagne, "at least it has bubbles!" she'd said to James.

By the time they've reached the peak, the sky now edged

into darkness and the city below awakening in a twinkle of light, she and James are floating—above the pedestrian concerns of their city, above the street corners and the apartment buildings and the cars honking and the sprawling mansions and the dirty stars.

James pops two beers open on the side of a rock. They toast.

"To you," she says to James.

"To you," he says back.

"To 1999," James says, clinking his bottle against hers again.

"To 1999," she replies, and then, "To New York City."

"To New York City," James says, and they both laugh, making a game of it. "To your photographs."

"To pawnshop cameras and ocean pictures," she counters.

He meets her gaze. "To the color of your eyes."

"To your perfect smile."

"To favoritest Christmas presents ever," James says with a grin, and she blushes.

"To James Brown."

"To Joan Didon."

"To being at our best."

"To love."

"To love."

A firework explodes in the distance, as if it had only been waiting to celebrate the sky's final darkness. And then another, and another, scattered across the city.

"I won't leave you, you know," she says.

"What do you mean?"

"I mean, next year. No matter what, I want us to be together."

James puts his hand on hers. "We just have to wait and see, Mari. I wouldn't let you give up everything you've been working for."

"It's *you* I don't want to give up," she insists, her voice rising.

"Okay, shh," he says, wrapping his arms around her. "It's you and me, kiddo. Whatever happens, we'll figure it out."

She stares into his eyes. "Promise?"

"I promise."

James unwraps their burgers and pulls a single white votive candle from his backpack, lights it.

Marilyn grins. "A romantic picnic." The tiny flame burns between them as they eat, watching the bursts of light on the horizon, popping open new beers.

"To man-made miracles." "To tiny colored clam shells." "To libraries." "To Pink Panther popsicles." "To Romeo and Juliet." "To broken bottles." They go on toasting, celebrating the moments and objects and feelings that have made up their months together.

"To the first night you kissed me," Marilyn says.

"Did I? I thought *you* kissed me." He grins.

"Not so, but I'll toast to that anyhow." She laughs.

They both sip, and she can feel her head starting to fill with bubbles. Her desire for him arises with immediacy; it is something she can almost taste, like the air before a thunderstorm. She puts her lips on his lips, and she knows—this will be the night. This is right.

She reaches into her purse, pulls out a single condom that she bought at the corner store, imagining this moment would come. She offers it to him.

James takes it and raises his eyebrows at her, a small smile blooming across his face.

Marilyn stands, her hands against a railing for balance, the City of Angels spread out below her, the heat of his body behind her. She feels his grip on her shoulder, pulling her against him, his hand resting gently on her throat.

"You want this?" he whispers.

"Yes."

She stretches her arms out like wings, looking out as he pushes himself inside her, little by little, and then all at once. She feels herself opening into the horizon—and it hurts. It hurts in her body. It hurts the way that it hurts to let someone in.

"Are you okay?" he asks.

"I need to see your face," she says. And she does, suddenly, urgently. He spins her around, pushes her back against the railing. She gasps as he's inside her again, a groan in the back of his throat, his expression one she's never seen before—lucid and concentrated, stars spreading behind his head as he looks at her, as he looks *into* her.

She runs her hands over the muscles of his back, his shoulders, pulling his body closer, pulling him deeper. The diamond in her mind has become a thousand diamonds and they belong to her and to James. The future is no longer a single point of light but a whole sky. Scattered and shot through.

"I love you."

"I love you."

For the rest of her whole life, she will never have a story that's not his too.

• • • • • *"Hold me like a bear," James says, and she squeezes*
him with all her might.

"Hold me like a lion," she answers in a whisper, and he squeezes
her back, his arms locking her body to his.

"Grrr," James growls to her.

"Grrr," she growls back, and paws gently at his chest.

"Hold me like a tyrannosaurus," James says.

Marilyn laughs. "Tyrannosauruses have tiny arms!"

"Like you!" James says.

"My arms are not tiny!"

The midday light spills in through the window, catching itself in Marilyn's hair, on James's cheekbone, now in his laughing
eyes. Woody hasn't returned from his stint at the casino, and
Sylvie's off at work. When she woke at noon, Marilyn called
James and he rushed upstairs, body still smelling like sleep.

He wraps his hand around her bicep. "Rar," he says, his face
inches from hers, scrunched up playfully as he grabs her waist.
"Rar," she growls back, half giggling.

"You're fierce, though." James smiles. She gently bites at his
neck and he shuts his eyes, lets out a throatier growl and pushes
her onto her back. He kisses down her stomach, quick, playful
kisses, and pauses at her cotton underwear, dotted with cherries

and tearing at the seams. He looks up at her, and a stillness falls over the room, the sunlight now making a hot spot over her heart.

As he rests his head on her belly it promptly growls.

"Who's there?" He laughs.

"Hungry."

"Hungry who?"

"Hungry me!"

"Let's feed you."

Her stomach growls again and James picks up Braveheart, her stuffed lion, moving his head as if he were speaking to Marilyn's tummy.

"Rar!" James says in a high voice.

Marilyn giggles and looks down at him. This is what it's like to be in love with James Alan Bell on the first day of 1999.

"Wait one second. Stay right there," she says, and gets up to take her camera from the corner of the room. She frames the image of him tangled in her My Little Pony sheets, face tilted upward, light playing over his skin.

Click.

And then another sound. The front door opening. Marilyn's heart spikes in panic. The footsteps are Woody's.

"Wait here," she whispers to James as she quickly dresses. James reaches out and grabs hold of her hand, but she pulls away and slips out the door, where she finds Woody in the kitchen. Marilyn knows by his demeanor that the outing at the casino wasn't a winning one. The faint smell of booze seeps from his body and travels across the room.

"Hey," she says.

"There's no beer."

Shit. In the haze of James, she'd somehow forgotten to replace the six-pack they took last night.

"You want me to run out and grab you some?"

"Where's the one that was here." His question sounds like a statement.

"I don't know."

Woody slaps her across the face. It's so sudden, at first her brain cannot process what's happened.

"Don't you lie to me."

Marilyn raises her hand to her cheek, starting to feel the pain.

"You want free rent and now you think you can take what's not yours and lie about it? You and your mother ever come to see me for eight years until your broke asses needed a place to stay? And if you get one of those fancy houses she wants, think I'll be invited? Y'all will disappear into thin air again, like I was nothing, like I am nothing. You don't love me. You don't *love me*. You don't give two shits about me, and now you wanna steal my fucking beer and lie about it—"

James rushes into the room.

"What the *fuck* are you doing in my house?" Woody explodes.

James puts a hand on Marilyn's shoulder, starts to pull her away. "I was just going," he says coolly, though she can feel the heat coming off him.

"If your father saw what a little slut his daughter's become—"

This is the last thing Marilyn hears before James closes the door behind them.

He keeps his arm around her, keeps walking. He won't let her collapse. He guides her down the stairs. The orange tree in the yard is full of fruit. The glints in the cement remind her of the shattered glass in the moonlight, the night they broke the bottles. He opens the door to the passenger side of his red Dodge, parked just outside the apartment. Marilyn steps into the car, smells the leather air freshener, the softer scent of his body. She sees the raindrop-shaped stains of dirt on the windshield, a brochure advertising carpet cleaning. An old cup from In-N-Out on the console, the *Hard Knock Life* tape on the dash. She tries to notice these things, each thing.

James starts the ignition, his body still tense, his energy bent toward self-control as he pulls off down the street, taking Marilyn away from there.

· · · · ·

They drive in silence. James gets on the freeway, and without asking she knows he's going to the ocean.

Finally she turns to him, and her voice comes out in a whisper: "I'm sorry."

"For what?"

"For my uncle. That you had to see that. That he talked to you like that—I should've known he'd come home . . . I should've been more careful."

"It's not your fault he's a fucking asshole," James replies. He's squeezing the wheel so tightly he could be choking it. "But you can't live with him, Mari. I can't let that happen to you."

"I know," she says. "You're right. But I don't know what to do. We have nowhere else to go, and my mom will blow it off. She'll say he's just volatile, she'll tell me we'll be out of there soon, up in our house in the hills."

James inhales, holds it in.

"It's only a few more months. I just have to make it a few more months, and we'll both be . . . somewhere else." She brushes his hand with hers. "Together. Starting our own lives."

He takes another deep breath. "He ever does that again, I'm going to fucking kill him." By the look in his eyes, Marilyn almost believes he might.

"You promise me," he says. "You promise me that if he ever does that again, you'll tell me."

"James . . ."

"Promise me."

"Okay."

· · · · ·

When they arrive at the ocean, Marilyn tries to let the sound of the waves soothe her, but she can't rid herself of the old feeling that she's somewhere else, not really there at all. She tries to focus on the facts of the world: water receding from the shore, shards of iridescent mussel shell, tangled masses of seaweed beached in the rough shape of bodies. Beside her, James stares out at the horizon, his hands clenched into fists.

As the sky begins to dim, she gets up, leading them to the spot beneath the pier. Surrounded by the old wood smell of the cedar boards mixed with the salt air, Marilyn brings her body against his.

"I don't have anything," he says.

"Just, pull out?" she suggests in a whisper, already running her hands over his back.

In the salt dark of five o'clock on New Year's night, sex feels like a fire hot enough to transform her rage, his rage, into something else, something hot and clean, something sacred. It is an absolution. An answer.

• • • • • *"You can't go upstairs by yourself,"* James *says when* they arrive back at the apartments. "Come over and have dinner with us. You can stay the night if you need; I'm sure they'd let you sleep on the couch. Or at least wait till your mom's back."

So Marilyn follows James to his front door, noticing Woody's car in the drive, wondering if he's watching through the window. His slap has left a soft red stain across her cheek, which Rose spots as soon as they come in.

"Baby, what happened to your face? Are you okay?"

"Yeah," Marilyn says. "I'm fine." She glances at James. "I fell asleep on the beach. I must've gotten too much sun."

Rose frowns, but maybe because Justin's right there, she only nods. A moment later she reappears with her blanket from the couch—the soft fuzzy one with fringe at the ends, which smells like muddled roses, and puts it around Marilyn's shoulders. The scent of it reminds Marilyn of crushing petals for "perfume" when she was a child.

She sits at the kitchen table, wrapped up in it, snapping green beans, the fragrance of rice and chicken filling the room, *Jeopardy!* on the television, Alan calling out the answers and slapping his knee at every right response, James lying on the couch quietly next to his grandfather, offering responses only when Alan doesn't have one of his own. Justin stealing bites from the kitchen before Rose swats him away, Justin coming to sit by Marilyn and telling her about his math teacher with a prosthetic leg who has a policy of tossing Starbursts to the kids who raise their hands and get the answers right. He runs into his room and comes back with a huge collection carried in his T-shirt that's pulled into a pouch, and shows them off to her proudly.

"You haven't eaten any of them?" she asks.

"Nu-uh." He grins.

"I'm very impressed."

As they sit down to dinner, Marilyn can hear footsteps above— her mother's, she guesses, because it sounds like heels. She tries to concentrate on her food, which is delicious. The feeling in the Bells' house is so warm, so full—she wants to crawl inside of it, to stay wrapped up with them.

And then, a knock. Quick and insistent. James gets up to answer and finds Sylvie standing there, still wearing her heels from work, her hair coming out of its bun and sticking to her neck. Alan follows his grandson to the door.

"Hi, Ms. Miller," James says politely, flatly.

"Hello. I'm assuming my daughter's here?" she asks with a tight-lipped smile, peering between James and Alan to get a glimpse into the apartment.

Marilyn slowly rises.

"Hi, Mom."

"Come on, first day back at school tomorrow. You need your beauty sleep," Sylvie calls in a voice that's forcefully bright.

"I'll be right up," she says.

But Sylvie makes no move to leave. Instead she waits, hovering in the doorway.

"We were just eating dinner," Alan says. "Would you like to come in?"

"Oh, no. We've got to be going."

Marilyn gets up, not wanting the scene to escalate.

"Thank you for dinner, Nana," she says as she moves to hug Rose good night.

"At least take your food with you, baby." Rose stands abruptly and gives Sylvie a sharp glance as she goes to the kitchen. She comes back with a Tupperware container, and they all wait in awkward silence as she packs Marilyn's mostly uneaten dinner into it.

"Thank you," Marilyn says softly, and kisses her on the cheek.

She can feel James's eyes following her. She doesn't touch him in front of her mom, but she meets his gaze, trying to say, *I love you. It's all going to be okay.*

"See you tomorrow?" she asks.

He only nods as Sylvie shuts the door behind them.

Marilyn heads toward the steps to their apartment without a word, when she feels Sylvie's hand on her arm.

"I was thinking we'd have a little mother-daughter time."

"I thought I needed my 'beauty sleep.'"

"Marilyn . . . come on." She gestures to Rose's Tupperware with a wave of her arm. "You don't need that. Let's go get something really good."

Marilyn clutches the container when Sylvie tries to take it from her hands, but she follows her mom to the car. Sylvie drives them to Johnny Rockets—a surprise, because she's hardly allowed Marilyn to eat a whole meal, much less a burger and fries, since Ellen-obviously's entrance into their lives.

Marilyn eats from the giant basket, one fry after another, as her mother sips her iced tea, looking into the glass as if it were a crystal ball.

"I heard what happened this morning," Sylvie says, setting down her drink.

"He hit me, Mom."

Sylvie's quiet for a long moment, her mouth drawing downward, the bags beneath her eyes visible through her makeup. "I'm sorry," she says finally. "But you know you shouldn't have had James in the house. I warned you."

At once Marilyn's heart begins to thud its protest.

"Listen," Sylvie continues, reaching for Marilyn's hand across the table. "I know what it's like to be your age, and to think you're in love, but—I don't want to see you settle the way I did."

Marilyn turns away from Sylvie, stares out the window.

"Are you—are you having sex with him?" Sylvie asks.

Marilyn eats another fry. "No."

"Okay," Sylvie says. "That's good."

Marilyn swallows and turns back to the window, focusing on wrapping her rage in a tightly contained ball in her stomach. She watches an old man in a walker being helped along by a chubby nurse. A young mom struggling with a stroller and a tiny fluffy dog on a leash. A trio of teenagers smoking cigarettes against the neighboring building.

"James," Sylvie presses on, "is a nice boy. Good-looking too. But, Mari—you have your whole life ahead of you. If you can just wait—I promise you, the world will become your oyster. You can't even imagine the choices of men you'll have." Sylvie allows herself a small smile. "Men like the ones you see on television, Mari. And they could be yours. You're that beautiful. You're that special. You just have to be patient with life, you have to believe . . ."

Marilyn opens her mouth to speak, but before she can, Sylvie continues, "It's not that I'm against the fact that he's—well, I actually, perhaps I shouldn't be telling you this, but I slept with a black man once, just before I met your father."

Marilyn feels suddenly ill.

"If that's"—Sylvie clears her throat—"what you want, give it a little bit of time and I'm sure you can find one who's more—well—suitable for a rising young star."

"Can you even hear yourself? I cannot believe you're saying this right now! I LOVE JAMES. *James.* It has nothing to do with wanting to be with someone of a particular skin color, it has to do with falling in love with a *person.* And there is no one else like him in the whole world, there is no one else more right for me than he is, and you don't even know him—not at all—so you have absolutely no right to talk about this. You don't even know *me.* I am not a rising young star. I am not your payday. I'm a high school kid who's going to college next year. I want to become somebody, but not because of how I look. Because of how I *think.* You have *never* respected that. You have *never* encouraged that. James does. James has known me for six months, and he knows more about how I feel than you ever have, because you never listen. Our lives have nothing to do with what I want, or what's good for me—it's all about what *you* want, and using me to get it, and you can't even see that, is the worst part."

Sylvie stares back at Marilyn, her mouth half open. Finally she moves her lips, as if to speak, but nothing comes out.

At that moment, the waiter arrives with two cheeseburgers, and Marilyn becomes aware of the furtive eyes of the other diners watching them. Sylvie asks for the check and gets up, leaving the uneaten food on the table. She doesn't say a word to Marilyn the whole way home.

• • • • •

Marilyn's wide awake in the dark. It's too early for sleep, but all she can think to do is to try to remove herself from the world. She's been shaky, literally, since they left Johnny Rockets, feeling as if the ground were moving below her feet, as if her body were changing shapes. Finally she sits up, takes out Rose's Tupperware, and eats the chicken, now cold but still good. Marilyn hears the phone ring in the living room, then Sylvie's voice through the thin wall, though she can't make out the words. A moment later, her mother opens her door.

"You got it," she says flatly. "If you even want it."

"What?"

"The Levi's commercial."

"I did?"

Sylvie nods and shuts the door.

Marilyn stares after her mother, angry at herself for half

wishing Sylvie were wrapping her up in her arms like she'd done when Marilyn was a little girl, in this same bedroom, and Sylvie had come in to give her the news about My Little Pony.

She tries to remember how clear, how hopeful everything had felt with James just yesterday—mailing in their college applications, the night at Runyon and the sky bursting open. She wishes she could run downstairs, tell him everything. Instead she pushes open the window, though the night is biting, and hears Aaliyah's voice, sweet and clear in the January air—*Let me know, let me know . . .* The song ends and begins again. Marilyn knows he's playing it for her.

She gets up, knocks on Sylvie's bedroom door. Sylvie doesn't answer, but Marilyn can hear shuffling inside. She peeks her head in to find Sylvie in her satin pink nightgown, flipping through *US Weekly*. When she looks up, Marilyn sees the tears running down her face.

"Mom . . ." she starts, and takes a deep breath as she sits at the edge of the bed. "Listen, I wanna do the commercial, and I want you to keep half the money—to put toward a new place, or for whatever you want—and I want to take the other half to put in an account to use for college. Okay?" She does her best to keep her voice even, matter-of-fact.

Sylvie looks back at her, with the eyes of a girl who's been left alone at school for too long, waiting for someone to come and pick her up. Marilyn calls up a memory from her own childhood—days blurred into a single afternoon.

She's home from school sick, a cool washcloth on her forehead (she learned to relish the feeling of fever coming on, just to feel her mother's love like this), eating toast sprinkled with cinnamon and sugar, sipping ginger ale through her twisty straw, her head resting in Sylvie's lap, watching daytime soaps while Sylvie strokes Marilyn's head and smokes her Salems. Marilyn can still hear the voice—*Like sands through the hourglass, so are the days of our lives . . .* During those afternoons, her mom would talk to her in ways she never did otherwise. Twirling a lock of Marilyn's hair between her fingers, she'd light a cigarette and stare into the distance and tell stories of her girlhood in Bishop Hills, the tiny dust-blown town outside of Amarillo, flat red dirt as far as the eye could see, Sylvie would say. She told of waiting for her own mother to come and get her from school, watching the clouds changing shapes in the blue, blue sky. How some days her mom wouldn't come, and Sylvie would walk home two miles, her worn, patent-leather shoes blistering her feet, to find her mother in bed, the shades drawn, smelling of alcohol. On days like these, she would turn on the TV and escape into the same soap operas she still loves, or, even better, she might walk to the town's one-screen theater and sneak in after the film had started. She would hide in the back all night, quickly picking up people's half-eaten buckets of popcorn or boxes of Jujubes between showings, watching and rewatching the film, memorizing the lines that she would then act out in whispers when she couldn't sleep at night. Her favorite: *Gone with the Wind*. Marilyn can still see her, exhaling smoke, performing the lines from her childhood, her voice turning soft and girlishly fierce even as she spoke Rhett's part—*That's what's wrong with you. You should be kissed and often, and by someone who knows how.*

She talked, also, of her high school days—she'd been a grade-A cheerleader, she said with a wistful smile, and based on the old Amarillo High School yearbook—one of the few nostalgic items from the past that she carries with her—she'd been beautiful. Her childhood love of the screen transformed into a dream of becoming an actress, though perhaps, even then, she hadn't really believed it would come true. That was her problem, she said. You must believe in yourself. You must be around people who believe in you.

She told of Marilyn's dad. They'd met when Sylvie, at seventeen, drove into Amarillo with her girlfriends. He managed the hotel whose bar they liked to go to for its bowls of free peanuts and lack of vigilance in checking IDs. Patrick had comped three rounds of pink drinks the first night, and though Sylvie wouldn't agree to go out with him right away, slowly he won her over. She hadn't been interested in the football players at school; she knew the reign of their royalty would fade after graduation. Patrick was not the most handsome, but not ugly, either. He was sturdy, ambitious (already managing the hotel at twenty-three), well-groomed, smelling of detergent and Old Spice. He was the kind of man who'd stay with you, she thought. He bought her dinners, opened doors for her, and most of all he seemed full of the promise of a new life. The kind of life she saw all around her, on television, in movies, in magazines—a pretty white house with a green lawn, nice clothes, a diamond on her finger, and a baby in her belly. So she made what she'd thought was a solid choice in marriage. A man who could take care of her. Until he died and left her with nothing but an upside-down mortgage, as she'd often repeat to strangers in the checkout line at the grocery, holding tightly to Marilyn's then tiny hand.

It had been Sylvie's television shows—the same shows that she and Marilyn watched together on her sick days—that had comforted Sylvie through the long empty afternoons after his death, through the loneliness that was loud enough to be deafening, the sudden sense of purposelessness. She wanted her little girl to have a chance at something better, better than the dustbowl they came from.

Sylvie, stubbing out her cigarette, kissing young Marilyn's hot cheek: "So I packed up my baby and headed for the city where dreams come true." The washcloth refreshed, newly cool, and Sylvie's voice: "I believe in you."

Marilyn now looks at her mom in her nightgown—lace unraveling at the edges, a soft brown stain on the chest, her blond hair flattened against her head—and conjures, best as she can, the image of her mother as a child in her dusty patent-leather shoes, alone on the open Texas roads, repeating movie lines. She thinks that young version of Sylvie is not so different than she herself—both of them dreaming of somewhere else.

"You're going to leave me," Sylvie says finally, with the sharpness of grief. "I don't think I can stop it."

"Mom," Marilyn tries, "I'm just going away to school. That's normal. I'll still be your daughter."

"I'm sorry," Sylvie says, looking off into some invisible horizon. "I'm sorry I couldn't give you more."

Marilyn can see now that it's not only the money her mother

has wanted for so long; she'd wanted to buy them a new life, one she imagined they'd share. Perhaps she wanted Marilyn to have those things she'd always dreamt of—the pool, the castle on the hill, the prince—because she had believed they would make Marilyn happy too.

Sylvie looks back at her open magazine page, tears spilling onto a picture of Tom Cruise and Nicole Kidman. "It's your money," Sylvie says. "You can do what you like with it."

• • • • • *Marilyn is one of three girls dressed in identical Levi's* low-rise jeans and crop tops. Her hair hangs long over her shoulders, her skin leveled by makeup. Under hot lights, she's instructed to walk: up an escalator, down a hall, across the street. Walk this way, walk that way, shoulders back love, chest out, okay, but move your hips, I mean, can you hear the music?

During her My Little Pony commercial, she'd been called "Little Princess," looked after by a woman whose hand she instinctively felt safe holding on to, and taken on constant trips to the craft services truck, where she was given snacks—Skittles, peanut butter sandwiches, and chocolate kisses. But here, the obvious has become more obvious—she's a body, meant to sell a product. She's a prop. All the organs that operate within her—the heart that pounds at James's touch, the stomach that growls when hungry, the bladder that is right now full—they are invisible, unreal, unnecessary. She is flattened to her image on-screen.

It's for us, for James and me, she tells herself when they ask her to sway her hips (aka stick out your ass), when they shout, "Number three, cross left!" It's for their future—for the flights to New York, for the books they will buy at the student bookstore, for all the rolls of film she will be able to afford to develop.

And. It's for her mother—if not the house on the hills, it's for what she hopes will be the consolation prize of a clean apartment of her own where she can watch her soap operas in peace, maybe a little pool where she can lie in the sun.

James has stayed on at the pawnshop and now makes a small salary, so he lent Marilyn the twenty-five dollars she needed to open her own account at Chase—a place to receive the Levi's check when it arrives. But her newfound freedom has not come without consequence. Since their fight, Sylvie's changed. Her glasses of wine have gotten bigger, her eyes more absent. Sometimes she doesn't come home after work in the evenings, and Marilyn hears her return at one or two a.m. Marilyn doesn't know where she's been, where she goes. Maybe she's dating a man, Marilyn suspects, but doesn't ask. The wound between them is still open, and their words to each other, no matter how brief, no matter how softly spoken, are salt.

Since the day he hit her, Woody has spoken to her only to make requests. Sylvie, listless from drinking, no longer bothers to cater to his demands, so he calls upon Marilyn for trips to the store, dinner, cleanup. But his fits of rage have become worse, more frequent. In the dark of the house, he often looks as if he's shadowboxing with a ghost. Many nights, after he's safely passed out, she'll go into the living room and quietly sweep shattered glass.

• • • • •

The Levi's commercial wraps. It rains for days on end. The California sunshine goes into hiding, the streets flood. At school, the days feel dreary, but the January afternoons become lovely when Marilyn's with James, the gray of the sky making the colors of the city look saturated: the greens of the trees deeper, the purple flowers more purple. The patter of droplets on the windowpane makes his apartment all the cozier. She most often has supper there, and she's begun to think of his family almost as her own, as the place where she belongs.

The weather breaks just in time for Justin's birthday, and the three of them spend the first Sunday of February at the beach. The storms have left the air piercingly clear, the morning sunlight incisive. Justin wants to take pictures in color, so Marilyn has loaded up the camera, and she and James watch him on the pier, stealthily aiming his lens. He captures a little girl rising on tip-toe to measure herself against the smiling wooden shark who will determine if she's tall enough for the Ferris wheel, a man sleeping in the sand, a boy whose ice cream has just fallen from his cone.

James buys them corn dogs and fries for lunch and they sing happy birthday to Justin, sitting on the wooden slats at the edge of the pier, feet dangling over the water. As Marilyn swings her legs to the tune of the song, one of her brown moccasins goes flying into the ocean.

"Shit!"

Justin bursts into giggles. It's contagious, and soon all three of them have erupted with laughter. Justin insists she shouldn't walk barefoot. "You might get splinters," he warns. "I got a splinter in my foot over here when I was a baby—"

"You were four," James interjects.

"And it got in so deep, I had to go to the doctor for them to cut it out, and then I couldn't walk for a month."

"A couple days," James corrects, but Justin wins the argument anyhow, and Marilyn hops along the boardwalk with one arm around each of their shoulders. (Justin's nearly as tall as she is now—how could that be? It seems as if he's grown more than a foot in the six months since she met him.) The three of them laugh all the way to the vendor selling knock-off sunglasses and flip-flops whose soles are stamped with white palms and the words LOS ANGELES. Marilyn asks for Justin's input on color and ends up with a red pair. James pays for the shoes while Marilyn tries on oversize sunglasses.

"You're channeling Joan Didion in those," James tells her. She replies with a grin and puts the glasses back on the spinner rack, but a moment later James appears behind her, places them jaggedly on her face.

"You got them?"

"They were made for you. I had to."

Marilyn turns, kisses him. "I love you," she whispers into his ear. He smiles, and she smiles at his smile.

"This way," Justin says, and they turn to see he's aiming the camera at them. *Click.*

They must look happy, Marilyn thinks. They are happy. And this is only the beginning: next year, they'll stand together on a New York City rooftop, the city spread below them. When Justin comes to visit, they'll show him the neon lights of Times Square and the museums full of art. They'll stay up all night studying in the library; they'll watch the leaves go golden in

Central Park; they'll sneak into bars to hear music. They'll graduate, proud in their sky-blue gowns. James will write his essays; she will take her pictures; they will travel and see the world together. And, she hopes, they will one day have a daughter and call her Angela.

ANGIE

• • • • • *Angie wakes alone in a bed she doesn't recognize, her* head throbbing, the light too bright. She looks at the mural of Cherry on the wall and slowly remembers where she is. Welcome to LA.

She opens her palm, sees the black ink smudged on her hand— 179 Sycamore.

Today she'll go to knock on Justin's door. She'll meet her uncle, and he will tell her where her father is. So why does she feel as if something inside of her has been lost? The mold of her body, the very shape of her seems somehow askew. Her head— Jesus, it hurts. She tries to walk through the events of the night before, but it goes by in a blur. She tries to remember Justin's face, but can't.

"Hey, sleepyhead. You're awake."

She rolls over, slowly, to see Sam sitting up in bed, holding a cup of coffee, reading.

"What's that?" Angie asks.

Sam tilts the book to show her the cover: *Citizen: An American Lyric.* Claudia Rankine. There's a picture of the hood of a black sweatshirt, cut off from the body.

"It's poetry. My dad's teaching it next year."

"Oh."

"She's writing about racism, like the microaggression kind of stuff that can just build up."

"Oh."

"Here, listen. This is really good. *The world is wrong. You can't put the past behind you. It's buried in you; it's turned your flesh into its own cupboard . . .*"

Angie nods. "That is good."

"How are you feeling?"

"Okay," she says, trying to maneuver around the shame that's settled in her center, running into nausea. "What time is it?"

"One thirty."

"Where are Miguel and Cherry?"

"They took an Uber to Cherry's place last night."

"Oh."

"Want some coffee?"

"Some water maybe."

Sam stands, and brings her a glass.

"We should talk," he says, as she sits up, sips. It occurs to Angie with a rush of anxiety that she's wearing only a T-shirt and underwear.

"Did we—"

"No. Nothing happened. You just—you just got undressed before bed. I didn't have anything to do with it."

"Oh."

"But you know, you *did* kiss me the other day—"

"Sam—I—"

"Just—let me talk. Don't 'Sam I' me."

Angie looks back at him, her heart knocking insistently against her chest like an impatient visitor.

"Angie, do you love me? Did you mean that?"

"What? I—" Angie's heart now pounds so hard it could knock down the door. "I can't—I can't talk about this now. It's all going to be okay—it's all going to get better."

It's all going to get better. She's going to meet Justin. She's going to find out the truth about her dad. Her dad, whom she hopes will fill in the gap between her and the world.

But she can see Sam's face shutting down, the hope in his gaze replaced by desolation.

"What am I to you?" he asks after a moment, his voice hard-edged.

"You're—you're someone I care about. You're—my friend."

"Your *friend*? 'Cause sometimes it feels a lot like you don't give a shit about me. Like you think you can just walk right into my heart whenever it's convenient, whenever you need something. But it doesn't work like that, Angie. You're not the only one in the world with problems."

"Sam, I know! I *know* I am not the only one in the world with problems, I know in the grand scheme of things I'm meaningless—"

"You're not! Maybe if you could wrap your head around the fact that you matter, you'd start learning how to treat other people like they matter too."

"Listen, I'm sorry that I'm not ready to—to talk about our relationship right this second, but, Sam, I am *this close,* closer than I've ever been, to finding my dad, and I—"

"Fine. Go."

Sam gets up and pulls the keys from his jacket pocket, throws them to her from across the room.

Angie picks up the keys, which have landed on the floor. She pulls on her jeans. She steps into the bathroom and splashes water on her face. She tells her heart to stop knocking, to stop pounding against her chest. She is not going to open the door to let it out, not going to let it escape her. They are going together, in one piece, to find her father.

• • • • • *Angie steps into the too-bright sunlight, Sam's keys in* hand. A car honks. A siren in the distance. A mother pushing a stroller up the sidewalk veers around her. She has no memory of where they might have parked last night and begins to circle the block, but she gets only a few steps before she leans into the gutter and throws up. Two kids on skateboards clatter past her. She shuts her eyes and takes a deep breath. *Get it together,* she tells herself.

She stands and continues walking until she sees Sam's Jeep parked around the corner, in front of a small stucco house. As she goes to unlock the door, she watches a hummingbird land on the trumpet vine that grows over the chain-link fence, and at once, she's lost in a memory.

She and Marilyn are unpacking boxes in the kitchen at their new house, when Marilyn gasps. "Angie, come here!" she whispers, peering out the window. A hummingbird, beating its wings a million times a minute, stares back at them. Her mom squeezes her hand and says, "It's a sign. We're home." Angie can't tell if her mom is sad or happy, or something in between, but Marilyn insists they abandon the boxes and drive to the hardware store. She lets Angie pick out a feeder, made of blue glass and decorated with cheerful red flowers.

Get. It. Together, Angie tells herself again, and opens the door to the car. She pulls her phone from her bag to find her battery's at ten percent. Ugh. Of course she didn't plug it in last night. She types Justin's address into Google Maps: seventeen minutes away. But she can't go like this.

Siri guides her to the nearest CVS, where she buys a bottle of Smartwater, a toothbrush, and travel-size toothpaste. She asks to use the bathroom, waits for the door to be unlocked by the clerk, and brushes her teeth.

When she finishes off the water she buys another, along with red lip gloss and mascara. Back in the Jeep she applies the makeup using the rearview mirror, hoping she looks better than she feels. She follows the directions to 179 Sycamore, driving carefully on the city streets, trying her best not to be rattled by the honking cars that veer around her. The Miss Mari Mack tape plays on the stereo. She fast-forwards to "At Your Best," and lets Aaliyah's voice soothe her. At a stoplight, she stares up at the twinkling palm leaves, a billboard tagged BLANK FACE, the empty blue sky, and tries to imagine her mother—the mother from the picture, the mother with the golden smile—listening to this song in the car with James. *Stay at your best, baby . . .*

She turns onto Sycamore, parks, and walks up the block. An Orthodox Jewish family with three small kids crosses the street, two black girls in designer dresses get into a Prius, a white dude jogs past them. A huge eucalyptus tree grows beside the pathway to 179, its roots pushing up against the bricks.

She knocks on the door that Justin disappeared into the night before.

She waits. And waits.

She knocks again.

She glances at the second-story window but can't see anything behind the curtain.

She waits.

But he doesn't come.

It's okay, she tells herself. *He's just out. He's just not home right now. He'll come home.*

Angie gets back in the Jeep, her hands shaking. She starts the song again, and closes her eyes.

• • • • *Angie blinks her eyes open to find the last of the sun* draining from the sky. Shit. How long did she sleep? Her mouth is dry. She searches the floor of the Jeep and comes up with half a bottle of purple Gatorade. Sam loves purple Gatorade. *Sam.*

She pushes the thought of him away and chugs the liquid. Now she can see Justin's black Mustang parked across the street ahead of her. Angie gets out and quickly retraces her steps to his apartment, tugging at her jeans, squeezing at her curls, inhaling the smell of jasmine on the warm evening air. The window on the second story is open, the lights on behind the curtain. Music drifts out: *I tried to dance it away . . .*

Solange, "Cranes in the Sky." Angie *loves* this song. It must be a sign—there's already a thread tying her and Justin together. As she reaches the door, she can hear voices from inside. She knocks before she can think about it—a good, hard knock—and exhales, not realizing she'd been holding her breath.

A moment later, the door swings open. It's him. Justin, right in front of her.

His eyes look like her father's in the photo, the eyes she'd stared into so many times.

She stands there taking in every detail: the Smog City beer in his hand, the sugar skull tattooed onto his ring finger, the baseball cap that says COFFEE, his faded gray hoodie, the smell of pot smoke wafting out of the apartment.

"What's up?" he says.

But her voice has fled. She'd assumed he'd recognize her. She'd been expecting—what?—that he'd wrap her into an embrace, that he'd say—what?—*Oh my god, your father, he's going to be so excited to meet you?*

He focuses on her more fully, his eyes squinting. "You alright?" he asks.

"Yeah," she manages. "Sorry. Hi. I'm Angie . . ."

He looks back at her quizzically. "You look familiar but I can't place it. We met?"

"I think you might be, well, um . . . my uncle."

Almost in slow motion, his face changes first into a look of recognition and then into one of shock.

"Shit," he finally says. "Fuck. Wow . . . Yeah. You look . . . so much like him."

"So do you."

"I had no idea," Justin says. Angie can see he's blown open, can see him trying to gather himself as if he were chasing leaves in the wind. "I had no idea," he says again. "You're—you're Marilyn's kid?"

Angie nods her confirmation. ". . . Can I come in?"

"Um, yeah. Yeah. Just—hold up."

Justin goes inside, leaving Angie standing alone beneath the eucalyptus tree, its papery bark peeling off. She peers through the half-open front door and spots him partway up a flight of stairs, resting his head against the wall.

After a moment he disappears into another room. She can hear his voice calling, "Yo! Put that out!"

He returns and leads her inside. "Sorry, I—wasn't expecting you. Obviously," he says, trying for a laugh as he leads her up the steps. "I just have a few people over, but we can bounce if you want? Are you hungry? I can take you to get some food, or . . ."

Before Angie can answer, they arrive in a living room that smells like a recently extinguished joint. The apartment has creaky hardwood floors and high ceilings. A marquee sign that says OPEN leans against the wall. A French poster for a movie she doesn't recognize hangs beside a Basquiat print. A small crowd sits around a table—the girl with the curly hair from last night, a black guy with baby dreads and a collared shirt, a white guy with glasses and stubble. A girl with pink hair sitting on the lap of another girl with a buzzed head and big earrings. They've paused their poker game, it seems, to stare at her.

"This is . . . Angie," Justin says.

Choruses of "What up, Angie." "Nice to meet you." "Welcome to the Sycamore Lounge."

She raises her hand in an uncertain half wave.

"Can I get you something? Are you hungry? Did I ask you that already?" Justin watches Angie. She watches the room. Could her father be there too, around the corner? Perhaps he's in the bathroom?

"Sorry," Justin says. "This is just . . . a trip . . . Come on, come in the kitchen with me."

324

She follows him into the kitchen, which smells faintly of cooked steak. She sits tentatively at a wooden table as Justin pours a Coke from a glass bottle into a mason jar and hands it to her.

"So you live in LA?"

"No, I . . . I live in Albuquerque . . . with my mom." She pauses, checks his face for a sign. She thinks she catches a small grimace before he goes back to neutral. "I'm here with a friend. Visiting. I—I saw your 'Some Dreamers' video," Angie goes on. "I recognized your name, and I—I just knew it was you. I loved it, so much. I mean, I really loved it."

He smiles. "Thanks, kiddo."

"So, what are you working on now?" Angie asks, wiping her sweaty palms on her pants, trying for a semblance of normalcy— as if they were just two people having a conversation.

"A bunch of different stuff. I'm editing a new Fly Boys video. And prepping for a feature I'm shooting this fall."

"Oh, cool."

"Yeah . . ." Justin trails off, and a sudden silence falls over them. "Sorry. I'm not sure what the protocol is here. I . . . Jesus. I wish I'd known about you sooner."

"Me too," Angie says quietly.

"What's up with your mom?" Justin asks after a moment. "How is she?"

"Um. She's okay."

Angie reaches into her purse and pulls out her photograph of Marilyn and James at the beach. She offers it to Justin, hoping it will create a bridge to the answers she's afraid to ask for.

"Oh my god. Wow. That's a trip. I took that picture."

"You did?"

"It was my twelfth birthday . . . Who could have imagined one day their daughter would be looking at it." His eyes search Angie's. "Marilyn was the one who got me into photography, back in the day. I haven't seen her since . . . yeah. I was just a kid. So was she, I guess . . ."

"Justin?"

"Yeah?"

"So my dad—is he here? In LA too?"

"What?"

Angie begins to talk quickly. "I mean, I thought he'd died in a car accident, but my mom said you'd died too, so I thought—I mean, that if she's lying about that, then my dad might also be alive, right?"

She stares down at her hands folded in her lap, not able to look at Justin.

"Oh, Angie. He's not alive. He died before you were even born. I don't think he ever knew . . . that he'd have a daughter."

All at once Justin's house feels like a stranger's house—the cast-iron pan left unwashed on the stove, the dim smell of marijuana, the laughter from the other room, the Edison bulb dangling in a cage overhead. What is she doing? Why is she here? She looks at Justin, Justin who looks like her father, Justin who looks like her, and he looks like a stranger too.

"Sorry," she whispers, afraid that if she speaks too loudly her voice will crack. "I don't know what I was thinking. I—I have to go." She gets up from the table.

"Angie, wait." He follows her as she walks out of the room. "Let's—do you want to talk about it?"

"No, no thanks."

"But—how did you get here?"

"I drove. Sorry to bother you," she mumbles.

She hurries down Justin's stairs without looking back and steps into the thick night. As soon as her feet hit cement, she breaks into a run. She cannot get back in the car. She cannot go back to Miguel's, cannot face Sam, not now. She runs in her ballet flats, scuffing them on the pavement. She runs blindly through the dark neighborhood streets, through the smells of blossoms and cigarettes, trash bins and barbecue, air heavy with distant ocean water. She runs over cracks in the cement pushed up by roots, through stop signs without stopping. She'd been so close; she'd come so far. She'd known, felt, that he was just around the corner. But at the end of the road, there was only the same fact that has been true for her entire life. *He's dead.* LA is just a city, a single city on the planet earth, where her father died more than seventeen years ago. *He's one of one hundred and seven billion*, Angie tells herself. *He's one of one hundred and seven billion dead humans. He's dead, just like he's been since I was born. We're both just tiny drops in the ocean of humanity anyway, our earth is just a tiny planet in a vast solar system, our solar system just one of countless solar systems, our whole universe probably a single universe in an ocean of universes—*

"Angie!" The deep voice comes from the black Mustang pulling toward the sidewalk just ahead of her. "Angie, slow down!"

Angie does not. She keeps running, past the car.

"Fuck! Angie!"

Angie does not want to see Justin, her dead dad's brother. She cannot face the shame of the naïveté—a child's—that led her to believe somehow she would find her ghost alive and walking through the City of Angels.

And then there are footsteps behind hers, and suddenly arms around her, grabbing her shoulders from behind, slowing her, strong arms.

Arms like a father's.

As Justin holds her in his grip, the sob inside of her breaks loose at once.

"Okay, come here. Okay." He pulls her into an embrace. It feels like being hugged by her dad. He lets her cry.

"Where did you learn to run like that, girl?" he asks eventually. "You are fucking fast."

Angie looks up at him and, through her tears, she laughs.

"I wasn't gonna meet my niece for the first time and let her just take off, but there was no chance I would have kept up with you on foot!"

"You shouldn't smoke pot," Angie says. "You'd be a better runner."

Justin laughs. "Okay, I'm sorry you walked in on that. If I'd have known you were coming, obviously, I would have . . . done it differently. *You* shouldn't smoke pot; you're still a kid, but I happen to be an adult with a prescription. So."

Angie raises her eyebrows at him.

"Listen, I don't know about you, but after that chase scene I'm starving. Have you been to In-N-Out yet?"

"No."

"Alright, let's go. I may not be your father, but far as I can see I'm the closest thing around to a guardian, legal or not, so for now I'm in charge. And I guarantee the best medicine for you at the moment is a Double-Double."

"Okay," she says. "But only 'cause you've got a cool car." Before he can open the door for her, she gets in.

Remembering her promise to her mom, Angie pulls out her phone. *I'm safe,* she types, and perhaps for the first time since she's arrived in the city, she feels it could be true.

• • • • • *Angie sits in the passenger seat of Justin's Mustang,* parked outside of In-N-Out. The tray in her lap holds an order of Animal Fries (smothered in cheese, grilled onion, and sauce), a Neapolitan milk shake, and a Double-Double (double meat, double cheese), which she takes the last bite of.

"So, tell me about yourself," Justin says as he starts in on a second burger. "What are you into?"

Angie shrugs. "I'm kinda boring."

"No you're not. Nobody's boring. Everyone's got a whole universe inside them."

"Okay, um . . . I like running."

This gets a laugh from Justin. "Clearly."

"And soccer. And music. And . . . and I don't know what I want to do with my life, and this is the first time I've ever been out of New Mexico."

"And next year? What about college?"

"I don't know."

Justin raises his eyebrows. "You don't sound too enthusiastic."

"I guess it seems like it's all kinda pointless anyway. There are more than seven billion people in the world. We walk around feeling like we're so important, but we're just this invisible fraction of humanity."

"You think about that a lot?"

"Yeah," Angie admits. "Anyway, even if you *do* know what you want to do with your life, even if you manage to have some big dream, like my mom did, there's no guarantee it's gonna work out that way. I mean, she was supposed to become a photographer, but instead she had to became a waitress, then a banker."

"And a mother," Justin adds. "Don't forget about that."

"But maybe she'd be better off if she weren't," Angie blurts out.

"What do you mean?"

"I know I was a mistake. Nobody gets pregnant at seventeen on purpose. She's always saying I'm her greatest joy—but maybe, if she'd never had me, she'd have other joys . . . Maybe if my dad hadn't died, she wouldn't have felt like she had to keep their baby." Angie stares out the window. "Maybe if my dad had lived, I wouldn't exist."

Justin looks at her for a long moment. "Listen, you could argue all of us came into this world by chance. Maybe you're right—maybe if James had lived, maybe you wouldn't have been born. But at this moment, you're here. You might be one of seven billion and counting, but so was he. So does that mean his life didn't matter? Do you think it's no thing that he died unfairly?"

"No. Of course I don't think that."

"But isn't he only an invisible fraction of humanity?" Justin pushes.

Angie looks back at him. "Yeah, but . . ."

"It's a question of perspective, isn't it?"

"Right." Angie pauses. "If you're looking at the world all

zoomed away—if you're thinking about one of seven billion—
he seems small. But up close, to the people who love him—his
life was everything."

Justin nods. "And we'll never know what he might have done,
how it might have impacted others . . ."

"Yeah," Angie agrees, wondering now what she might do
one day.

"Listen, it's a good thing—an impressive thing, even—for a
kid your age to be able to get outside of yourself, to see the bigger picture, but don't lose the ability to look at things up close
too. You find a lot of the important stuff in the details. The thing
is to be able to have multiple points of view—to see both how
small and how enormous our lives are. You got me?"

"Yeah."

"I'm gonna be straight with you. I spent a lot of my time feeling like I could never be enough to make up for the life that James
didn't get to live. And I spent a lot of time furious that he's gone.
After fucking up and almost dropping out of high school—after
all the drugs and the girls and whatever else I could use to numb
myself out—the thing I've figured out along the way is that you
can't let yourself off the hook. There are some wounds that don't
close, and some losses that will never be okay. But you've got to
let that be a force that drives you, not an excuse not to try. His
life got taken, and mine didn't. So how could I throw mine away?"

Angie looks at him. "Can I ask you something?"

"Yeah?"

"What happened to him?"

A pained expression passes over Justin's face. "He didn't die in a car accident. I don't know why your mom lied to you, Angie, but that's between you and her. You'll have to talk to her about it—"

"But—" Angie feels a burst of flame licking at her chest.

"Hey," Justin says. "Take a deep breath."

"Why won't you tell me the truth?"

"I am telling you the truth. The truth is that your mother lied. I'm mad about that too. I think she made a huge mistake, keeping you away. But the truth is also that I don't know what it's like to be a parent. The truth is that I don't feel like it's my place to step into that. The truth is that I'm sorry you had to grow up without your father, and I'm sorry that I didn't get to be in your life sooner, and I'm sorry that there are parts of where you come from that you haven't gotten to uncover yet—but you will, okay?"

Angie stares back at him.

"Okay?" he asks again.

"Okay."

"I get the sense that you're a kid who's gotten used to hiding a lot of what you're feeling, but if I'm gonna be your uncle, you have to promise to be real with me. I promise I'll be real with you."

"Okay."

"Promise?"

"I promise."

"It's alright to freak out if you need to, and you can be pissed at me for sure, but no more running away."

"Alright. I promise."

"I'm working at my studio downtown tomorrow, if you wanna come check it out."

"I'd love to."

Justin pulls out of the In-N-Out parking lot, scanning through music on his phone until the first notes of "DNA" begin. He looks over at Angie and smiles. Angie smiles back and puts her arm out the window, leans her head on the sill as the warm wind drifts over her . . . Looking up at the palm trees in the dark, she lets the thoughts drain from her mind, allowing the grief for her lost father to take up space, to shift inside of her, changing its shape.

• • • • • *When Angie gets back to Miguel's the lights are out,* the main room illuminated only by the faint glow of the ambient city. She finds Sam asleep on the floor beside the pullout. At the sound of her, his body shifts, but he says nothing. She takes off her sneakers and lies back on the bed, trying to keep her breath quiet, as if she could erase everything that had gone wrong between them with silence.

The next morning, Angie wakes to the sound of Miguel making breakfast. She sits up as Cherry appears in a nightshirt and boxers.

"Want some coffee?"

"I'm okay," Angie answers uncertainly. "Where's Sam?"

"He went for a run. Come outside with me."

Angie stands at the edge of the little balcony as Cherry lights a cigarette. "Listen, Sam asked if you could stay at my place for the rest of the week. Which is fine with me."

"He did?"

"Yeah. I think he needs . . . a little space. And it sounds like you do too. Maybe you've gotta just figure out your family stuff on your own. I think it's not fair to drag him into it, unless you're ready to be responsible."

"Responsible?"

"He's a good kid, Angie. He deserves someone who will take care of his heart, treat it like it matters. Like it's one, whole, beating heart—a universe of its own."

Before she can think how to respond, Angie's phone buzzes with a text from Justin. *Hey niece. You still want to come by the studio today? I can pick you up or you can meet me over there.*

Angie looks back at Cherry, her red hair brilliant in the morning light, last night's mascara smudged under her pale eyelids, and she feels her insides grip hold of themselves, as if she were balancing on a tightrope. "Okay," she says. "I'll stay at your place if that's alright. Thank you for offering."

"No problem." Cherry extinguishes her half-smoked cigarette. "I'm mostly over here anyway, so you'll have it to yourself. Sam said to tell you you can keep the car."

Angie nods and takes Cherry's key, which has a butterfly print on it. Inside, she gathers her belongings, and refuses the eggs that Miguel politely offers. She says goodbye, okay, thank you so much, and steps back into the morning sun, texting Justin on her way to the car. *Yes, tell me where and I'll meet you.*

When she looks up, there's Sam running up the sidewalk, his face reddened with sun, glistening with sweat. He sees her and slows, half a block away. She waves. He nods. They walk toward each other until there is no option but to cross paths.

"Hey," he says.

"Hey." Angie looks back at him, searching for an edge of familiarity, for a crack in the wall between them. But he's as much a stranger to her as she is to herself right now. When did she become a person who ran away?

"I found him," Angie blurts out. "I mean, we met."

"Cool. You like him?" Sam asks, and Angie can hear the slightest softness creeping into his words.

"I do. A lot. My dad, though, he's gone."

Sam just nods. Angie stares off. Across the street a man sells fruit from a cart. A mother with gold hoop earrings buys mango on a stick for a little girl in a wagon. Something about her movements, her smile, remind Angie of her own mom.

"I'm gonna go in and shower," Sam says. "Be careful, alright?"

"Okay. I will."

"Later."

As she watches Sam jog past her, up the block, she realizes, with a sinking regret, that she's treated their relationship as if it were a room she could always walk into and out of. But the private world you live inside of with someone else—it's a space you have to hold open. She feels as if she has so little strength left; she can't keep the door from closing.

Her phone buzzes with a text from Justin: *984 Pico Blvd.*

And so she steps forward, away from Sam, toward a version of family she doesn't yet understand.

• • • • • *After checking the address Justin gave her twice, Angie* parks in front of what looks like an old warehouse. But when she walks into the building, nervously tugging at her T-shirt, she sees it's perfectly polished inside: high ceilings, skylights, white gallery walls displaying huge canvases with faces that have been scratched into thick paint.

"Can I help you?" the girl at the reception desk asks. She wears curly hair and a purple leotard and couldn't be too much older than Angie.

"I'm here for Justin. Justin Bell? I'm his niece." She likes the way the words sound in her mouth. *I'm his niece.*

The girl smiles. "Right. He said you were coming. I'll let him know you're here." She gets up and disappears down a hall, her low heels clicking on the shiny concrete floors.

Angie moves to the wall to study the huge canvases.

"They're dope, right?" Justin says when he comes up behind her.

"Yeah, they are."

"A friend of mine from RISD did them. He and I and a few other dudes went in on this spot together. We all have offices here, but we also use it as a sorta museum space—we host readings and music and that kinda stuff."

"That's super cool," Angie says.

"Here, I wanted to show you something," Justin tells her, and he takes Angie into another, smaller gallery room. On the walls is a collection of photos mounted against black backgrounds—Justin sitting on a beach wearing a hoodie over his head, Justin on a hiking trail, Justin drinking a beer at a dining table, Justin floating on his back in a pool, Justin leaning against a streetlamp. They're all perfectly lit, enchanting, but from each there's been the shape of another person cut out of the picture. Something about the crude simplicity of the absence feels acute—a gaping hole in the center of an otherwise normal moment.

"Wow," Angie says. "These are so beautiful."

Justin smiles, and she can see her opinion matters to him. "Thanks. I did this series way back when—it was my senior thesis in college. I called it Brother."

After he gives her the rest of the tour—including his office where he's working on storyboards for his movie, and a pretty garden in the back—Justin declares it's time for lunch, and he and Angie walk several blocks through downtown LA, crowded with tall buildings and traffic, tiny shops selling cheap leggings, the occasional upscale restaurant tucked haphazardly into the bustle.

"I talked to my nana last night and told her about you," Justin says. "She was so excited she practically had a heart attack . . . I said I'd bring you by for lunch tomorrow so she can meet you, if you're free?"

"Of course!" Angie says. "Are there more people to meet?"

"Our mom died when I was just a baby, and our granddad a couple years ago . . . Our dad lives in Texas. I'm sure you could meet him eventually. You'll love Nana Rose, though."

Angie's never really had a grandma before. She feels a tiny bit guilty about how excited she is by the idea that her family's becoming so much bigger than just her and her mother.

They arrive at Grand Central Market, a space with open-air entrances, filled with smells of Chinese, barbecue, pizza, Mexican food. People gather at little tables to eat their lunches near stalls selling fruits, vegetables, and spices. They sit at the counter at Justin's favorite spot—Belcampo Meat Co. He orders them both burgers.

"This is delicious," Angie manages, her mouth full.

"They sing to the cows before they slaughter them, like whisper in their ears and shit. That's what makes their meat so good."

Angie cracks up.

"God, you sound just like him," Justin says. "You have the same laugh. It's crazy."

This makes Angie go quiet. "Do you—believe in heaven, or anything like that?" she asks after a moment, over the din of the crowd.

"I do believe that there's so much beyond our understanding. If there is a heaven, I don't think it's like anything we can imagine. But I guess what I hope is that the people we've lost are somehow part of things now—the air and sky and all the way out to the stars—and that one day James and I will be part of the same stuff . . ."

Angie smiles. "Yeah. I like that."

"James used to tell me that our mom was watching over us. Whenever a hummingbird would come by our window, he used to say it was her, sending them to look in on us. He was so into those birds—always filling up the feeder for them and all."

Angie thinks of the day the hummingbird appeared when they were moving into their new house. She can still hear her mom's voice—*It's a sign.*

"I think what I believe in is ghosts," Angie says. "I don't mean like haunted-house ghosts, but ghosts like the idea that all the lives that've been lost are still part of the world we live in—almost like traces of energy. I mean, we inherit everything—our language, our countries, even our DNA . . . But also things that are harder to name. I think we all carry the ghosts of people who came before us . . ."

Justin studies her for a moment. "You're such a smart girl. Hard to believe you're only seventeen."

Angie grins down at her plate. "Thank you."

"Maybe you don't know what you wanna do, but there's a start—what you're saying is that history matters. Why not make it a project, to find out all you can about what you've inherited from this country, from your ancestors, from the centuries of humanity? Make the invisible things visible. Tell the ghost stories. We need them."

"Like what you do through your art."

"Yeah, I mean, I guess that *is* what I try to do."

"You're easy to talk to," Angie says. In fact, she hasn't been able to talk to anyone else the way she can talk to Justin.

"You're easy to talk to too," Justin replies. "There are too many horrors in this world for me to believe things happen for a reason, but if I did, I'd say you came here because I was meant to meet you."

Angie smiles.

"Anyway," Justin goes on, "that's what your dad wanted to study, you know. In college."

"History? Really?"

"Yep. Let's go back to my place after this. I have a few books I want you to borrow."

"Okay."

"Where are you staying, anyway?" he asks.

"Um, I was staying with my ex-boyfriend and his cousin, but we fought, and so I guess tonight I'm gonna stay at his cousin's girlfriend's place."

"Aw, hell no. Why would you do that? You can stay with me."

"Really?"

"Of course, silly. You're family."

• • • • • "*Ta-Nehisi Coates is a dude you should definitely read,*" Justin tells Angie as they walk up the block to his apartment. "He does an amazing job of showing how history is key to understanding our present. He published this article a few years ago called 'The Case for Reparations.' It's about how to heal as a country, we've got to finally address the truth of our collective biography. Not just slavery, but Jim Crow, red-lining—"

Suddenly, Angie stops. Justin turns back, to find her staring down the street.

There's her mom, sitting on the hood of her car under a sycamore tree, watching Angie and Justin as they come up the sidewalk. She wears her Montezuma Elementary T-shirt and jeans, her long blond hair pulled back into a girlish ponytail. Out of context, she looks suddenly young, too vulnerable. Almost like a kid who doesn't know where to belong on her first day of school.

"Mom?" Angie hears the word come out, shaky. "What are you doing here?"

"I came for my girl," Marilyn says.

And then Marilyn's arms are around Angie, holding too tight. She smells like her Paul Mitchell Awapuhi shampoo, like laundry detergent, like Easter Sundays and Fourth of July and movie nights and mornings waking before sunrise. The child in Angie wants to burrow into her mother; the other half of her wants to push her away, to be Angie in her new world, Angie in LA.

When Marilyn finally releases her grasp, Angie turns to see Justin watching them. As he and Marilyn meet each other's eyes, they become heavy storm clouds, barely able to contain their rain.

"Well, if it isn't Miss Mari Mack."

"Jus—you're—you're all grown up."

"So are you."

"You look—just like he would've . . ." Marilyn reaches out, as if she'll brush her hand across his cheek, but he takes a step backward and she retreats.

"There's not a day I haven't thought of you," Marilyn says in a whisper.

He stares back at her.

"I'm sorry," Marilyn says. "I had to—I had to go."

"Who am I to say. You've got a helluva daughter. Must've done something right." His voice is taut like a bow, but the arrow goes unreleased. He tilts his head up to Angie, turns, and walks away.

Angie's heart begins pounding its protest, her breath quickening as he disappears into his apartment. She wants to run after him, to beg him not to go. Justin was *hers*, her uncle. Now what if her mom's scared him off?

Angie looks at Marilyn standing there on the sidewalk, her face naked as she stares at Justin's back.

"How did you find us?" Angie asks.

"Your phone was off, so I called Sam. He gave me the address."

"Oh."

"Come on. Get in the car."

"I have Sam's car. I know you're probably mad at me, I get that, but I'm not ready to leave LA yet. I can't."

"Get in the car. I'm not asking you." Angie doesn't remember her mom ever sounding like this before, at least not since Angie was a little girl, refusing to go to bed.

"You don't get to tell me what to do right now. Not after you've spent my whole life lying to me," Angie says.

"Please, Angie. This isn't easy for me, either."

"So why did you even come, then?"

"Because you are my daughter and I love you. I didn't want you to have to do this alone."

"I wasn't alone. I was with Justin. My uncle. You know, the one you told me was dead?"

Marilyn pauses. "I've had a long drive, across that desert, thinking about the best way . . . I thought I'd take you to a place that your dad used to like—I thought—"

"Fine. Let's go." Angie gets in the car and pulls the door shut behind her.

Marilyn gets in after her, starts the engine, and drives off in silence.

As they turn into slow traffic moving down La Brea, Angie stares out the window at the coffee shops and sneaker shops, yoga studios and restaurants where people lounge with glasses of wine.

"The city's changed," Marilyn says, as if they could just have a normal conversation. "It has and it hasn't. There's something about the light here. And I see these palm trees in my dreams . . ."

Angie glances over to see her mom gripping the wheel too tightly.

"When you left, Angie, I was angry and scared. I missed you terribly . . . I went to look at the photos in my drawer, but they were gone. When I found the charges from the White Pages on your debit card, I put it together and realized you'd come looking for Justin. I just wish you would have told me the truth. Why didn't you tell me?"

"Why do you think? I didn't trust you."

Marilyn brakes suddenly as an Audi makes a left turn, cutting them off. "I know it might be hard for you to understand, but I—I was trying to protect you," Marilyn says.

"From *what*? Don't you think it would've been good for me to know another black person in my family? Don't you think it would've been good for me to have someone who could've been like, a father figure or whatever, since I didn't have a dad? I could've grown up knowing Justin."

Marilyn keeps her eyes on the road. Someone honks as she merges into the right lane. "Angie, I—"

"You *lied*! About one of the most important things in my whole life!"

"I may not be perfect, but I've done my best! I'm doing my best!" Marilyn pulls over against the curb, traffic rushing on around them, and wipes tears from her eyes.

"I can't ask you anything or talk to you about anything 'cause you just start crying," Angie blurts out.

Marilyn stares out the windshield for a long moment, tears still streaming down her cheeks. "I wanted to make a world for you where you would feel safe, where the horrors of life would be distant. I didn't want you to grow up with the pain that I felt, the rage. I thought if I could carry all the weight of it, you wouldn't have to."

Angie has to know the truth or she will forever be chasing ghosts.

"What happened?" she asks, and the words taste too hot in her mouth. "How did my dad die?"

. . . . .

I think we are well advised to keep on nodding terms with the people we used to be, whether we find them attractive company or not. Otherwise they turn up unannounced and surprise us, come hammering on the mind's door at 4 a.m. of a bad night and demand to know who deserted them, who betrayed them, who is going to make amends.

Sitting by the entrance to the 10—the freeway to the ocean she used to drive with James—Marilyn remembers the quote from the Joan Didion book that she'd loved: the words that had led her, back then, to open the doors to herself, to eventually let him in.

The girl of seventeen, the girl who fell in love with James Alan Bell, who took pictures with the camera he bought her, who lost her virginity to him at the top of Runyon Canyon, who planned their futures together . . . she's been pounding down the door of Marilyn's heart since the day Marilyn abandoned her in Los Angeles and drove off through the desert.

Marilyn looks into their daughter's face, and for the first time sees her there—the self she left behind. For the first time she sees that to understand Angie the way she needs to be understood, Marilyn will have to let that girl back in, her own self at seventeen, ravaged as she ended up by grief, drowned as she was in guilt; she will have to learn to love that girl again as she loves her own daughter, or she may lose Angie along with her.

And so she begins to speak. She tells Angie the story that she's told to no one, since the night that shattered her all those years ago.

MARILYN

• • • • • *James and Justin sing along to "Rosa Parks" on the* radio as they turn onto Gramercy Place, on the way home from the beach. The music is effervescent, and Marilyn feels herself starting to bounce along with them, loosening, lightening, almost levitating. But when they park, she spots Woody getting out of his truck across the street, and she crashes back to the ground. James reaches over, puts his hand on her leg, looks into her eyes. *It's okay,* he's saying, without needing to speak. Justin jumps out of the car, not realizing what might be wrong.

Marilyn silently reminds herself that it doesn't matter what Woody thinks. She only has a few more months here, anyway. What's the worst he can do? She takes the camera—just a couple photos left on the roll that Justin shot—and follows James to his door.

"Where the hell do you think you're going?" Woody comes up behind Marilyn and grabs hold of her arm, his face red with fury or booze or likely both. She hates that her voice is gone.

"We're having dinner, for my brother's birthday," James says. She can see his muscles tensing, the fight gathering itself into his body. Justin, luckily, has already slipped inside.

"I need you to clean up upstairs," Woody says to Marilyn. "Come on."

"She's not going upstairs right now." James takes a step forward. "And if you ever hit her again," he says, voice low, "you won't survive it."

Marilyn sees the wild fury flashing in Woody's eyes, but she allows herself to feel sheltered by the certainty in James's voice. James matters; their love matters; Woody doesn't matter. Before Woody can respond, Marilyn yanks her arm back and follows James into his apartment.

She forces air into her lungs, promises herself that she won't let the incident get in the way of Justin's birthday night. James keeps his hand on her back, guides her to the couch, brings her water. She can smell the chocolate cake just out of the oven. They have mac and cheese casserole, Justin's favorite. They sing happy birthday, and Justin blows out candles, opens presents. Marilyn gives him a photo book she made for him, where she's pasted copies of her favorite pictures, with room for him to add his own. She hears her mother's footsteps upstairs; she must be back from work. But she knows Sylvie won't come looking for her, not now. Now she acts as if Marilyn's just a shadow of herself, a Marilyn impersonator there only to remind her of the daughter she's already lost. When it's time to go home, James asks to walk her up, but she doesn't want to provoke Woody further, or hear whatever Sylvie might have to say about it, under her breath. She's hoping they're both asleep or passed out from too much to drink, anyway.

The apartment is dark—not a single light left on—so she lets her eyes adjust, relieved as she makes her way to her bedroom. It is not until she's beneath the covers, beginning to drift off, that she hears the door open. And there's Woody, stepping—no—staggering—toward her.

"How dare you embarrass me like that, after everything I've done for you."

She tries to get up, but he pushes her back with a force she didn't expect he had. It's the look on his face that chills her most: as if somehow, all that he's been unable to control has concentrated itself in her body.

"Mom!" she screams, but there's nothing. "Mom!" she screams louder. Sylvie doesn't come. Why doesn't she come? Too drunk, too deep in sleep to be woken, or maybe she went out again, as she's been prone to do lately. Maybe she's not there at all.

"James!" she screams into the dark night, out the open window, the kind of scream that slices her chest open, before Woody puts the pillow over her face, faded My Little Ponies printed on its case. She tries to knee him, but it doesn't land. She digs her nails into his skin, ready to draw blood.

"You won't get away with what you're doing. The party's over. You're going to learn some discipline, and I'll teach it to you myself."

He lets the pillow up and she gasps for air before he pushes it back down again. She tells herself to stay inside of her body, but she's drifting, scattering into the night.

The pounding at the front door brings her back.

"Mari!" James's voice calls out.

She knees Woody, successfully this time. As he falls back, she bursts up, runs to the door, and swings it open to James.

"Are you okay?" he asks, pulling her close.

353

But then Woody's right behind her, grabbing her by the hair.

James punches Woody in the side of the face, causing him to loosen his grip. Marilyn runs for the phone. She dials 911. It's pure instinct; the single move one is meant to make in the face of disaster, embedded into her mind by childhood training. She speaks quickly: *1814 Gramercy, number two, upstairs. Please, come as fast as you can.*

When she hangs up and turns back, she sees James struggling to contain Woody. He gets Woody in a headlock. But then, with a free hand, Woody pulls his switchblade from his pocket, presses it to James's stomach.

"Let him go!" Marilyn screams. She tears a lamp from its socket and runs toward them.

"You made a mistake, boy," Woody says to James, icy. "This is my home."

James releases his grip and quickly pushes Woody backward, separating the knife from his body, but Woody launches toward Marilyn.

James intercepts, throws Woody to the floor. He tries to pin Woody, but Woody slashes the knife at the air, flailing in a desperate bid to regain control. Marilyn hears sirens in the distance. *Hurry*, she prays.

James finally wrestles the blade from Woody's hand.

And then the policemen, two of them, storm through the door, guns drawn. Marilyn turns to James—the sweat on his perfect face glistening in the dim apartment, his breath ragged, the rage, the adrenaline not yet drained from him, the knife still hanging in his grip.

Before he even registers their presence.

The sound of the shot splits the world open, and splits it again. Marilyn launches herself onto James's body, collapsed to the floor. She wraps her arms around him, pulls him toward her. He does not sit up. He does not make a sound. His body is the dead weight he'd playfully get her to try to pull up from the couch. "James!" She screams too loud, and not loud enough. He is dead.

ANGIE

• • • • • *Angie can feel her mom's panic, the fear that cuts into* her center, the feeling of not being able to get enough air. She watches Marilyn fold into herself, head bent onto the steering wheel, breaths shallow, rapid.

"Mom," Angie says—the voice of a child. She rests her hand on Marilyn's, laces their fingers together, desperate to grab hold of her, to pull her back.

Marilyn sucks in another breath, this time longer. She exhales, and Angie feels her grip tighten.

"Angie. I'm so sorry, Angie. I'm so, so sorry. I'm sorry I called the cops that night."

The weight of what her mother has told her settles in Angie like a boulder that will not break down, that insists only on its own absolute gravity.

"Mom," Angie says again, and doesn't know what else to say.

Across the street a man pumps gas into a green Range Rover at an Arco station. A line of cars wait at a Carl's Jr. drive-through. A man at the corner holds a sign: HOMELESS, HUNGRY, ANYTHING HELPS, GOD BLESS.

Learning the truth of her father's death has not changed the fact that Angie will never know what it's like to feel the scratch of his beard on her face, to eat Chinese food for dinner together, to run beside him, to feel him grip her hand, to see the shape of her own eyes when she looks back at his. To hear him tell her, "I love you."

The fact is the same as it's always been. He's gone.

And Angie still does not know where her story begins. With the invisible ancestors, whose ghosts she cannot see? With a Los Angeles love story, between the boy and the girl in the photograph? With a murder. With a single mother, working impossible hours, singing her to sleep. With a gesture, a dream, a whisper.

Angie thinks of that piece of the poem Sam had read—what did it say? *You can't put the past behind you. It's buried in you; it's turned your flesh into its own cupboard* . . .

That's the truth, isn't it? Her father's life, the history that led to his death—it's stored within her.

This then: a place to begin. With anger, with devastation, with heartbreak. At least it's real.

MARILYN

• • • • • *Her body understands before her brain will.* She's sick to her stomach, dizzy and weak, but she's listening for his music, she's waiting for him to come home. No matter that she's now in a stiff motel bed, the only sounds the sterile hum of cars on the freeway, the tumble of the ice machine. It's been three weeks.

Sylvie had gathered their belongings and checked them into a Motel 6 in Orange, as if she thought they could go back in time, simply erasing the seven months since they'd left the OC. She treats Marilyn like porcelain, like she could shatter (she already has—can't her mother see?), turning her pillows, stroking her forehead, leaving Marilyn alone only to go to work or, on her days off, to look at apartments. When she returns she tells Marilyn cheerfully about the places she's seen that day, describing the pools, the pale yellow walls, the kitchen islands.

Neither Sylvie nor Marilyn have any interest in the idea that she should return to school; though there are only three months left, graduation seems irrelevant. Marilyn wishes she'd already died with James. The grief is unbearable; there are no words for the pain.

She'd made her statement to the investigating officers through sobs: *James wasn't doing anything, he'd had the knife only because he was protecting me from Woody, he didn't pose any threat.* But the cop who shot him was cleared after a three-week leave. Woody was brought in on a domestic battery charge the last she knew; a no-contact order had been issued at the arraignment. Sylvie had not called the Bells for details about the service; Marilyn had not, either, had not felt capable of facing them. The guilt weighs more than she does; she can't keep herself afloat.

During the days, the sound of the television fills the silence of the dim room with the soap operas from her childhood. Perhaps Sylvie hopes that they will be an antidote to her daughter's despair, as they had once been to her own, but Marilyn only stares at the images, uncomprehending.

She throw ups in the mornings, in the afternoons, at night. The sound of James's voice is everywhere, already distant, the way an echo fades and softens, comes back to you changed. She doesn't notice when her period doesn't come, not right away, but finally a couple weeks after the fact she has a premonition. When Sylvie leaves for work, she dresses herself and steps out of the hotel room.

The sun outside is too bright, filling her with sudden fury. Why should it shine on, indifferent, as if nothing had happened? She manages to walk across two parking lots until she finds a Walgreens. She buys a pregnancy test, not caring about the eyes of the other shoppers in line behind her.

"That'll be seven eighty-five," the cashier says.

She wants to cry out—*he's dead.*

The cashier stares back at her. "Honey?"

Marilyn pushes the money across the counter without a word and carries the test back to the hotel.

It is positive.

She had not considered whether she'd hoped it would or

wouldn't be, but the sight of the pink plus sign ignites a spark in her chest—light piercing the heaviest fog.

When Sylvie comes back that evening, Marilyn tells her without preamble. "I'm pregnant."

Sylvie momentarily freezes—thin lips parted, eyes peeled open too wide. Marilyn expects her to scream, but then she fixes her face, sits beside her daughter on the bed, strokes her head. "It's okay, baby. We'll get it taken care of. It's okay."

Marilyn's jaw clenches. For the first time since his death, the fight begins to return to her body; she now has something to protect.

Sylvie sees the look on her face. "Oh, Marilyn, you can't possibly—you can't keep it, honey. You can't. I know you're hurting now, but you're going to put all of this behind you. It's not too late."

"I want the baby, Mom."

Sylvie's eyes are frantic. "Marilyn, sweetie, I didn't want to tell you until you were feeling better, but I've spoken to Ellen and there's a lot of excitement about you, after the Levi's commercial. There's lots of new opportunities. You're still so young, there's so much life ahead. The future we always wanted, it's here. You're going to be okay."

Marilyn turns away, lies back against the pillow.

"If only you listened to me," Sylvie's saying now. "If only you listened to me and stayed away . . . this all could have been avoided. Listen to me now, honey. You're in no state to make these kinds of choices."

Marilyn shuts her eyes and lets her racing mind leave the room.

What will she do? Where will she go? She can't stay with her mom, that much seems clear. No, she can't stay in this city at all. She will have to start over. She and her baby.

Marilyn pacifies her mother by agreeing to let her set up a consultation. The following day, when Sylvie is at work, Marilyn asks the hotel manager—a greasy-haired man who lets his eyes wander over her—for directions to the nearest Chase. She walks the mile and a quarter. The Levi's money has been safely deposited into the new account she'd set up, residuals to follow. She gets a cashier's check for half of the amount, made out to Sylvie. Marilyn's half will be enough to get her out of here, to allow her to survive until she finds a job.

On the way back to the motel, she sees an old Dodge with a for sale card in the back window, not red like James's, but white. Still, she takes it as a sign. An hour later, she pays cash to a kind older couple from Mexico in exchange for the keys, and drives to the Walgreens, silently thanking James for her lessons.

She drops off the roll of film from Justin's birthday, pays the extra five dollars for one-hour processing, and mills the cold, air-conditioned aisles aimlessly until the photos are ready. In the car, she opens the envelope and looks through. She arrives, finally, at the photograph of her and James, her head on his shoulder, his arm around her, both of them smiling.

She bursts into racking sobs.

A bird flies from a phone wire. A palm tree sways. Golden sun glints from the windshield. A mother exits the store holding her daughter's hand. The world feels at once too empty and too full, everything overly bright, impossibly close. When she can breathe again, Marilyn gently, tentatively lays her hand on her belly. She is carrying his baby. The only part of James that will remain alive.

She looks through the negatives and finds the one for the picture of them. She carries it back inside and asks the woman behind the photo counter to make another copy, which she tucks into her purse, saving it, she imagines, for a future when she will be able to make sense of their faces.

· · · · ·

The next day, after Sylvie leaves for work, Marilyn packs her belongings into the white Dodge in the early-morning fog. She places the cashier's check on the dresser, along with a note. *I'm sorry, Mom, I can't stay here. Please leave an address with the motel desk once you find an apartment. I'll call for it. I'll write. I love you. Marilyn.*

She gets onto the 405, driving back toward the apartments on Gramercy, barbed sunlight puncturing the layer of cloud. She pulls off the freeway, turns left on Washington. Cars honk. Her hands begin to shake. She turns right onto their block. But how could the streets be the same without him—the city, the sky?

Marilyn rests her hand on her stomach to remind herself of her purpose. She runs quickly up to the Bells' door with a package containing the camera, Justin's photographs, and a note:

Justin, I don't know how to tell you how sorry I am. This camera is yours now—please keep taking pictures. I have to go, and I'm sorry for that, too. Perhaps one day I'll find your photos in a magazine, or read about your display in a gallery, and I will be so proud of you. I already am. I know your brother is too.

Love, Marilyn

She sets it below the mailbox. And that's when she sees it, sticking out. An envelope from Columbia. Fat, thick. The kind that means you got in. He got in. Her heart beats into her head. She runs up to Woody's mailbox, where weeks' worth of mail has piled up, and sees the matching one for her. She touches its surface—the ticket to the future that belonged to her and James. The future they would have lived together.

Devastation chasing her, she rushes back to her car, starts the ignition, and drives away, through the sharp maze of the city, out into the land of strip malls and palm trees, and through the expanse of desert torn from her childhood.

ANGIE

• • • • • *Justin opens the door to Angie and Marilyn. "Looks* like you guys had a rough afternoon."

They only nod.

"You told her?" Justin asks Marilyn. Marilyn confirms with another nod.

"You guys hungry?" he asks. "I was thinking of making some food." His voice sounds raspier than usual.

"That would be great, thanks so much," Marilyn says in a near whisper. Angie follows as her mom carefully climbs the stairs into the apartment, tiptoeing over the creaky wood floors as if she wanted to make herself weightless, as if she didn't want to take up space.

They'd never made it to wherever it was Marilyn had meant to take her. Instead, Angie had sent Justin a message, telling him she needed help, asking if her mom could stay with them tonight.

They both sit at Justin's wooden table as he pulls steaks from the fridge, takes out onions, peppers, sweet potatoes. After a moment Marilyn goes to him, still stepping softly. She puts the palm of her hand on his shoulder. "Can I help?"

"Sure." He moves aside, leaving her with the vegetables and cutting board, and goes into another room. When he returns, James Brown's voice follows. Marilyn looks up and stares out the window, past the little cactus on the sill, past the crisscrossing phone wires and into the distant Hollywood sign set against the Santa Monica Mountains. Justin turns on the burner, gives Angie another cutting board and asks her to chop the potatoes. The space begins to warm, the air saturated by the smell of cooking and by the music: *Try me, try me* . . . Angie recognizes the song from the tape; she glances at her mom, but Marilyn is still somewhere else.

· · · · ·

From where she is now, standing in Justin's kitchen, onions burning tears from her eyes, Marilyn can hardly remember the Motel 6 where she and Sylvie once stayed, the Walgreens, the couple who sold her the white Dodge. What she remembers, clear as water, is the feeling of the child inside her, the child who would not have a father.

And she remembers the way Sylvie had said, "If only you'd listened to me . . ." as if Marilyn herself were to blame. She remembers how Sylvie's words stuck with her across the stretches of open desert. She remembers thinking that if James had never met her, his grandparents would still have two grandsons, Justin would still have a brother. James would still have his life.

She remembers how the weight of the injustice, of the guilt, of the pain became something she believed she must bear alone.

· · · · ·

But Angie has inherited her own legacy of injustice, of brutality, of children without fathers, of fathers robbed by violence. Marilyn had not wanted to give it to her, had wanted to shield her from it, but it is Angie's right. She understands that now, even as it leaves her speechless, even as it leaves her lost.

Curled inside a sleeping bag on the couch in Justin's living room, she begins counting the leaves on the sycamore tree out the window—an old trick she hopes will help her finally sleep.

Marilyn sits up on her air mattress beside Angie and starts fumbling through her suitcase. She takes out a tattered copy of *The White Album*, pulls a folded sheet from between the pages.

"I wanted you to have this."

Angie recognizes her mother's cursive—though it is slightly loopier, more girlish—written on a Motel 6 pad. She reads in the moonlight:

You have no name yet, no gender. You are as a big as a raspberry, moving your tiny arms and legs, growing taste buds. Inside of my broken body, you are all that is still alive in me.

Sometimes, when I wake in the mornings, there's a split second when I've forgotten, when the sun is just the sun falling across my skin, when I know, without even thinking it, that he's just downstairs sleeping. A moment when he's still here and we're still in love, going to college together.

And then, the sudden reality—the impossible blow all over again.

The tears rush to my eyes. I run to the bathroom to throw up, sick from grief or the pregnancy, I don't know.

You are the part of him that will live on. I will carry you. We will leave behind all that is unspeakable, the quicksand I am sinking under; we will become new. Me like you.

Both of us together. Tomorrow, I'm going to take you to the place from my memory, the place where I was a child. I'm going to retrace the highway across the desert, and bring you to the place I was born. Though it will only be us two, I promise to make you a home; together we'll be a family. I promise to teach you as much as I can, about what is still good in this world, about what is still beautiful. I promise to love you fiercely, with all of me.

He wanted a daughter one day. He wanted to name her after his mother. If you come out a girl, I will call you Angela.

• • • • • *People think ghosts are for the night, but the dead are* haunting us, even on bright summer days. This is the feeling Angie has as she stares out the window from the back of Justin's Mustang, turning onto Gramercy Place. Palm trees rise tall in the distance, bending in the breeze, as Justin pulls up to the end of the block, parks outside of 1814. Angie recognizes the steps from her mother's photograph. An orange tree grows in the yard, a child's tricycle beside it, casting its shadow onto the dried grass. One hundred and seven billion lives have passed from this earth, and traces of the dead are everywhere, even if they're invisible to us.

"Here we are," Justin says.

When they get out of the car and step into the air thick with heat, Marilyn's eyes are wide, her skin pale. "We lived just above," she murmurs as they walk up the path. "I could hear him. I used to listen to his music at night."

As they arrive at the porch, Angie glances back to see her mom staring at a hummingbird feeder that hangs from a hook below the storm gutter, its faded red flower waiting.

Justin knocks and the door swings open. As Angie's eyes adjust from the bright sunlight to the dim room beyond, she sees a face creased with wrinkles, dancing eyes, hair in braids. The old woman wears a flowered dress draped over her tiny frame, big gold earrings.

"Hi, Nana," Justin says, and kisses her cheek. "I brought you a surprise." He turns to Angie, his hand extended in a flourish.

"Hi," Angie says, and before the syllable has left her lips, Rose pulls her into an embrace, the grip of her small arms surprisingly strong. She smells like rose water and more faintly of cooking oil, garlic, thyme.

"My baby girl. You're here." She keeps hold of Angie's hand as she searches her face. "You look so much like him."

Angie turns to Marilyn, who hangs back a few feet, watching. She knows that this place is haunted, that her mom sees not only her father's ghost, but the ghost of the girl she once was.

"Hi, Rose," Marilyn says in a whisper—the kind of whisper that didn't mean to be a whisper, but got stuck somewhere along the way.

But Rose looks away from Marilyn, at an invisible point in the distance. "Well. Come in," she says finally, still not meeting Marilyn's eyes.

They follow Rose into the apartment, where Justin waits on the couch. Angie takes in the walls full of photographs, the pretty glass lamps, the thick flower-printed curtains, the smell of roasting chicken. She can feel the weight of the memory contained within the space almost as if it were her own.

"It's just the same . . ." Marilyn says.

"She refuses to leave," Justin says. "I've tried to move her out, but she's stubborn, aren't you?" Rose only frowns in response before she disappears into the kitchen.

Angie follows her mom as Marilyn goes to look at a photograph on the wall: Justin, a baby; her dad, a boy, grinning that perfect grin; and a woman with his same smile—a radiant woman in a red dress.

"That's her, your grandma," Marilyn says to Angie.

Angie looks again at the woman in red. She remembers filling in Angela's and Rose's names on Ancestry.com not so long ago. She'd yearned to know who they were, but they'd seemed no realer than fiction, tucked into a past she'd never be able to find. And now, here they are: Rose, coming up behind them with a tray of lemonade, and Angela looking out from her photograph—a daughter, a mother, Angie's own grandmother. Someone she can see herself in.

"Do you have more pictures?" Angie asks Rose.

Rose's face peels open into a grin. "You don't know who you're talking to." She disappears and comes back with a stack of photo albums that reaches almost to the top of her head.

Marilyn watches as Angie settles between Rose and Justin on the couch, paging through. There's Angie's dad, a child in his mother's arms. There's him and Justin dressed as Ninja Turtles for Halloween.

The albums go backward in time, and soon they are looking at a faded color photo of Angela as a girl, barefoot and beaming outside a rural North Carolina home. Angela on Alan's lap. Angela in a school portrait, hair in braids, a front tooth missing.

There's Rose and Alan on their wedding day. Rose, a pretty

teenager in black and white. And then, Rose, a little girl with her family: mother, father, and three brothers, crowded onto a wooden porch.

"These are amazing," Angie says to Rose. "I wanna hear all about where you grew up and everything . . ."

Her great-grandma pats her leg. "I'll tell you everything you want to know, baby. But now, let's eat."

Rose moves slowly through the kitchen, refusing Justin's help as she sets out plates of chicken and rice.

"This is delicious, Rose," Marilyn says. "It tastes—just like I remember."

Rose only nods.

"Yeah, it's great," Angie says, filling the silence. "Thank you."

Rose smiles at Angie. "You're welcome, honey."

In fact, it tastes very much like a dish her mom used to make. They had this—chicken and rice—for dinner many nights when Angie was a girl.

"Your great-grandmother is the woman who taught me to cook," Marilyn says. She offers a smile to Rose, but it goes unreturned.

From upstairs there comes the sound of children's feet pattering, the muted laughter of a little boy.

"There's a couple really cute kids that live up there now," Justin says.

Marilyn nods. "Where—where's Alan?" she ventures.

"He died," Justin says. "Two years ago. A heart attack."

"Oh, no."

"It's a shame," Rose says, with a pointed look to Marilyn, "that he never got to meet his great-granddaughter."

"I'm sorry," Marilyn blurts out, her voice breaking. She gets up and turns away, wiping her eyes. Angie's about to push out her chair to follow, but then Marilyn sits back at the table and looks to Rose. "I'm sorry," she says again. "I should have had the courage to tell you that a long time ago. I just—"

"They killed my boy. And you *just* disappeared. Like it was nothing. Like we were nothing. And now we find out you kept his daughter from us?"

"You all were everything. But I didn't know how to face you after what I did. I knew you must have hated me—"

"I'm not angry at you for his death, Marilyn. But we lost everything when we lost him. How could you leave us too?"

For a moment, Marilyn looks back at her in astonishment. "I shouldn't have. But the pain was too much," she says quietly. "I thought it would swallow me—"

"It was too much for all of us."

"I thought the only way to be strong enough to be a mother was to start over—"

"Ignoring something does not make it disappear. And it doesn't do your daughter any good to lie about the world she's living in. She's her father's too. I see him in her smile. I hear him in her voice. She should have grown up knowing his family. You should have let us love her. You should have let us help you."

"She's right, Mom," Angie says.

Marilyn turns to Angie, and her face fractures.

"It doesn't mean that I don't think you're an amazing mom . . . but I wish we could've talked about this stuff. I wish you wouldn't have kept me away."

Marilyn takes in a ragged breath and tilts her gaze toward the sky, perhaps weathering a private earthquake. "All these years," she says, when her eyes find Angie's again, "I've known you were growing up in a world that took away your dad, that never accounted for the injustice of his death. I wanted, somehow, to shield you from that reality. And I thought I was protecting you, but I see now that I was also protecting myself—from my own sorrow, my own guilt.

"Rose, I know you have every right to be angry. But even if you can't forgive me, I'm coming to you now, and to you, Justin, and asking for your help. To finish raising my daughter. I know I might not deserve it, but I'm asking you to let me back into your family."

Angie reaches under the table and wraps her fingers through Marilyn's, willing Rose to say yes, for both her sake and for her mother's.

"I'm in," Justin says, breaking the silence. He squeezes Angie's shoulder. "I'm not missing out on any more time with my niece."

"Okay, then," Rose says finally. "Come here." Marilyn goes to Rose and wraps her arms around her—timidly at first, but then she's holding on as if to a life raft. Angie watches her mom become a child, crying in her great-grandmother's arms, and she knows these tears are different: they are a release.

· · · · · ·

An hour later, the four of them sit together on the porch, watching the neighbor boy circling the lawn on his tricycle, as Rose tells the story of meeting Alan as a teenager: at the grocery store where he worked as a cashier, he used to slip a Sugar Daddy into one of her bags every week.

"Look!" Angie exclaims at once. A hummingbird hovers near the feeder, seeming to watch them, its wings beating so quickly they blur into air. Marilyn's face breaks open into brightness as the bird flies up to them, tilts its head, and disappears into the sky.

• • • • • *Angie wakes on Justin's couch, her mom's air mattress* empty on the floor beside her. She smells eggs and coffee in the kitchen, hears her mom's and Justin's voices. She walks in just as Justin's handing Marilyn a 35-millimeter camera.

Marilyn lifts it slowly to her face, looks through the lens. "It was a Christmas present," she tells Angie, "from your dad."

"Your mother," Justin adds, "gave me the camera years ago."

He studies Marilyn for a moment. "Took me six years to use it," he says. "For so long I was too angry at James's death. Angry at you for leaving me. Furious at your uncle, and at the cop who shot an innocent kid. I was so angry it could have swallowed me. Almost did."

Marilyn meets his eyes, nods.

"I had a rough time of it for a while. Nearly dropped out of high school. Some part of me thought if James never got to go to college, I wasn't gonna go either. It was my eighteenth birthday. And I was there, in Nana's house, depressed as fuck. I thought back to the last birthday I could remember being happy, all those years ago. That day at the beach with you and James, taking pictures, and just like that, I reached under the bed, past a few balled-up T-shirts, and pulled out that camera. The moment I looked through the lens, I felt . . . like I could breathe again. I started shooting as much as I could, going to museums every day. I applied to art school the following year, and got in to RISD."

"I just had this memory of watching you at the pier—I was so proud. And now look at you. I saw your video. It's beautiful, Jus—just as good—better—than I'd hoped you'd become."

"I've still got a lot to learn. The point is, even if there's part of me who's still that twelve-year-old boy mad you left him behind, that camera saved my life, and I'm grateful to you for it. But I'm ready to give it back. And that girl I used to know—the one who was always taking these weird fake pictures, the one who was able to see so much—I bet she's still in there, waiting to come out."

"Thank you," Marilyn says, and Angie watches her mom carefully place the camera into her backpack, trying to see the girl that Justin sees.

"Get dressed," Marilyn tells Angie. "I've got a big day planned."

· · · · ·

At the downtown library, Marilyn shows Angie the table where she and James used to study, and the bench outside where they'd sit in the evenings to read *Slouching Towards Bethlehem*. They go to James's favorite taco truck and picnic in Elysian Park. It is not, after all, the facts of her father's death, but the details of his life, the stories that Marilyn tells her about their time together, that begin to give Angie's dad new dimension.

Over the next couple days Angie and Marilyn visit colleges too: USC, UCLA, and, Angie's favorite, Occidental. She can imagine herself there, among the white buildings with red

Spanish tiles, the palms and purple-flowered trees, the bustle of students that will come when school resumes in the fall. She could go to Justin's house on the weekends; he'd only be thirty minutes away. She could visit Rose for home-cooked dinners. Outside one of the many campus cafes, she and Marilyn agree to add it to Angie's list of places to apply.

As they hike up Runyon Canyon in the evening, Angie thinks back to the camping trip she and Marilyn had taken when Angie was in first grade—the one in which Angie stuck her head out the window, singing at the top of her lungs to her CD of children's folk songs. They spent the days exploring the forest and the nights sleeping outside the tent, making wishes on the shooting stars. She remembers now that they hadn't gone back to their old apartment after that trip, but instead had moved into another, smaller place. She remembers that Marilyn had told her they were going on an adventure, that the back of the car had been stuffed up with so many possessions that Marilyn joked they'd have everything they could need to survive the wilderness.

"You know that time we went to the Sangre de Cristos?" Angie asks her mom.

"Yeah," Marilyn answers.

"Was it really 'cause we had to leave our apartment?"

"It was."

"I never knew. I mean, I never realized until now."

"It was Manny who found us the new spot when we got back. He had a friend who owned the building. I didn't know what we were gonna do."

"You must have been so scared . . . but I couldn't tell. That camping trip is a really happy memory for me," Angie says.

"I *was* scared," Marilyn answers. "But in a way, it's a happy memory for me too. You were so wide-eyed. So full of wonder. It was contagious."

"Do you ever—" Angie starts, and then pauses. "Do you ever wish maybe you didn't have a baby?"

"Oh, Angie, no! Why would you think that? Having you is the single decision I could never regret."

"But, I mean, you never got to go to Columbia, or become a photographer, or even actually date anyone. You never got to do anything you were supposed to."

"Well, I've got some time left, you know." Marilyn smiles. "And I would not trade you for anything in the entire universe. Not for a lifetime at Columbia, or photographs in a million galleries, or Idris Elba in my bed."

Angie laughs. "Mom! Gross!"

Marilyn pauses on the trail and turns to Angie. "There was a part of me—a big part of me—that didn't believe I deserved to live after your father died. So, I think, in a way, I've lived for you— for our girl—instead. And that's not—I don't think I've understood, until now, how big a burden that's been on you. I'm sorry."

Angie nods, and she feels the familiar tension in her chest loosening its grip.

They reach the top of the cliff just in time for the sunset. Angie stands at the brink and stretches her arms out wide, as if to open herself to the city below. She remembers her first view of

LA in the car with Sam, and the sense of hope she'd felt. Perhaps her father has been here all along, hidden in the light, just as she'd thought.

When she turns, she sees, with surprise, her mom looking through the 35-millimeter camera.

Click.

"It's like you're getting ready to fly," Marilyn says quietly. She glows against the pink of the evening sky. "There were nights here when I felt like I could . . ."

Angie looks out over the City of Angels and remembers the question Sam had asked her: *If your dad were here, if he could talk to you, don't you think he'd tell you that love's worth it, for however long it lasts?* Yes, Angie thinks now, she believes he would.

Her mom walks up beside her, and they stand like that, together, each of them at their own edges.

• • • • • *Marilyn and Justin follow Angie to Miguel's, Justin's* car packed with beach supplies. Her mom and Justin say they'll go to the park to wait for her, so Angie walks up the block alone and knocks on Miguel's door.

A moment later, Cherry appears.

"Hey," Angie says. "Here's your key. Thanks so much for offering me your place."

"It's nothing."

"Is Sam here?"

"He is, but I . . . don't think he wants to see you, to be blunt."

"I just," Angie stutters, "I . . . really need to apologize to him, in person. Can you—can you ask?" Sam hasn't replied to a single one of the string of texts she's sent over the past three days.

Cherry pauses for a moment. "Sure," she says, and disappears inside.

Angie sits on the stoop to wait. It feels like ages ago that she walked up this street with Sam on their first night in LA, though it's been only a week. She counts the palm trees peeking their heads over the buildings to distract herself from her anxious heart.

"What's up," Sam says as the door swings open.

Angie stands to face him. "I brought your car back. Thank

you so much for letting me use it. My mom's here. She has to work, so I'm gonna go back to Albuquerque with her tomorrow."

"Okay."

"I'm sorry, Sam."

"No worries," he says flatly, and turns to go.

"Wait," Angie says. "I was wondering—what are you doing right now? I mean—what I meant to ask is if you'd want to go to the beach with us? To Venice? My mom and me and Justin."

"Um. I don't think so."

Angie takes a deep breath. So far, the conversation she's been practicing in her head hasn't gone as planned. "Sam, I know that—that I've been really selfish. Something about the night I found that photo of my parents—it's like suddenly my dad was real, and I wanted to know him so badly. I missed this person I'd never met so much, it's like there was a hole inside me. And it brought up all these questions I didn't know how to understand myself, so I didn't know how to share them with you, which made me run away, I guess.

"I used to have this feeling that there was something wrong—that something awful was just around the corner, but now that I can see what it is, even if it's worse than I imagined, at least I can start to try and figure out how to look at it . . . Getting to know Justin has helped. And especially finally talking to my mom. She told me. My dad was shot, by cops that came in the middle of a fight with her uncle. They didn't even ask what was going on. They just—killed him."

"Jesus, Angie. I'm so sorry."

"There's a lot that I still don't understand. But you're the best friend I've ever had. And the truth is, I love you," she says. "I love you," she says again, "but I didn't know how to say it before."

Sam stares back at her for a long moment. "Come here," he says finally, and pulls her into a hug. Angie's not sure how long they stand like that, still inside of each other's arms as the car horns and distant sirens and passing songs of the city rush on around them.

"Give me a minute," Sam says. "I'll get changed for the beach. I'm gonna see if Miguel and Cherry wanna come too."

As he disappears inside, Angie feels as if she's just stepped out of an ice-cold pool on a hot summer day—half shocked and shivering, but awake, alive, trusting the sun to warm her.

• • • • • *Justin's Mustang moves west on the 10. When he pulls* off the freeway and drives them over a hill, a sudden, endless expanse of blue water appears, glittering. Angie follows him and Marilyn out of the car, and she's overcome at once by the smell of the sea, the sound of the waves, which she'd imagined so often as she stared at the picture of her parents.

She watches her mom, trying to see the grinning girl with the golden hair as Marilyn takes a deep breath, looks out at the horizon. On a path running parallel to the sand, a little girl on a scooter pushes ahead of her father, who follows with a stroller. Someone rides by on a bike, playing "Ultralight Beam." Angie catches hold of the fleeting music: *Deliver us loving . . .* Two old women sit on a bench, doing arm lifts while looking out at the water.

Angie watches as her mom bends to take off her flat black ballet shoes, the edge where her big toe sticks out starting to wear toward a hole. The shoes are such a familiar thing—Angie's momentarily surprised by seeing them in this context, struck by a strange tenderness toward them. She unties her sneakers and the three of them walk across the sand.

Angie's finally here, on the beach where her parents stood together all those years ago.

Justin sets up blankets and umbrellas, and Sam arrives with Miguel and Cherry a few minutes later.

"You remember," Justin says to Marilyn, "when you dropped your shoe off the pier?"

Marilyn laughs. "Yeah. I still have those red flip-flops James bought me."

"We had some good times," Justin says.

"We did."

While the others get up to play football, Marilyn begins *The Year of Magical Thinking* by Joan Didion and Angie starts *The Fire Next Time* by James Baldwin, one in a stack of books that Justin gave her to take home.

When she turns around, she sees Marilyn texting, smiling at her phone.

"Who are you talking to?" Angie asks.

"Manny," Marilyn says. "After you left—I was such a mess. I didn't know who else to go to. He's always been a great friend."

Angie raises her eyebrows.

"I just wanted to let him know everything's alright. We're going to have dinner this week." She reaches out and tugs at Angie's toe. "Take a walk with me?"

"Okay," Angie says, and lets her mom lead the way, the sun dipping toward the water, the colors of sky reflected in the wet sand. They pass kids building castles, families playing Frisbee, a woman in a tiny gold bikini, a toddler running from the waves, people of all ages bobbing in and out of the sea.

When they reach the pier, Angie thinks they'll climb the

steps, but instead, Marilyn walks beneath. The dark of the shadow makes the water ahead so bright. Even on a busy beach day like today, it feels private, almost secret. Angie takes in the salt-stained smell of the old wood.

"This," Marilyn says, "was one of your dad's very favorite spots. His own mom first showed it to him." She pauses. "It was where we'd go to talk, to dream, to be alone with each other . . ."

Angie puts her arm around her mom. "You miss him, huh?"

Marilyn nods. "Always." She rests her head against Angie's. "He would be so proud of you."

Angie wonders if her mom's right. This trip did take courage; actually, she thinks, for the first time she's proud of herself. She's still not sure what she wants to "be"—maybe a journalist, she thinks now, or a teacher, or a lawyer, or a documentary maker—but she knows she doesn't want to feel too small to make a difference.

On the walk back, Marilyn suggests they stop at Hot Dog on a Stick. Angie remembers it from the food court in the mall; now she sees the root of her mom's love of the place. The little stand by the beach is the original, Marilyn tells her—another discovery she'd once made with James. They get as many hand-dipped corn dogs and cups of fresh lemonade as they can carry, and return to the others.

"I wanna get in the water," Sam says after he eats his corn dog in three bites. He looks to Angie. "You?"

Angie grins and jumps up.

She steps out timidly at first, the waves breaking and foaming around her stomach, but with Sam's encouragement finally she dives under.

You can't understand how wonderful the ocean is, Angie thinks now, until you've been swimming in it. She and Sam float on their backs, contained in the endless blue of water and sky.

How many of the seven billion people in the world are seventeen years old? How many are pregnant with a future child, and how many still feel like children themselves? How many are squinting into the same sun? How many are floating in the sea? How many are mourning lost loves, and how many are falling for the first time?

As they make their way to the shore, Angie reaches out, tentatively, for Sam's hand. He lets her take it. She thinks of what Justin had said: it's all a question of perspective. She and Sam— two tiny drops of water, but here, together, suddenly they are an ocean. Maybe it's true that there are no happy endings. But, right now, Angie is grateful to be at what feels like a beginning.

Seventeen years is too short to see on the cosmic timetable of our universe, of our planet, or even of our species. But it's the time Angie's dad had on this earth. Angie doesn't know how many years she'll get, but right now, she's here, among the living. Conscious and breathing. She's alive on this day, in this world full of violence and unthinkable horror, cruelty and kindness, wonder and so much love.

Epilogue

MARILYN

• • • • • *Marilyn means to head to Amarillo, the city where* she was born. She's made it ten hours from LA with only gas station food and bathroom breaks, but by six thirty the road is starting to go bleary ahead of her and she's starving again. So she pulls off I-40 in Albuquerque—the Central Avenue exit seems like a good bet. After checking into an Econo Lodge, she asks the clerk—a sweet, pimply-faced kid who couldn't be much older than she is—about a place for dinner. He recommends the 66 Diner down the road, so she walks the few blocks to stretch her legs. She likes the low brown buildings, the epic sky, the sudden mountains. She likes that it is quiet; she likes that there is space. The desert heat has begun to soften with the evening, and the air feels clean and thin and smells like memory.

When she walks into the diner, a pretty girl in a poofy blue dress greets her and guides her to a sparkly vinyl booth. She's suddenly so tired, she could fall asleep right there. Marilyn asks the girl what's good to eat, and the girl brings her a green chile cheeseburger and a mint chocolate chip milk shake. *This is the best meal I've ever had*, Marilyn thinks, and she eats it all, down to the last french fry. "My Girl" plays on the jukebox. A little boy with his mother devouring a sundae at the counter sends her a grin. A young couple nods to her on their way out the door. The kindness of strangers means everything now.

Manny, the midtwenties junior manager (so says his name tag) cashes her out at the register. She notices the help wanted sign beside the vintage Coke ads, the jar of Bazooka bubble gum on the counter.

"You have a nice evening." He smiles, and he has a wonderful smile—the kind that belongs to someone who believes the world is good.

When she steps outside, the sky has turned into an unbelievable riot of color: purples you could swim in, oranges you could eat, distant, streaking rain lit pink. This sunset is the first beautiful thing she has seen—*actually* seen, really taken in—since James's death. She feels her chest tear open where it had closed, compelled to let such beauty inside. It is painful. It is necessary.

She rests her hand on her stomach and she swears, for the first time, she can feel the baby move. Maybe it's a sign, she thinks, and turns to go back into the diner. Manny is still standing behind the register.

"Did you forget something?" he asks.

"Um. No. I was just—I noticed you guys are looking for help? I wondered if I could apply?" She wipes her sweaty palms on her jeans.

The restaurant is beginning to fill up with a dinner rush. A man with two young kids waits behind her.

"Take a seat at the counter," Manny says. "I'll be right over."

Marilyn spins subtly back and forth on the stool until he returns.

"You have any restaurant experience?" he asks.

"No, but I promise I'm a hard worker. I had a 4.0 GPA in

school, and . . ." Marilyn feels stupid. Who quotes their grades? "Well, I've had other jobs."

"Okay, what did you do?"

Marilyn's cheeks grow hot. She unconsciously reaches her hand to her stomach. "Modeling stuff. I was in a few commercials. I've come from LA." As soon as the words leave her mouth, she realizes she could have lied. Why not say she'd worked in a clothing store?

Manny studies her. "We can start you as a hostess," he says, finally. "It's five fifteen an hour, plus the waiters will tip you out. Can you come back tomorrow at noon?"

"Yes, of course," Marilyn says. "Thank you so much." Her first real job, on her own in the world.

When she steps out and turns to walk back to the hotel, she sees the Sandia Mountains glowing an impossible pink, the colors of the sunset softening but holding on, a streak of heat lightning flashing ahead. The air smells as promising as electricity. She makes a wish, that her and James's baby will live a life full of this much beauty.

ACKNOWLEDGMENTS

To my editor, Joy Peskin, thank you for pushing me and for trusting me, for your sensitivity and your insight, for your clear eyes and sharp mind. *In Search of Us* wouldn't be itself without you. Thank you to Richard Florest, my stellar agent, for helping me create the space to bring this book into the world, and for seeing the girls of the golden west so clearly. And a huge thank-you to Nicholas Henderson, Molly Ellis, Lauren Festa, Brittany Pearlman, Kristin Dulaney, and the amazing team at Macmillan: I feel so lucky to work with such lovely, smart, passionate people.

I'm grateful to have wonderful friends who've supported me in big and small ways through the writing process: thank you to you all. Thank you, especially, to Heather Quinn, who knows how to nurture newborn stories, and to Hannah Davey, my day one, whose brilliant brain helped shape this book from beginning to end. Thank you to Stephen Chbosky, who suggested I write my first novel and has been an incredible support ever since. To Lianne Halfon, who sees poetically and incisively at once, thank you for always reading every sentence. To Khamil Riley, a hugely talented reader and writer, thank you for lending your smarts to this story.

A monumental thank-you to my family, who are all part of

this book in both visible and invisible ways. To my dad, Tom Dellaira, thank you for your memoir that gave me such a poignant a picture of your past, and of the love you and Mom shared before we were ever there. Thank you for reading, for listening, for your encouragement and your counsel. Laura, my beautiful, brilliant sister-pie, my bestie, my bipster, thank you for your insight, and, as always, for your love and support. Denise Hope Hall, my little sister-in-law, thank you for *Citizen*, for Christine and the Queens, and especially for *you*: you are an inspiration in so many ways. Thank you to my stepmom, Jamie Wells, for your compassion and care. To Tammi and Gloria, thank you for welcoming me into your family with open arms from the very beginning. I am so lucky that I have such an amazing new momma and granny.

Thank you to my mother, Mary, who showed me what a mother's love can mean. Who taught me to chase my dreams. Who dedicated herself to my sister and me. Whom I would give anything to meet at seventeen. I miss you every day.

And thank you to my husband, Doug, for more than I can say. I didn't know there was love like this until I found you.

Finally, a humble thank-you to several authors whom I deeply admire, whose brilliant work taught and inspired me as I was writing this story: to Ta-Nehisi Coates for his incisive journalism in *The Atlantic*, to Joan Didion for *Slouching Towards Bethlehem* and *The White Album*, to Claudia Rankine for *Citizen*, to James Baldwin for *The Fire Next Time*, and to Jesmyn Ward and the contributing authors of *The Fire This Time*. Thank you to Wesley Stephenson, who wrote a *BBC News* article titled "Do the Dead

Outnumber the Living?" published February 4, 2012, which formed the original inspiration for Angie's ghosts.

In support of the ongoing fight for racial justice, a portion of the author's proceeds from this book will be donated directly to the NAACP Legal Defense and Educational Fund.

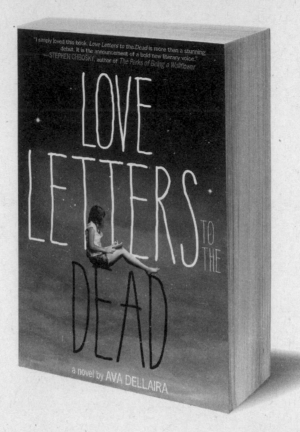